BY JACKIE COLLINS

Jackie Collins

LADY BOSS

A NOVEL

SIMON AND SCHUSTER
New York London Toronto Sydney Tokyo Singapore

SIMON AND SCHUSTER
SIMON & SCHUSTER BUILDING
ROCKEFELLER CENTER
1230 AVENUE OF THE AMERICAS
NEW YORK, NEW YORK 10020

DESIGNED BY EVE METZ
MANUFACTURED IN THE UNITED STATES OF AMERICA

1   3   5   7   9   10   8   6   4   2

LIBRARY OF CONGRESS CATALOGING IN PUBLICATION DATA
COLLINS, JACKIE.
LADY BOSS/JACKIE COLLINS.
P.   CM.
I. TITLE.
PR6053.0425L3   1990
823'.914—DC20   90-45840
CIP
ISBN 0-671-61937-3

For Tracy, Tiffany
and Rory.
Girls can do anything!

LADY

BOSS

PROLOGUE
September 1985

"Kill her," the voice said.

"Who?"

"Lucky Santangelo, that's who."

"It's as good as done."

"I hope so."

"Don't worry—the lady is already dead."

1

From the very beginning they were destined to be a lethal combination—Lucky Santangelo and Lennie Golden. Two stubborn, crazy, smart people.

Lennie was tall and lanky, with dirty-blond hair and ocean-green eyes. He was good-looking in an edgy offhand way. Women loved his looks. At thirty-seven, he'd finally made it as a movie star. He was the new breed—a comedian of the Eddie Murphy/Chevy Chase school. Cynical and funny, his films made big bucks—the bottom line in Hollywood.

Lucky Santangelo Richmond Stanislopoulos Golden was the thrice married daughter of the notorious Gino Santangelo. In her early thirties, she was darkly, exotically beautiful, with a tangle of wild jet curls, dangerous black eyes, smooth olive skin, a full sensual mouth, and a slim body. She was a fiercely independent, strong-willed woman who never compromised and always took chances.

Together they generated blazing heat. They'd been married for nearly a year, and both looked forward to their wedding anniversary in September with a mixture of delight and amazement. Delight, because they loved each other very much. Amazement, because who'd ever thought it would last?

Currently Lennie was in Los Angeles shooting *Macho Man* for

Panther Studios. The film was a comedy takeoff on all the Hollywood superheroes—Eastwood, Stallone, and Schwarzenegger.

They'd rented a beach house in Malibu, but while Lennie was filming, Lucky chose to stay in New York where she headed a billion-dollar shipping company—left to her by her second husband, Dimitri Stanislopoulos. She also had wanted Bobby, her six-and-a-half-year-old son by Dimitri, to be educated in England, and being in New York meant she was closer to his English school.

On most weekends she either visited Bobby in London or Lennie in Los Angeles. "My life is one long plane ride," she joked ruefully to friends. But everyone knew Lucky thrived on activity, and to sit by Lennie's side playing movie star's wife would have bored her. As it was, they had a volatile and passionate marriage.

Macho Man was causing Lennie nothing but problems. Every night he called Lucky with a litany of complaints. She listened patiently while he told her the producer was a jerk; the director was a has-been lush; his leading lady was sharing her bed with the producer; and Panther Studios was run by money-mad grafters. He wanted out.

Lucky listened, smiling to herself. She was working on a deal that —if all went according to plan—would free him from the restrictions of answering to a director he didn't respect, a producer he loathed, and a studio run by people he never planned to do business with again—even though he'd foolishly, against her advice, signed a three picture contract with Panther.

"I'm about ready to walk," he threatened for the hundredth time.

"Don't," she said, attempting to soothe him.

"I can't make it with these assholes," he groaned.

"Those *assholes* can sue you for a fortune. *And* stop you working elsewhere," she added, the perfect voice of reason.

"Fuck 'em!" he replied recklessly.

"Don't do anything until I get out there," she warned. "Promise me that."

"*When*, for crissakes? I'm beginning to feel like a virgin."

A throaty chuckle. "Hmm . . . I didn't know you had that good a memory!"

"Hurry it up, Lucky. I really miss you."

"Maybe I'll be there sooner than you think," she said mysteriously.

"I'm sure you'll recognize me," he said dryly. "I'm the guy with the permanent hard-on."

"Very funny." Still smiling, she replaced the receiver.

Lennie Golden would be shocked and delighted when he found out her surprise. And when he did, she planned to be right there next to him, ready to enjoy the expression on his face.

Once he put the phone down, Lennie felt restless. His wife was the most exciting woman in the world, but damn it—she pissed him off. Why couldn't she say, "Lennie, if things are tough I'll be right there." Why couldn't she forget everything else and be with him?

Lucky Santangelo. Drop dead gorgeous. Strong. Determined. Enormously rich. And too independent.

Lucky Santangelo. His wife.

Sometimes it all seemed like a fantasy—their marriage, his career, everything. Six years ago he'd been just another comedian looking to score a gig, a few bucks, anything going.

Lennie Golden. Son of crusty old Jack Golden, a stand-up Vegas hack, and the unstoppable Alice. Or "Alice the Swizzle" as his mother was known in her heyday as a now-you-see-'em, now-you-don't Las Vegas stripper. He'd split for New York when he was seventeen and made it all the way without any help from his folks.

His father was long dead, but Alice was still around. Sixty-five years old and frisky as an overbleached starlet, Alice Golden was caught in a time warp. She'd never come to terms with getting older, and the only reason she acknowledged Lennie as her son was because of his fame. "I was a child bride," she'd simper to anyone who'd listen, batting her fake lashes and curling her overpainted lips in a lascivious leer. "I gave birth to Lennie when I was twelve!"

Lennie had bought her a small house in Sherman Oaks. She wasn't thrilled at being shunted out to the Valley, but what could she do? Alice Golden lived with the dream that one day she'd be a star herself, and then, as far as she was concerned, they could all watch out.

"You're wanted on the set, Mr. Golden," said Cristi, the second assistant, appearing at the door of his trailer.

Cristi was a California natural blonde with an earnest expression and extra-long legs encased in patched dungarees. Lennie knew she was a natural blonde because Joey Firello, his friend and cohort in *Macho Man* had been there, and when it came to women, Joey had a notoriously big mouth—not to mention a notoriously big dick, which he'd affectionately christened Joey Senior.

Lennie, however, wasn't even interested. Since Lucky had entered his life he couldn't be bothered to look, and he really didn't appreciate Joey's giving him a rundown of the sexual habits of every female on the set. "You're just jealous, man," Joey had laughed when he'd complained. "Out of action an' gettin' no action, huh?"

Lennie had merely shaken his head and given Joey a "Why don't you grow up?" expression. Once he'd been a serious cocksman. "If it's blond and it moves, nail it" had been his motto. For years he'd explored every possibility, managing to avoid any lasting commitments.

Along the way there'd been a few women who'd left their mark. Eden Antonio, for one.

Ah, Eden, he thought ruefully. She was something else, a real operator.

Poor Eden. In spite of all her dreams she'd ended up living with a vicious mobster who had used her in a series of porno movies. Not exactly the future she'd planned for herself.

And then there was Olympia. He'd married the plump, spoiled shipping heiress because he'd felt sorry for her. Unfortunately, even he was unable to save her from her self-destructive excesses. Eventually she and spaced-out rock star Flash overdosed in a sleazy New York hotel, and Lennie was a free man.

Now he had Lucky, and life didn't get any better.

Grabbing a pack of cigarettes from the dresser, he said, "O.K., Cristi, I'm on my way."

The girl nodded thankfully, earnest expression firmly in place.

This was not an easy movie to work on, and any cooperation at all was a definite plus.

On the set Joey Firello was arguing with the old-time director Grudge Freeport about the next scene. Grudge wore a bad rug and chewed tobacco, spitting great gobs of it indiscriminately wherever he pleased. As usual he was almost drunk.

Marisa Birch, Lennie's leading lady, who doubled as the producer's girlfriend, leaned against a slant board idly picking her cuticles. She was a startling-looking woman, six feet tall, with spiky silver hair and frighteningly huge silicone breasts—a present from her former husband, who hadn't considered thirty-six inches enough. Marisa was a terrible actress, and as far as Lennie was concerned she was helping to ruin the movie in a big way.

Macho Man, he thought sourly. A comedy destined to be dead on arrival at the box office, in spite of his presence. His other movies had been hits; now he was stuck in a real disaster waiting to happen, and there was nothing he could do about it. The trouble was he'd been dazzled by the astronomical amount of money Mickey Stolli— the head of Panther Studios—had offered him. And like a greedy fool, he'd gone ahead and made another three-picture commitment.

"Don't do it," Lucky had warned him. "The lawyers only just got you out of your other deal, and now you're tying yourself up again. When are you going to learn? I'm telling you, keep your options open—it's more of a challenge."

Sure, his wife loved a challenge. The trouble was he couldn't resist the lure of megabucks. And megabucks put him one step closer to his wife's unbeatable fortune.

Oh, yeah, he knew he should have listened to Lucky; she had the Santangelo knack of knowing all the right moves and when to make them. Her father, Gino, had made it all the way from nothing. The old guy had style, and Lennie admired him. But what the hell—big bucks were big bucks, and he never wanted to be the poor relation.

Fortunately they were back in the studio shooting interiors. The week before they'd been on location in the rugged Santa Monica mountains—a real pain. And coming right up was a five-week location shoot in Acapulco.

With a sigh he entered the fray.

Marisa puckered up luscious swollen lips and blew him a kiss. She'd been after him from their first meeting. He'd managed to remain totally uninterested. Even if he didn't have Lucky, he'd never been turned on by silicone.

"Hi, Lennie, cookie," she crooned, erect nipples straining in his direction.

Shit! he thought. Another fun day at the studio.

Lucky hurried from the tall chrome-and-glass Park Avenue building that still bore the Stanislopoulos name. She had no desire to change it. One day everything would belong to her son, Bobby, and Dimitri's granddaughter, Brigette, so the name stayed.

Lucky was extremely fond of Brigette. The sixteen-year-old reminded her of Olympia, the girl's mother, at the same age. Olympia and Lucky had once been close friends. But that was long ago and far away, and a lot had happened since their out-of-control teenage years when they'd attended boarding school in Switzerland and ended up getting expelled.

Olympia's young death had been a senseless tragedy. Its only positive aspect had been the release of Lennie from a lifetime of burdensome responsibility.

Occasionally she'd felt guilty that everything had worked out so well. But what the hell—that was life. Hers hadn't exactly been a day at the beach. At the age of five she'd discovered her mother's body floating in the family swimming pool. Then, years later, Marco, her first love, was gunned down in the parking lot of the Magiriano Hotel. Shortly after, Dario, her brother, was shot to death. Three tragic murders.

Lucky had taken her revenge. She was a Santangelo after all. *Don't fuck with a Santangelo*—the family motto.

As soon as she walked out of the building she spotted Boogie lounging against the side of a dark green Mercedes. When he saw his boss striding purposefully toward him, he leaped to attention, quickly throwing open the passenger door.

Boogie was her driver, bodyguard, and friend. They'd been together many years and his loyalty was unquestioning. He was long-haired, tall, and skinny, with an uncanny ability to be there always when she needed him. Boogie knew her better than almost anyone.

"The airport," she said, sliding onto the front seat.

"Are we in a hurry?" he asked.

Lucky's black eyes flickered with amusement. "We're *always* in a hurry," she replied. "Isn't that what life's all about?"

2

When Gino Santangelo took his morning constitutional he invariably followed the same route: straight out of his apartment building on Sixty-fourth Street, across Park to Lexington, and then a brisk walk along Lexington for several blocks.

He enjoyed his routine. At 7 A.M. the streets of New York were not crowded, and in the early hours the weather was usually bearable.

He always stopped for a Danish at his favorite coffee shop, then picked up a newspaper from the corner vendor.

As far as Gino was concerned, this was the most pleasurable hour of his day, except when Paige Wheeler visited from Los Angeles—which was not as often as he'd like.

When Paige came into town his morning stroll was put on hold while he spent lazy mornings rolling around with her on his comfortable king-size bed. Not bad for an old guy in his seventies. Suffice to say Paige brought out the best in him.

Goddamn it, he loved the woman, even though she still steadfastly refused to leave her producer husband of twenty years.

For a long time he'd been asking her to get a divorce. For some unknown reason she wouldn't do it. "It would destroy Ryder if I wasn't around," she'd said simply, as if that was explanation enough.

"Bullshit," Gino had exploded. "What about me?"

"You're strong," Paige had replied. "You can survive without me. Ryder would crumble."

My ass, he'd crumble, Gino thought to himself as he walked along the street. Ryder Wheeler was one of the most successful independent producers in Hollywood. If Paige dumped him, he'd jump the nearest bimbo and that would be that.

What made Paige think she was so goddamn indispensable? To Gino she was indispensable. To Ryder she was just a wife he'd had for twenty years. The guy would probably *pay* for his freedom.

Gino had seriously thought about sending in a third party to plead his case. Offer Ryder a million bucks and goodbye schmuck!

Unfortunately, in the last eighteen months Ryder Wheeler had fathered two movie megahits and had no need of anyone's money. The jerk was shoveling it in.

"Screw the sonofabitch," Gino muttered aloud, well aware of the fact he was not getting any younger, wanting Paige by his side permanently.

There was a crisp breeze as he stopped at his usual newsstand and schmoozed for a moment with Mick, the dour Welshman with one glass eye and a bad set of yellowing false teeth. Mick ran his little kingdom with unfailing gloom and bad humor.

"What's goin' on in the neighborhood?" Gino asked casually, pulling up the collar of his windbreaker.

"Hookers an' cabdrivers. They should bloody shoot the lot of 'em," Mick replied, a malevolent gleam in his one good eye. "A couple of 'em bastards nearly got me t'other day. It's a good thing me wits are about me—I paid 'em back good."

Gino knew better than to question further. Mick was given to telling long, imaginative stories. Throwing down change, he picked up a *New York Post* and hurried on his way.

The headlines were lurid. Mob boss Vincenzio Strobbinno gunned down outside his own home. There was a picture of Vincenzio face down in a pool of his own blood.

The jerk had it coming, Gino thought with hardly a flicker of surprise. Young turks. Hotheads. The assholes never waited to see if they could work things out, they just blew each other away as if that was the answer to everything. Today Vincenzio—tomorrow another one. The violence now was relentless.

Gino was relieved he was out of it. Many years ago he would have been right in the middle, loving every minute.

Not now. Now he was an old man. A *rich* old man. A *powerful* old man. He could afford to say nothing—merely observe.

Gino did not look seventy-nine years old. He was amazing—easily able to pass for a man in his mid-sixties with his energetic gait, thick mop of gray hair, and penetrating black eyes. His doctors were constantly surprised at his energy and enthusiasm for life, not to mention his remarkable physical appearance.

"What about this AIDS problem I keep hearin' about?" he'd recently asked his personal physician.

"You don't have to worry about that, Gino," his doctor had replied with a hearty laugh.

"Yeah? Says who?"

"Well . . ." The doctor cleared his throat. "You're not still . . . active, are you?"

"Active?" Gino roared with laughter. "Are you shittin' me, Doc? The day I can't get it up is the day I lie down an' die. *Capisce?*"

"What's your secret?" the doctor asked enviously. He was fifty-six and a tired man. He was also full of admiration for his feisty patient.

"Don't take no crap from no one." Gino grinned; most of his strong white teeth were still intact. "Hey—'scuse me, Doc—correct that. Do not suffer fools. I read that somewhere. Sounds more like it, huh?"

Gino Santangelo had obviously led a fascinating life full of adventure. The doctor thought gloomily of his own five years in medical school, followed by over twenty years of private practice. The only adventure *he'd* experienced was when one of his patients fell in lust with him and they'd enjoyed a furtive six-week affair. Not much to get excited about.

"Your blood pressure is perfect," he assured Gino. "The cholesterol test turned out fine. Uh . . . about your sex life. Maybe you might consider investing in some condoms."

"Condoms, Doc?" Gino began to laugh. "We used to call 'em rubber joy-killers. Y'know—like takin' a swim in your boots."

"They're much improved today. Thin latex, a smooth feel. You can even get them in different colors if you're so inclined."

"No kiddin'?" Gino laughed again. He could just imagine Paige's face if he slipped a black johnny over his cock.

Oh, boy! Not such a bad idea. Paige loved variety. Maybe he'd try it. Maybe . . .

The airport was a mob scene as usual. Lucky was met by an efficient young man in a three-piece business suit who escorted her from her car to the private TWA lounge.

"Your flight's running fifteen minutes late, Miz Santangelo," he said apologetically, as if he were personally responsible. "Can I get you a drink?"

Automatically she glanced at her watch. It was past noon. "I'll have a Jack Daniel's on the rocks," she decided.

"Coming right up, Miz Santangelo."

Leaning back, she closed her eyes. Another lightning trip to L.A. she couldn't tell Lennie about. Only this time she hoped to close the deal that would make her husband a free man again.

This journey west would be the final clincher.

3

Abedon Panercrimski—or as he'd been known to a world that had all but forgotten him—Abe Panther—was eighty-eight years old and looked it, even though he didn't act it. Abe still had his balls, although many women—including two ex-wives and countless lovers—had tried to cut them off.

Abe arose every morning promptly at six. First he showered, then he put in his new set of brilliant white teeth, combed his few remaining strands of silver hair, swam the length of his pool ten times, and feasted on a hearty breakfast of steak, eggs, and three cups of bitter, black Turkish coffee.

Next he lit up a formidable Havana cigar and proceeded to read the daily newspapers.

Abe loved reading everything. He devoured *The Wall Street Journal* and the English *Financial Times*. With equal enthusiasm he scanned the gossip rags, enjoying every juicy item. It pleased him to acquire knowledge, however useless. From world affairs to idle chit-chat, he absorbed it all.

After his marathon reading session he was ready for Inga Irving, his longtime companion, to join him on the terrace of his Miller Drive home.

Inga was a big-boned, straight-backed Swedish woman in her early fifties. She never used makeup and had allowed her shoulder-length, club-cut hair to gray. Inga always wore loose fitting slacks and a shapeless sweater. In spite of her indifference to fashion she was still a striking woman who had obviously once been a great beauty.

Long ago, when Abe was *the* Hollywood tycoon to beat all Hollywood tycoons, including the Misters Goldwyn, Mayer, Zanuck, and Cohn, he'd attempted to make Inga into a star. He had not succeeded. The camera didn't like Inga Irving. The public didn't like Inga Irving. And after several tries in three big Panther Studios productions, Abe had finally given up. Every contract producer, director, and leading man on the lot had breathed freely again. Inga Irving was not destined to be the new Greta Garbo, in spite of Abe's valiant efforts.

When she so desired, Inga could be a prize bitch, moody, rude, and insulting. Those qualities might have been acceptable if she'd possessed talent and star potential. Alas, she didn't. And during her rise to nowhere she'd made many enemies.

Inga had never forgiven Abe for not persevering in promoting her career, but she'd stayed with him anyway—companion to the once great Abe Panther was better than anything else she could think of.

When his last divorce took place he didn't marry Inga. She refused to blackmail or beg. She was a proud woman; besides, as far as she was concerned, she was his common-law wife, and when Abe died she had every intention of claiming what was rightfully and legally hers.

Every day around noon, Abe partook of a light snack. He favored oysters when they were in season, accompanied by a glass of dry white wine. After lunch he had a nap, awaking refreshed after an hour, to watch two of his favorite soaps on television, followed by a solid dose of Phil Donahue.

Abe Panther never left his house. He hadn't done so for ten years —ever since his stroke.

Six weeks in the hospital, and he allowed his sons-in-law to take over running the studio. Although technically he never lost control —and was indeed still president and owner of Panther Studios— he'd not had the inclination to return. Making movies wasn't the same as it once was. Abe had been in the picture business since he was eighteen, and at seventy-eight he'd decided taking a break was no big deal.

The break had lasted ten years, and nobody expected him to return.

What they did expect, Abe realized, was for him to drop dead and leave everything to them.

His living relatives consisted of two granddaughters—Abigaile and Primrose—and their offspring.

Abigaile and Primrose were as unalike as two sisters could be. They couldn't stand each other. Sisterly love and affection failed to exist between them.

Abigaile was pushy and grasping. She loved entertaining and big parties. She lived for shopping and glitzy social events. A true Hollywood princess.

Primrose, the younger of the two, had opted for a different kind of life in England, where she was able to raise her two children in what she considered a more wholesome atmosphere.

And then there were the sons-in-law: Abigaile's husband, Mickey Stolli, who ran the studio, and Primrose's spouse, Ben Harrison, who took care of Panther Studios' overseas operation.

Mickey and Ben also loathed each other. For the sake of business, however, they had formed an uneasy truce. It helped that they lived on different sides of the Atlantic.

Abe considered both sons-in-law—or scums-in-law as he had christened them—to be cheating connivers who stole whenever they could.

It amused him to discuss the scums-in-law with Inga. She hardly ever cracked a smile, although she was certainly an avid listener, missing no detail of what he imagined were the scums-in-laws' latest scurrilous activities.

Abe had a loyal employee firmly ensconced on the studio lot. His name was Herman Stone, an unassuming man with the useless title of Personal Assistant to Mr. Panther. Herman visited Abe once a month and gave him a rundown of studio activities. Everyone knew he was Abe's spy, so therefore he was left alone and never privy to any important information. He had a comfortable office and an elderly secretary, Sheila. Herman and Sheila were both relics of the Abe Panther reign, perfectly harmless and absolutely unfirable until the day Abe Panther dropped dead.

Which would be soon, Mickey Stolli hoped. For then he would have complete control and could set about getting rid of his brother-in-law, Ben Harrison.

Yeah, soon, Ben Harrison also hoped. For then he was going to move back to Hollywood and grab the studio from his conniving brother-in-law's grasp.

When Abe Panther dropped, Abigaile Stolli and Primrose Harrison knew they were destined to become two of the most powerful women in Hollywood. Abe had never gone public with Panther Studios. He owned it—all one hundred and twenty glorious acres of prime land. So the girls would inherit everything.

Mickey Stolli planned to rule his inherited kingdom like the studio heads of the old days.

Ben Harrison planned to sell off parcels of the valuable land, just as 20th Century-Fox had done, and become a multibillionaire.

The "scums-in-law": they couldn't wait, and old Abe Panther knew it.

That's why he had other ideas: ideas that if Abigaile and Mickey, Primrose and Ben knew about, they would commit hara-kiri in the middle of Chasen's on a Sunday night.

Abe planned to sell his studio.

And the sooner the better.

4

In New York, Steven Berkeley kissed Mary Lou, patted her lovingly on the stomach, and headed for the door, pausing only to ask, "Are we in or out tonight?"

"Out," she replied.

Steven groaned. "Why?" he asked plaintively.

" 'Cause when that baby starts to bulge, I ain't goin' *nowhere*, man."

They both laughed. Mary Lou was a glowingly pretty black woman, a few months away from her twenty-third birthday, and two and a half months away from giving birth to their first child. They'd been married nearly two years.

Steven Berkeley had skin the color of rich milk chocolate, black curly hair, and unfathomable green eyes. Six feet three inches tall and forty-six years of age, he kept himself in great shape, visiting the gym three times a week and swimming at an indoor pool every other day.

Mary Lou was the star of a popular television sitcom. And Steven was a highly successful defense attorney. They'd met when her managers had approached his firm to represent her while she sued a low-life magazine for publishing nude photos of her taken when she was sixteen. Steven had accepted the case, won her an award of 16 million dollars—since appealed and reduced—and married the girl.

In spite of a twenty-four-year age difference, both of them had never been happier.

"And what kind of an incredible, exciting evening do you have planned for us tonight?" he asked sarcastically.

Mary Lou grinned. Whatever it was, she knew Steven would sooner stay home. He loved to cook, watch television, and make love—not necessarily in that order.

"We were supposed to see Lucky," she said. "But her secretary phoned to say she had to go out of town. So . . . I called my mother and asked her to join us."

"Your mother!"

Mary Lou shook her head in an exasperated fashion. "You *looove* my mother. Quit giving me a hard time."

"Sure I *looove* your mother," he imitated. "Only I *looove* my wife even better. Why can't we spend a quiet evening at home? Just you and me?"

Mary Lou stuck out her tongue and wiggled it at him. "That's all you ever want to do."

"Anything wrong with that?"

"Get outta here, Steven. Go to work. You're *such* a nag."

"Who, me?"

"Good*bye*, Steven."

He continued to defend himself. "Is it a criminal offense to want to be alone with my wife?"

"Out!" Mary Lou said firmly.

"One kiss and I'm history," he promised.

"One kiss only," she said sternly.

One kiss turned into two, then three, and before either of them could help it they were back in the bedroom pulling off each other's clothes and falling breathlessly on the bed.

Making love to Mary Lou was a sweet wild ride of mutual passion. Steven tried to be gentle with her. He was frightened of hurting the baby. Mary Lou didn't seem to care; she was full of exuberant love, pulling him close, wrapping her legs around his waist, rocking and rolling until she climaxed with a series of little screams.

By the time they were finished he was ready for another shower and already late for an appointment.

"Not my fault," Mary Lou said primly as he raced from the house.

"Not your fault!" he yelled, running for his car. "Face it! You're an uncontrollable sex machine! How am I ever expected to get any work done?"

"Will you shut up!" Mary Lou scolded, standing at the door wrapped in a silk kimono, her pretty face alive with pleasure. "People will hear you!"

At the office, Jerry Myerson, his closest friend and partner in the law firm of Myerson, Laker, Brandon and Berkeley, waited impatiently in the reception area. "You're late," Jerry reprimanded sharply, tapping his watch as if he were anticipating an argument.

"I know," Steven replied, straight-faced. "Had to make love to my wife."

"Very funny," Jerry snorted. He was a forty-seven-year-old playboy bachelor with the unshakable belief that once you got married your hard-on shriveled up and died forever. "Let's go," he said impatiently.

It wasn't often that Jerry Myerson and Steven Berkeley made house calls. Sometimes there were exceptions. The client they were on their way to see was an extremely rich woman called Deena Swanson. Deena was married to billionaire Martin Z. Swanson, president and owner of Swanson Industries, an all-powerful organization that owned major New York real estate, hotels, cosmetic companies, and publishing firms.

Martin Z. Swanson was Mister New York, a charismatic man of forty-five with unlimited power and an insatiable thirst for even more. Deena had parlayed her position as his wife into one of importance. Early on she had hired a press agent to make sure she was known as much more than just the wife. From social butterfly and fashion plate, she had risen to fame, lending her name to everything from perfume to her own line of designer jeans. She figureheaded Swanson Style, one of her husband's many companies. Deena made sure the name Swanson was always in the columns.

The Swansons had been married ten years. They suited each other. Deena's appetite for even more fame, money, and power was just as voracious as her husband's.

When Deena Swanson called and requested their presence, Jerry was delighted. The firm had been representing her for several months on minor matters, but Jerry figured that being summoned to her home meant things were definitely looking up—maybe they were going to get her husband's account. He liked that idea a lot.

"Why do I have to come along?" Steven grumbled as they sat in the back of Jerry's chauffeured town car on their way to Deena's Park Avenue apartment, one of the Swansons' three permanent residences.

"Because we don't know what she wants," Jerry replied patiently. "It could be simple. Maybe it's complicated. Two minds are better than one." A pause, and then a sly "Besides, the rumor is she likes her coffee black."

Steven narrowed his eyes. "What?" he said sharply.

Jerry was unperturbed. "You heard."

Shaking his head, Steven said, "You're an asshole, Jerry. Sometimes I don't think you ever took it out of college."

"Took what out of college?" Jerry asked innocently.

"Your fucking brains."

"Thank *you.*"

The car stopped at a red light. Jerry studied two girls crossing the street. One, a bouncy redhead, really got his attention. "Do you think she sucks c—"

"Don't even say it," Steven interrupted grimly. "Y'know, Jerry, you should get married and stop behaving like a dirty old lawyer."

"Married?" Jerry's voice filled with undisguised horror. "What makes you think I'd ever be that stupid?"

Every so often Steven wondered how their friendship had endured since college. They were both so different, and yet he couldn't imagine a more loyal and supportive friend than Jerry Myerson. Jerry had seen him through so much—including a disastrous marriage to a wild Puerto Rican dancer named Zizi, his many years as a crusading assistant D.A., and finally the long, painstaking years trying to find out the identity of his father. When he finally discovered his father was the infamous Gino Santangelo, Jerry had congratulated him.

"Hey—now you've got one white ball and one black," he'd joked. "The man can play in both courts. Not bad, Steven. There's a little larceny in you after all."

The discovery was a shock, but life went on, and Steven weathered the revelation. With Jerry's help he threw himself into his work, deciding to specialize in criminal law. He'd discovered his vocation and loved it. Soon he developed quite a reputation as one of the best defense attorneys in New York. He was the first to admit that without Jerry he certainly wouldn't be a partner in one of the most successful law firms in New York. Jerry had supported him all the way. So what if he conducted his personal life like the ideal *Playboy* subscriber? Beneath all his sexist front the man had heart, and that was what really counted.

Deena Swanson was a coolly attractive woman with chiseled features, dead blue eyes, and very pale red hair cropped in a thirties bob. She was one of those women of indeterminate age—taut white skin without a line in sight, perfect makeup, and a slim figure beneath a tailored gray skirt and an expensive silk shirt. Steven figured her to be anywhere between thirty and forty—it was impossible to tell. What he could tell was that she didn't look happy.

She greeted them with a limp handshake, receiving them in a spacious living room filled with African artifacts, sculpture, and fine paintings. Above the mantel hung an impressive oil painting of Mr. and Mrs. Swanson. In it, she wore a pink ball gown and her husband sported a white tuxedo; both held the same expression—bland indifference.

A Lebanese houseman hovered, waiting to take their order for coffee before backing respectfully from the room.

Deena indicated that they were to sit on an overstuffed couch, and when they were settled, she said in a slightly accented voice, "The meeting we are about to have must be absolutely confidential. Am I assured of this?"

"Of course," Jerry replied quickly, offended that she might think otherwise.

"My husband is not to know of this conversation either."

"Mrs. Swanson, you are a valued client. Whatever you say to us is strictly for our ears only."

"Good." She crossed impressive silk-clad legs and reached for a thin black cigarette in a silver box.

Jerry leaped to attention with his lighter.

Deena drew deeply on her cigarette, stared first at Jerry, then at Steven, and said, "I don't believe in wasting time. Do you?"

"Couldn't agree more," replied Jerry, ever obliging, and quite attracted to this cool, expensive-looking woman, even though she wasn't his usual type.

Deena silenced him with a look. "Kindly hear me out," she said imperiously. "No interruptions."

Jerry's back stiffened. He wasn't used to being spoken to as if he were hired help.

Deena spoke again, oblivious to his hurt feelings. "Gentlemen," she said calmly, "it has recently come to my attention that one of these days I might be obliged to commit the perfect murder."

A heavy silence hung over the room while Deena paused for a long moment, allowing her words to register. When she was satisfied they had, she continued, "If this situation ever arose, and I failed in my attempt to make it perfect, I would naturally expect you—as my attorneys—to do everything in your power to defend me." A long white finger decorated with a huge diamond ring pointed straight at Steven. "*You.* I would want you to defend me. I understand you're the best."

"Now wait a minute," Steven interrupted heatedly. "I can't—"

"No. *You* wait a minute," she snapped, a woman used to getting her own way. "Allow me to finish." She glared at them both, cold blue eyes daring either of them to interrupt again. "A retainer of one million dollars was transferred into your company's account today. All you have to do, Mr. Myerson, Mr. Berkeley, is to be there *when* and *if*—and I emphasize the *if*—I need you." She gave a brittle laugh, before adding with slow deliberation, "For all our sakes, we should hope that day never comes."

5

Abe Panther sat behind his large walnut desk, a fierce Inga positioned in the background.

Lucky Santangelo entered the room, accompanied by Morton Sharkey, her West Coast lawyer.

Abe greeted Lucky with a friendly nod. They had met only once before and he'd warmed to her instantly, recognizing in her the true spirit of a maverick and an adventurer. She reminded him of himself when he was young.

"You're looking well, Mr. Panther," Morton Sharkey said politely, still in a mild state of shock that Lucky had been able to get this far with her deal. When she'd first come to him with her wild proposition, he'd almost laughed in her face. "Don't you know you're asking the impossible?" he'd warned her. "Panther Studios is controlled by Mickey Stolli and Ben Harrison. And let me tell you, I know for a fact they'd never even consider selling."

"Aren't you forgetting they merely run it?" Lucky had replied coolly. "And from what I hear, they're mostly in business for themselves. Don't worry, Morton, I've had every detail checked out. Abe Panther owns the studio one hundred percent. He can do whatever he likes. And I want him to sell it to me."

"The man is a hundred and six," Morton had joked.

"The man is eighty-eight, and in full possession of all his faculties," she'd replied, full of confidence.

Morton Sharkey had never thought it possible. But then, Morton Sharkey had never dealt with a Santangelo before. When Lucky put something in motion she was behind it all the way, and instinct had immediately told her Abe Panther would love to dump on his two thieving sons-in-law and pull the studio—*his* studio—out from under them.

Secret negotiations had taken place. At first Abe hadn't seemed interested, until Lucky had insisted on flying out to Los Angeles for a face-to-face confrontation.

Abe Panther might be an old man, but she had known they were kindred spirits the moment her black Santangelo eyes met his canny, faded blues at their first meeting.

"What the hell you know 'bout runnin' a studio an' makin' movies?" he'd snapped at her.

"Not much," she'd replied honestly. "But I *can* smell garbage when I'm near it, and that's what your studio is turning out. Cheap, exploitive garbage." Her eyes burned bright. "So, I reckon I can only do a better job, right?"

"The studio's turnin' a profit," Abe had pointed out.

"Yes, but you're still making shit movies. I want to make Panther great again, as it once was. And let me tell you something—I *can* do it. That, I can assure you, is a Santangelo promise. And the Santangelos do not break promises." She'd paused and stared at him, mesmerizing him with her dangerous black eyes before adding, "Bet on it."

He'd warmed to her immediately. She had spirit and ballsiness, refreshing qualities in a woman.

And Lucky had guessed right—Abe would enjoy nothing more than to screw his sons-in-law out of what they took for granted as their rightful inheritance.

A deal was put into motion. All that was needed now was Abe's signature.

"Let me talk to Lucky alone," Abe said, shifting in his chair.

They were almost there, but Morton sensed a curve ball coming.

"Certainly," he said, far more easily than he felt. He glanced over at Lucky.

Imperceptibly she nodded, indicating he should leave.

Morton walked out of the room.

Inga didn't budge. She remained behind the old man's desk, a stoic Swedish monument.

"Out!" Abe commanded sharply.

A twitch of her thin lips was the only indication that she minded. Leaving the room, she slammed the door behind her, a signal of disapproval at being dismissed.

Abe cackled. "Inga don't like me telling her what to do. Still blames me for never makin' her a star." He shook his head. "Not my fault. No screen presence. Movie stars gotta have two qualities— without 'em they're dead." He cocked his head on one side. "Know what they are?"

Lucky nodded. She knew Abe Panther's credo by heart. "Likability and fuckability," she recited without hesitation.

He was impressed. "How'd you know that?" he demanded.

"Because I've read everything about you. Every press clip, studio release, three unauthorized biographies. Oh, and a few personal biographies by some very beautiful female stars who couldn't help but mention you." She grinned. "You sure got around in your time, didn't you? You're a very famous man, Mr. Panther."

He nodded, pleased at her assessment of his standing. "Yup. I'm the last of 'em," he said proudly. "The last of the movie dinosaurs."

"I wouldn't call you a dinosaur."

"Don't need your flattery, girlie. You've almost got your deal."

"I know." Her black eyes shone brightly. "I'm ready to meet your price. You're ready to sell to me. So come on, Mr. P. What exactly is holding us up?"

"Just a little something I need from you."

She tried to suppress the impatience in her voice. When Lucky wanted something she wanted it immediately. "What?" she asked edgily.

"Retribution."

"Huh?"

"The scums-in-law an' all the bloodsuckers around 'em."

"Yes?"

"I want you to nail 'em, girlie. Nail 'em good."

"I plan to."

"My way."

She continued to check her impatience. "What's your way?"

"Before you gain control, you take a job at the studio. You'll be assistant to Herman Stone, he's my man." Abe sparkled as he felt excitement creeping back into his life. "An' when you're there— right in the thick of it—you'll catch 'em all doin' what they shouldn't be doin'." He cackled with delight. "Six weeks on the inside, an' then whammo, girlie, you're the new boss, an' you can dump 'em all. Some good plan, huh?"

Lucky could hardly believe what she was hearing. It was an insane idea. How could she vanish for six weeks and assume another identity? She headed an empire; there was no way she could just disappear. What about Lennie? And Bobby and Brigette? Not to mention all her numerous business commitments?

"Impossible," she said, shaking her head regretfully.

"If you want my studio you'll do it," Abe retorted, clicking his false teeth. "If you *really* want it."

She brushed a hand through her dark hair, stood up and began pacing around the room.

Sure, she wanted the studio, but she wasn't about to jump hoops to meet the whims of a demanding old man. Or was she?

Hmm . . . Maybe it wasn't such an insane idea. Maybe it was quite a tempting proposition—a challenge. And there was nothing Lucky enjoyed more than a challenge.

Undercover she could catch everyone doing what they weren't supposed to be doing.

Abe watched her carefully, crinkling his shrewd eyes as he reached for a glass of prune juice on his desk. "No undercover . . . no sale," he said, just to make quite sure she understood his rules.

Lucky spun around and stared at him. "You mean you'd blow this deal?" she asked incredulously. "All that money?"

Abe smiled, clicking his teeth into a neat porcelain row. They didn't fit his leathery, lined old face. They looked too new. "I'm eighty-eight years old, girlie, what am I gonna do with the money? It ain't gonna buy me a hard-on, huh? *Huh?* It ain't gonna raise my *schnickel.*"

Lucky grinned. "Who knows?"

"*I* know, girlie."

"Nothing in life is a certainty."

Abe clicked his false teeth in and out of his mouth one more time —not exactly an endearing habit. "Six weeks," he said with surprising firmness. "Or we got no deal."

6

Brigette Stanislopoulos was just seventeen years old and undeniably pretty. She had long, naturally blond hair and a rounded, well-developed figure. She was also an heiress, due to inherit half the Stanislopoulos fortune left to her by her grandfather Dimitri. She already had her mother's vast estate in trust, and when she reached twenty-one she was destined to become one of the richest women in the world. A sobering thought—for Brigette, although still a teenager, had already lived a life filled with pain and confusion, and instinctively she knew her huge inheritance was only going to add further complications.

Money had failed to bring her mother happiness. Poor Olympia —discovered in a seedy New York hotel with the famous rock star Flash, both of them drugged out and dead. Not a very fitting end for Olympia, the girl who should have had everything.

Brigette was determined *her* life would be different. She had no intention of following her mother's treacherous path to unhappiness: three husbands, and an excess of selfish pleasures.

Brigette was thirteen when Olympia died. She'd never known her real father, an Italian businessman whom her grandfather had always referred to as "the fortune hunter." Olympia had divorced him shortly after Brigette was born, and several months later he'd been blown to pieces by a terrorist car bomb in Paris. Losing her mother and natural father at such an early age had been bad enough; more tragedies, however, loomed ahead. Several months later she and Lucky's son, Bobby, were victims of a kidnapping. Santino Bonnatti —a infamous crime czar and a lifetime enemy of the Santangelo family—had the two children trapped in the house of his girlfriend, Eden Antonio, and was intent on sexually molesting them. Before he was able to succeed, Brigette managed to grab his gun and fire three times, just as Lucky arrived to the rescue. Almost immediately the police were at the front door, but by that time Lucky had made sure Brigette and Bobby were hustled out the back, and taken safely home. Lucky had then proceeded to accept responsibility for Santino's death.

Months later at Lucky's trial, Brigette had gathered all her courage, jumped to her feet, and publicly confessed. It was a brave thing to do, but she had been unable to sit back any longer and allow Lucky to take the blame. Fortunately, there had been a videotape proving Bonnatti's death to be a clear case of self-defense.

Brigette was placed on probation for a year and sent to live with her grandmother Charlotte, Dimitri's first wife.

Charlotte was no comfortable grandmother figure. She was an elegant society matron, now married to her fourth husband, an English stage actor ten years her junior. They divided their time between a house in London's Eaton Square and a New York brownstone.

Looking after Brigette's welfare was not exactly Charlotte's dream come true. She had immediately enrolled her granddaughter in a strict private boarding school an hour's drive from New York.

All Brigette wanted was to be left alone. She felt like the original poor little rich girl with a scandalous past.

She kept to herself, shunning any offers of friendship, for above all, Brigette had learned the true secret of survival—and that was never to trust anyone.

"Hey, Stanislob—it's the phone for you."

Stanislob was one of the better names they called her. Brigette didn't care. She knew who she was. She was Brigette Stanislopoulos.

Person. Human being. Not the spoiled brat some of the tabloids liked to make her out to be.

They never left her in peace, the gutter press. There was always someone around lurking, spying. A photographer hiding in the bushes, an insolent reporter tracking her every move. They watched her relentlessly.

The tabloids had their favorites. Lisa Marie Presley, Princess Stephanie of Monaco, and Brigette Stanislopoulos. Three young heiresses. Always good for a story.

Ignoring the stupid nickname, Brigette took the phone from a tall girl with frizzed hair and an abundance of freckles. Maybe they could've been friends—another time, another life.

"Yes?" She spoke hesitantly into the receiver. Her calls were supposed to be monitored, but nobody ever bothered.

"Hey, pretty girl, it's Lennie. As usual I've come up with a sensational idea. What are your plans for the summer?"

"No plans."

"I like it. I'm gonna speak to Lucky about you coming out here and spending time with us in Malibu. We've rented a sensational house. How about it?"

Brigette was delighted. Lennie Golden and Lucky were the only two people she really cared about—Lennie, her ex-stepfather, now married to Lucky, who had once been married to her grandfather. What a tangled web of relationships! The Stanislopoulos clan made the Onassis family tree seem simple.

"I'd love that," she said excitedly.

"Great. I'll have Lucky persuade Charlotte to let you go for a few weeks."

"God! The last thing Charlotte needs is persuading. Just tell her. She'll be thrilled to get rid of me."

"Now, now, don't be nasty, little girl," he teased.

"It's true, Lennie!"

"And then, when I finish the movie, maybe we'll all take off for Europe."

"Brilliant!"

"Tough. No enthusiasm, huh?"

"C'mon! I'd kill for this trip."

"You don't have to. It's almost settled."

"I can't wait!"

"Good."

"How come you're not working? Isn't it the middle of the day in L.A.?"

"What about you?" he countered.

"It's five-thirty. I'm a free person."

"So get out an' run riot."

She giggled. "I can't. It's a weekday. We're not allowed out on weekdays."

"Break a rule or two, live dangerously."

"You're not supposed to tell me to do things like that," she said, remembering the one time she had broken the rules and suffered the consequences.

"No shit? If I were you I'd go for it."

Go for what? She had no friends. No one to cut school with. Besides, she was not like her mother—she had no desire to break loose. The price, she'd discovered, was far too high.

"How's the movie going?" she asked, hurriedly changing the subject.

He groaned. "Don't ruin my day."

"Is Lucky in L.A. with you?"

He feigned exasperation. "What is it with the questions? Are you needlin' me because you've nothing better to do, or what?"

She smiled. "Don't you know? I live to piss you off."

Laughing, he said, "Well, keep on livin', and I'll call you next week with more plans. Okay, bait?"

"Okay, dirty old man."

Lennie always made her feel terrific. Especially when he called her "bait," an abbreviation of "jail bait"—his pet name for her. She always retaliated with "dirty old man." It was their private game. Their way of saying the past meant nothing. "You gotta laugh about something an' it'll go away," Lennie had often told her.

Maybe he was right, but it didn't mean she had to let her guard down. She was Brigette Stanislopoulos. Person. Heiress. Always an heiress. No getting away from *that*.

With a deep sigh she returned to the dormitory room—a prison shared with three other girls. There was a stack of homework piled on the table next to her bed, and on her side of the wall hung a single poster of Boy George, smiling shyly, wearing full makeup and ringlets. She liked his music, and she liked the fact that he didn't seem to give a damn. Her kind of person.

The other girls had posters and pictures of everyone from Rob Lowe to an almost naked Richard Gere. So what? Romantic involvements were something Brigette never wanted to experience again.

For a moment she allowed her mind to drift back in time. First there was Santino Bonnatti's face—always there—that evil, sneering face. And then there was Tim Wealth. Handsome and young. A would-be-famous actor who'd had the bad luck to try and pull a scam with Bobby and her as the central characters. The newspapers had never connected the murder of the young actor with the Bonnatti events.

Thank goodness, Brigette thought with a shudder. She'd loved Tim, and he'd tricked her. Unfortunately he had paid with his life. No fault of hers. Bonnatti's men had done what they were told, and they were told Tim Wealth was in the way.

Don't think about it. She scolded herself silently. For two months they'd made her see psychiatrists. "Don't think about it," the last one had told her. The only good advice she'd received. All that talk about her real father being dead and then her mother leaving her, causing her to feel like an abandoned child, meant nothing.

She wasn't abandoned—she was strong. A survivor. Brigette Stanislopoulos didn't need anyone.

7

Sitting still for an interview had never been Lennie's favorite pastime. Especially when the interviewer insisted on intruding on the set, watching everything, eavesdropping, and making copious notes.

Shorty Rawlings, the P.R. on the movie, had talked Lennie into it against his better judgment. It was a cover story for *People* or *Us*—he couldn't remember which—and the interviewer was a horse-faced woman who kept skirting dangerously around his private life—a subject he never discussed, a fact always made very clear up front.

Not that his private life was a secret. Marrying Olympia Stanislopoulos and then Lucky Santangelo did not exactly help him maintain a low profile. What the hell—he refused to fuel the gossip; better to keep quiet.

Lucky was paranoid about staying out of the press. She refused to give interviews, and like her father, Gino, she went to a great deal of trouble to avoid being photographed. "I'm not a public person," she'd warned Lennie before they were married. "And I intend to keep it that way."

Not that easy when you marry a movie star, he'd wanted to say. Especially when your previous husband was one of the richest men in the world and your father made plenty of headlines in his day.

43

Despite everything, Lucky had somehow succeeded in holding on to a certain amount of anonymity. Not many people knew what she looked like—her name was better known than her face.

"How's your wife?" horse-faced reporter threw in casually, tracking his thoughts. "Is it true you're separated?"

Lennie fixed her with his disconcertingly green eyes. "I gotta get back to work," he said, rising from his canvas chair. He'd had enough.

Undaunted, the reporter pressed on. "Lucky Santangelo—quite a woman. Is she in L.A.?"

"Ever thought of getting a tongue job?" Lennie asked sharply.

The woman was startled. "I *beg* your pardon?"

"Y'know, a little snip at the end? Just to stop you asking those personal questions you've been told not to ask?"

Before she could respond, Shorty Rawlings appeared, and Lennie stalked off without saying another word.

"Well, really!" the woman said, her face flushed, "did I hit a nerve?"

"I sure hope not," Shorty replied anxiously. This movie was giving him ulcers, what with Joey Firello laying everything in sight; Grudge Freeport drinking himself into oblivion; Marisa Birch shacking up with her female stand-in as well as with the producer; and Lennie Golden behaving like he didn't have to do publicity. And this was on home ground—Christ knows what they'd all be like on a five-week location in Acapulco.

Shorty frowned. Lennie Golden wasn't Nicholson or Redford, for crissakes. He was just the new schmuck on the lot with a couple of money-making movies behind him and no solid track record.

Shorty Rawlings was fifty-two years old; he'd seen them come and he'd seen them fade—real fast. Plenty of publicity kept you up there, and Lennie Golden better wise up.

Shorty threw his arm around the journalist's shoulder. She was a tall woman with greasy hair and a bad nose job. Probably a failed actress—Hollywood was full of 'em, and they all ended up doing something else. "C'mon, honey," he said expansively. "I'll buy you a drink." *An' maybe you'll give me a blow job*, he added silently. After all, this was Hollywood, and the perks of the job were many.

"What's going on, man?" Joey Firello caught him on the way back to his trailer.

Lennie shrugged noncommittally. "Some stupid cow of a reporter."

"Fuck 'er," Joey said, cavalier as ever.

"No. *You* fuck her," Lennie retaliated.

Joey was not adverse to the idea. "What does she look like?"

Lennie couldn't help laughing. Joey would screw a table if it eyeballed him nicely. "I'm going home," he said. "See you tomorrow."

"Home." Joey repeated home as if it were a dirty word. "How about my party?"

"I told you, I can't make it."

"You're missin' out on a wild time."

Lennie was not into Joey's bad behavior. "I've had enough wild times to last me several lifetimes, thank you."

"You don't know what you're missing!"

"That's just it, Joey. I do."

He bumped into Cristi on the way to his car. She certainly was a prime California girl, all bronzed limbs, pale hair, and gleaming white teeth. He couldn't help noticing that her legs ended at her neck.

"Good night, Mr. Golden," she said politely.

Mr. Golden! Was he that old?

Climbing into his Ferrari he realized he not only missed Lucky, he needed her. She'd promised to spend a couple of weeks at the Acapulco location, and he couldn't wait.

Being together. Wasn't that what marriage was supposed to be all about? For eighteen months they'd spent most of their time apart. O.K., so he'd known up front Lucky wasn't the kind of woman to drop everything just to be with him. She had a multibillion-dollar business to watch over, and a son and a father she liked to spend time with. But somehow he'd always imagined he could handle it, that it wouldn't bother him. Lately he'd been realizing things weren't exactly turning out that way. He'd been missing her plenty. And a more traditional marriage didn't seem like such a bad idea. He enjoyed being married. It gave him security and balance, made him feel centered in his life, for once. And after *his* crazy childhood he needed a stabilizing influence. He certainly hadn't found it with Olympia. Lucky was supposed to be it.

Maybe the time had come to think about having a kid of their own. A Golden kid—with Lucky's looks and his humor. He'd mentioned it a couple of times, and Lucky had changed the subject before they'd really had a chance to get into it.

Yes, he decided, Acapulco was the time and the place. And the more he thought about it the more he was sure. Fun times in the Mexican sun, talk her into a baby, and after the movie was finished they'd spend a couple of weeks in Malibu with Brigette and Bobby, and then take the summer off and drift around Europe doing nothing.

He remembered the first time he and Lucky had made love. What a memory! It was a late afternoon in Saint-Tropez. Calm sea, deserted beach, balmy weather. Some great trip!

Goddamn it! The memory was making him horny.

He screeched the Ferrari to a stop at a red light, suddenly craving a cold shower.

"Hi!" A girl in a white convertible pulled alongside him. She wore a purple tank top and matching visor.

Before he could decide whether he knew her or not, she solved his problem. "I *looove* your movies," she purred. "You're *sooo* funny and *sooo* sexy."

If he'd wanted to he could have hit on her with no trouble. She was certainly pretty enough.

But those days were over. He was a happily married man with an incredible wife and a baby on the way. Well . . . almost.

Flashing her a smile, he muttered a quick "Thanks," and without a second thought floored the Ferrari, making a fast, clean getaway.

8

Back in New York, Lucky made her decision. She would do it. Goddamn it, if that was the only way she could get Panther Studios, she would do it! Go in undercover and find out everything Abe Panther wanted to know. In fact, while she wasn't about to tell Abe so, she was beginning to think it was a great idea. This way, when she took over the studio she'd know everything. A great advantage.

Immediately after the meeting with Abe, she'd caught a plane back to New York. Morton Sharkey had accompanied her in the limousine on the drive to LAX. He'd talked all the way, telling her how ridiculous Abe's idea was, how it would never work, how it was quite obvious that Abe Panther was finally getting senile.

Morton couldn't help but notice her silence. "You're not actually thinking of doing it?" he'd asked incredulously.

She'd smiled a slow inscrutable smile. "I'll let you know, Morton."

Now she was ready to tell him Yes, we're going for it.

Naturally, Mr. Morton Sharkey would throw a fit, lawyers were always creating problems, studying every legal angle, pointing out the pitfalls.

So what? Lucky Santangelo did what she wanted. And this caper was just the kind of adventure she craved. She was already thinking of ways to change her appearance so no one would recognize her. As Gino's daughter, the widow of Dimitri Stanislopoulos, and Lennie Golden's wife, she'd had her photograph in the newspapers from time to time, but not that often. And she'd never cooperated with the press—there were no official posed pictures, only random paparazzi shots.

A wig would take care of her hair. And glasses for her eyes. Dowdy clothes and a subservient attitude. This was going to be fun! Six weeks of play-acting and then Panther Studios would be hers.

The only catch: How was she supposed to take six weeks off from normal life? How was she going to explain it to Lennie?

First she decided to confide in Gino.

The Santangelos: black-eyed Gino and his wild daughter. They'd been through a lot together—more than most families in ten lifetimes. Lucky loved him with a fierce and enduring passion.

She called, saying she had to see him urgently. They usually dined several times a month. Unfortunately she'd had to cancel their last dinner because she'd been in L.A.

"Paige is in town," Gino said, over the phone. "Can't it wait?"

Lucky was insistent. "Urgent means urgent."

"And Paige in town means an old man's feelin' pretty damn good."

"So feel good later. This can't wait."

"Lucky, Lucky, you're a difficult woman."

"So what else is new?"

"Hey—how about I bring Paige with me?" he suggested.

Lucky stood firm. "Absolutely not."

She wasn't being possessive, but the last thing she needed was Paige Wheeler knowing what she planned. Who could guess what kind of mouth the woman had? She was, after all, married to a Hollywood producer. One word in the wrong direction could blow the whole setup.

Lucky was determined to make sure nothing went wrong. Acquiring Panther Studios was all-important to her. There could be no tripping up along the way.

They met at a small Italian restaurant on Lexington. Father and daughter. Lucky, dark haired, black-eyed, and exotically beautiful. Gino, still walking with a swagger, a certain energy and cockiness about him that belied his years.

The man's still got it, Lucky thought admiringly as he approached their table. *He really must have been something when he was young.*

She'd heard enough stories about him from Uncle Costa, her father's dearest and oldest friend. Costa Zennocotti, who'd once been Gino's lawyer, was now a retired and respectable old gentleman living in Miami.

Ah . . . when Costa got to talking about the old days it was a treat. To hear Costa tell it there'd never been anyone quite like Gino the Ram. What a nickname! Lucky couldn't help smiling.

"What are *you* grinnin' at?" Gino demanded, sitting down and winking at their regular waitress—a big, surly woman who saved all her good moods for Gino.

"I was reflecting on your lurid past."

"Sweetheart, you don't know nothin'."

"Bull . . . shit."

"My daughter, the lady."

"Just what you wanted, huh?"

Their eyes met, full of warmth. Gino summoned the waitress and ordered his favorite red wine and hot crusty bread to be brought to their table immediately.

"It's on the way," the waitress said triumphantly.

He pinched her big ass, making her day. "What a girl!" And then he turned his full attention to Lucky. "How's Bobby? An' more important—when am I gonna see him?"

Gino was crazy about his grandchild, and never stopped complaining about the boy's being educated in England.

"Bobby is fine," Lucky replied. "I speak to him every day. Naturally he sends you his love. You're his favorite, as if you don't know."

"The kid would be better off in New York," Gino grumbled. "He's an American, he should be here. What's he gonna learn in one of them fancy-shmancy English schools?"

She did not feel the time was right to remind her father that Bobby was half Greek. "Manners," she said.

"Ha!" Gino snorted his amusement. "I sent you to Switzerland to learn manners, an' look what happened to you!"

"Yeah, look what happened to me. I *really* bummed out, didn't I?"

The waitress poured a drop of wine for Gino to taste. He sipped, nodded. "You're one hell of a Santangelo," he said, facing his daughter. "You got my street smarts, your mother's class, *and* you're a looker on top of it all. We did O.K. by you, kiddo, huh?"

"Thanks a lot. Don't *I* get any credit?" Lucky asked good-naturedly.

"It's all in the genes, kid."

"Sure."

Gino's eyes scanned the restaurant as he drank his wine and tore into the freshly baked bread. "So," he said slowly, "tell me, what's so important that I had to leave Paige? She thinks I got another broad stashed away."

"At your age?" Lucky asked, raising a skeptical eyebrow.

"Listen, kid. Age has nothin' t'do with nothin'. Just remember that. In your head you're always whatever age you wanna be—an' I'm stickin' to forty-five. *Capisce?*"

My father is a remarkable man, Lucky thought. *He's probably going to die on the job—humping his way to heaven!*

"You're grinnin' again," Gino said. "What's up? Are you pregnant? You an' Lennie hit the old jackpot, huh? Is that what you got to tell me?"

"No way!"

"O.K., O.K., so don't get excited. It's about time Bobby had a brother or sister. I'm only askin'."

"Why is it that whenever a woman has a secret, every man in the world naturally assumes she's pregnant?"

"So stab me in the back. I came up with a bad guess."

Taking a deep breath she made her announcement. "I'm going to buy a movie studio."

"You're gonna do *what?*"

"I'm buying Panther Studios," Lucky continued excitedly. "The studio that has Lennie tied to a three-picture deal." Her eyes spar-kled. "You see, the truth is he's hating every minute of the movie he's shooting now. He wants out, and *I'm* going to arrange it. Not out—but control. All the control he wants! Isn't it a sensational idea? *I* own the studio, and *he* gets his freedom."

"Slow down, kid. An' correct me if I'm readin' you wrong. But the

LADY BOSS

thought here seems to be that you're gonna buy a film studio just 'cause your old man is not havin' a day at the beach. Am I hittin' it straight on?"

"You got it!" Lucky was on a roll. She felt the adrenaline coursing through her body. Telling Gino was a kick. When she'd financed and built the Magiriano Hotel in Vegas by herself, and her father had seen the results, it had been a real triumph. Somehow, purchasing a movie studio was even more of a thrill.

Gino laughed derisively. "What the hell do *you* know about makin' movies?" he asked.

"What did *you* know about running a hotel when you put up the Mirage in 1902?" Lucky countered.

"It was 1951, smart ass, an' I knew plenty."

"Like what?" she challenged.

"Like more than *you* know about the goddamn picture business."

"What I don't know I'll find out. I plan to surround myself with professionals. If you look around at some of the jerks in charge of major studios you can see it's no big challenge. Panther is coasting along on cheap exploitation flicks and stars' ego trips. I'm going to turn the studio around and make it hot again."

Gino shrugged, sipped more wine, and shook his head. "Yeah, you're my daughter, all right. You're a Santangelo."

With a smile she charmed him. "Was there ever any question?"

Three hours later they'd finished two bottles of wine; eaten a mound of spaghetti and clam sauce; dallied with a dish of homemade pastries; and were now on hot, whiskey-laced Irish coffees.

"Cholesterol heaven!" Lucky murmured happily. "Are you *sure* you're supposed to do this at your age?"

He winked. "I'm forty-five, remember?"

She leaned forward to kiss him on the cheek. "I do love you, Gino . . . uh . . . Daddy." It was only on very special occasions she called him Daddy.

Basking in her affection, he said, "It's mutual, kid. You never doubted it, didja?"

Yes, lots of times, she wanted to say. *When Mommy was murdered and you withdrew from your children. And how about the time you paid to marry me off to Senator Richmond's dumb son*

51

when I was only sixteen? And shutting me out of the family business. And treating me like women were an inferior species. And marrying that Beverly Hills bitch Susan Martino, and almost adopting her scuzzy, fully grown children. . . .

Oh, yes, there were plenty of bad memories. But now things couldn't be better. They were a team. And somehow she knew it would never change.

9

"**Y**ou've been edgy for the last three days," Mary Lou said, massaging Steven's left foot. "What is it, honey? Are you ever going to tell me, or have I just got to carry on tiptoeing around your bad mood like a zombie?"

Steven roused himself from Johnny Carson's monologue. "What bad mood are you talking about?"

Mary Lou dropped his foot and let out an exasperated sigh. "Either you're going to tell me or you're not. Obviously you're not, so quit with the short answers and long silences, otherwise I am out of here." She raised her voice. "You hear me, Steven? O—U—T."

He looked faintly amused. "Where would you go?"

"Go? Me? I'm a star, honey, I can go where I want. So there!"

Lazily he reached for her. "With that big belly?"

She pulled away. "Don't try and sweet-talk me now. You're too late."

His hands found their way to her swollen breasts, where they lingered.

She didn't move. A good sign. Maybe he could shortstop a fight and get lost in her warmth. He needed comforting and nurturing, not a damned argument.

"Steven," she murmured in a low voice that was neither denial nor acceptance.

With practiced ease he continued to fondle her breasts, springing one of them free from the confines of a lacy nightgown, and bending his head to play small circling games with his tongue.

"Steven Berkeley," she sighed breathlessly, "I *really* hate you."

There was no more talking after that. Two years of marriage and they were both still hopelessly turned on by each other.

On television Johnny Carson continued to entertain.

In the Berkeley household no one was watching.

The next morning Mary Lou was up first. She showered, dressed in a sensible track suit, and sat on the side of the bed waiting for Steven to wake up.

He rolled into consciousness, foggily aware it was Saturday, his favorite day.

As soon as he opened his eyes Mary Lou pounced. "About time, lover-boy," she said matter-of-factly. "Now let's continue that conversation we never finished last night."

Piece by piece she dragged it out of him until eventually he confided the whole story to her. What else could he do? She was relentless when it came to extracting information.

He told her about Deena Swanson and their bizarre meeting. And then he told her about Jerry—the fool—who'd laughed the whole thing off and claimed they were dealing with a crazy woman, and no way was he handing back a million bucks retainer—no damn way.

"Perhaps she *is* crazy," Mary Lou mused. "She must be, to even tell you she's considering murdering someone. I'm sure she's putting you on."

"Great. Just great. *You're* sure she's putting us on," Steven replied sarcastically, jumping out of bed. "That solves everything. Now I can go about my business with a clear conscience." He stalked into the bathroom. "Let's not worry about the poor victim, huh?" he called over his shoulder.

"There *is* no victim," Mary Lou pointed out sensibly.

"Yet," Steven replied ominously.

"And there won't be."

He was aggravated. "For crissakes, Mary Lou. Don't come off as if you know what the hell you're talking about."

Slamming the bathroom door he stared at himself in the mirror. *Satisfied?* his inner voice lectured. *You've betrayed a client/lawyer confidence and hurt your pregnant wife's feelings. All in one morning too. How clever can you get?*

By the time he emerged, Mary Lou had left the house, leaving behind a terse note saying she would not be back until late.

Steven was really pissed off. They always spent Saturdays together, shopping for food, catching a movie, dropping by Bloomingdale's, and finally, when they came home and she began to do things around the house, he was able to collapse on the couch in front of the television and watch sports.

Now their day was ruined, thanks to Mrs. Deena Swanson.

He considered calling Jerry and telling him exactly what he could do with Deena Swanson's million bucks. But then again, maybe Jerry was right: Keep the money and wait for nothing to happen. Deena Swanson was no dangerous killer. She was a very rich woman with a grudge against someone—and there was no way she was ever going to go through with her plan to commit the perfect murder.

Besides, what could either he or Jerry do? Talk was talk, and lawyer/client privilege was supposed to be sacred.

So why had he spilled the goods to Mary Lou and spoiled a perfect day?

Because it bothered him. He didn't like it. He felt caught in a trap.

On the other hand, there was absolutely nothing he could do about it.

Impulsively he picked up the phone and dialed Lucky's number. He hadn't seen her in a few weeks, and he wouldn't mind talking to her. She was something else, his half sister. A really incredible woman who'd added so much to his life, especially since the death of Carrie, his mother, who'd died peacefully in her sleep of a heart attack.

He really missed Carrie. She'd raised him alone, and in spite of terrible beginnings had managed to give him a sense of values, a great education, and a chance to succeed.

For many years she'd lied to him about his father—claimed that he died when Steven was a small boy. One day he found out the truth. His real father was Gino Santangelo, a man Carrie had slept with only once, and never told him the result of that union.

The truth was difficult to accept—for Gino, too—but gradually, over the last eighteen months, they'd forged a relationship. Hardly father and son, but a strong bond of mutual respect.

Lucky was different. She'd accepted him as her half brother with immediate warmth. And when Carrie was alive she'd welcomed her into the family, too. He would always love Lucky for that. She was a very special woman.

The answering machine picked up at her apartment. Steven left a message and then tried Gino. "How about lunch?" he asked.

"What is it with my kids this week?" Gino demanded gruffly. "I got Paige in town. Don't that mean nothin' to any of you?"

Steven was delighted to be called one of Gino's kids. It was taking time but he was getting there. "How about I buy you *both* lunch?" he suggested.

"When Paige is here I don't eat," Gino replied. "Y'know how it is."

"Hey, sorry I asked."

"Don't be sorry, call me Monday."

Paige Wheeler wore a lacy brown garter belt, silk stockings, very high heels, a push-up bra, and nothing else. Although nearing fifty, she was still a very attractive woman with her pocket Venus figure, abundance of copper-colored, frizzy hair, husky voice, and sensual smile.

Gino, who'd had more women in his life than most rock stars, couldn't get enough of her. To him she was the perfect companion to grow old with—a smart, sassy broad who appreciated Frank Sinatra, enjoyed sex, and could hold a more-than-decent conversation.

"Who was that?" Paige asked, as soon as he put the phone down.

"Steven. He wanted to take us to lunch. I told him to forget it."

"Why?" She paraded in front of him, spreading her legs in a dancer's stance.

"Why the hell d'you think?" he replied, grabbing her. "Has anyone ever told you you're one hot number?"

She smiled. "Yes, you, Gino. Constantly. And I love it."

He put his hand down the top of her stocking. "Get down on your knees an' say that."

"If you insist. However, let me remind you—a lady *never* speaks with her mouth full!"

When they were done, Gino collapsed on the bed, his heart pounding at a roaring pace.

Better take it easy, old man, he warned himself. *You're not as young as you used to be.*

No shit?

When his heart resumed its normal rhythm he remembered Steven and regretted having been so abrupt with him. Reaching for the phone he called him back. There was no reply.

Paige slept face down on his rumpled bed. The woman was an original. No shadows of the past to haunt him when she was around.

He got up and went to his dresser, unlocked the top right hand drawer and took out a Harry Winston box. Opening it, he gazed at an Elizabeth Taylor-sized diamond ring.

He'd bought Paige gifts before, usually from Forty-seventh Street, where he had connections and could get a deal. But this ring was different. This ring he'd gotten retail.

If Paige wanted it she could have it. Only one small catch. *If* she wanted it, she had to finally divorce Wheeler—no more excuses—and marry him.

Gino Santangelo had waited long enough.

Brigette was counting the weeks until vacation. June the fifteenth and she was a free person for the rest of the summer. What a relief to escape the daily grind of suffocating, boring school. She'd already spoken to her grandmother about spending a good chunk of her vacation with Lennie and Lucky.

Charlotte had not objected. "Whatever you like, dear," she'd said vaguely, probably thrilled to be rid of her.

Sitting in English class she daydreamed about all the fun she'd have. There had to be more than getting up in the morning, mingling with a bunch of stupid, unfriendly girls, and listening to a succession of uninspirational teachers drone on about nothing that interested her. Malibu with Lennie and Lucky was sure to be a major blast.

"Stanislopoulos!" Mr. Louthe, her English teacher, interrupted her reverie. He was a gray-haired man with ferret teeth and a droopy mustache. "What did I just say?" he asked sharply.

Brigette looked at him blankly. "Huh?"

Two of her classmates whispered an exaggerated "Huh?" at each other and giggled.

"Silence!" Mr. Louthe said sternly. "See me after class, Stanislopoulos."

Inwardly she groaned. She'd be late for tennis practice—her one pleasure. And Mr. Louthe was notorious for his sanctimonious lectures.

After the class was over she went and stood by his desk. He was attending to paperwork and made her wait for fifteen minutes. Finally he looked up. "Stanislopoulos," he said, "I'll make this brief."

Thank goodness, she thought.

"You are an intelligent girl. A pretty girl—"

Oh, no! Was he coming on to her? After Santino Bonnatti, she was never going to allow anybody to do anything to her again— unless she wanted it.

"And you are also an extremely isolated and unsociable girl."

Thanks a lot! she thought sourly.

"In life," Mr. Louthe continued in a sonorous tone, "there is always a price to pay. And I do not mean a monetary price. You must realize, young lady, that with all your money and connections, you will not end up a very happy person if you go through your days and weeks and months living in your own cocooned little space. Learning, sharing, reading, mixing with other people, giving of yourself—these are all growing experiences. Learn to grow, Miss Stanislopoulos, and your life may have some meaning. Thank you. You are dismissed." He bent his head and resumed work.

Brigette was stunned. How dare he talk to her like that! She knew how to learn—only it wasn't something she cared to do. She knew how to share—but why should she? And as for mixing with other people—well it was they who didn't want to mix with her. Wasn't it?

Returning to the dormitory, she continued to fume. What did he know about her life anyway? What did he care?

Dumb man.

Dumb *old* man.

Dumb *old* man with a stupid mustache!

Inexplicably she began to cry, and suddenly it was a deluge of tears, as if all the pain and frustration and hurt of the last few years came pouring out.

It occurred to her that this was the first time she'd cried since Tim Wealth's death and the following nightmare events.

When the tears were over she felt better, until she noticed Nona, one of her more recent roommates, standing inside the door. God! On top of everything else she would now have a reputation as a crybaby.

"Are you O.K.?" Nona asked, sounding sympathetic.

She rubbed her eyes. "Just a choking fit—nothing terminal."

"I know what you mean," Nona said casually. "I get 'em all the time. Especially when I have to endure one of Louthe's lectures."

"It wasn't too bad."

Suddenly they were having a conversation, something Brigette had managed to avoid until now.

"O.K.," Nona said brightly. "I'm out of here. I've got a pass for town." She picked up her purse and hesitated for a moment. "You wouldn't like to come, would you?"

Normally Brigette would have said no, and that would be that. But today was different. Today was the start of something new— making friends.

"I'd love to," she answered shyly.

Nona was surprised. The other girls would kill her for dragging along the poor little rich kid, but she couldn't help it—Brigette looked so lost and lonely.

"Come on," she said warmly, grabbing her by the arm. "I don't know about you, but the sooner I'm out of this prison the better."

10

It was a go situation, and Lucky felt incredibly elated. First she made a short trip to London via the Concorde to visit Bobby. He was in fine shape—small and handsome, with an endearing British accent. Gino would have a shit fit!

After visiting Bobby, she flew out to Los Angeles to spend a couple of days with Lennie before embarking on her adventure. If she was to successfully vanish for six weeks, everything had to be carefully coordinated.

Arriving at their rented house in Malibu, she was met by Miko, their diminutive Japanese houseboy. Miko informed her he was expecting Mr. Golden home at seven.

She was pleased. She'd told Lennie she wasn't flying out until Sunday, figuring a surprise would enhance the mood nicely. Now she'd have time to relax for a few hours.

"O.K., Miko," she said, handing him a wad of bills. "Here's five hundred bucks to do a vanishing act. This'll pay for your hotel and expenses. I don't want to see you for forty-eight hours. Do we understand each other?"

Miko accepted the money with a small, formal bow. "I am gone, madam," he said in perfect English.

With Miko out of the way, she threw open the doors to the beach, plumped up the cushions on the large rattan couches, put Luther

Vandross on the stereo, called Trader Vic's to request Lennie's favorite Indonesian lamb roast to be delivered at 9 P.M., and prepared a mean Margarita.

When that was all done, she indulged in a leisurely shower and slipped white shorts and a T-shirt over nothing. Lucky rarely bothered with underwear; she didn't see the point. Piling her long dark hair atop her head, she added a touch more gloss to her lips and some tawny blusher to accentuate her sharply defined cheekbones.

In her thirties, Lucky Santangelo had only grown more beautiful, a beauty she treated very casually, for ego was not her thing.

The beach looked inviting. It was almost dusk, and several people jogged along the shoreline with their dogs, while a single swimmer braved the cool Pacific ocean.

She'd spent only a few weekends at the house, but there was something about it she was beginning to get attached to. It was so peaceful and quiet. You couldn't hear the cars racing by on the nearby Pacific Coast Highway—only the soothing rhythm of the waves hitting the beach.

Maybe they should buy it, she mused. Not that she was crazy about California, but once she owned Panther Studios they would obviously be spending more time there.

Mental note: Call the real estate agent and find out if the house was for sale.

It was nearing seven. She poured the Margaritas into tall frosted glasses, and sat outside on the deck overlooking the beach.

Luther serenaded her with "Superstar."

Leaning back, she closed her eyes and drifted off into a jet-lagged sleep.

Cristi was definitely coming on to him in her all-California-girl way. She'd been doing it throughout the day. Nothing too overwhelming, but Lennie was more than aware of her interest.

"I'm takin' the twist to Spago, why don't you come with us?" Joey suggested, enjoying the possibilities. He referred to all women as twists or grunts. The twists were the delectable ones, and Cristi was certainly edible.

Lennie said no.

"You prefer drivin' back to an empty beach house rather than a fine pizza with two of your best friends?" Joey tried to look hurt. The expression did not take.

Joey Firello was short and wiry, with rubbery lips, an ethnic face, and lots of nervous energy. Not traditionally good-looking, he was seemingly irresistible to women. "They want to mother me," he deadpanned. "Hey—the day I say no to tit is the day it's over, man."

Joey had been very supportive when Lennie had first arrived in L.A. fresh from being fired out of a gig in Vegas, stone-cold broke. Joey—who at that time was just beginning to make it himself—had gotten Lennie a job at the legendary Foxie's club on Hollywood Boulevard and had been there for him all the way.

Lennie did not forget favors, so when his own career began to surpass Joey's by a long streak, and Joey's was on a downward spiral due to a serious cocaine problem, he'd always made sure there was a role for his friend in everything he did. Right now Joey's career was on an upswing.

"You comin' for dinner or what?" Joey demanded.

"Maybe I'll let you buy me a pizza," Lennie relented. After all, the house in Malibu was distinctly lonely with just Miko and himself for company. And he was tired of trying to make improvements on a script that was going nowhere.

Joey seemed pleased; he'd been trying to get Lennie out for weeks. "We'll go back to my place, you can grab a shower, an' then we'll *paaarty* all night long! Yeah?"

"Dinner, Joey. That's it."

Joey pulled a disappointed face. "Dinner, Joey," he mimicked. "Hey, hey, hey. Whatever happened to the wild guy I used to know? Whatever happened to the king of the party scene?"

"He got married," Lennie said.

"Yeah, he got married—not dead."

The doorbell woke Lucky. Asleep on the outside deck she came to with a start and shivered. A brisk wind whipped along the beach, and now the ocean was black and the waves sounded thunderous.

A quick glance at her watch revealed that it was nine o'clock.

She hurried through the dark house to the front door and let in the waiter from Trader Vic's. The food was sealed in cardboard cartons. She had him place them on a counter in the kitchen before he left.

Nine o'clock and where was Lennie? Miko had told her he was expecting him at seven, and like an idiot she hadn't thought of checking because she'd wanted to surprise him. Obviously not so smart. Lennie was out and about, and she had no idea where to start looking.

It's your own fault, Santangelo, she scolded herself sternly. *That'll teach you to go for the unexpected.*

She wondered if Abe Panther was awake, or did the fierce Inga put him to sleep at eight o'clock? She wouldn't mind talking to the old guy. He was sharp and canny. She liked him.

Morton Sharkey had insisted that two separate psychiatrists and an independent doctor examine Abe before allowing Lucky to go ahead with the deal. "What if he drops dead?" Morton had asked. "Or even worse—what if *when* he dies the family steps forward and challenges his state of mind? We need to have this covered."

Abe had not objected. Like Lucky, he was enjoying the game. He brought his own lawyer into play, and every intricate detail was worked out.

Now they had a deal set in concrete. Starting Monday, Lucky was going in undercover. She couldn't wait!

Joey knew almost everyone in the restaurant, so what started out as a quiet dinner for three gradually grew into chaos.

"I'm getting out of here," Lennie announced at ten-fifteen. He'd had enough.

Joey grimaced. He was surrounded by women of all shapes, hues, and sizes. "I may be talented but I need help," he complained. "You can't leave me, man."

"Watch me." Lennie was already on his feet.

"Can you drop me off at my car?" Cristi asked hopefully. "I never was one for group auditions."

How could he say no to Miss California? "Aren't you staying with Joey?" he asked halfheartedly.

She eyed the seven other girls hanging onto Joey Firello's every breath. "Give me a break, Lennie." With that she pushed her chair away from the table and stood up, allowing him no choice but to take her with him.

"Bye, Joey," they said in unison.

Joey signaled a thumbs up. After four vodkas and several lines of cocaine (surreptitiously snorted because after numerous dry-out periods he was supposed to be reformed) he was flying on a solo journey.

Instinctively Lennie steered Cristi toward the back entrance, which led directly to the parking lot. Sometimes fans and photographers nested outside the front, and he didn't want to get caught. Even though this was a perfectly innocent situation, being photographed with Cristi wouldn't look right, and he had no wish to put Lucky's understanding to the test.

Once in the passenger seat of his Ferrari, Cristi let out a little sigh and said, all Miss California Clean-cut, "I'd really enjoy having sex with you, Lennie."

She made it sound so matter-of-fact he almost didn't get it. But when she joined the words with a silky hand on his crotch, cleverly missing the gearshift by inches, he had no doubt of her intentions.

Pulling on a thick sweater and a pair of faded Levi's, Lucky walked along the beach. It was deserted, windy, and dark. She stuck close to the shoreline, listening to the waves hitting the sand.

The solitude was enjoyable, giving her a great feeling of peace.

Being alone had never bothered her. Apart from her brother, Dario, she'd spent most of her childhood by herself and gotten quite used to it.

Thinking about Dario made her shiver. Once they'd been each other's lifelines, sharing every secret until she was sent away to boarding school. And then, after she was expelled, Gino had forced her into an arranged marriage with Senator Peter Richmond's dumb son, Craven.

Gino had thought he was doing her a big favor.

Ha! Some big favor. She'd shown *him*.

She remembered the first love of her life—Marco. Gorgeous Marco, with the dark, curly hair, Mediterranean features, muscular build, and brooding good looks.

Ah, Marco . . . she'd loved him when she was fifteen, and bedded him when she was twenty-two. He'd first worked for Gino as a bodyguard, and risen to casino manager.

When Marco was brutally gunned down, she had held him in her arms and felt his life slip away.

Taking revenge was satisfying. Above all, she was a Santangelo. She was Gino's daughter.

Gino had always labeled her a wild child. Now she was all grown up and had everything she'd ever wanted. Including Lennie. He made her laugh. He was her rock, her steadying influence. He was funny and warm and loving. She felt safe and protected when they were together. Lennie gave her more strength than she'd ever believed possible, and she loved him for it. That was why she wanted to give him something back—and what better prize than a movie studio?

The wind whipped the pins from her hair and it flew around her face.

Time to head back.

There was that split-second, almost automatic masculine reaction. *Why not? Who's going to know?* Then Lennie removed Cristi's enthusiastic hand, changed gears, and said, "Thanks, but no thanks. I'm not interested."

Obviously this was the first time in her young and delectable life Cristi had been turned down. To her credit she took it bravely. "My car's at Joey's," she said without losing a beat.

Lennie swung the Ferrari left on Sunset and again at Laurel Canyon. They rode in silence.

Joey owned a large house halfway up the hill—a ramshackle place with a breathtaking view and hidden snakes slithering around in the bushes.

When they drew into the driveway Lennie leaned across and opened her door. "Don't take it personally," he said, feeling that some acknowledgment was necessary. "I'm a very happily married man."

Cristi was not at all put out. "Why should I? You'll change your mind," she replied, confident and pretty as she climbed out of his car and walked toward the front door, turning for a final wave, her pale hair catching the light on the porch.

Hey, before Lucky, things might have been different. Now he couldn't wait to get home and call his beautiful wife in New York.

Lucky turned around and began the long jog back. The beach was still deserted. The waves continued to hit the sand with monotonous regularity.

With a shudder she wondered what was out there hiding in the vast, dark ocean. A recent news report had mentioned sharks venturing closer inland. Not that they were going to come sliding out of the sea onto the beach, but suddenly she felt an overwhelming desire to hurry back to the safety of the house.

The Ferrari made a noise that expensive Italian sports cars are never supposed to make, and spluttered to a standstill in the middle of Sunset, opposite the Roxy, where groups of stoned, long-haired rock fans waited for the next Heavy Metal concert.

"Shit!" Lennie muttered. He needed this like he needed the clap.

A patrol car cruised by and pulled up in front of him. The policeman who emerged was better-looking than Tom Selleck and wore his uniform well. He exhibited plenty of attitude as he sashayed toward Lennie. Big cock with a big gun. An unbeatable combination.

"We got a little problem here?" the cop drawled, a Southern import.

"Nothing that a new engine won't fix," Lennie replied.

"Aren't you—?" The cop hesitated for a moment, determined to get it right. "Lennie Golden!" he announced triumphantly. "You're some funny guy."

Happiness is finding a policeman who's a fan, Lennie thought. Sometimes it was just the opposite, and they broke your balls because of your celebrity.

"I guess we gotta get you outta here before the crowds discover you," the cop said, doing nothing except to stand by the stalled car while a traffic jam built up in the lane behind them and impatient horns began to blast.

"That would be nice," Lennie agreed.

"I came out to L.A. ten years ago," the cop continued conversationally. "Wanted to be an actor. I guess it didn't work out." He fingered his holstered gun. "Being a cop ain't all that bad. Sometimes I *feel* like an actor. Women really get off on the uniform." He smiled, pleased with himself. "Y'know what I mean?"

"I know," Lennie said amicably, wishing this schmuck would get his shit together.

"I bet you got a lotta women chasin' you," the cop said with a lewd wink. "Famous ones, huh?"

Lennie ignored the comment. "Do we phone the Automobile Club or what?" he asked, trying not to sound too irritable.

The policeman ran a stubby finger along the shiny part of the Ferrari. "Any time you got a part for a real live cop y'can call on Marian Wolff," he said casually.

Lennie frowned. "Who?"

"Marian Wolff. That's me. That's my name. Y'see, my mom figured if they could give the name of Marian to John Wayne when he was born, then it was O.K. enough for me. An' y'know something? My old mom was right. I kinda like the name Marian. It's got character. What d'you think?"

Lennie shook his head, already working this whole routine into some future comedy shtick. Not that he did stand-up anymore— he'd passed on that a long time ago. But this could be a funny set piece for Letterman or Carson.

An older policeman emerged from the patrol car—a grizzled guy with a mean stomp to his walk. "Marian," he yelled gruffly, "what the fuck is goin' on here? Ya want the whole of Sunset to grind to a fuckin' stop or fuckin' what? Get this Italian piece of shit tin outta here."

"Wally," the first cop announced proudly, "this here's Lennie Golden."

The old cop spat on the ground in disgust, completely unimpressed. "Marian," he said wearily, "who gives a flying fuck?"

It occurred to Lucky that Lennie might be out screwing around. The thought had never entered her mind before because she knew they had something very special, and it was not to be put at risk by either of them. Jealousy was an emotion she wasn't comfortable with. However, she couldn't ignore the fact that Lennie was a very attractive man, a very *famous* man, a very *fuckable* man, and she'd been neglecting him the last few weeks because she'd been so involved in putting the Panther Studios deal in place.

"What if" thoughts kept creeping into her mind.

What if Lennie was with another woman . . . ?

What if there was more than one woman . . . ?

What if . . . ?

The telephone interrupted her reverie. "Yes," she answered sharply.

"Who's this?"

"Who's *this?*"

"Lucky?"

"Lennie?"

And together they both yelled, "WHERE *ARE* YOU?"

It was almost an hour before his cab pulled up in front of the house.

Lucky raced out of the front door to greet him, throwing herself into his arms.

He hugged her tight and kissed her, a long, lingering soul kiss that excited the entranced cabdriver no end.

"Pay the man," Lucky said at last, extracting herself from his arms. "Then come in the house, lock the door, activate the answering machine, and *do not* speak to another human being for twenty-four hours."

The cabdriver leered. "Sounds good t'me."

"Goodbye," Lennie said, seeing the leering man on his way.

And so they fell into bed immediately, each craving the touch and sound and smell of the other.

No conversation. First, sex. Fast, pure, exciting lust took over as he remembered her smooth body, her silky skin, the tangle of her black hair, and the wildness of her lips.

She lost herself in his rhythm, luxuriating in the passion of his arms and legs and body language, holding him in every way, a captive to her strong desire.

"I love you, lady," he said as they rode the crest.

"And I love you, husband," she managed, before losing herself in an orgasm that seemed to last an hour.

Later, in bed, there was warmed-up Indonesian lamb roast with thick peanut-butter sauce and Chinese pea pods.

They ate with their fingers from paper plates, tearing at the meat, dipping it into the creamy sauce, feeding each other and giggling like a couple of wired teenagers.

"I never want to leave this bed," Lennie said happily. "This is it, lady. This is *it*."

"We waited a long time to get here," Lucky murmured softly.

"We sure did. A lot of time wasted, huh?"

"Not wasted, Lennie. We're together now, and we'll be together forever. We both know that, don't we?"

Taking her face in his hands, he kissed her slowly and passionately.

She stroked his chest, delicate fingers touching his nipples, drifting down toward her real objective.

To her delight he responded immediately.

"I'd hate to have met you when you were nineteen," she teased. "I bet you were the horniest guy in the neighborhood!"

"Don't give me that story. You'd have *loved* to have met me when I was nineteen. Your life's greatest wish. Right?"

She laughed. "Right!"

"I love you, beautiful lady."

JACKIE COLLINS

"Yeah?"

"Yeah."

They held a long meaningful look.

"Pass me the peanut-butter sauce," she said at last, with a wicked smile. "I've got plans."

He feigned alarm. "What plans?"

"Lie back, Lennie, and don't ask so many questions."

In the morning they surfaced just before noon, automatically reaching for each other as if it were the most natural move in the world.

Outside, the sun attempted to break through the closed shades, and a dog barked incessantly.

They made love again, slowly, languorously. And when they were finally finished, Lennie said, "What would the love of my life like to do today?"

Lucky stretched and smiled. "Take a shower with you. Take a walk along the beach with you. And then come straight back to bed without passing Go."

"It sounds like the perfect day to me," he replied with a grin. "Only how about we cut out the shower and the walk?"

"Don't you think we need the exercise?" she asked innocently. "I have exercises for you even Jane Fonda doesn't know!"

"You do?"

"I'll be your personal instructor."

"Sounds good to me."

It wasn't until later they began to talk. Lennie had his usual list of complaints about the movie, and Lucky listened quietly, hugging to herself the knowledge that soon she was going to make everything O.K.

"I write new dialogue, the asshole director says, 'Great—fantastic stuff, Lennie.' And then he doesn't want to shoot it. I go to the dailies, I give my suggestions—they ignore 'em. Jesus H. Christ, they're getting my input for free—you'd think they'd run with it. Right?"

She nodded her agreement, stroking his back, lightly massaging his neck.

He lay facedown on the bed, completely relaxed for the first time in weeks. Lucky was the only woman in the world who was able to draw every bit of tension out of him and make him feel this good.

"We've got to think of a way to get you out of this contract," she said.

He admitted defeat. "As usual you were right. I'm gonna talk to my lawyer."

"Hold off until *Macho Man* is finished. That's the time to make a move."

"Yeah, I guess so. How come you're always right?"

She laughed. " 'Cause I'm Gino's daughter and he taught me good."

"Pretty damn good."

"*Very* good. And don't you forget it, husband."

He rolled over and grabbed her in a hug. "So—the big question. When are you coming to Acapulco? I need you there like immediately."

Now came the crunch. She took a deep breath. "Uh, Lennie, I've been meaning to talk to you about Acapulco."

"What?" he asked suspiciously.

"Don't get mad," she warned.

"What?" he repeated, getting mad.

She began the carefully rehearsed speech she'd planned. "There's a huge business deal in Japan I have to take care of. If all goes as it should, I'll be out of there in a couple of weeks, and then I'll stop off and see Bobby in London, maybe spend a few days at the office in New York. After that, I'm all yours."

His tone was bleak. "You've got to be kidding."

"I'm not."

"Lucky," he said forcefully, "you promised me Acapulco."

"I'll be there," she lied.

"When?" he asked accusingly.

"As soon as I can."

Angrily he sat up. "I don't fucking believe this."

"I'm not exactly thrilled myself. But the Japanese are very particular when it comes to deal-making." She reached for a cigarette. "Oh, sure, I could send one of the heads of the company—but it's me they want. Something to do with honor. The owner of their company will only deal with the owner of *our* company, and until Bobby and Brigette reach a legal age, that's me. This is an enormous deal, something we've all been working on for over a year. I can't risk blowing it."

Fortunately Lennie knew nothing about what went on at Stanislopoulos Shipping—he'd never shown any interest, and she'd never volunteered information. Her story sounded plausible.

"Shit!" he grumbled. "Why did I have to marry a business tycoon? I never fucking see you." He leaped off the bed and stalked into the bathroom.

"Because I excite the hell out of you," she yelled after him. "And with anyone else you'd be bored. C'mon, Lennie, admit it."

The sound of the shower drowned her out. Goddamn it, he wasn't taking this well.

Stubbing out her cigarette, she followed him into the bathroom and into the shower, wrapping her arms around his waist from behind.

"Quit," he said sternly, attempting to shake her off.

"Don't be a pain in the ass," she replied, hanging on. "This is only a delay. I'll be there. After all, it's not like you're going to be a free person. You'll be working every day, and you know I hate to sit around playing the wife role."

"I had other plans," he said, reaching for the soap.

"What other plans?" she demanded, sneaking her hands around to the front of his body, cupping his balls and going for the main event.

"Listen, lady, sex ain't gonna get you out of this one," he warned, turning to face her as the lukewarm water cascaded over both of them.

"*What* other plans?" Lucky demanded a second time, sinking to her knees.

"No you don't." Weakly he attempted to push her away. "You can torture me all you want, but I'm not telling."

She flicked his growing hard-on with her tongue. "Tell!" she insisted. "Give me the information or you're in big trouble!"

"No . . . way," he managed to groan.

Her tongue teased him lightly, causing him to change his mind. He began to thrust against her.

Now it was her turn to back away. "Tell," she repeated sternly. "Or suffer."

They were both beginning to break up; the crisis was over.

Urgently he grabbed the back of her wet hair, pressing her head toward him.

She wriggled free and slipped out of the shower.

With a quick lunge he caught her, and they both fell to the floor, naked, slippery, and laughing.

"Gotcha!" he muttered triumphantly, spread-eagling her arms and pinning her legs with his body as he maneuvered into position.

And then he was pounding into her, and the words came out, surprising both of them.

"I . . . want . . . you . . . to . . . have . . . our . . . baby.   And . . . I . . . don't . . . want . . . any . . . excuses.   O.K., Lucky? O.K.?"

11

Under the guiding hand of Mickey Stolli, Panther Studios was a changed place from the days when Abe Panther was in charge. Once one of the great old studios making tasteful, stylish films, Panther had moved with the times. Mickey had made sure of that. As he was so fond of saying at meetings, "It's the frigging eighties, for crissakes. Let's give the dumb unwashed what they *really* wanna see."

What Mickey wanted the public to see was multiple violence with an avalanche of tits and ass. Not harmless tits and ass, but the pornographic kind. Girls being stripped, terrified, mutilated, raped, and murdered. On film, of course. In fact, whatever he and his willing team of writers, directors, and producers could get away with.

These were not big movies, starwise. But they were huge money-makers all over the world—every one. Cheap to shoot, cost nothing to put out, and easy to produce.

America the great. They could kick the hell out of women up there on the screen any way they wanted, and as long as the sex wasn't too graphic, they could get away with murder. Literally.

Panther Studios had begun to specialize in these low-bucks, soft-core exploitation flicks. Thanks to Mickey Stolli, who liked the big bucks they generated. But as powerful as he was, even Mickey had to cover his ass, bolster his ego, *and* shut up his brother-in-law, Ben

Harrison, who was always bitching and complaining about the cheapos. So, aside from the exploitation cheapos, Panther Studios made deals with major stars, paying them more money than anyone else, and also giving them sweet development deals that included their own production companies and a suite of offices on the studio lot.

Every year Panther made three or four legitimate big-time movies, like *Macho Man*, the film currently shooting with Lennie Golden, Joey Firello, and Marisa Birch. And *Strut*, a dramatic movie about a charming con man and a street-smart young woman, starring Venus Maria—*the* hot property of the year—with Cooper Turner co-starring and directing. Quite a coup.

And in post-production they had the new Johnny Romano action comedy *Motherfaker*.

Abigaile Stolli insisted that Mickey make movies with big stars. It was good for her social life.

Quite frankly, Mickey didn't give a rat's ass. Movie stars were trouble, always causing problems, holding things up, and expecting more money and attention than they were worth. Their egos were beyond enormous.

Mickey preferred shooting his cheapos. A nice fast production with a guaranteed box-office bonanza at the end of it.

Of course, he had to take into account Abigaile's feelings. She was, after all, Abe Panther's granddaughter, and the reason he was where he was today.

And where was he, Mickey Stolli?

He was in an air-conditioned office bigger than the house he'd grown up in. He was forty-eight years old. He was five feet nine inches tall. He was bald and didn't wear a rug. He had a deep, permanent suntan, flashing white teeth (all his own—the teeth compensated for the lack of hair), a hard body (thanks to daily tennis—his passion), and a rough-edged voice tinged with memories of the Bronx only when he was angry.

Mickey had lived in Hollywood for thirty years, first coming out as an eighteen-year-old would-be actor. Giving that up when he lost his hair at twenty, and becoming an agent. Giving that up when he married Abigaile eighteen years ago and becoming Abe's right-hand man. Giving that up ten years ago when Abe had his stroke and Mickey took over.

Mickey Stolli was a happy man. He had a wife, a thirteen-year-old daughter, Tabitha (nobody knew about the illegitimate son he'd fathered when he was twenty-nine, just before meeting and marrying Abigaile), a black mistress, two houses (Bel-Air and Trancas), three cars (a Rolls, a Porsche, and a Jeep), and a studio.

What more could any man ask for?

Olive, his English personal secretary, entered the office. Olive was a slim woman of forty, cast in the Deborah Kerr mold. "Good morning, Mr. Stolli," she said crisply.

Mickey grunted. On Monday mornings Olive presented him with a private and confidential report of all the studio activities from the previous week. She handed it to him as usual. It never bothered him that she had to work all weekend to get it ready for their 8 A.M. meeting.

He skimmed it quickly, jotting notes in the margin with a thick red pen. When he finished he handed it back to her to be retyped with his notes included. After this was done, she filed it in a locked cabinet in his office.

"Juice," Mickey snapped. "Carrot."

Olive hurried into the small gleaming kitchen adjoining his office and prepared freshly blended carrot juice for her boss. Mickey Stolli had a health-and-cleanliness fetish. He allowed nobody but the fastidious Olive to fix his fruit and vegetable drinks.

While Olive busied herself at the blender, Mickey called his head of production, Ford Werne, at home. He told Ford he wanted a private discussion before the regular Monday morning meeting of all the department heads.

Ford agreed, although he wasn't happy about having to leave his house in the Palisades an hour earlier than usual.

Mickey sipped his fresh carrot juice and studied the list of stars with current production deals at Panther. It was quite a list. There were six of them. Six superstars. And Mickey Stolli had them all tied up.

. . .

At one time Virginia Venus Maria Sierra was nothing more than a scrawny American-born Italian kid who lived in Brooklyn with her widowed father and her four older brothers. She worked like a modern-day Cinderella, looking after them—cooking, cleaning, shopping, washing and ironing—whatever there was to do. It was her job.

Virginia Venus Maria Sierra was a conscientious girl; she devoted her young life to her family of males, and in return they took her totally for granted. As far as they were concerned, it was her mission to attend to their every need; she was a woman. So, naturally, it came as a nasty surprise and quite a shock for all of them when one day she left home and ran off with Ron Machio, the long-haired gay son of a neighbor, who danced for a living in Broadway shows.

"What kind of a whore slut have I raised?" shouted her father in an almighty rage.

"We'll beat the fag punk's brains out," screamed her brothers, equally angry.

Virginia Venus Maria Sierra was no fool. She and Ron took to the road at once, hitching their way cross-country until they reached California—the promised land. And eventually, after many adventures, Hollywood.

Ah . . . Hollywood. Nirvana. Paradise. Palm trees, sunshine, and agents. Virginia Venus Maria Sierra and Ron were at peace. They knew they'd found heaven. Destiny hovered overhead, and all they had to do was reach up and touch.

Actually they had to do a lot more than that. They had to scrape the bottom and rise slowly, Ron as a choreographer, and Venus Maria (the adaptation of her name she'd decided on) as a movie extra who performed in underground clubs as a singer/dancer/actress.

Between gigs they sampled a variety of jobs. Ron attempted waitering, messengering, and chauffeuring; while Venus Maria worked in a supermarket, a bank, and finally as a nude model for an art class.

"Surely all those strange people staring at your naked body makes your flesh shrivel?" Ron shuddered.

"No way. I get off on it," Venus Maria replied confidently, shaking her newly dyed platinum-blond curls, while pursing freshly glossed lips. "I *looove* to watch 'em drool! It's a real kick."

It was at that precise moment Ron Machio knew for certain Virginia Venus Maria Sierra was going to be an enormous star.

It took a while, but sure enough it happened. Eventually Venus Maria was discovered by a small-time record producer who hung out at the same all-night clubs she and Ron frequented. With some heavy persuasion she got him to cut a record using her, and then she and Ron put together an outrageous, sexy, and controversial video to go with it. Venus Maria planned the look and the style, while Ron came up with all the right moves.

Overnight she scored—a lightning strike, for within six weeks the record was number one and Venus Maria was launched.

Now, three years later, at the age of twenty-five, she was a superstar, a cult figure, an icon.

Venus Maria had it made.

Caught in a seventies time warp, Charlie Dollar was permanently stoned, a joint never far from his reach.

Charlie was hardly your average matinee idol. He was overweight, with a comfortable gut, fifty years old, and balding. But when Charlie Dollar smiled, the world lit up, and every female around got itchy pants, for Charlie possessed a particular wild, stoned charm that was irresistible to both men and women.

A Charlie Dollar movie was a guaranteed box-office smash, thanks to his quirky presence and brilliant offbeat performances. Charlie had a way of taking on a role and bending the character until it fit him to perfection.

Some said that Charlie Dollar was a genius. Others claimed it was just old Charlie up there on the screen jerking off over anyone who'd pay attention.

Nobody knew the real story about Charlie. He'd burst upon the scene as a burnt-out, thirty-five-year-old in an underground rock-and-roll movie, playing the crazed manager of a heavy metal group. After that one brilliant, insane performance, he never looked back. And he never wanted to.

Charlie Dollar—the hero of stoned America. He enjoyed fame, but pretended to hate it. Life was simpler that way. After all, a guy had to look like he had some ethics.

Susie Rush came up through television. Sweetly pretty, with a neurotic girl next door quality, she'd parlayed two hit television series into an important big-screen career as a light comedienne.

Susie was an intensely competitive, driven woman who allowed no one to get in her way. She admitted to being thirty-two years old, although she was actually nearer forty, a fact that petrified her.

Susie was into many good causes, ecology, and channeling. She believed she'd lived many previous lives, and was not shy about telling people so.

The public considered her to be above reproach.

The folks who worked with her had christened her the bitch of the lot and loathed her. Her nickname around the studio was Rent-a-Cunt.

On-screen, Susie was sugary sweet with her delicate looks and helpless demeanor.

Off-screen she was a tyrant. Her husband had long ago hung up his balls and lived meekly in her shadow. It suited him. He was an unsuccessful actor—where else was he going?

Susie Rush was known as America's sweetheart.

Poor America.

Johnny Romano was Hispanic, six feet tall, and of slender build, although he'd developed his upper body enough to boast a powerful set of muscles. He had thick, sensual lips, a sly smile, and deep-set brown eyes—mocking eyes, challenging eyes—but most of all, sexually inviting eyes. Women couldn't get enough.

Johnny Romano was twenty-eight years old. He had starred in three extraordinarily successful films. *Hollywood Dick*, *Lover Boy*, and *Hollywood Dick 2*. These blockbuster movies had made him a very valuable property, and also extremely famous. In case anyone was in doubt, he traveled with an ever-present entourage consisting of two sassy female assistants, one white, one black; two formidable bodyguards whose main function was to proposition women for Johnny; a yes-man uncle; and a best friend/stand-in/chief procurer of any young lady who caught Johnny Romano's fancy.

One sweet, nubile female a day was not unusual. Ever aware of the perils of AIDS, Johnny Romano protected himself with two condoms and a cavalier attitude. After all, AIDS could never happen to him. He was a megastar, for God's sake. And what's more, he was a *straight* megastar. The condoms were merely a gesture in the right direction, a nod to the good Lord.

Yes, Johnny Romano was a responsible human being who liked to get laid a lot. And why not? He'd worked hard for the privilege of bedding any piece he wanted.

Right now he wanted Venus Maria. But the woman didn't want him. Unheard of! Ridiculous! Nobody turned down Johnny Romano.

Oh, sure, she was riding way up there, certainly the most successful young female star around. Venus Maria left Madonna, Pfeiffer, and Basinger trailing in her wake. There was no doubt she was in demand. But to turn Johnny Romano down? The woman had to be crazy!

And then there was Cooper Turner. The handsome, mysterious, insomniac Cooper Turner, who lived in a Wilshire high rise penthouse and had made only a few movies over the years, but was still regarded as a major player.

Cooper's looks belied his forty-five years. He was boyishly handsome, with brownish hair, penetrating ice-blue eyes, and a well-preserved body.

Cooper refused to give interviews. He kept his private life very private indeed, although there was always one special woman in residence, usually a breathtaking beauty or great talent. Cooper enjoyed discovering the woman of the moment. His sexual prowess was legendary.

In spite of his attachment to women, Cooper had never married, although there'd been a few close calls. He definitely preferred the perennial bachelor life. Cooper Turner was not the marrying kind.

Currently the tabloids were alive with news of his supposed affair with Venus Maria. He was directing and co-starring with the young superstar in *Strut*, and tongues were busy all over town. The latest rumor concerned a very public fight they'd had on the set, and the way they'd supposedly made up. According to *Truth and Fact*, one of the more scurrilous tabloids, Venus Maria had apparently quieted his anger with a somewhat public blow job on the set in front of everyone. Enough to deflate anyone's temper tantrum.

Cooper would neither deny nor confirm the scandalous story. He liked to keep a low profile.

Also tied to Panther with a three-picture deal—the first of which he was currently shooting—was Lennie Golden. Tabitha's favorite. She nagged Mickey constantly: "I wanna meet him, Daddy. All my friends love him. What's he like? Can I marry him some day?"

Mickey couldn't understand the attraction. As far as he was concerned, Lennie Golden was just another comedian going through a hot streak. Part of the Billy Crystal/Robin Williams syndrome.

But since he *was* so hot, Mickey had signed him. It was good business.

And if there was one thing Mickey excelled at, it was business.

Six superstars. And as far as he was concerned, all six belonged to Mickey Stolli. He had them tied to Panther Studios with the best deals in town. They were his. All the way.

Panther Studios. Mickey Stolli. What a team!

His brother-in-law, Ben Harrison, hardly counted. And as soon as old Abe Panther died, Mickey Stolli planned to buy Ben out, whether he wished to sell or not.

Panther Studios. Mickey Stolli. A winning combination.

And beware anyone who got in his way.

12

Panther Studios was one of the last of the great landmark Hollywood studios. Over the forty-five years since it was originally built, occasional modernization had taken place. There was a brand-new six-story gleaming steel-and-chrome office building that was Mickey Stolli's pride. He regarded it as an architectural statement. Naturally, it housed his sumptuous suite of offices. And those of Ford Werne, his chief of production. Plus the offices of the heads of marketing, distribution, and international production. Mickey Stolli's team. His A-team, as he liked to call them. Sometimes the A stood for Ace Achievers, other times for Asinine Assholes. The title depended on Mickey Stolli's mood and his team's performance.

Hidden behind Mickey's building was the old publicity structure, complete with photographic studios and rabbit-hole office spaces. And a long way behind that, right at the back of the lot, stood the oldest building of all—the main administrative block, nicknamed Alcatraz, because it was gloomy and depressing, and did indeed remind one of a prison. Alcatraz was sandwiched between two of the largest sound stages—massive towers that cut off all light. It was a building due for demolition. And it was also the building that housed the office for Herman Stone, Abe's faithful man on the lot. Sheila, his secretary, had been sent off on a six-week cruise. The story was —if anyone asked or even cared—that Sheila was visiting a sick relative, and that Lucky (rechristened Luce for the gig), her niece, was helping out on a temporary basis.

On Monday morning Lucky reported for work at the gates of Panther Studios at exactly ten o'clock. She wore a long, shapeless dress, a loose cardigan, and flat shoes. Her jet hair was hidden beneath a badly styled mousy-brown wig with heavy bangs, and very thick pebble glasses covered her eyes, causing her to squint.

She was driving Sheila's car, of which she had temporary possession, along with Sheila's apartment, a depressing two rooms in West Hollywood that she'd used to change in after she'd left Lennie early in the morning, supposedly to fly to New York, and then on to Japan.

Lennie had kissed her long and hard. "Don't forget what you promised me, sweetheart," he'd said.

How could she forget? She'd promised him a baby, but she hadn't said when. A couple of years down the line—maybe. Right now she had a studio to think about.

Lucky felt a shiver of delight as she stopped Sheila's modest Chevrolet by the security guard's window and stated her business.

Entering Panther Studios was a Hollywood historian's dream. Huge arched gates, intricately carved in stone, with fancy Art Deco iron railings. And on top of the gates perched a sleek, black granite panther, just about to take flight. MGM had its lion—but Panther Studios had the *real* power symbol.

One of these days all of this was going to be hers—a stimulating thought.

The guard was rude. He questioned her brusquely, giving her vague directions about where to park her car.

"Well, buddy, we know what's going to happen to *you* in six weeks," she muttered under her breath, when, after driving around the vast studio twice, she realized she was completely lost.

Stopping the car on what seemed to be the main street, she asked a slim woman in a floral print dress where the parking for Herman Stone's office was.

"Isn't this Sheila's car?" the woman asked. She spoke with a strong English accent.

Test number one. "Yes," Lucky replied without losing a beat.

"Sheila had to go and care for a sick relative. I'm Luce, her niece. I'm helping out for a couple of weeks."

"I do hope it's nothing serious," the woman in the floral print dress said, looking concerned.

"I don't think so."

"Good." The woman then proceeded to give her directions before entering a nearby building.

Lucky found the parking lot, left the car, and walked quite a distance. It seemed that secretaries were not allowed the privilege of parking their cars close to their bosses' offices.

Hm . . . better start making notes, Santangelo.

Trekking briskly past a group of bare-chested workmen, she couldn't help noticing that none of them whistled or catcalled. There were no anguished cries of "Give it to me, baby. C'mon, sweet stuff, *give it up!* I *waaant* your fine ass!! I *neeed* to taste pussy!"

This was a first. Her disguise was better than she'd anticipated. She really had managed to turn herself into a dowdy, nondescript drone. Even Lennie would fail to recognize her if they came face to face. Not that it was likely, for he was due to leave for the Acapulco location that very afternoon, and would be away five weeks. At least her timing was impeccable.

She quickened her step and headed for adventure.

Herman Stone was a nervous wreck. He hustled Lucky into his dark office, arms flailing, muttering to himself, practically pushing her into a chair in front of his desk. "You're late," he fussed.

"I had to walk ten miles to get here," she complained. "Why can't I park outside the office?"

"Executive parking only," Herman explained.

"My ass," Lucky muttered.

"Excuse me?"

Herman Stone was in on the scam, and Lucky wondered if he'd last the six weeks. A small, wizened man, he looked older than Abe and frightened out of his shiny blue suit.

She wanted to give him a shot of brandy and tell him to calm down. Instead she leaned back in her chair and spoke slowly and reassuringly. "Mr. Stone—all I need from you is information. Everything you have on everyone who works here. And then, after I familiarize myself with the players, you're to send me out into the field to play. O.K.?"

Herman breathed sharply—short, jerky gasps, as if at any moment someone was going to shut off his air supply.

"Don't worry," Lucky continued reassuringly. "This entire exercise is going to be easy. And since your job is totally secure, let's just relax."

Herman gasped another breath. "Whatever Mr. Panther requires," he said sourly, glaring balefully at her.

Lucky nodded. "Yeah." And for the first time she realized that maybe it wasn't going to be as easy as she'd imagined.

The morning passed slowly while Herman repeated everything she'd already learned about the key executives. Mickey Stolli was number one. Followed by Ford Werne, his head of production; Teddy T. Lauden, chief of business affairs; Zev Lorenzo, head of the television division. And three senior vice presidents: Buck Graham, marketing; Eddie Kane, distribution; and Grant Wendell, worldwide production.

These were the most important players, although there were other influential figures on the lot—several producers with multipicture deals. The two most important were Frankie Lombardo and Arnie Blackwood.

And then, of course, there were Mickey Stolli's six resident stars.

"C'mon, I'm after the *real* dirt," Lucky pressed. "I can get all this stuff you're telling me from their studio bios."

"What real dirt?" Herman asked blankly, fiddling with his heavy horn-rimmed spectacles. "I've told you everything I know."

Some spy Abe had stashed on the lot. Herman was either too old or too out of touch. Probably a combination of both. Lucky realized she was going to have to figure out who was doing what to whom all by herself.

"What do you usually do all day?" she asked. She'd been sitting in his office for two and a half hours and the phone hadn't rung once.

"I look over papers."

"What kind of papers?"

"Deal memos."

"And whose deal memos would these be?"

"Various."

"I don't see any today."

"They're usually sent over at the end of the week."

"Can I look at last week's?"

"If you wish."

Herman Stone was a tired old man. It was quite obvious that he felt his nice, ordered life was being threatened. She could understand his discomfort, but she couldn't accept it. He had to know where at least *one* body was buried.

The deal memos turned out to be a stack of duplicates dealing with mundane everyday affairs at the studio. None of them meant anything.

Lucky decided it was time to get started. "Call Mickey Stolli and tell him you want to see copies of the budgets for *Motherfaker, Strut,* and *Macho Man,*" she said briskly.

"Why would I do that?" Herman asked, blinking nervously.

"Because you're supposed to be looking after Abe Panther's interests at the studio, and you're entitled to see anything you want. Tell him you're sending your secretary over for the papers."

Herman Stone blanched visibly. Reluctantly he did as she requested.

Marching across the studio lot was no fun, especially at midday. By the time Lucky reached the outer limits of Mickey Stolli's quarters she was exhausted. The dowdy clothes clung to her body, and the heavy wig didn't help. Sweat moistened every inch of her, and she could hardly stop the thick pebble glasses from sliding off her nose. Playing dress-up was not exactly dinner with Al Pacino.

"Oh," said Olive, the woman with the English accent and floral print dress who'd given her directions earlier. "It's you again."

Lucky attempted a pleasant expression. " 'Fraid so. Mr. Stone sent me over to collect some papers."

"Yes." Olive appeared flustered. "Mr. Stolli will get them to Mr. Stone later in the week."

"Why?" Lucky wanted to ask. "What's wrong with now?" Instead she mock-groaned. "Don't tell me I've come all the way over here for nothing."

Olive put on a suitably sympathetic face. "It is hot, isn't it?"

Noticing a watercooler in the corner, Lucky asked if she might have a drink.

"Certainly," Olive said crisply, although her eyes darted toward the door to the inner sanctum, as if she needed Mickey Stolli's approval.

Lucky approached the watercooler and took a long, refreshing drink, using the time to check out her surroundings. The outer office was painted a cool light beige, with matching wall-to-wall carpet, and a large modern window overlooked fancy landscaping. Quite a difference from Herman Stone's dreary space. On the walls were perma-placqued pictures of Mickey Stolli with various celebrities and politicians.

A sudden commotion took place as a woman swept through the door, paused dramatically, and said, "Olive, dear, is he here?"

Olive jumped to her feet. "Miss Rush. He's expecting you."

A tinkling, phony laugh. "Of *course* he is."

Susie Rush was petite and slim, with straggly yellow hair artfully arranged in neat curls, wide pale blue eyes, porcelain skin, and thin lips. She was almost pretty, certainly petulant. She did not have the presence of a movie star. More girl next door than Marilyn Monroe.

Olive buzzed her boss, who apparently didn't hesitate once he got the news. Throwing open the door to his office, along with his arms, he exclaimed, "Susie my pet! Come in."

Susie my pet ran straight into his welcoming gesture and nuzzled for a moment or two. Small mewing sounds could be heard. Then the two of them, still in full embrace, entered his office and slammed the door shut.

Olive's nostrils flared. A sign of disapproval? Lucky couldn't be sure. "Wasn't that Susie Rush?" she asked brightly.

"You must *never* ask for autographs," Olive admonished sternly. "It's a studio rule."

"I wasn't planning on doing so," Lucky couldn't help responding.

Olive ignored her, busying herself with a pile of papers on her desk. Susie Rush's being in her boss's office was obviously not a thrilling happening.

"Is there somewhere around here for lunch?" Lucky asked in her best polite voice, hoping to win Olive over.

"The commissary," Olive replied, without looking up.

"Maybe we can lunch together," Lucky ventured.

"I rarely eat lunch," Olive replied brusquely. "The commissary is halfway between here and your office. Do give my regards to your aunt." It was a dismissal, firm and proper.

So . . . English Olive had a thing about her boss, who was very obviously kissing Susie Rush's ass—if not other parts of her anatomy.

Veree interesting.

And Mickey Stolli did not want to hand over the budget sheets on his three big movies in production. Even more interesting.

These weren't important discoveries, but it was a start. And at least she'd got a look at the first scum-in-law, Mickey Stolli, a bronzed bullet of a man with cobra eyes and a phony whiter-than-white smile.

Outside the gleaming structure there was a pleasant walkway lined with shady trees, banks of flowers, and in the middle, an elaborate fountain. There was also a bench, where Lucky stationed herself, all the better to catch the action as people hurried in and out of the main building.

A few secretaries came and went. A couple of executives, recognizable because of their California Casual attire. A tall woman in a tightly belted yellow Donna Karan suit. And finally Susie Rush emerged, hiding behind large white-rimmed sunglasses.

Susie stood on the steps for only a minute before a sleek chocolate-brown limousine slid into position, and she vanished inside it.

Five minutes later Mickey Stolli appeared, accompanied by two other men. The three set off at a brisk pace.

Lucky trailed them all the way to the commissary, where they were ushered into the private dining room. She found herself a table for two in the crowded main restaurant and sat down.

Now that she looked like a drudge, she felt almost invisible. People didn't seem to notice she existed—a good way to get a massive inferiority complex. Fortunately she knew that if she took off the disguise, things would change instantly. The power of appearance was potent indeed. Luce and Lucky. Two different people inhabiting two different worlds.

What have I got myself into? she thought. *One morning and I'm ready to rip off this stupid disguise and run back to real life. How am I going to last six goddamn weeks?*

Because it's a challenge.

Right.

"You're sitting at my table." A man. Slight, bespectacled, undernourished. He spoke in an agitated voice.

Lucky checked him out. She judged him to be somewhere in his fifties. "I didn't see a reserved sign," she replied coolly.

He was clearly irritated. "Everyone knows this is my table."

"Then why don't you sit here? There *is* another chair," she suggested, quite reasonably.

He hesitated for a moment, then realizing he had no alternative, he pulled out a clean handkerchief, dusted off the vacant chair, and sat down. His close-set brown eyes, covered by wire-rimmed spectacles, darted around the room looking everywhere except at her.

A plump waitress appeared at their table. "The usual, Harry?" she asked cheerfully, adjusting her diamanté-tipped wing glasses.

"Yes, thank you, Myrtle," he replied, rubbing a spot on the brightly checkered tablecloth.

Myrtle turned her attention to Lucky, pad poised. "Yes, dear? Have you decided?"

"Can I try a Susie Rush salad?"

"Why not? Everyone else has." Myrtle guffawed at her own joke. Harry didn't crack a smile. "Beverage?" Myrtle asked.

"Fresh orange juice," Lucky replied.

"Canned or frozen? Take your pick."

"I'll just have water."

Myrtle glanced from Lucky to Harry. "You two make a fine pair. The last of the big spenders!"

"She's friendly," Lucky remarked, as Myrtle departed.

"Myrtle's not the best waitress here," Harry confided. "Leona is. She would never have let my table go. Unfortunately she's in the hospital at this time attending to her varicose veins. I hope she'll return soon."

He was definitely a strange one. "Can't wait," Lucky said flippantly.

He peered across the table, finally looking at her. "I beg your pardon?" he said.

Stop being smart, Santangelo. Shape up and act the way you look.

"Do you work here?" she asked nicely.

Harry considered her question before answering. "I have been at Panther Studios for thirty-three years," he announced at last. "Panther Studios is my home."

"Your home?"

"It seems I have spent more time here than in my own house. My wife left me because of it."

"Really?" She tried to look interested. "And what do you do around here?"

If Harry had been standing he would have pulled himself up to his full height. As it was, he squared his shoulders and answered proudly, "I am the chief projectionist."

Oh, yeah. Like he was going to tell her a lot. "How interesting."

"I worked for Mr. Abe Panther himself when he was here," Harry continued with dignity. "This studio was different then, I can tell you." Realizing that this might sound like a complaint, he stopped himself from saying more.

"I bet you miss the good old days, huh?" Lucky encouraged.

Harry found a new spot on the tablecloth and began to rub it vigorously. "Things change. I understand," he said in a noncommittal voice. "Are you visiting? Or are you employed here?"

"Sort of both," Lucky replied. "I'm Luce, Sheila Hervey's niece. Y'know, Sheila, Mr. Stone's secretary? Well, she's off sick, and I'm kind of filling in for her."

"Sheila doesn't have a niece," Harry said, blinking rapidly several times.

Sonofabitch! "You're looking at her," Lucky replied without losing a beat.

"She has one sister, childless. And no other living relatives," Harry said, adjusting his spectacles. "I make it my business to find out about people."

"I guess Sheila kept secrets," she said lightly.

Harry shook his head as if he still didn't believe her, but he didn't question further. In fact, he lapsed into silence.

Myrtle brought two glasses of ice water, placed them on the table, and pointed out Johnny Romano as the flamboyant star made his way into the private dining room, flanked by his ever attentive entourage.

"Isn't he a big hunk of real man? And *sooo* sexy," Myrtle gushed, nudging Lucky. "I can tell you this, honey. I wouldn't mind crawling into *his* tent one long dark night. How about *you?*"

"Where's my fish?" Harry demanded testily.

"Still swimming." Cackling heartily, Myrtle hurried off.

An hour later, Lucky sat in front of Herman's desk again. "Why doesn't Mickey want to send you the budgets?" she asked.

Herman tapped a heavy glass paperweight. "I have no idea," he admitted.

She reached for a cigarette and lit up. "You'll just have to keep on pressuring him."

Herman didn't like her tone, but he said nothing.

"Oh, and by the way, who's this projectionist guy, Harry something or other?"

Herman thought for a moment and then said, "Do you mean Harry Browning?"

"I guess so." She exhaled a thin stream of smoke. "Skinny man in his fifties—maybe heading full tilt for sixty. Finicky little guy."

Herman coughed, letting her know the smoke bothered him. "Yes, that's Harry Browning. He's one of the oldest employees on the lot. Why do you ask?"

"Because when I told him who I was, he couldn't wait to tell *me* that Sheila doesn't *have* a niece."

Herman clucked nervously. "Harry thinks he knows everything. Ignore him, he's a strange one."

"Shit, Herman. If Harry knows everything, maybe *he* can give me some info on Mickey Stolli. What do you think?"

"I'm not sure exactly what you're looking for," Herman said tightly, offended not only by her smoking but also by her unladylike language.

"All the things *you* missed," she replied pointedly.

In six weeks she was going to have to put this old guy out to gaze at the stars. His days as a studio executive were definitely numbered.

"O.K., Herman, I'll tell you what to do; call Harry whatsit. If he asks you, assure him I'm Sheila's niece—make up a 'long-lost' story or something. And while you're at it, arrange for a screening of all the dailies on *Macho Man*. I want to see what it's like."

"But—"

She stubbed out her cigarette. Smoking was a bad habit she had to give up. "Don't even fight it, Herman. You're supposed to have the clout, use it for once. Let us not forget you are Abe Panther's representative, and it's about time you started kicking ass, because if *you* don't, *I'm* going to be awfully tempted."

Herman twitched.

"Right now I'm out of here," she continued. "I am hot. I am tired. And tomorrow I'll start again. I'll see you in the morning."

Sheila's car broke down on Hollywood Boulevard. Lucky got out, gave it a vicious kick, hurting her foot in the process, and strode into the porno theater the car had chosen to die in front of.

"Can I use your phone?" she asked the gum-chewing blonde behind the ticket counter.

"Out on the street," lisped blondie. "Two blocks down."

"You don't have a phone here?"

"S'private."

Lucky pulled off the hideous glasses that were driving her crazy and stared at the woman with her deadly black eyes. "Will ten bucks make it public?"

The woman didn't hesitate. "Gimme the money."

Lucky waved a ten in the air. The woman grabbed, stuffed it down mottled cleavage, and produced a filthy white phone hidden on the floor.

A customer buying a ticket for *Hot Tight Lust*, the current movie on show, nudged closer to Lucky as she punched out a number.

"Wanna come in with me?" he offered suggestively. "I'll spring fer ya ticket, cutie."

She smiled a cold smile. "Take your ticket *and* mine. Roll them tightly, then shove them up your dumb ass. Okay, *cutie?*"

He snatched his ticket and ran.

Lucky spoke into the receiver, a plaintive cry for help. "Boogie? Come get me. School's out and I've had it."

13

"**W**here *is* Lucky?" Steven asked impatiently. "I've been trying to reach her for days, and nobody seems able to give me an intelligent answer."

"Japan," Gino lied with a straight face. "You know how she likes to make the big deals herself. And I understand this one is some killer."

The two men sat companionably next to each other in a steak house with sawdust on the floor and autographed photographs of boxers on the walls.

The more time Gino spent with Steven the more he enjoyed his company. Steven was a no-bullshit guy, like himself. They didn't share the same set of morals, but that was O.K. too.

When Gino had first learned of Steven's existence it had been a tremendous shock. Not only did he get the news, "You have a son," but "Your son is black" really sent him reeling.

Lucky couldn't have been more thrilled. "I always wanted another brother," she'd said. "And now I've got a *black* brother. Hey, thank you, Gino. You really come up with wild surprises. You're the best!"

He'd searched his memory for the one time he'd slept with Steven's mother, Carrie, and finally he'd remembered. A few hours of pleasure, and—forty-five years later—a son.

The revelation had been a year earlier. Now he was over the

shock. Steven had arranged a reunion with him and Carrie before she died. She'd turned out to be an elegant woman in her sixties who bore no resemblance to the young teenage girl he'd once made love to. They'd gotten along just fine.

Gino had reconciled himself to the fact that while Steven could never replace Dario—the son he'd lost to the Bonnatti family's murdering hands—he was certainly a true comfort to have around. Not to mention Mary Lou, his pretty and talented wife, who made the best pasta this side of Little Italy.

"Why do you need to reach Lucky?" Gino asked.

"Nothing important. I like to talk to her every so often. Usually she calls me back."

"I may be speaking to her in the next few days. Shall I give her a message from you?"

Steven shook his head. "It can wait. When is she expected back?"

"A week. Maybe longer, maybe sooner." Gino attacked his steak. "So, tell me, how's the pregnancy going? Is Mary Lou bad-tempered? Good-tempered? What?"

Steven grinned. "It ain't easy," he said.

Gino nodded knowingly. "When my Maria was pregnant with Lucky, she drove me insane! All the time it was somethin'—I could hardly keep up. And that's when I was young and strong!"

"C'mon, you'll always be young and strong," Steven said affectionately. "And by the way, isn't it about time you handed over the family secret of your sex life? From what I hear, you're unbelievable!"

"Words of advice," Gino said sagely. "A hard-on keeps you young, an' I don't *ever* intend to get old!"

Mary Lou was in bed when Steven arrived home. She was propped up against several lace pillows watching a "Taxi" rerun while devouring a box of Reese's Peanut Butter Cups.

"What are you doing?" he demanded.

"Watching gorgeous Tony Danza and having a great time," she replied, happily munching chocolate. "How was Gino? Did you give him my love?"

"I sure did. He was sorry you couldn't make it. I told him if you left the house you'd frighten women and horses! He understood."

She pulled a pillow from behind her and threw it at him. "I don't look *that* bad."

"You look sensational, babe."

"Babe?" she questioned, smiling. "Has Gino been teaching you a new vocabulary?"

He loosened his tie as he approached the bed. "Gino's been teaching me that the secret of staying young is maintaining a constant hard-on. How about that?"

"Steven! You're beginning to sound like Jerry!"

"Wanna feel what I got for you?"

Mary Lou began to giggle. "I love it when you talk dirty! It's so un-you."

"Hey, who's talking dirty? I'm just trying to get you horny."

"Try some butter pecan ice cream and *mucho* chocolate. That's my big turn-on. Sorry, sweetheart. I promise I'll make it up to you the day I leave the hospital."

"Yeah, yeah." He strolled into the bathroom, dropping his clothes on the way. "You know, I almost told Gino about the Deena Swanson deal," he called out.

"I hope you didn't," Mary Lou replied disapprovingly.

"No. I kept it to myself."

"Good thing. You're a lawyer, Steven. You're supposed to be able to keep your client's secrets. Remember?"

"Yes, ma'am."

Sometimes Mary Lou felt twenty years older than Steven instead of it's being the other way around. She knew the Deena Swanson situation was worrying him, but why couldn't he relax about it like Jerry? It was no big deal. It was just some rich woman showing off and paying for the privilege.

Steven had to learn to lighten up. When they had the baby, she would teach him. Oh, how she would teach him!

Paige Wheeler had not turned Gino down. But she had not said yes to his proposal either.

"Your kids are grown, the time has come," he'd told her. "This once-in-a-while shit don't work for me no more."

Paige had studied the huge diamond ring he'd presented her with. She'd tried it on and admired the way it sparkled on her finger. "I can't live in New York," she'd stated.

"No problem. We'll live wherever you want. Tahiti, Tokyo—you name it."

She'd returned the ring to its box and reluctantly handed it to him. "Give me some time, and I'll give you an answer."

"Do I pay for the ring?" he'd joked.

"Make a deposit," she'd joked back.

Now two weeks had passed and no word. Gino tried to pretend he didn't care, but there was no mistaking it—he did. Getting old did nothing to diminish the strength of his feelings. He might be seventy-something, but he certainly wasn't dead yet, although he had a few aches and pains—more than a few, but complaining had never been his style.

He'd had some life. Yeah! A real adventure. And goddamn it, he had no regrets. Gino Santangelo had managed to live every minute of it. Now all he wanted to do was settle down with Paige and live quietly ever after.

Lucky had called him the night before. She was his daughter all right. Ready to try anything. He recognized so much of himself in her.

"What have I let myself in for?" she wailed over the phone. "I'm finding out nothing. I need *action!*"

They'd talked awhile. She'd told him about Olive, Mickey Stolli's English secretary, Harry, the projectionist, and no-balls Stone—her nickname for Herman.

"Get friendly with the projectionist," Gino had advised. "He'll know a lot more than you think."

"How come?"

" 'Cause he's always around, y'know? He's in that small dark room where nobody sees him. And I can bet you *he* sees everything."

"You may be right," Lucky had replied slowly.

"Sure I'm right, kid. When I was datin' that movie star, Marabelle Blue, she made it her business to get friendly with the little guys. That way she always had a bead on what the big guys were gonna do next. *Capisce?*"

"Capisce."

He wondered how Lucky was making out her second day on the job. Maybe he'd fly out to California and see for himself. Or maybe the real reason he wanted to visit L.A. was to force an answer out of Paige.

Whatever . . . a trip to the Coast wasn't such a bad idea. He had his routine, but routines could become boring. Sometimes it was healthy to shake things up. There was nothing wrong with surprising Paige on her own territory.

Reaching for the phone, he called his travel agent. Gino never had been good at sitting still and waiting.

"Didja score?"

"Did I what?"

Joey leaned closer. "Didja score with Cristi? Miss legs-up-to-her-eyeballs."

"*C'mon*, Joey."

"I'm serious, man."

"Get real. I went home to my wife."

"Lucky ain't here."

"She flew in for the weekend."

"Yeah?"

"Yeah."

"Ya missed out."

"On what?"

"Cristi's a trip."

Lennie gave a weary sigh. "Let's get this straight. I am not in the ball park for any trips. I'm married and I like it. Can that fact penetrate what I laughingly refer to as your brain?"

Joey shrugged. "What the cow don't know, the bull don't tell her."

Lennie shook his head in amazement. "You have no idea what being with one woman is all about, do you?"

Joey mock-shuddered. "Don't ever let me in on it, it's too frightening!"

They were on the private Panther plane en route to Acapulco. Attractive flight attendants served drinks, while Marisa Birch sucked

up the attention of her producer boyfriend, Ned Magnus. Grudge
Freeport and Shorty Rawlings also formed an admiring audience.
The three men all had a hot nut for her.

"You want to talk frightening—how about shacking up with that?"
Lennie nodded down the aisle toward the amazonian Marisa. "She
could crush Schwarzenegger with those knockers!"

"Maybe I should go for it," Joey mused.

"Maybe you wouldn't have a chance. She's screwing for a part,
and the part she's screwing for is definitely not yours, Romeo."

"If she saw it, she'd want it," Joey boasted. "They all do. Joey
Senior gets 'em every time!"

Lennie sighed. "You got anything else to talk about?"

"Not really," Joey said with a casual shrug.

There were press waiting at Acapulco airport, and more at the
hotel. Lennie hated it. He couldn't get off on the attention anymore,
although in the early days it had been a kick. He didn't enjoy smiling
for photographers and making nice for the assorted journalists. In
his next contract he was going to insist on a no publicity clause.

What did it all mean anyway, this celebrity crap? Sometimes he
thought about taking all this stardom shit and shoving it. So he was
having a terrible time on *Macho Man*—so fucking what? It was only
a movie.

Marisa Birch reveled in the attention. She gave herself to the
photographers. She gave them her eyes and her teeth and her hair.
She gave them her forty-inch silicone breasts barely covered by a
thin silk top, nipples erect, thrusting their way into the public's
consciousness.

Ned Magnus gazed lustfully on from the sidelines. Mister producer. Mister married man. Mister asshole.

Lennie had met his wife, Anna, a tight-lipped Wasp with an an-
orexic body and a penchant for good causes.

Thankfully, Lennie thought about Lucky. He couldn't imagine
being with anyone else. She was the best, everything he'd ever
wanted. And soon she would be pregnant with his baby and they'd
be a real family.

He made a decision. After this film he was going to take a year off.
Relax and do nothing except be with Lucky. And if Panther Studios

sued him, let them. He deserved the time with his wife. Since their marriage they'd both done nothing but work. It was getting to be too much.

As soon as Lucky arrived in Acapulco he planned to tell her. He could convince her. He knew she'd understand.

One year. No responsibilities. No work. No nothing.

Yeah!

14

Deena Swanson and her husband, Martin, were one of the most sought after couples in New York. They had what everyone else seemed to lust after—money, position, power, good looks, and invitations to every major event and party in town.

Deena, with her ice-cold appearance, trademark pale red bobbed hair, frosty blue eyes and famous-for-being-famous demeanor, created envy in other women, and a certain kind of desire in men. She was so cool she was hot. The Grace Kelly syndrome. Rip off the Chanel suit, the lace teddy, the silk panties, and crack the zero-temperature facade.

Everyone thought Martin must be a fortunate man, for surely, between the satin sheets, Deena was an untamed tigress, enough to make any man crazy with her passion. And Martin must be something too. The manly profile, ready smile, toned body, and charismatic charm.

Were the truth to be made public, sad to say, a different story lay beneath the glossy exterior of the very visible Swansons. Deena loved her handsome husband and was prepared to do anything he wanted. But Martin enjoyed sleeping only with star achievers, and famous as his wife might be, she was famous only because of him, and as far as he was concerned that didn't count. Besides, everyone knew Deena was merely a figurehead. She didn't design the jeans she lent her name to, or create the perfume that bore her signature.

When Martin married her he thought she showed terrific potential. Deena had arrived in New York from her native Holland a few years previously and soon became a partner in a small interior design firm that seemed to be going places. She was beautiful, smart, and appeared to be everything Martin was looking for in the woman who was going to be his wife. His own career was taking off, lifting him above his wildest expectations, and it was time to connect with the perfect partner.

On their honeymoon in a secluded villa in Barbados, Deena had told him that as soon as they got back to New York she was leaving her job.

"You can't do that," Martin had objected strongly. "You're a full partner. They need you there."

"Well, actually," she confessed, "I'm more an employee. They used my image as one of the partners because it seemed to be good for business. You don't mind if I leave, do you?"

Yes, he did mind. Deena was not the woman he'd thought she was. And discreet inquiries revealed she didn't come from one of the wealthiest families in Amsterdam. Her father, it turned out, was an innkeeper. And her mother worked at the American Embassy as a translator. Furthermore, Deena was six years older than she'd told him, making her only two years younger than him, instead of the eight years he'd believed.

Martin Z. Swanson was not a happy man when he discovered all this information. He angrily confronted his bride. She nodded, perfectly composed. "Yes, it's true. But what does it matter? Besides, if I can fool a smart man like you, then I can certainly fool the rest of the world, making me the perfect wife for you, don't you think?"

She happened to be right. The image was there—why care about the past?

So the Swansons embarked on married life, both determined to reach the top. Deena became pregnant twice and miscarried on both occasions. After the second time, Martin took his first mistress, a Tony Award-winning stage actress with a jutting lower lip and insatiable sexual appetite. The important thing was, she was famous, extremely talented, and her achievements really turned Martin on in a big way.

After the actress came a prima ballerina. And then a voluptuous blond author who wrote about sex and had topped *The New York Times* best-seller list several times. The author was followed by a female racing-car driver, and then a particularly skilled lawyer.

By this time, Deena had grown used to Martin's indiscretions. She didn't like it, but what could she do? Divorce was not even a consideration. She was Mrs. Martin Z. Swanson for life, and let no one forget it. Especially her erring husband.

When Deena decided to parlay her social celebrity into real bucks, Martin was unimpressed. After she showed him how much money her various products were making, he was still unmoved. "Money is not talent," he said flatly.

"Ah, but that's *all* you've got—money," she answered triumphantly.

"The truth is, I'm closer to real talent than you'll ever be," he replied.

"If you think sleeping with sluts is being close to real talent, then you're deluding yourself."

Martin had an infuriating, self-satisfied smirk. "Try it. You'll see," he said.

She tried it. She had an affair with a sleek black soul singer. Naked, he was the most magnificent man she'd ever seen. But he wasn't Martin, and although the affair satisfied her physically, it wasn't enough, so she dropped him.

Just in time, for when Martin found out he was truly furious. "If you wish to stay married to me, you'll never sleep around again," he warned her. "You are my wife, Deena. Do you understand me? *My wife.* And you will *not* make me out to be a fool."

She stared at him angrily. "And you're my husband. Yet you expect me to accept your screwing around without question. I'm only doing what *you* do all the time. Why do you object?"

"Because you're a woman. And for a woman it's not the same. No more affairs."

"What am I supposed to do? *You* never sleep with me," she cried. "I'm hardly going to become a nun."

So they struck a bargain. Every Sunday night Martin would take care of his husbandly duties. And in return Deena would remain the faithful wife.

She welcomed him back into her bed with every trick she could think of. Not that Martin was such a great lover. He did not believe in foreplay unless it was for himself. And his action was short, sharp, and clinical.

Deena comforted herself with the thought that at least he was in *her* bed again, and wasn't that what really mattered?

Although Deena had no love for the women her husband slept with, she couldn't help feeling the tiniest bit sorry for them. Anyone who knew Martin at all was fully aware his work came first. The man had an insatiable lust for more money and power. He also enjoyed the headlines on the financial pages.

Over the last few years the name Swanson was everywhere. There was a Swanson Sports Stadium, a chain of Swanson shopping malls, Swanson Publishing, and in development there was a new luxury automobile to be named "the Swanson."

Yes, Martin got off on seeing his name in print, but only in a positive way. He abhorred scandal and gossip, regarding them as a major embarrassment. When the newspaper columns hinted at some of his affairs, he was furious, and since they couldn't prove anything, he immediately threatened legal action.

The press had learned to leave the great Martin Swanson alone unless they had something positive to write, or could prove his infidelities.

One of these days, Deena was sure Martin would tire of being unfaithful, and then he would be all hers. No more talented whores. No more superachievers. She couldn't wait.

And then along came The Bitch, and Deena knew her almost perfect existence was seriously threatened.

At first she didn't take the intrusion of another mistress as anything more than a passing fling. They came, they went, and usually a month or two was enough to rid Martin of his newfound passion.

But this latest one was different. This one was here to stay, and Deena recognized her as putting the great Swanson marriage at risk.

She'd thought of many ways to handle it. Perhaps pay her off—

no good, because The Bitch made megabucks and had no need of anyone's money.

Threaten her with physical violence. No good either, because she'd merely run to Martin for protection.

Kill her.

Extreme, but if she became too much of a threat—the only answer.

Deena had thought about this solution for many months. At first the idea of hiring a professional had seemed best. There were men for hire, and she knew of acquaintances who could probably arrange a contact. But the risk involved was extreme. And how convoluted did the trail have to be before it led back to her?

She was also opening herself up to lifelong blackmail, and that would never do. There was no way she could allow her position to be jeopardized.

There was only one answer. If she wanted The Bitch dead, she was going to have to do it herself.

Once she reached that momentous conclusion she felt secure.

But there remained three big questions.

How?

Where?

When?

The how was easy. Growing up in Holland, she'd always been exceptionally close to her father, a handsome man, with two passions in life—hunting and fishing. He'd taught his only daughter to do both, and she'd learned well. Very well. Deena was a crack shot. She knew about guns. Disposing of The Bitch with a single bullet through the head would be simple.

The where was another question. It all depended on timing.

And the when was entirely in Martin's hands, for if he stopped seeing The Bitch, none of the above would have to take place.

Unfortunately, Deena did not think this would happen. Her instincts told her that eventually Martin was going to come to her for a divorce, and if and when that day ever arrived, she was ready to put her plan into operation.

She had already taken out insurance. Jerry Myerson's firm was one of the best. But the real reason she'd chosen them was because of Steven Berkeley and his reputation as being the finest defense attorney in town. If and when she was ever forced to act, she had a plan. Of course, she had no intention of getting caught. But events took strange turns, and Deena wished to be fully prepared.

She knew one thing for sure, and one thing only: Nobody was going to take Martin away from her. Absolutely nobody.

15

For some time Harry Browning had been considering inviting Olive Watson, Mr. Stolli's English secretary—or personal assistant as she referred to herself—out. Not exactly on a date—more like an evening of shared companionship, although he certainly had every intention of picking up the check should they go to a restaurant. He'd been thinking about this for eight months—ever since Olive had wished him a happy birthday on his big day. However, these things could not be rushed, so it was quite a disappointment when she'd announced, calmly and coolly, that she was engaged.

"Engaged?" Harry had questioned blankly. They were on the phone at the time, arranging the hours Mr. Stolli would require the screening room that week.

"Yes," Olive confirmed happily. "My fiancé proposed long distance from England last night. It's quite a surprise."

It was quite a surprise for Harry also, for he'd always imagined Olive was there for the taking whenever he decided to take.

Now this ruffle. It annoyed Harry. All those wasted hours thinking about Olive, only to discover she was no longer available.

When Lucky Santangelo—whom Harry knew only as Luce—sat herself down at his table in the commissary for the third consecutive day, Harry impulsively blurted out, "Would you like to go out one night?"

Lucky stared at the small, bespectacled man who'd so far told her nothing, in spite of the fact that Gino seemed to think Harry Browning held the knowledge to all of Panther Studios' secrets. Did he actually imagine she'd go out with him? Wow—her disguise must really be spectacular.

"Where?" she answered carefully, not wishing to offend him.

Harry hadn't expected a "Where?" He'd expected a "Yes," or a "No." Certainly not a "Where?"

"I don't know," he admitted honestly.

"Perhaps," Lucky replied, giving him hope.

Harry peered at her. She was certainly no Olive. In fact, she was rather strange-looking with her frumpy clothes, dowdy hairstyle, and impenetrable glasses. But still, had she been more attractive he would not have dared to invite her out, or even have wanted to. Harry knew his limitations. Once he'd dated a pretty, redheaded extra, a date that had ended in disaster when she'd turned on him publicly, screaming in a bansheelike voice, "If you can't get me in to see Mickey Stolli, what the fuck am I doing out with a dumb creep like you anyway?"

That nasty and humiliating incident had taken place five years ago. Harry had never forgotten it.

He was wary of women. Most of the secretaries and female staff around the studio were what he termed "loose." They wore revealing clothes and slept with anybody. On four separate occasions during the last year he'd discovered couples "at it" in the screening rooms when they thought these were not in use. Each time he'd got rid of them with the same ominous words: "Mr. Stolli is due here in five minutes."

He could get away with telling that to the minor players. With the majors it was another game. They could do what they liked, and they did. Frequently.

Gino Santangelo was right. There was not much Harry hadn't seen in his years of standing in the projection booth looking out over the moguls and producers, the directors and movie stars who always seemed to forget his very existence and to do exactly whatever they pleased in the darkened screening rooms.

Harry often mused that one day he might write a book. A pleasant dream—it made his secrets very valuable. He'd never told anyone of the goings-on he'd witnessed.

Lucky drew a deep breath. She was getting nowhere. If she met with Harry away from the studio, maybe he *would* have stories to reveal. It was worth a shot.

Leaning across the table, she fixed him with a friendly stare. "As a matter of fact, I'm making . . . uh—salmon mousse tonight. Why don't you come by Sheila's apartment? I know you like fish."

Sure she knew he liked fish, he'd eaten it three days in a row.

Harry considered her invitation. There was something about her he found slightly odd. However, a night away from his Sony television and three cats was a tempting prospect. And salmon mousse . . . his favorite. "Yes," he said, nodding decisively.

"Good," Lucky replied, thinking to herself, *What the hell am I doing?* "Shall we say seven-thirty?"

Harry looked almost eager. "Yes," he repeated, blinking rapidly.

A man of not many words. Lucky forced a smile and stood up. How the hell was she going to get hold of a salmon mousse? Why hadn't she said pizza or pasta or something sane?

Her glasses rolled down her nose and she pushed them up in exasperation.

"Later, Harry," she said, going for the fast getaway. "I'll be expecting you."

Herman Stone was horrified. "Seeing someone away from the studio is dangerous."

Lucky raised a cynical eyebrow. "Dangerous, Herman? I'm not cocaine busting, I'm just trying to get a little insight into what's really going on around here."

"You're leading Harry Browning on. He's a decent man."

Lucky was outraged. Herman was such a stuffed asshole. "I'm not planning to fuck him," she said coolly. "Merely pump his tongue a little."

Herman stood up. He was red in the face. "I can't be a party to this folly. I'm phoning Abe. You talk like a . . . a . . ."

"Man?" she offered helpfully.

Herman sat down again. He picked up a pen and banged it on the table. For ten years he'd led a quiet life. Two hours in the office, four hours on the golf course. No pressures. No headaches. No foulmouthed woman to harass him.

"Call Abe if you want," Lucky said. "Remember though, it's *me* you're going to be working for."

They both knew this wasn't true. Lucky would retire him the moment she took control. And he wouldn't work for Lucky Santangelo if she trebled his salary.

"Do what you wish," Herman muttered.

"Thank you *sooo* much. Your permission has made my day."

"Sherry?"

"I don't drink," Harry Browning replied.

"Never?" Lucky asked.

He hesitated. "Only if it's an occasion."

She poured him a glass of sherry and handed it to him. "This *is* an occasion," she said firmly.

The occasion of Olive's engagement, Harry thought dourly as he drank the pale brown liquid. He deserved one drink.

Lucky decided Sheila Hervey's tiny apartment was the most depressing place she'd ever had to spend time in. The walls were painted a particularly dreary shade of maroon, and the oppressive furniture was a mixture of heavy oak combined with cheap plastic modern—all of it too big for the small apartment. Voluminous velvet drapes completed the claustrophobic effect. And an ancient record player offered only Julio Iglesias for entertainment. Lucky was fed up.

While Julio crooned something incomprehensible in broken English, Harry Browning gulped two glasses of sherry in quick succession and waited patiently for his salmon mousse.

Boogie had delivered the mousse fifteen minutes before deadline. "Now I *know* you can do anything," Lucky had complimented him. "It'd better be good."

Boogie had merely shaken his head in exasperation. Like Herman

Stone, but for different reasons, he did not approve of his boss's adventures. But then, working for Lucky had never been dull.

"Did you bake it yourself, Boog?" she'd asked with a sly grin.

"Try the best fish restaurant in L.A. You'll get the bill," he'd replied laconically. "Call me in the car when you're ready to go home."

She was ready to go home the moment Harry Browning arrived. But as she'd gone this far, she couldn't back out without giving him a chance to tell all.

Somewhere real life was going on while she was busy playacting with a mild little projectionist called Harry Browning, who probably couldn't tell her anything she needed to know anyway.

Damn! And on top of everything else she was now going to have to eat salmon mousse, which she hated. What a night!

Eventually Harry Browning started to talk. Like a hooker revealing how she first got into the business, it all came rushing out.

For two hours Lucky had babied him along, flattering and feeding, plying him with a good white wine Boogie had thoughtfully provided, and after that, brandy. Now it was paying-off time.

After his first sip of Courvoisier, quiet little Harry Browning turned into Harry the Mouth. Lucky could hardly believe it. This was going to be worthwhile after all.

"When Abe Panther was in charge we had a decent studio," Harry said forcefully, sounding proud. "Mr. Panther was a *real* boss. People respected him."

"Don't people respect Mickey Stolli?" Lucky murmured.

"Him!" Harry spat in disgust. "He doesn't care about making movies. All he cares about is money."

"At least he's honest. Mickey is looking after Abe Panther's interests, isn't he?" Lucky asked innocently.

"The only interests Mickey Stolli cares about are his own."

"How do you know that?"

"I see plenty," Harry said, reaching for the bottle of brandy. "I hear plenty."

"Like what?"

Fuzzily Harry realized he might be saying too much. So what? He could talk if he wanted to. He felt pretty damned good. This woman was fascinated by everything that came out of his mouth, and it was a long time since he'd had a woman spellbound. Maybe he would impress her even more with his knowledge. "Do you know who Lionel Fricke is?"

Lucky tried to sound suitably impressed. "The big agent?" she asked.

"Yes, that's right." He peered at her through his wire-rimmed spectacles. Her image swam before his eyes. She wasn't Olive, but she was a woman, and if she got rid of those godawful glasses . . .

"What about Lionel Fricke?" Lucky pressed.

Harry wondered how far he could go. He took another gulp of brandy and placed his hand on her knee. "I saw the two of them together, Lionel Fricke and Mr. Stolli. I heard 'em make a deal for Johnny Romano. A *big* deal."

"Yes"—Lucky leaned toward him, eyes gleaming excitedly.

"A five-million-dollar price for Johnny Romano—only *he* never sees the full payout. Lionel Fricke sells Johnny to Panther for four million. And then he sells a script to a shell company for one hundred thousand. A month later Panther purchases the same script for one million."

"And Lionel and Mickey split the million minus the hundred thousand, and put it in their own pockets. Right?" Lucky finished.

Harry nodded. "I heard 'em. No mistaking what I heard."

"I'm sure you did," Lucky said matter-of-factly, removing her hand from her knee. "So tell me," she added casually, "who else is stealing?"

"Everyone. Eddie Kane, Ford Werne, most of the producers on the lot. They all have their ways, you know."

"I bet," she said, topping his glass with more brandy.

Suddenly he sat up straighter. "Why are you so interested?" he asked suspiciously.

"Wouldn't anyone be? You've seen so much. You should write a book."

Harry was flattered. She had touched his secret dream, this odd-looking woman. He nodded. "Maybe . . . one day." Reaching for

his glass he took a healthy swig. "I could tell you about drugs, sex
. . . the loose women and the things they do."

"What sort of things, Harry?"

"They lean on women for sex. They use them."

"Who uses them?"

"Everyone," Harry said darkly. "They promise a girl a part in their
movie if she'll perform certain disgusting acts."

"How do you know?"

"Because they do it in my screening room. In plain sight."

"I guess you *have* seen it all."

He mumbled on some more, complaining about the quality of the
films Panther produced and the low level of management. He particularly loathed Arnie Blackwood and Frankie Lombardo. The two
producers were apparently the worst offenders when it came to sex
in the screening room. After a while his eyes began to roll.

"Do you feel all right, Harry?" she asked anxiously.

"Not so good."

Helping him to his feet she said, "Maybe it's time to put you in a
cab. There's no way you can drive your car."

"They sit in my screening room an' I see everything," Harry repeated. "Some people have no shame."

Putting her arm around him, she steered him toward the door.

"Drugs," he mumbled, "an' sex. That's all they think about." He
hiccoughed loudly. "Don' feel so good."

"Can we talk another time?"

"We'll see." He hiccoughed again and stumbled.

She managed to get him outside, hailed a passing cab and bundled
him in. There was no point in letting him pass out on her floor. If
he did, she'd have to stay the night and look after him—and that
was the last thing she needed.

Harry Browning had given her enough for one session. At least it
was a promising beginning.

16

Two more weeks and she would be out of school! Brigette was marking the days. Two weeks ago she'd been counting seconds. Now it was O.K. She had a friend, and what a difference it made.

Her newfound friend, Nona Webster, was the funny, vivacious daughter of a New York publisher and his fashion-designer wife. Nona had long naturally red hair, slanted eyes, and an interesting face covered with freckles. She was slender and quite tall. Like Brigette, she'd seen plenty of the fast life, and once they got to talking they soon found out they had lots in common. Nona had lived in Europe, had met many famous people, slept with a man ten years older, and tried cocaine on more than one occasion.

Brigette confided about her own troubled past, including the kidnapping and her mother's death from a drug overdose. They'd both decided drugs were useless, causing nothing but heartache and trouble.

"We're cosmic twins," Nona explained excitedly when she found out their birthdays fell in the same month. "It's amazing we didn't get to talking before. I never bothered, because everyone told me you were such an unbearable snob. And let's face it—you don't exactly encourage friendships, do you?"

"Right," Brigette admitted. "It's not easy being who I am." She looked embarrassed. "Y'know, with the money thing and all."

"God! I wish *I* was going to inherit a fortune," Nona said enviously.

"Your family has money," Brigette pointed out.

"Compared to you we're bloody paupers!" Nona complained. "And my parents don't believe in passing it on to their kids. They spend everything they make. It's not fair. My brother is furious. He's threatened to murder them both before they get rid of it all!"

Brigette giggled. "How old is your brother?"

"Twenty-three and much too cool-looking for his own good. He's into rich older women and money. In that order. I'm trying to save his soul. Trust me, it's a pitiful battle."

Brigette was immediately intrigued. "Save his soul from what?"

"Booze, coke, and women. He's a real loser, but I love him."

"I wish I had a brother," Brigette sighed wistfully.

"I'll let you share mine if you promise to help me save him," Nona offered.

"How can I do that?"

"Marry him. All your money will surely make him a very happy man!"

They both giggled. Ridiculous conversations could be fun.

The other girls did not change their attitude toward Brigette. "You gotta ignore them, they're just jealous," Nona said one afternoon as they took off for town.

"Why?" Brigette asked. She couldn't understand how anyone could possibly be jealous of her.

" 'Cause you're pretty, *and* you've got big boobs!" Nona joked. "That's quite a combination."

Brigette was glad Nona thought she was pretty. But they both knew it wasn't that. It was the money. The money was an impenetrable barrier separating her from the rest of the world.

"What are you doing this summer?" Nona asked, as they trudged along the country lane on their way to the bus stop.

"Some of the time I have to spend with my grandmother. Then I'm joining my ex-stepfather and his wife in California. They're renting a house in Malibu. How about you?"

Nona kicked a pebble. "Montauk some of the time. We've got a place there. It's really boring. Malibu sounds more like it."

"Hey—I've got a sensational idea. Why don't you come with me?" Brigette suggested impulsively. "Lennie and Lucky won't mind— really—they're terrific."

"Lennie, as in Lennie Golden?" Nona asked, raising her eyebrows. "Lucky, as in Lucky Santangelo?"

"She's Lucky Golden now," Brigette pointed out.

"Wow! That makes all the difference."

Brigette laughed. "Well?"

"Well, how can I possibly turn down an invitation to meet a real live movie star?" Nona said. "Lennie Golden is gorgeous."

Brigette smiled. "He's O.K."

Nona looked pleased. "It sounds like a cool idea. But only if you come stay with us first. You'll meet Paul, my brother. What a thrill! Maybe even marry him. Can you do me that small favor? Get him off my case forever."

Brigette went along with the joke. "Yeah, sure. Why not? Anything to oblige a friend."

They both laughed.

"I'll call Lennie tomorrow," she promised.

And for the first time in ages she felt she really had something to look forward to.

"Oooh, Lennie, you're *sooo* cold. Why are you so icy to me? What have I done to upset you?"

Marisa was all over him, and she was big. Long legs and arms, huge breasts, thick gooey lips, and an overly active tongue that slid into his mouth every time they had to kiss for the camera.

Love scenes were the worst, especially with someone you didn't like, and there was a Berlin Wall between Marisa Birch and Lennie Golden. He didn't respect what he considered she represented—the phony glitz and so-called glamour of show business. And he also thought she was an abysmal actress. Not to mention that she was screwing Ned Magnus, *and* managing to put in time with her stand-in, Hylda—another amazon with large knockers.

The crew were in pussy heaven. Marisa wore nothing except a flesh-colored G-string as she thrashed around under a sheet with

Lennie. She got off on giving the boys a show, and it annoyed her that she couldn't turn Lennie on too. Marisa was used to instant drool. She felt insecure when a man didn't react to her all too obvious charms.

"We've got a scene to do, Marisa," Lennie said patiently, trying not to notice an erect nipple thrust dangerously close to his face. "It's called acting. Isn't that what you are—an actress? Remember?"

They were on location in the bedroom of a spectacular villa perched high on a cliff.

"Darling, when I'm making love, I'm *never* acting," Marisa confessed, waving away her dresser, who wished to cover her undulating flesh between takes.

"Let's roll another one," Grudge Freeport said, striding over to confer with his stars. "Lennie, you're supposed to be enjoying yourself. The broad is naked. Go for it, for crissakes." He turned to spit a great gob of tobacco into a yellow dish, handily carried by his young female assistant.

"Don't call me a broad," Marisa scolded. "Call me a star." She stretched languidly and spotted Ned Magnus, who'd just arrived. "Hi, honey." She waved and blew him a few kisses.

Ned looked pleased.

"Does honey's wife know about you?" Lennie asked.

Marisa smiled. Her teeth were big and white. Lethal teeth. Man-biting teeth. "Wives are always the last to know," she said sweetly. "And if it's the wife who's fooling around—then it's the husband who finds out last. Didn't you know that?" Another stretch. Another treat for the crew. "By the way, Lennie. Where is *your* wife? I'd heard she was joining us on location. Did something more exciting come up?"

"Action!" Grudge Freeport yelled.

Gino Santangelo checked into the Beverly Wilshire Hotel and called Paige.

"Mrs. Wheeler, she out," a maid informed him. "You lika Mister?"

No. He would not lika Mister. He hung up.

The Beverly Wilshire held all sorts of good memories. Afternoon trysts with Paige. Nonstop champagne and sex—long, throbbing marathon sessions.

Gino grinned and fingered the faded scar on his cheek, a souvenir of his youth. Ah, if Paige had known him in those days, she would not have hesitated. Gino the Ram was his nickname then.

Gino Santangelo . . . the first boy in the neighborhood to discover the secret of pleasing women.

He was twenty-two and horny when he met the incredible Clementine Duke, wife of an elderly Senator. What a lady! She'd taken raw street material and molded him into something. She taught him how to dress, what to drink, how to make polite conversation. She *really* taught him how to make love. And he allowed her to tutor him willingly, because he wanted to learn. More than anything else he'd had a strong desire to succeed, and Clementine and the Senator had helped him achieve every one of his goals.

Now, all these years later, he could still remember her sensuous silk underclothes, the smoothness of her firm white thighs, and the musky scent of her hair.

There had been many women, but only a few he remembered. His first love was Leonora, who turned out to be a bitch on wheels. Next came Cindy, his first wife. Another winner. Followed by Bee, a woman he almost married. And then Carrie—a short one-nighter resulting in Steven. And then his second wife, Maria, the true love of his life, innocent and beautiful mother of his other two children.

When he thought about Maria and the tragic way she'd been taken from him, it was almost too much to bear. But he'd carried on without her, although there was always a deep sadness buried in his soul.

After Maria there were countless women. A fling with Marabelle Blue, the movie star, had kept him busy. The widow Rosaline had looked after him in Israel. Finally he'd married for the third time— Susan Martino, a perfect Hollywood wife.

The only good thing about Susan was that she introduced him to Paige. Actually he'd caught them together, enjoying each other in bed. Paige had never offered an explanation or an apology, although at the time he and she had already embarked on their affair. He understood that Paige had a voracious sexual appetite. It didn't faze him. He was no slouch himself.

Now he wanted to marry her. And the sooner the better.

Grabbing the phone, he tried her number again.

This time Ryder Wheeler picked up.

"Is Paige around?" Gino demanded, deciding he'd had enough game-playing. If *she* wasn't going to get it out in the open, *he* would.

"Who wants her?" Ryder asked abruptly.

"*I* want her, Ryder. This is Gino Santangelo. Remember me?"

17

Lucky Santangelo knew how to kick ass; she'd had enough experience over the years. First the hotels in Vegas, then Dimitri's business empire, which she ran with steely confidence, never depending on management, always going on her own instincts, which were rarely wrong. Now, to sit back in her little corner of Panther Studios, to merely watch and have no power, was driving her crazy.

Herman was hardly any help. If she gave him a chicken he couldn't make soup, the man was that incompetent. No wonder Mickey Stolli didn't mind having him around as Abe's spy. He knew Herman was incapable of doing any harm.

She'd told Herman to get copies of the budgets on the three big movies Panther was shooting. So far—nothing. She'd requested that he arrange screenings of the *Macho Man* dailies. He hadn't even done that. They fed him an excuse and he bought it.

Arriving for her second Monday of work at Panther Studios, she was determined that this week things would be different.

Since dinner with Harry Browning—the famous salmon mousse night—he'd hardly spoken to her. A mumbled, embarrassed hello was all she could get out of him. He'd changed his lunch hour, and he fled whenever he saw her coming. So much for Harry.

In the meantime she'd put in serious work on Olive: congratulating her on her engagement with a bottle of mediocre champagne;

popping in whenever she could to see if the budgets were ready for Mr. Stone; staying to chat idly about inconsequential matters.

Olive had gradually warmed to her. "You're different from the other secretaries around here," she confided. "Most of them are only interested in men, money, and makeup."

They had a laugh at that. "What are *you* interested in?" Lucky had asked, trying to gain her confidence.

"I pride myself on being the best personal assistant Mr. Stolli has ever had. We English girls are very dedicated, you know."

"How long have you worked for him?"

"Five years," Olive replied proudly. "And he appreciates me. He gave me a car for Christmas."

"A car! How wonderful!"

"Yes. Mr. Stolli is a fine boss."

Any probing as to what Mickey Stolli was like as a person got her nowhere. Olive was close-mouthed and loyal. A particularly annoying English trait.

Lucky managed to have an interesting if somewhat exhausting weekend. On Friday afternoon she flew to London, arriving at noon on Saturday. She spent the rest of the day and Sunday morning with Bobby. And then she'd taken the Concorde to New York, where she'd made a fast connection back to L.A.

She'd needed the break, and Bobby had been thrilled to see her. They'd taken a boat out in Hyde Park, eaten hamburgers at the Hard Rock Café, visited Harrods toy department, and seen a movie.

Bobby was an incredible kid. At six and a half, he looked just like a small Gino. Same black eyes and hair, with a jaunty little walk and a sharp, inquisitive personality.

"I miss you, Mommy," he'd told her, just before she left.

"You'll be with me all summer," she'd promised, hugging him. "You're coming out to California, and we'll all be together in a big house right on the beach. You, Lennie, Brigette, and me. Okay, baby? Does that sound like fun?"

He'd nodded solemnly, and she'd left him with his nanny and two permanent bodyguards. It was sad that Bobby had to lead such a protected life, but after his kidnapping she couldn't take chances. Anyway, it wasn't so bad. He enjoyed his school, and he adored Cee

Cee, his pretty Jamaican nanny who'd been with him since he was a baby.

Back in L.A. Lucky felt invigorated. She called Lennie in Acapulco on Sunday night and covered herself there.

"How's the deal going?" he asked.

"Slowly," she replied, setting him up for a delay. "You know what the Japanese are like."

"Are you having a good time?"

"Without you? No way."

"This movie sucks."

"You've told me that seven thousand times."

"Make way for seven thousand and one."

"I love you, Lennie," she said wistfully, aching to be with him.

"Prove it."

"How?"

"Dump your deal and get on the next plane."

"Have you ever heard of the word patience?"

"I'm trying."

"Keep trying."

When he eventually found out she'd bought the studio, it was all going to be worth it. Oh, boy, would he regret his relentless nagging!

Now it was Monday morning, Herman was staring at her, and she was ready for action.

"Mr. Panther wishes to speak to you," he announced, as soon as she arrived.

"He does? Why?"

Herman fidgeted in his seat. "I don't know."

It was a particularly hot day. Lucky pulled at her awful wig in disgust. Two days of freedom, and being back in disguise was a burden. She flopped into a chair and called Abe.

Inga answered the phone. Clipped, unfriendly tones. "Who's this?"

"Lucky Santangelo."

"I'll see if Mr. Panther is available."

"*He* called *me*, Inga. I'm sure you'll find he's available."

"I'll see."

Tight-assed dragon lady!

A short wait, and then Abe on the phone, talkative, excited. "What's goin' on, Lucky? What's happening? How come you haven't phoned me? Did you forget about keeping in touch?"

"Our deal is six weeks, Abe. I didn't realize you expected me to check in."

"I'm anxious for a report, girlie. I want to hear it all."

"Nothing much yet."

"Come for dinner tonight. Six o'clock."

"Just you, me, and Inga?"

"Yes, yes," he said impatiently.

"I wouldn't miss it," she drawled sarcastically.

As soon as she hung up, Herman couldn't wait to ask what Abe wanted.

"My body," Lucky replied dryly.

Her humor was lost on poor Herman. He gazed at her blankly.

She reached for a cigarette and lit up. "Have they sent the budgets over?"

He shook his head.

"Pick up the phone and tell Mickey Stolli personally you want them today or else."

"Or else what?" Herman asked, wheezing.

"Good point." Thoughtfully she sucked on a pencil. "Or else you tell Mickey you're going to have to inform Abe Panther you can't get any cooperation, and that maybe Abe had better put a younger guy in your position. Mickey won't like that."

Herman loosened his tie. He had a chicken neck etched with wrinkles. "It's so warm today," he grumbled.

"Tell me about it." Lucky sighed, tugging at her wig again. "It's only going to get hotter. Let's make the call, Herman. Are you ready?"

He nodded reluctantly.

Lucky reached Olive, who told her that Mr. Stolli was in conference and could not be disturbed.

"Mr. Stone needs to talk to him about the copies of the budgets he asked for a week ago. I *have* reminded you, Olive. When can we expect them?"

"Doesn't he have them? I was under the impression they were sent over," Olive said, sounding quite put out.

"Not yet."

"Oh, dear."

"I can drop by and collect them," Lucky offered helpfully.

"Let me check with Mr. Stolli when he leaves his meeting. I'll get back to you."

Lucky put down the phone. "You are getting what is commonly known as the royal runaround," she informed Herman. "Or, as my daddy used to say—fucked."

Herman winced.

"But I," Lucky announced grandly, "will take care of it." She leaped to her feet, full of sudden energy. "Today we will have the budgets in our possession. Sit tight, Herman, and trust me. I'll see you later."

Over at the main building there was the usual activity. People coming and going. Executives in tight jeans with open shirts. A sprinkling of gold chains. A ton of hair spray. Tennis tans and toned bodies. And that was just the men.

The women were divided into two categories: business and pleasure. The business ones wore suits with no-nonsense jackets, silk shirts, and determined expressions. The pleasure seekers let it all hang out in clinging tops, sexy tanks, and miniskirts, with no visible panty line.

It was sometimes difficult figuring out who did what. One of the secretaries, conservatively dressed, was so drop-dead gorgeous you would have sworn she was a movie star. And an expensive-looking young man, featuring all the right gold accouterments, worked in the mail room as a runner.

The two hottest producers on the lot, specializing in the sex/horror megabucks movies so dear to Mickey Stolli's heart, resembled a couple of bums off the street. Lucky recognized them from a recent photograph in *Variety* as they made their way into the building.

Frankie Lombardo and Arnie Blackwood were partners. Arnie was lean and lanky, with greasy hair pulled back in a ponytail, and mirrored shades covering watery eyes. Frankie had freaked-out brown hair, an unruly beard, small eyes, bushy eyebrows, and a rolling gut.

They were nicknamed "the Sleazy Singles," and most female employees went out of their way to avoid them. "Sexist pigs" was a kind description.

Lucky kept her distance as she followed them all the way to Mickey Stolli's office, where Olive promptly stopped them at her desk.

"Gentlemen," Olive said crisply, "kindly take a seat. Mr. Stolli will be with you in a moment."

"What an accent!" Frankie exclaimed, perching on the corner of her desk, his big bulk dislodging a framed photo of her fiancé.

"What class! What an ass!" Arnie joined in. "I want a Limey broad to do *my* dirty work, Frankie. How about it?"

"Whatever Arnie wants—Arnie gets," Frankie promised, and then he noticed Lucky lurking in the doorway. "Hello, gorgeous," he said in a loud, arrogant voice. "You ever given any thought to changing your hairdresser?"

Arnie guffawed. "Looks like a wig t'me. Gives a whole new meaning to the word head—huh?"

This broke Frankie up.

Lucky had to bite her tongue to prevent herself from zapping these dumb assholes into the ground. She recalled Harry Browning's reports of their scurrilous activities in the screening room.

Olive jumped to her feet, two bright red spots highlighting her very English complexion. "Mr. Stolli will see you now," she said in a strained voice. "Please go in."

Frankie removed himself from her desk and ambled toward Mickey's office, closely followed by Arnie. When they opened the door, Mickey Stolli could be spotted behind his enormous desk, leaning back in an oversized leather chair speaking on the phone. He waved a greeting to his two out-of-control producers, and then Arnie kicked the door closed with an unpolished cowboy boot.

Olive turned to face Lucky. "I'm so sorry," she said, obviously embarrassed. "They don't mean any harm. They're like two big naughty schoolboys."

Lucky found it hard to keep her mouth shut. She'd heard about Frankie and Arnie from Lennie. "A couple of major zeros," he'd told her. "They run around the lot with T-shirts emblazoned 'I Eat Pussy if It Don't Eat Me First.' "

"They sound like real charmers," she'd replied.

"Put it like this—I'd have to be dead to do a movie for 'em," Lennie had said laughing. "They make Ned Magnus look classy."

Olive was staring at her, waiting for a response. "You're upset, aren't you? Please don't be. Your hair looks very nice."

Oh, Olive, Olive. You are full of shit. Speak out. My hair—wig— is a disaster. Arnie called it like he saw it.

"That's all right," Lucky managed in a low voice, hoping she sounded suitably hurt.

"How about lunch?" Olive said brightly. "One o'clock. My treat."

"You said you didn't eat lunch."

"Certainly not every day. I don't get engaged every week, either. We'll call it a celebration. Yes?"

Lucky agreed, deciding not to bother Olive about the budgets. If she didn't mention them now, it would give her an excuse to come back tomorrow. They arranged to meet in the commissary, and Lucky departed.

Outside she observed the tall, striking woman she'd seen entering the building the week before. Last Monday the woman had been wearing Donna Karan. This Monday it was Yves Saint Laurent. There was something about her that didn't quite jell.

Instinct made Lucky turn around and follow her back inside. The woman walked fast and knew exactly where she was going. High heels clicked their way down the marble hallway, stopping in front of a door marked "Eddie Kane, Senior Vice President of Distribution." She entered and vanished.

Lucky waited a few minutes before pushing open the door. Two secretaries were carrying on a conversation about Tom Selleck. One of them glanced up. She had blood-red talon nails and lips to match. "Can I help you?" she asked tartly.

"I think I'm in the wrong place. I'm looking for Mr. Stolli's office."

"One floor up," Talon Nails said, generously adding, "you can take the elevator if you like."

As she spoke, the tall woman emerged from Eddie Kane's private office. Close up she had a face carved in granite, decorated with perfect makeup. Her eyes were hard and unrelenting. Lucky recognized the look—she'd seen it on hookers and gamblers and druggies. Vegas was full of expensive whores; Lucky had grown up observing them.

"Thanks," she said to the secretary, and followed the woman outside.

Johnny Romano was on his way toward the building. He walked with a pelvic thrust. Cock first, everything else trailing behind, including his entourage.

The woman didn't even glance in his direction. She hurried over to a gray Cadillac Seville, climbed inside, and took off.

Feeling like a detective, Lucky made a note of the license plate before hurrying back to Eddie's office.

Talon Nails was now on the phone, while the other secretary, a pretty black girl, flicked through a copy of *Rolling Stone*.

"Excuse me," Lucky said. This playing meek and mild was getting her down, and the fucking wig stuck on top of her head was driving her insane, especially on this exceptionally hot and humid Monday morning.

The girl reading *Rolling Stone* lowered the magazine and managed a desultory "Yes?"

"The woman who was just in here—does she work at the studio?"

"No. Why?"

"Uh, because I just saw someone damage her car, and I thought I ought to tell her."

Talon Nails got off the phone and said, "What's up, Brenda?" to the other girl.

Brenda shrugged. "Something about a car accident."

"I need to reach the woman who was just in here," Lucky said assertively. "Do you have a number I can call?"

Now it was Talon Nails's turn to shrug. "Dunno. Maybe Eddie does."

"Mr. Kane," Brenda interrupted with a warning look.

Talon Nails pulled a face. "I hate calling anyone Mister anything," she snapped. "It's so demeaning. Like we're inferior or something. I'll call him Eddie if I want."

"Do what you like. I'm just reminding you what he said."

"Yeah, like he's going to fire me if I forget," Talon Nails sneered. "Sure. He's lucky to *have* a secretary the way *he* carries on with his horny hands. They're everywhere. Bending down is a hazard in this office!"

Brenda couldn't help giggling.

They both suddenly remembered Lucky was standing there.

"I seem to remember her name is Smith," Talon Nails said, all business. "Let me check the Rolodex."

"If you can't reach her, she'll be here next Monday," Brenda joined in helpfully. "She comes in once a week to look after his fish."

"I'm sorry?"

"Tropical fish. He keeps them in a tank in his office."

"Really? And what exactly does she do to them?"

"Who knows?" Brenda yawned. "Feeds 'em, I guess. He *is* kind of obsessive about it, though. One Monday she didn't turn up, and he just about threw a fit. Screaming and yelling like Stallone on a rampage."

"Very good, Brenda," Talon Nails said admiringly. "You should be writing scripts."

Brenda giggled and picked up *Rolling Stone* again. She'd had enough conversation for one day. She was more interested in whether David Lee Roth bleached his hair or not.

"Here we are," Talon Nails said. "J. Smith, Tropical Fish." She scribbled on a piece of paper and handed Lucky the number. "Do you work here?"

"I'm Mr. Stone's temporary assistant."

"Who's he?"

"An executive."

"Of what?"

"He was around in Mr. Panther's day."

"Yeah?" Talon Nails was bored.

Lucky made her escape. *Tropical fish, my ass,* she thought, trudging back to Herman's quarters.

So far it had been an interesting morning. She'd observed the Sleazy Singles in action. Elicited Olive's sympathy. And come across a woman who—if her gut instinct was anything to go on—was quite obviously Eddie's Kane's drug supplier.

Not bad. Not bad at all.

And now she had lunch with Olive to look forward to, and dinner with Abe and Inga. How exciting could one day get?

18

Abigaile Stolli was entertaining, or at least preparing to do so. She marched around her Bel-Air mansion checking every little detail, closely followed by her two Spanish maids, Consuela and Firella.

Abigaile was a short woman with thick shoulder-length auburn hair, snubbed features, and an abundance of designer clothes. She was not a beauty, but as Abe Panther's granddaughter, she had no need to be. Abigaile was true Hollywood royalty.

At the age of forty she had managed to keep a girlish figure (thanks to Jane Fonda), a smooth complexion (thanks to Aida Thibiant), and a keen sense of competitiveness with every other Hollywood wife in town.

When Abigaile did something, it had to be the best. She strived to give the best big parties, the best charity premieres, and the best intimate little dinners. The food was always wonderful, the service impeccable, but her true secret was putting together the right mix of guests.

Tonight was a perfect example. A simple dinner party for twelve people, and the mix was dynamite. One black politician—male. One famous feminist—female. A legendary rock singer with his darkly exotic wife, who happened to be a successful model—another plus. Two movie stars—Cooper Turner and Venus Maria. A hot young director and his girlfriend. And to round out the group, the fast-talking, newly appointed head of Orpheus Studios, Zeppo White, and his eccentric and mildly stoned wife, Ida.

Zeppo—a former top agent, and Ida—a so-called producer who never produced anything, were mainstays of any good dinner party. Zeppo with his snobbish ways and acid conversation. Ida, chicly turned out, with all the latest outrageous gossip. Abigaile always tried to include them. They were insurance against boredom.

Abigaile was especially pleased that Cooper Turner had accepted her invitation. He was known for never appearing anywhere, so it was a coup to get him. And Venus Maria was another hard-to-get guest.

Abigaile was satisfied that this was going to be a talked-about evening. She would call George Christy personally to inform him of the guest list. Let the town read and weep.

"Hmmm . . ." Abigaile spotted a Lalique wineglass with a tiny chip in the rim. She picked it up and turned to her two maids, glaring at them accusingly. Words were not necessary.

"So sorry, madame," gasped Consuela, immediately accepting responsibility along with the offending glass. "I will take care of it, madame," she promised.

"Yes, and perhaps you can find out who is responsible," Abigaile said testily. "These glasses cost over one hundred and fifty dollars each. *Somebody* should pay. And that somebody is certainly *not* going to be me."

Consuela and Firella exchanged glances. One hundred and fifty dollars! For a glass! American women were surely crazy.

Abigaile finished her inspection without further incident and set off for the beauty salon in her cream-colored Mercedes.

Speeding down Sunset, she used her cellular car phone to catch Mickey at the studio.

"I'm on my way to lunch," Mickey said, sounding harassed. "What is it?"

"You were supposed to send over three dozen bottles of Cristal from your office. Where are they?"

Here he was running a major studio, and his wife spoke to him like he was a goddamn liquor salesman. Wonderful! "Talk to Olive," he snapped.

"No, *you* talk to Olive," Abigaile snapped back.

In most Hollywood marriages the men sat in the power seat and the women danced carefully around their delicate egos. In the Stolli household, Abigaile held the real chair of authority. She was Abe Panther's granddaughter, and let no one forget it, especially Mickey.

"And while you're speaking to Olive," she added, "make sure she confirms the time and place with Cooper Turner and Venus Maria for tonight. I don't want any no-shows."

"Yeah, yeah," Mickey said impatiently, tagging on a sarcastic "Anything else? Maybe you'd like me to pick up your dry cleaning, or stop by Gelson's?"

"Goodbye, Mickey dear." The way Abigaile said goodbye spoke volumes.

She pulled up to the valet parker in front of Ivana's, the hot new beauty salon, and hurried briskly inside.

Abigaile Stolli was giving one of her famous intimate dinners. She had no time to waste.

19

Olive Watson spoke glowingly of her fiancé, a computer systems analyst. She'd met him on her annual vacation trip to England a year ago, and they'd corresponded ever since.

"How much time have you actually spent with him?" Lucky asked curiously.

"Ten days," Olive replied. "It was quite the whirlwind courtship."

I bet, Lucky thought. She was mildly curious to know if they'd slept together. But there was no way demure Luce would go for an intimate question like that, so she discreetly shut up and settled for "What's his name?"

"George." Olive sounded in love. "He's an older man. Very distinguished-looking."

"How old is older?" Lucky ventured.

Olive pursed her lips. "Fifty-something," she revealed.

"There's nothing wrong with an older man," Lucky said reassuringly, thinking of her own marriage to Dimitri Stanislopoulos when she was twenty-something and he was in his sixties.

"You're very understanding," Olive replied, picking at a light salad. She hesitated a moment and then said, "I hope you don't mind me saying this, but actually your hairstyle could be improved, and I'd be willing to take you to my hairdresser. That's if you want me to," she added hastily, anxious not to offend.

"Thanks, I like it this way," Lucky said quickly, automatically touching the hideous wig.

"Oh. I don't mean that it's not very nice. It is. Very nice," Olive said, obviously flustered, and lying as best she could.

For the first time Lucky felt like a fraud. Olive was genuinely concerned, and maybe it wasn't fair to be playing games with her.

No problem, she decided. When she took over the studio she'd give Olive a hefty raise and a promotion. The woman deserved it after working for Mickey Stolli all these years.

Changing the subject, she asked, "When are you planning on getting married?"

"George wants to do it at once," Olive said with a worried frown, thinking of the difficulties. "I told him it's impossible. There's so much to discuss, and I have no desire to leave my job. I'm not sure if George is prepared to live in California."

"Shouldn't you find out?"

"Yes." Olive nodded vigorously. "George is going to be in Boston for two days next week on business. It would be a perfect time to talk things over." She sighed. "He wants me to join him. Unfortunately it's impossible."

Lucky sensed an opportunity. "Why?"

"Because Mr. Stolli can't do without me. He's a very particular man. Everything has to be just so."

"Really? He won't accept a temp?"

"Certainly not."

"Or one of the girls in your building?"

"Absolutely out of the question."

"How about me?"

"You?"

This was a hard sell, but she could do it. "Yes, me. I can take over for a couple of days. You'll show me what to do, and I promise you he'll have no complaints."

"You work for Mr. Stone," Olive pointed out.

"He's off on vacation next week. Besides, even when he's around I have nothing to do. It's a boring job. To tell you the truth, I was thinking of leaving."

Olive lapsed into silence for a moment. It was a tempting offer.

Luce certainly seemed competent enough. "I'll have to ask Mr. Stolli," she said unsurely. "After all, it's his decision, and as I said before, he's a very particular man with cast-iron habits."

"O.K.," Lucky said, willing Olive to go for the idea. "I understand."

Olive nodded. "I *will* ask him," she decided. "This is such an important trip for me, and it's best to get things settled as soon as possible."

"Quite," agreed Lucky.

Olive nodded again. "I'll let you know," she said.

Lucky had Boogie run a trace on Eddie Kane's tropical fish lady's car. It was registered to one Kathleen Le Paul. J. Smith never entered the picture. Well, anyone with half a brain would have guessed that.

She instructed Boogie to check Ms. Le Paul out and to get her the information as soon as possible.

"It's done," Boogie assured her.

Herman immediately wanted to know what was going on. The air-conditioning in his office had broken down, and he was feeling the heat in more ways than one. He was red in the face and stressed out.

Lucky felt sorry for him. "You're taking a vacation," she said firmly.

He became agitated. "What?"

"A vacation. You need it. You deserve it. A week in Palm Springs. You're to get out of here so I'm free to fill in for Olive. O.K.?"

Herman wasn't about to argue. Anything to get away was welcome. "When shall I leave?" he asked stiffly.

"Stick around until Thursday. Maybe we can get to see the dailies you requested. In fact—" she grabbed the phone—"I'm going to arrange that right now."

The screening room was comfortably decorated in plush green leather, with thick carpeting and blowups of some of Panther's biggest stars on the walls. There was Venus Maria, clad in black leather, with a mocking expression. A full close-up of the very handsome Cooper Turner. Susie Rush, pert and coy, hiding beneath a pink parasol. Charlie Dollar, maniacal grin in place. Johnny Romano, surrounded by girls in low-cut dresses. Marisa Birch, standing tall with her crew-cut hair and enormous bosom. And Lennie Golden, laid back and quirky, with his longish dirty-blond hair, penetrating green eyes, and cynical smile.

Lucky lingered in front of his photograph. He looked great. As always. She missed him with a vengeance.

Harry Browning came out of the projection booth to greet Herman Stone personally. Ignoring Lucky, he shook Herman by the hand and said, "How very nice to see you, Mr. Stone. It's been a long time."

"What do you have I can look at?" Herman asked gruffly, playing his part, just as Lucky had instructed him to.

"I've got the latest dailies on *Macho Man*. And a rough cut of *Motherfaker*," Harry offered.

"That'll do," Herman said, making his way to the center of the back row of seats, where there was a telephone to issue orders to the projection booth and a small cooler containing a selection of soft drinks.

"What would you like to see first?" Harry asked.

"The dailies on *Macho Man*," Lucky replied, adding quickly, "Mr. Stone would like to see the *Macho Man* dailies first."

"That's right," agreed Herman, continuing to play his part.

"Certainly," said Harry stiffly, avoiding eye contact with Lucky.

When Lennie's presence dominated the screen, Lucky was filled with pride. Apart from being funny and intelligent, he was so goddamn horny-looking. And he was her husband!

The first scene was a brief setup between Lennie and Joey Firello. They worked well together. Their dialogue played fast and snappy. Lucky recognized Lennie's beat on the material. Why was he complaining? This was good stuff.

And then Marisa Birch took over the screen in more ways than one, and Lucky knew exactly what Lennie was bitching about. Marisa's physical appearance was overpowering, but there was not an ounce of talent to back it up. Her acting, such as it was, seemed to be a giant put-on.

The scene where she was in bed with Lennie was a joke. Grudge Freeport had obviously got his rocks off directing it. Marisa's huge tits were the only focus he was interested in. They managed to take over every shot—great big bouncy things, large enough to do serious damage.

Lennie was not happy, and it showed. Talk about no chemistry! Marisa and Lennie did not create sparks. There was no sizzle— merely fizzle.

Watching the five takes Grudge had ordered printed, Lucky began to feel acutely embarrassed. No wonder Lennie was complaining all the time—this was worse than she'd imagined.

"What kind of films are they making now?" Herman said, looking distressed. "I'm watching pornography."

"When did you last see one of Panther's movies?" Lucky asked curiously.

Herman failed to reply.

He probably hasn't seen a movie since *Gone With the Wind*, she thought. Poor old Herman. What a shock he's in for if he ever gets out into the real world.

The rough cut of *Motherfaker* hit the screen with an opening shot of a tough, leather-jacketed Johnny Romano strutting down a rain-slicked street and practicing the old familiar cock-thrust swagger.

Suddenly a man steps in his path, blocking him.

"Whattya want, mothafucker?" Johnny Romano asks.

"I want what's mine, shithead," the other actor replies.

"Man, whyn't you take your dick an' shove it up your ass, 'cause you ain't gettin' shit from me, prickface."

"What ya call me, fuckhead?"

"Prickface, mothafucker. You want I spell it out for you?"

"You're fuckin' with the wrong dude, spic."

"Yeah?"

"Yeah, ya dumb cocksucker."

A tight close-up on Johnny Romano. His eyes hold the screen.

Deep-set and brown, they draw you into the character. His eyes register anger and a lurking danger. His eyes are lethal weapons.

The camera pans back to show the other character reaching for a gun.

Johnny kicks the gun from the man's hand, produces a weapon of his own and blows him away.

Loud rap music blares and the credits begin to roll.

"This is appalling!" Herman gasped.

"Welcome to the eighties," Lucky said dryly.

20

Ivana's was a den of gossip. Everyone knew something that nobody else knew. "I can tell you this only if you *promise* not to tell anyone else," was the battle cry.

Naturally everyone promised, and everyone told.

The story about Venus Maria giving Cooper Turner a blow job on the set was still circulating. Only now the tale was embellished. It wasn't just Cooper she'd attended to—it was half the crew she'd obliged at the same time.

"Nonsense!" snapped Abigaile, when the skinny black girl who shampooed her hair recounted the story.

"Oh, it's true, Abigaile," the girl assured her, nodding solemnly.

"Kindly address me as Mrs. Stolli," Abigaile said grandly. "And, dear, please be aware that my husband is the head of Panther Studios, where this event is supposed to have taken place. And, if you continue to spread malicious gossip, you will be sued."

Wide-eyed, the girl wrapped a towel around Abigaile's wet hair and fled.

When Saxon, the owner of Ivana's, came over to style her hair, Abigaile complained.

Saxon did not kiss ass. Saxon was tall and muscular with shoulder-length blond curls. He had the body of a weight lifter and the look of a heavy metal rock star. Having arrived from New York and opened his salon a mere ten months ago, he was now, at age thirty, the most popular hair stylist in town.

"Stop bitching, Abby, I hate it when you whine," Saxon said in a deep, gruff voice. Nobody had managed to figure out whether he was gay or straight. And nobody dared ask.

"I'm not whining," Abigaile replied tartly. "And I don't think it's too much to ask for your transient staff to address me with some respect. I am Mrs. Stolli to them. *Mrs.*"

"Yes, dear," Saxon said, with a notable lack of respect.

"Thank you." Her eyes dropped to his crotch. Saxon wore the tightest jeans known to man.

He caught her checking him out. She quickly glanced away.

"So, and how does *Mrs.* Stolli want to look today?" he asked, tossing back his mane of enviable blond hair.

"Do your best," she replied shortly.

"I always do, dear, I always do."

Boogie was a whiz at getting fast information. By the time Lucky returned from the screening there was a message waiting for her to call him.

Herman was slumped behind his desk. He had left the screening twenty minutes into the picture, muttering to himself.

Lucky was certainly no prude, and she abhorred any kind of censorship, but *Motherfaker* had managed to offend almost everyone. Every other word was "motherfucker," the violence was relentless and mostly pointless, and women were portrayed as either whores or dumb victims.

Johnny Romano had written, executive-produced, and starred in this piece of crap. Some message he was putting out there.

"Does Abe know what kind of sexist violent junk this studio is making?" Lucky demanded.

Herman shrugged hopelessly. "A Johnny Romano film makes money," he said.

"So does a thousand-dollar-a-night hooker, but that doesn't mean you have to fuck her, does it?"

Herman pushed his chair away from the desk and stood up. "I'm leaving."

And don't bother coming back, she wanted to say. *Stay at home, Herman. Grow roses and play golf. Home is where you belong.*

"Don't forget you'll be taking a vacation next week," she reminded him.

He nodded and walked slowly from the office—a tired old man being dragged reluctantly into the present.

For a moment Lucky almost felt sorry for him. But then she thought, what the hell—he was being paid a fat paycheck to sit on his can and do exactly nothing. The least he could have done was view the product once in a while.

Boogie answered her call immediately. "What's up?" she asked. "Can it wait, or should I hear it now?"

"You're right, as usual," Boogie said admiringly. "You should be at the racetrack picking horses."

"Give me the story," Lucky said impatiently, cradling the phone under her chin while she reached for a cigarette.

"Kathleen Le Paul," Boogie announced, "alias Cathy Paulson, alias Candy Ganini. Thirty-four years old. She started out as a sixteen-year-old stripper, married a hood, became a call girl, then started to run dope across borders for anyone who'd pay enough. Arrested in 1980 for transporting drugs. She had three bags of cocaine stuffed up her snatch."

"That's pleasant!"

"Did time, came out, married a small-time agent, had a child, then went back to her old ways. She's now the Los Angeles girlfriend of Colombian drug lord Umberto Castelli, and one of the chief suppliers of the show-biz community. They trust her. She dresses in designer clothes."

"I noticed," Lucky said dryly.

"Anything else?" Boogie asked.

"What color panties does she wear?"

"Blue. Pink on Tuesdays."

"Fun–nee."

"Incidentally, your father is here."

Lucky was surprised. "Gino's in L.A.?"

"At the Wilshire. He wants you to have dinner with him tonight."

"I can't do that, Boog. Tonight is Abe Panther time, I'm going up to his house. Call Gino and tell him I'll be in touch tomorrow. Oh, and run a fast check on Eddie Kane, he's senior vice president of distribution at Panther. I want to know it all."

"You got it."

She thought about Bobby and missed him like crazy. "Did you call London?" she asked anxiously.

"Bobby's fine," he assured her.

"And my office?"

"Running smoothly."

She sighed. "I guess I'm not missed."

"You're always missed."

"Thanks, Boog."

She hung up the phone and contemplated this latest information. So Eddie Kane was a cokehead, and who else had the same little habit?

A cocaine high was expensive to support. Exactly what other scams was Eddie Kane into?

In the executive dining room Susie Rush laid her delicate white hand over Mickey Stolli's not so delicate hairy fist and said, "Next time we lunch, we should do it at my place."

She fluttered her eyelids at him, a flirtatious gesture he did not appreciate. This broad had been coming on to him for weeks, and he couldn't quite figure out how to handle it. She was a major Panther star, and a major pain in the ass. He had no desire to fuck her. But the problem was, how to get out of it gracefully? Because as each day passed, Ms. Rush was making her intentions undeniably clear.

"Susie, my pet," he said, clearing his throat, "if I ever had lunch at your place it would be all over." ·

"What do you mean, Mickey?" she asked, girlishly innocent, knowing perfectly well what he meant.

"I mean I couldn't stop myself from jumpin' your gorgeous bones, an' that wouldn't be right, would it?"

Susie giggled. "Why not?" she asked, a coquettish tilt to her head.

He couldn't help noticing the fine network of lines around her watery blue eyes, and the two deeper furrows between her brows.

141

This broad was no longer in the first flush—it was miraculous what a great lighting cameraman could do.

"We're both married, Susie. Gotta remember that," Mickey said, trying to sound sincere.

She rubbed her fingers lightly across his clenched fist. "You're tense, Mickey. Relax, it's only little me."

This had gone far enough—better snap this back onto a business level. "I'm very married, Susie," he reminded her. And then, just to keep her in a good mood, "If I wasn't, who knows. . . ."

Susie patted his fist and withdrew her hand. "Do you know something, Mickey?"

"What?"

"In spite of your *fierce* reputation, you really are a very sweet and loyal man." She honored him with a sugary smile.

Mickey Stolli had been called a lot of things in his life. "Sweet" and "loyal" were a definite first. He sincerely hoped nobody was eavesdropping. Sweet and loyal could blow his entire reputation.

"Let's talk about the script," he said, firmly changing the subject.

"Which script?" Susie replied, delicately picking the leaves off an artichoke and dipping them in a buttery sauce.

"*Sunshine.*"

"I don't want to do *Sunshine*," Susie replied, getting quite snappish. "If you ever listened to me, you'd be aware I have no intention of doing *Sunshine*." She paused for dramatic effect. "I wish to play the lead in *Bombshell*."

Mickey laughed. A mistake.

Susie glared. "What's so funny?"

He recovered quickly. "Nothing's funny. Venus Maria is set for *Bombshell*."

"She hasn't signed."

"She will."

Susie's eyes hardened. "I want a shot at that role, Mickey. And I will not be happy if I don't get it."

He put on his best jerk-off voice. "C'mon, pet. What are we talkin' here? *Bombshell* is all wrong for you, it's not your image. The public wouldn't want to see you in it. You're Susie Rush, America's sweetheart. Stick to type. Right now you're queen of the box office."

Not strictly true. Her last film had been a disappointment, making a mere 60 million, as opposed to breaking the 100 million mark, a goal her movies usually achieved.

"I need a change of pace," Susie said, all business.

Where was the hand-holding of ten minutes ago? Mickey thought sourly, realizing this whole come-on for the last few weeks didn't mean shit. She had no wish to get into his pants, she merely wanted to get into his movie.

He sighed wearily. They were all the same, these actresses. Big star or minor player, they'd all drop their panties for the right role.

Everyone knew *Bombshell* was his special project, a script developed and written from an idea he'd suggested, a movie he was going to personally produce. *Bombshell*—the true, shocking story of a Hollywood sex symbol. He could see the billboard on Sunset now—preferably the one overlooking Spago. And with Venus Maria in the lead role it was a movie that couldn't miss. Venus Maria was the hottest actress in America. She had a fascinating chameleon quality, a new open sexuality that seemed to turn everyone on. Little girls copied what she wore. Big girls admired her feisty style of sticking her tongue out at convention. And all males, whether sixteen or sixty, felt the musky heat she exuded. Most of all she was *now*. A true woman of the moment.

"Well?" demanded a pursed-lipped Susie, obviously waiting for some comment on her desire to star in his movie.

"You're not right for it," Mickey repeated.

"I'm prepared to test," Susie said stubbornly.

Mickey shook his head.

She glared at him. Hell hath no fury like an actress scorned. "*I'm* willing to test and *you're* saying no?"

"Honey, I wouldn't put you through it. Venus Maria is set. It's a done deal."

"She's too cheap-looking—too obvious."

Mickey was smart enough to make no comment when one woman was putting down another. Dealing with Abigaile had taught him that. He shrugged noncommittally.

Susie sighed, a deeply put-upon type of sigh, and played her trump card. "Zeppo White has a script he wants me to read for

Orpheus. I hardly wish to be disloyal, but I guess I'll take a little peek. What do *you* think?"

I think you're a blackmailing cunt. "Go ahead if it makes you happy, Susie. But I'd still like you to think about doing *Sunshine.*"

A phony smile. "Thank you, darling, I knew you wouldn't mind."

Olive called Lucky three times during the afternoon. The first time she thanked her for listening to her problems over lunch. The second time she informed her she'd made a decision—she was definitely going to broach the subject of Luce's taking over for her a couple of days the following week while she visited her fiancé in Boston. The third time she sounded dispirited. "Mr. Stolli's in a dreadful mood," she said. "I daren't mention my plans until he calms down."

"What's the matter with him?" Lucky asked curiously.

"It's Susie Rush," Olive confided in a low voice. "She's refusing to commit to the film Mr. Stolli wants her to do next." Olive's voice got even lower. "And she's threatening to move over to Orpheus."

"Really?"

"He's very upset. Not a word to anyone, Luce."

"Wouldn't dream of it."

"I must go now. I have to send champagne over to his wife."

"Can't she call the liquor store?"

Olive snorted derisively. "Three dozen bottles of Cristal. If she gets it from the studio she doesn't have to pay."

Another petty scam. "Really?"

"Oh, dear," Olive fretted, "I shouldn't have told you that."

"Don't worry. Who am I going to tell?"

"Thank you, Luce. You're a good friend for putting up with all my carrying on. Perhaps we can lunch again tomorrow."

"I'd like that," Lucky said agreeably.

Shortly after Olive's final call, she took off. The heat was unbearable in the stuffy little office, and she couldn't wait to strip off her dreary clothes, dump the wig and glasses, and return to her real self.

Harry Browning was in the parking lot.

Harry Browning was watching her.

21

Virginia Venus Maria Sierra stared at her reflection in the mirrored wall of her all-white gym next to her all-white bedroom in her Hollywood Hills home. She was on her Stairmaster, a lethal machine that simulated climbing stairs. Clad in pale blue sweats, a headband holding back her platinum-blond hair, she worked diligently.

Stereo speakers cleverly concealed in the ceiling entertained her with the latest Eurythmics. Much as she admired Annie Lennox, she wasn't really listening—she had other things on her mind.

Like Ron.

Like Emilio—one of her brothers.

Like Cooper.

And like this stupid dinner party at the Stollis' she'd rashly agreed to attend tonight.

Oh, God! How she hated Hollywood dinner parties. They were such pretentious affairs. And she'd have to make nice to the Stollis —especially Mickey, Mr. Mogul himself.

She and Ron had christened Mickey Stolli "Mr. Mogul" the moment they'd met him. He was the perfect Hollywood studio-head prototype. Central Casting couldn't do better. He had the mogul look. The mogul voice. And the mogul bullshit charm.

She suspected the charm lasted only as long as one was hot.

Venus Maria was no fool. She was savvy and street smart. She even kept a watchful eye on her money—no smooth-talking "I'll just take twenty percent of your income" business manager for her. She knew where every dollar went and signed all her own checks, along with Ron. Early on, she and Ron had formed a company together. They'd called it MARO Productions, and they were fifty-fifty partners. At the time it had seemed like a wonderful idea. Two best friends, joined forever. Now Ron had acquired a new busybody boyfriend, and Ken—that was his name—was pissing Venus Maria off.

Not that she was jealous. Lord knows Ron had gone through enough different boyfriends since they'd arrived in Hollywood three years ago. But this one was definitely a pumped-up pain in the butt. A handsome (if you enjoyed the I've-got-a-hot-poker-up-my-ass-look), know-all male model. Behind his back she called him the Ken Doll. He was twenty-eight and acted as if he were fifty.

Ron was in love. Ron was buying the Ken Doll suits and jackets and paintings and sculptures and jewelry, and finally—a Mercedes. A fucking Mercedes for crissakes! *She* didn't even have a Mercedes.

Angrily her legs worked the Stairmaster. She'd made up her mind she had to split the partnership, and although she realized it was the only sane thing to do, it still hurt. Ron was her family, her spiritual brother, and she loved him. But she couldn't sit back and allow him to spend her money on some loser he had a hot nut for.

She'd turned to Cooper Turner for advice. "Do it," he'd advised her. "It's a foolish arrangement anyway. He makes plenty, it's not like you're leaving him with nothing."

This was true. Ron was an extremely successful choreographer, very much in demand since he'd done all the dance routines for *Danceflash*, a smash hit sleeper movie. And he always choreographed the top videos, including all of hers. So it wasn't like he was broke. He'd have plenty of money, and if he wanted to spend it on the Ken Doll, that was his prerogative. As long as it was *his* money buying the presents, there would be no need for her to be angry.

Now all she had to do was tell him.

Next problem. Her brother Emilio had turned up at her front door uninvited and unannounced. "I've come out to Hollywood t'be a star, just like you, little sis."

Little sis! Was this the same Emilio who used to scream at her all the time? The brother who used to whack her across the face if his Saturday night date shirt wasn't pressed exactly the way he liked? The very Emilio who'd called her ratface in front of his friends and repeatedly told her she was the ugliest, shittiest little turd he'd ever seen?

Yes, it was the same Emilio. Thirty years old and too fat to be anything but a slob.

"Get out of my face," she'd told him. "Go home. I can't help you."

He'd shoved his way inside her house, checked it out, settled down in front of the big-screen T.V., and said, "I'll only stay a few days, just till I get a job, little sis."

Big chance of that. Five weeks later he was still comfortably ensconced in front of her television with no intention of moving.

Another situation she was going to have to deal with.

One thing Venus Maria hated was confrontations. She wasn't good when it came to a showdown. Ever since she was a little girl she'd wanted to run away and not face up to conflict. It was a weakness she was working on.

Fortunately the movie with Cooper was going well. She liked herself in the dailies; she looked better than she had in her other two films. The acting classes she'd taken had helped, and her new worked-out, worked-on body was a definite improvement.

It was a challenge to be up there on the screen with Cooper Turner. She clearly remembered—although she hadn't told Cooper because he was sensitive about his age—the first time she'd ever seen him. Her mother was alive then, and Venus Maria had been about eleven. Her mother was a big fan and had taken her to see Cooper in one of his early movies.

Venus had thought he was sexy even then. That night she'd ended up playing doctor with herself under the bedcovers.

Cooper would enjoy that part, but she wasn't about to give him the pleasure.

Right now Cooper was being too dictatorial for his own good. He thought he knew everything, but professionally Venus Maria had an instinctive knack of sensing exactly what move to make next, and nobody could alter that—not even Cooper Turner.

"Tone it down," he kept on advising her about her performance. "You're too stylized. Wear less makeup. Darken your hair. Don't come on so strong."

She had the savvy not to listen. She knew the way she was playing the role was right. And if all went according to plan—her plan—she would steal the film.

Cooper was not happy. They fought a lot. Venus Maria was wise for her years; she understood him very well. He was an aging matinee idol who didn't enjoy getting older. At forty-five he was twenty years older than she, and on screen it showed. Consciously or subconsciously he was trying to dilute her impact.

Too bad. She knew the Venus Maria her fans were expecting to see, and she refused to let them down. Not at this stage of her career.

Finishing her workout, she jumped off the machine, stripped off her sweaty exercise clothes, and stood under an icy shower for a good ten minutes. Cold water toned the skin. And after it was toned, she lathered on a Clarins body lotion, making sure she covered every inch of valuable flesh.

As she was doing this, the door to her private bathroom was rudely flung open, and there stood Emilio.

She was stark naked, with one leg up on a stool, as she diligently applied the creamy lotion.

"Oh, wow. 'Scuse *me!*" exclaimed Emilio, eyes taking in every inch of little sis.

Venus Maria did not move. She refused to give him the satisfaction of grabbing for a towel and covering herself. Instead she glared at him, a put-down, menacing glare. "Get the fuck out," she said coldly.

He thought about a smart reply, decided against it, checked out pussy and tits and everything else he could lay his eyes on, then backed slowly from the doorway.

She was furious. This intrusion was too much. Emilio was out.

Once, a long time ago, another of her brothers had come to her bed in the middle of the night, drunk and amorous. She'd kicked him in the balls so hard he'd walked with a limp for several days. A week later she'd fled the family home with Ron, her savior. Without Ron she'd never have had the courage to hitch across the country all the way to Hollywood. She owed Ron a lot. But she didn't owe him half her money.

With Emilio out of the room, she walked over to the door, slammed and locked it. Burning with anger, she decided five weeks was long enough. Emilio had to go, no more putting up with his shit.

The phone rang. She snatched it up quickly. Emilio had developed a habit of picking up the phone before either she or her housekeeper could get to it, and chatting to her friends. She'd overheard him speaking to her agent one day. "Hi, I'm Emilio, Venus's brother." Pause, while her agent probably said something polite. Then Emilio again. "Yeah, I'm good-lookin'. Sure, I'm talented. Hey man, I got more talent than she got in her—"

She'd removed the phone from his big fat fist. "Don't you dare pick up my calls!"

It had not deterred him.

"Who's this?" she asked in her best disguised voice.

"Hi, babe. It's Johnny. What's with the funny accent?"

Ha! *He* could talk!

Why did she have to be put in this position? Johnny Romano was a pest. He seemed incapable of acceping the fact that she had no desire to go out with him. "Johnny, I'll have to call you back, I'm on the other line," she lied.

"Don't give me that, babe. Hang up your other call. It's me. In person."

She tried to sound reverent. "I'm talking to Michael Jackson."

A touch of respect. "Michael, huh? How is the home boy?"

"I'll find out and get back to you."

"When?"

"Soon."

"How soon?"

"Sooner than you think."

"Hey, babe. You an' I—we gotta take this further."

"We will."

"When?"

"Goodbye, Johnny."

She knew it destroyed him that she didn't jump. And why should she? Johnny Romano was not for her. He was a stud factory, nailing everything that breathed.

She wished he'd get the message and leave her alone. There were too many guys like him in Hollywood—Johnny was just a bigger star than most.

It was time to get ready for the Stollis' dinner party. After applying an alabaster-white makeup, with darkened eyes and bright red lips, she pinned her platinum hair on top of her head and marched into her walk-in closet to survey the possibilities. Abigaile Stolli's secretary had stated ties for the men and pretty for the women. What the fuck did that mean?

Venus Maria selected a black suit with a thin pinstripe, cut masculine style. Under it she chose a matching vest which only just covered her breasts. On her legs she wore white stockings, and on her feet granny-style lace-up black boots.

She chose her jewelry carefully, deciding on silver hoop earrings, accompanied by three small diamond studs embedded in each ear, and eight thin silver-and-gold bangles on each wrist. The Venus Maria look was complete.

A star was ready to face the world.

22

The driveway leading to Abe Panther's house was shrouded in darkness. Talk about creepy! Lucky wasn't frightened of the dark, but surely the old guy could afford a few lights?

She'd decided against bringing Boogie; he'd only have to sit outside in the car all night.

From the studio she'd driven straight back to her rented house, bypassing Sheila Hervey's depressing apartment where Boogie had installed an answering machine with a remote so if anyone from the studio called her—such as Olive or Harry Browning—she would know about it.

Once at the house she'd thrown off the hated wig, dumped the heavy glasses, stripped off the disgusting clothes, and dived into the pool for a welcome and invigorating swim.

She swam twenty lengths before quitting, and then she hurried to get ready for an evening with good old Abe. There wasn't even time to call Gino.

Inga answered the door of Abe's Miller Drive house. Big-boned Inga with her cropped hair and sour expression.

"Hello," Lucky said pleasantly.

Inga merely gave a curt nod and stomped off, obviously expecting Lucky to follow, which she did.

Abe was in the dining room sitting at one end of an elaborate oak table. "You're late," he snapped impatiently, indicating that she should occupy the chair next to him.

"I wasn't aware we were running on a strict timetable," Lucky remarked.

Gnarled fingers beat out a rhythm on the table. "I always eat at six o'clock."

She glanced at her watch. "It's only twelve past."

"That means I've been sitting here for twelve minutes," he said crossly.

"C'mon, Abe, lighten up." Lucky attempted to put him in a better mood. "Eating dinner a few minutes late is hardly a disaster. And frankly, I wouldn't mind being offered a drink."

"What do you drink, girlie?"

"Jack Daniel's. What do *you* drink?" she replied, challenging him.

He admired her attitude. "Whatever I goddamn feel like."

"And what do you feel like tonight?"

"I'll join you. Two Jack Daniel's, on the rocks. Pronto! Pronto!" He issued these instructions to an uptight Inga, who stormed off without saying a word.

"Used to have a houseful of servants," Abe offered. "Hated it! Couldn't take a crap without somebody smellin' it."

Lucky laughed. It felt good to laugh. She realized she'd been taking the whole Panther Studios deal too seriously. It was time to lie back and relax. Not too much, just enough to let it all go for a night.

"Y'know, my father, Gino, is in town. I'd love to bring him up here one day," she said, thinking to herself how well the two old men would get along.

"Why?" Abe snapped. "He and I acquainted or somethin'?"

"Maybe. He built one of the first hotels in Las Vegas, the Mirage."

"I remember the Mirage," Abe said gruffly. "Lost ten thousand big ones at the crap tables. That was way back when ten thousand meant somethin'. Today you can't buy nothin' for ten thousand bucks."

"You wouldn't want to buy anything anyway, you never leave the house."

"Why should I?" he demanded excitedly. "You think I'm crazy? I know all about what goes on out on the streets today. You think I want t'get mugged an' shot at? No thank you, girlie. No thank you very much."

Inga appeared, carrying the drinks. She placed them on the table with a disapproving thump.

Abe cackled. "She don't like me to drink," he said, taking a hearty swig. "Thinks I'm too old. Thinks the old ticktock can't take it. Ain't that right, Inga?"

"You do whatever pleases you," Inga replied dourly. "I can't stop you."

"Don't even try," he warned, shaking a bony finger in her direction.

"You're only as old as you feel," Lucky said cheerfully. "That's what my father says. He's decided to stick at forty-five—he's actually seventy-nine, you'd never believe it. The man is amazing."

"Seventy-nine's not old," Abe scoffed. "I was still runnin' the studio in my seventies." Realizing Inga had remained standing beside him, he waved her away with his birdlike arms. "Shoo! Shoo! Go get the food. I'm a hungry old dinosaur, an' I want to eat *now!* Hurry, woman."

Once more Inga departed to do his bidding.

"Uh . . . how does she feel about our deal?" Lucky asked curiously.

Abe shrugged. "What do I care?"

"You must care," Lucky insisted. "Inga's been with you a long time. She looks after you. Surely you depend on her? I don't see anyone else around taking care of your needs."

"I employ two gardeners, a pool man who comes in twice a week, an' two maids," Abe said grandly. "Inga sits on her big Swedish bottom all day doin' nothin'. She should kiss my ass to have such a life."

Lucky got to the point. "I'm sure. But can you trust her? I mean we don't want her blowing my cover. She's not exactly friendly toward me, you know."

Abe began to laugh. "Inga does what's good for her," he cackled. "She's a smart one. She's thought it out, an' she knows it's better for her if I sell the studio *before* I die, that way she gets a stash of cash. If I don't sell the studio, she's going to have a fight on her hands with my granddaughters. Those two'll tie her up in court forever."

"Why?"

"Because they're greedy. It runs in the family. They'll want everything I've got. No sharing."

"But they'll still inherit all your money."

He cocked his head on one side—a canny old man with a plan. "Maybe. Maybe not. I could move to Bora Bora an' give it all away to a cats' home before I go."

"Then you'd *really* have a fight on your hands."

"Not me, girlie. I'll be ten foot under. I could care less." He tapped his gnarled fingers on the table. "Now, lets get down to business. I want to hear everything you've got. Every goddamn detail."

Mickey Stolli prepared to leave the studio early. "If my wife calls, tell her I'm in an important meeting and cannot be disturbed," he instructed Olive. "Whatever you do, don't let her know I've left."

"Yes, Mr. Stolli."

Mickey was not in a good mood, and he was wise enough to realize he had to do something about it before going home to Abigaile's perfect little dinner party. Christ! How he hated her parties. Phony conversations. Too much rich food. And everyone as secretly bored as he was.

Why did she have to do it to him? Just so she could see her name in George Christy's column? Big deal. He worked like a slave at the studio all week. Wouldn't it be nice to come home to much needed rest and relaxation?

Tonight Cooper Turner would corner him about the movie. Venus Maria would do the same. They both wanted to complain about something or other.

How did he know?

Movie stars. They were all the same. Their part was never big enough. Their percentage didn't satisfy. And their close-ups were too far and few between.

Zeppo White would also want to talk business. Fucking social-climbing ex-agent snob. Zeppo thought he was running Orpheus Studios. He couldn't run an errand! Mickey missed the days when Howard Solomon was in charge. Howard was a goer, a little wacked out maybe, especially when he had the coke problem, but a real studio man. Howard knew what it was all about. And it was about making money, not hosting lousy dinner parties.

Just as he was about to leave the building, Eddie Kane grabbed him.

"Gotta talk to you, Mickey," Eddie said urgently, hanging on to his arm. "It's important."

"Not now," Mickey replied, freeing himself with a quick shake. He didn't like being touched unless he instigated it.

"When?" Eddie demanded. He was a sandy-haired attractive man in his early forties, with a Don Johnson stubble, transparent blue eyes, and a penchant for crumpled sports clothes. A former child star, he'd once been famous for an innocence that had now settled into a kind of bemused adulthood.

Eddie and Mickey went way back—almost twenty-five years. For a while Mickey had been his agent, nailing his once hot career right into the ground. When Eddie had given up acting—or rather when acting had given up him—Mickey had found him a job at his agency. Too mundane for Eddie—after a while he got bored and took off for Hawaii, where he became a production manager on a private eye television series. The drugs were plentiful and good, but eventually they got him into trouble, and once again he was on the move. Back in L.A. Mickey helped him out. He used a little influence and fixed Eddie up with a job at Panther.

As Mickey rose to power, he took Eddie along with him. Mickey knew the wisdom of surrounding himself with grateful people.

Now Eddie Kane had plenty of clout; a gorgeous wife; a simple little 2-million-dollar Malibu beach house; and an out-of-control cocaine habit.

"Speak to Olive. She'll set it up," Mickey said, already on his way.

"Tomorrow?" Eddie asked anxiously. " 'Cause we gotta talk, man. This is serious shit."

"Check with Olive."

Mickey ducked out of the building and hurried to his car. He could, if he so desired, have a limousine and a chauffeur on twenty-four-hour call. But there were occasions for formality and times for privacy. Today he needed privacy. What he didn't need was Eddie Kane driving him crazy. Eddie was an asset who at any moment could turn into a major liability. Drug users were bad news. Mickey had given quite a lot of thought to cutting him loose.

A dream. Eddie knew too much.

Mickey made a mental note to call Leslie, Eddie's wife, and talk to her about getting her husband into drug rehab. Lately he looked stoned all the time, and that wasn't good for business.

Behind the wheel of his Porsche, Mickey felt in complete control. He had his stereo equipment, a C.D. player, a telephone, and emergency supplies in the trunk should he ever get caught in an earthquake.

Mickey thought about earthquakes quite a lot. He fantasied all sorts of scenarios. His favorite was the one where Abigaile was shopping at Magnin or Saks, buying just another little five-thousand-dollar evening purse, when the big one hit, and poor Abby was buried beneath a mountain of designer goods and suffocated by a rare two-hundred-thousand-dollar sable coat.

Fortunately, in his fantasy the earthquake bypassed the studio and both his houses. Tabitha was safe, and so were his cars. Only Abby got it.

Naturally he arranged a magnificent funeral. Abe Panther would have attended, but the shock of the earthquake was too much for him, and the feisty son of a bitch finally expired.

At last Mickey Stolli was a free man. And Panther Studios was legally his. When Primrose and Ben Harrison arrived in L.A. to claim their share, a freeway overpass collapsed on their limo and crushed them out of his life.

What a fantasy! The best!

Mickey waved to the studio guard as he shot out of the gates.

The man saluted him. They all loved him at the studio—he was their king, their ruler. He was Mickey Stolli, and they all wanted to be him.

. . .

Everything was in place—the china, the glassware, the finest linens and silver.

Clad in a sweeping silk robe, Abigaile prowled around her pristine mansion checking details.

An army of servants were all present. Her permanent staff—Jeffries, her English butler, and Mrs. Jeffries, his plump wife, who acted as housekeeper; Jacko, a young Australian who cleaned their cars and did driving duties for Tabitha—tonight he would be assisting Jeffries; and Consuela and Firella, her two Spanish maids.

Hired for the evening were three valet parkers, two bartenders, a cook with two assistants, and a special dessert chef.

The total was a staff of fourteen to look after twelve guests. Abigaile liked to do things right. She was Hollywood royalty, after all. She was Abe Panther's granddaughter, and people expected a certain level of style. Her own mother, long dead—killed along with her father in a boating accident—had been a fine hostess who entertained lavishly. When Abigaile and Primrose were children they'd been allowed to peek in at some of the extravagant parties. Grandfather Abe was always present, surrounded by the great movie stars of the time, often with a dazzling beauty on each arm.

Abigaile had always been in awe of her grandfather. It wasn't until after his stroke that she'd been able to deal with him at all. Now she visited him as little as possible and secretly wished he would fade quietly away so she could take center stage.

She loathed Inga, and Inga loathed her. They barely spoke when Abigaile arrived at the house with Abe's grandchild, Tabitha, a precocious thirteen. It was difficult for Abigaile to persuade Tabitha to accompany her, but a touch of bribery usually did it, for she refused to go alone.

"Why do I have to come every time?" Tabitha whined.

"Because one of these days you're going to be a very rich little girl indeed. And you'd better remember where the money is coming from."

"Daddy's got money, I'll take his."

Daddy couldn't take a piss in the moonlight if it wasn't for your great-grandfather, Abigaile wanted to say—but she always stopped herself just in time.

"Is everything to your satisfaction, Mrs. Stolli?"

Jeffries was dogging her footsteps, the old fool. The fact that he was English was a plus. He was also unutterably nosy, and so was his wife. Abigaile suspected that if the opportunity ever arose they would sell her secrets to the gossip rags without so much as a twinge of regret.

Not that they knew any of her secrets.

Not that she had any.

Well . . . maybe a few . . .

"No, Jeffries," she said tartly, spying a dead branch on an elaborate orchid arrangement. She plucked at the offending twig, pulling it out and scattering earth on the expensive Chinese rug. "What exactly is this?" she asked accusingly.

Jeffries had been waiting for this moment. "If you do recall, Mrs. Stolli, you gave the entire staff instructions we were never to touch the house plants or floral arrangements."

"Why would I do that?" she asked testily.

A small moment of triumph. "Because, Mrs. Stolli, you said that only the plant man was to tend them."

Aggravation. "I did?"

"Yes, Mrs. Stolli."

"And where *is* the plant man?"

"He only comes on Fridays."

God! Servants! Especially English ones. "Thank you, Jeffries. In the meantime, have someone clean up the mess before Mr. Stolli gets home."

When he gets home, she added silently. For Mickey had this bad habit of always being late for his own dinner parties.

It drove Abigaile crazy.

Mickey Stolli wore his socks, pale gray Italian silk. And nothing else. He had a thing about his feet—he thought they were ugly and never allowed anyone to see them.

Surprisingly enough, even though he was devoid of hair on his head, his body was covered with tufts of black hair. A patch here, a patch there—strange little outbreaks of hairiness.

"You're gorgeous," Warner, his black mistress assured him. She was tall and skinny, with huge black nipples on generous breasts, and cropped black hair.

She straddled him, riding his erect penis as if she were taking an afternoon trot on a horse.

"You're gorgeous," she repeated, as the action heated up.

Nobody had ever told Mickey Stolli he was gorgeous before. Only Warner, who'd been his mistress for eighteen months. She was a cop. One day she'd pulled him over for a traffic ticket, and the rest was the stuff wet dreams are made of.

The thing he liked about Warner was her uniqueness. The first time they'd slept together she'd had no idea who he was or what he did. It simply didn't matter to her.

Mickey felt the moment of truth was going to be upon him at any given moment. He let out a long, strangulated sigh.

Warner contracted the muscles that really mattered and gave him the ride of his life.

He felt the come from the tip of his toes to the back of his head— which he thought might explode one of these days if Warner kept doing what she obviously loved to do. With him. Only him. Mickey Stolli was the only man in Warner Franklin's sex life. She had told him so, many times, and he believed her.

"Was that a trip to heaven or *what?*" Warner demanded, climbing off. "You get better every time, Mickey. You're the greatest lover in the world."

Nobody had ever told Mickey Stolli he was the greatest lover in the world before. Only Warner—she knew how to make him feel like he could climb the Empire State Building from the outside and jump off without breaking a bone.

Warner Franklin was thirty-five years old and not particularly pretty. She lived alone in a small West Hollywood apartment with a skinny mongrel dog, and much to Mickey's relief she had no aspirations to be an actress.

She didn't want his money. She didn't want his favors. She'd turned down his offer of a Wilshire condo and a white Mercedes. And the only gifts she'd accepted were a giant-screen color television and a video recorder. She'd taken those presents only because she was partial to "Hill Street Blues" repeats and "Hunter." "Gotta do something when I'm not working and I'm not with you," she'd explained.

He thought he might love her. But the dreaded thought lurking at the back of his mind was so scary that he'd never taken it out to inspect.

"Abby's having one of her dinner parties tonight," he said, stifling a satisfied yawn.

"I know how you *looove* them," Warner drawled, rolling her eyes. "Don't worry, honey—you're always the smartest man in any room."

By the time Mickey Stolli left Warner Franklin's apartment he was walking ten feet tall. He was the most gorgeous, best lover, smartest man in the whole fucking world!

Screw you, Abby.

You never told me shit.

Lucky was fascinated by watching Abe eat. He picked at his food like a ravenous monkey, rarely using a knife or fork if his fingers could do the job. For a man of eighty-eight his appetite was quite extraordinary.

Inga did not eat. She did not sit. But she was around enough to eavesdrop on exactly what was said.

Lucky was curious to know if Inga and Abe discussed things later. In fact, what exactly *was* their relationship now? Failed movie star and former studio head. Was there a lot to talk about?

During her research on Abe, Lucky had come across quite a few photos of Inga. There were many studio shots, and a few casual photographs of Abe and Inga together.

Twenty-five years ago, when Abe was a mere sixty-three and Inga twenty-something, she'd been a ravishing beauty. Luminous skin, wide gray eyes, a lithe body, and a bewitching smile.

What happens to people? Lucky wondered. How come some, like Gino and Abe, are born survivors. And others, like Inga, wither away into a miserable shell?

It's just the way the crap shoot goes, she thought.

She'd told Abe everything she knew up-to-date. He'd been disappointed. He wanted more. So did she.

A few petty scams were not worth getting heated over. So Mickey charged the studio for his personal supply of Cristal. Big deal. And Eddie Kane was probably a cocaine freak. So what?

Mickey pulling a phony script scam with the agent Lionel Fricke —that was the only information worth getting excited about.

How many times had Mickey pulled that particular stunt? She'd have to look into it.

"Enjoyin' yourself, girlie?" Abe asked, cocking his head on one side. "You like the movie business?"

"I think I'm going to love it," she replied honestly. "When I'm in control."

Abe liked a woman who knew what she wanted.

23

There was not much Cooper Turner didn't know about women. He'd had the best, he'd had the worst, and anything in between he could get his hands on.

Growing up in Ardmore, a small town outside Philadelphia, Cooper had started experimenting with girls when he was thirteen. Not for Cooper the paper cutouts and other girlie magazines. Oh, no—one sniff of snatch and it became his life's pursuit. Girls, girls, girls.

"You should have been a gynecologist," his older sister joked when he was nineteen. "At least get paid for what you do."

If he hadn't become an actor he would have made a great male hooker—the kind that services only the female sex.

He moved to New York when he was twenty, lived in the Village and hung out at the Actors Studio. His contemporaries got themselves jobs waiting tables and pumping gas while preparing for the big break.

Cooper never had to do any of that. There was always a hot meal and a warm bed begging for his attention. Not to mention a woman.

When he finally got out to Hollywood he met a beautiful young screen actress his first week in town. Within days he became her live-in lover. The relationship led to his picture in the papers, and his picture led him to a female agent who secured him the second lead in a small-budget teen film.

At the age of twenty-four, Cooper Turner became a heartthrob. Over the years his career just got better and better, culminating in an Oscar nomination when he was thirty-two.

He didn't win. It soured him. He stopped doing publicity and shied away from the press. The films he decided to appear in were few and far between.

The less Cooper made himself available, the more he was wanted. He tried to lead a private life. It was impossible. Women came and went. Some stayed around almost long enough to drag a commitment out of him. He would have liked children, but the price of being with one woman wasn't worth it.

And then he met Venus Maria and things changed. With Venus Maria anything was possible. She was young and incredibly sexy. She had knowing eyes and a man-eating mouth. She was sharp and street smart. She had a body made to tango and the mind of an accountant. She was sensual, startling, and, above all, vitally alive.

One drawback.

Contrary to popular belief and the headlines in the supermarket tabloids, he was not fucking her and she was not fucking him. Not even the famous blow-job story was true, although he'd heard it from various sources—including Mickey Stolli, who'd laughed, punched him slyly in the ribs, and said, "I like to see my stars getting along. Makes for a happy set."

What Venus Maria *was* doing was fucking one of Cooper Turner's best friends. A married man. A *very* married man. And Cooper found himself in the ridiculous position of being the beard.

Cooper Turner!

The beard!

What a laugh!

He looked at himself in the mirror and shook his head. He was dressed for the Stolli dinner party in a dark blue Armani suit, a white shirt, and a loosely knotted silk tie. The well-cut suit got 'em every time. Women loved a man they thought they could rumple.

Cooper ran a hand through his brownish hair. There were traces of gray along the sides, but nothing a talented hairdresser couldn't disguise. His eyes remained an intense blue. His skin was lightly sunkissed.

Cooper knew he looked good. He wasn't twenty-five, but he was still a killer.

Venus Maria had no idea what she was missing.

24

Steven Berkeley took it upon himself to visit Deena Swanson. He didn't tell Jerry. He didn't even confide in Mary Lou. He phoned Deena and told her they had to meet. She started to object, changed her mind, and asked him to be at her house at ten o'clock the next morning.

He was there.

She greeted him in a lime-green track suit, a matching headband holding back her pale red hair, running shoes on her feet. She looked thin and attractive and not at all athletic.

She proffered a delicate hand.

He shook it.

Limp handshake. No character.

"I found our last meeting very disturbing," he informed her, getting right down to business.

She raised a thinly penciled eyebrow. "Why?"

"We're talking about murder."

"Survival, Mr. Berkeley."

"Murder, Mrs. Swanson."

She clasped her hands together and lowered her eyes. "You defend people all the time. What's the difference if you get a little warning up front?"

Her attitude was bizarre. The woman was strange. "Are you kidding me?"

"Would it make you happy to know that I didn't mean it?"

"Did you?" he persisted.

She looked up at him. Dead blue eyes in a pale face. "I'm considering writing a book, Mr. Berkeley. I needed a genuine reaction. I'm sorry if it disturbed you."

"So you're not planning to kill someone?"

A low throaty laugh. "Do I seem like the kind of woman who would plan such a thing?"

"How about the million bucks you deposited in our company account?"

"Now that the game is over, I'll expect it back. Naturally I'll pay a handsome fee for your time and trouble."

Steven was angry. "Your game is not funny, Mrs. Swanson. I don't appreciate being used for research."

He got up to leave.

She watched him go. A lawyer with principles, quite unusual. No wonder he was so good.

She waited a few minutes then picked up the phone.

"Jerry?"

"Who else?"

How sensible of Jerry Myerson to have a direct line.

"I said what you told me to."

"Did he believe you?"

"I think so."

"Sorry about this, Mrs. Swanson. The trouble with Steven is that he has a conscience."

"And you don't?"

"I abide by a rule I never break."

"And that is?"

"The client always comes first."

"I'm delighted to hear it." She paused for a moment, and then added casually, "Oh, and by the way, if anything *was* to happen . . ."

"Steven will defend you."

"Can I count on that . . . Jerry?"

"Absolutely."

Jerry Myerson replaced the receiver of his private line and considered what he'd just done. He'd jollied along an eccentric woman and saved the firm a million bucks. Not bad for a morning's work.

Later that night Steven regaled Mary Lou with the story of his visit to Deena Swanson.

Mary Lou was engrossed in watching a television movie starring Ted Danson. She was eating a Häagen-Dazs ice-cream bar. She was contented and pregnant and getting larger every week.

"One of these days you'll learn to listen to me, Steven Berkeley," she scolded. "I told you that woman was putting you on all along. And you've been worrying about it. What a stiff!"

He felt relieved, and yet . . .

"Yeah," he said, not fully convinced.

"Did you tell Jerry?"

"I sure did."

"And what was his comment?"

"He hated to lose a million big ones. You know Jerry."

Mary Lou licked her ice-cream bar. "Sure, who *doesn't* know Jerry. He must have been *very* disappointed."

Steven walked to the bedroom door. "I'm hungry," he said, lingering, hoping she'd offer to fix him something to eat.

"That's a good sign," she replied, not getting the hint.

He came right out with it. "Make me a sandwich?"

"Honey," she said patiently. "We ate dinner two hours ago. You had steak and fries. You had cake. You had ice cream. I'll make you a sandwich when I've had the baby!"

"I don't think I can wait that long."

She grinned. "Try, Steven. Try."

"I have to fly out to the Coast for a few days."

Martin Swanson walked into the bedroom to make the announcement. Deena stared at her husband. Mr. Handsome if you were partial to weak chins and watery eyes. Mr. New York if you could stomach the self-promoting charm. Mr. unfaithful, lying, cheating son of a bitch. But he was *her* son of a bitch, and she loved him. She had no intention of losing him.

Deena smiled. She had very nice, even teeth, all her own—no Hollywood movie-star caps for Deena.

"Perhaps I'll come with you," she suggested.

"Too hectic," Martin replied, cool and controlled. "I've got meetings on that studio takeover deal I told you about."

Oh, yes, the studio deal. The studio Martin wished to control so he could make movies starring his little tramp.

Martin didn't think she knew. It was better this way. Keep him in a fog. Confuse him with kindness.

"When will you go?" she asked.

"Thought I'd fly out tomorrow."

"Are you sure you don't want me to come?"

"I'll manage."

Oh, yes, he'd manage all right, with a hard cock and The Bitch waiting for him with her legs spread.

"You're going to throw half the hostesses in New York into a panic. There's the opera tomorrow night. A lunch for the mayor on Thursday. Gloria's party. Diana's dinner."

Martin could care less. "You'll go without me. They love you."

They love you better, Deena thought. *How many of them have you slept with? Only the famous ones, or do money and position count too?*

"I suppose so. If I feel like it."

He walked over and kissed her. More a peck, really, an unaffectionate peck on the cheek to say goodbye. "I'll be leaving early in the morning."

Deena stood up and with one fluid movement unzipped her dress. Underneath she wore a black lace garter belt, silk stockings, and a half bra.

Martin took a step back.

Deena could remember their early days together. Once upon a time she'd always been able to excite him.

"You won't be here on Sunday," she said pointedly, walking slowly toward him.

25

The dinner-table conversation was going nicely. Abigaile glanced around at her guests. They all seemed to be enjoying themselves. The black politician was in deep conversation with the famous feminist. The hot young director had zeroed in on Venus Maria, while his girlfriend enjoyed the attention of Cooper Turner. Ida White chatted in her stoned way to the rock star and his exotic-looking wife, while Zeppo and Mickey were head to head.

Abigaile breathed deeply. She could relax.

"CUNT!"

The forbidden word, said loudly and with great venom, shocked the entire table into silence.

"What did you call me, you black prick?" screamed the feminist, clearly in a fury.

"I called you a cunt, and that's what you are," the black politician yelled back.

It was quite obvious that neither of them gave a damn about the rest of the guests, let alone their host and hostess.

Witnessing a calamity about to happen, and a speechless Mickey sitting there with his mouth hanging open, Abigaile leaped to her feet. "Now, now," she said, in what she hoped was a conciliatory tone, "let's quiet our tempers down."

"Fuck you!" from the feminist, shoving her chair away from the table. She had alabaster skin, sixties straight hair, and a direct gaze. She was fifty, but looked ten years younger. "I've had it with this phony, full-of-shit, skirt-chasing bum!"

Mickey forced himself into action. "Mona," he said, taking the feminist's arm, "if you've got a problem here, let's go in the other room and discuss it."

Mona Sykes withered him with a look. "A problem, Mickey," she said sarcastically, "why would *I* have a problem? I *love* being called a cunt by this womanizing piece of excrement." She pointed accusingly at the black politician, whose name was Andrew J. Burnley.

Andrew J. did not take her latest remark well. He too rose to his feet. He was six feet three, with a semi-Afro hairstyle, a round face, protruding eyes, and a honeyed voice. He was fifty-two years old and had a wife and five children who resided in Chicago and never came with him on his frequent trips to L.A.

"You *girls* are all the same, baby. If you're not gettin' fucked you're lookin' to fuck everyone around you."

That did it. Mona picked up a full glass of red wine and hurled it across the table at him, glass and all. The glass fell to the Italian limestone floor and shattered. Unfortunately most of the wine landed on Ida White, sitting there pleasantly stoned, minding her own business as she waited to be taken home.

Now it was Zeppo's turn to jump to his feet. "Can't you people behave like human beings?" he snapped, waving his short arms in the air. He directed his scolding at Andrew J., who immediately took it as some sort of hidden racial slur and retaliated accordingly.

"I don' need this crap," he shouted, stalking toward the door.

"Neither do I," snarled an angry Mona, following him.

And before anyone could say another word they were both out the door.

Abigaile rose to the occasion magnificently. "Civilians!" she sniffed. "Never did like 'em!"

Venus Maria felt as if she'd been watching a particularly fast tennis match. And it was certainly more entertaining than the rest of the evening so far, although the young director on her left *was* kind of cute, and she'd been leaning toward him as opposed to her host, Mickey Stolli, who bored her into cross-eyedom.

"What was *that* all about?" the rock star asked quizzically, as Firella and Consuela mopped Ida White down.

"Peasants!" snapped Zeppo. "Hollywood used t'be a place where people had manners and knew how to entertain."

Abigaile wasn't going to take that kind of typical Zeppo White remark without a fight. The man was the most appalling snob. "My grandfather told me you started your career selling fish from a cart in Brooklyn," she said sweetly. "Is that true? I find it a most fascinating story, Zeppo. *Do* tell us all about it. I'm sure we'd *love* to hear."

Zeppo glared at her. He could make a good story out of almost anything except his humble beginnings, which he preferred to forget.

Cooper Turner saved the moment. "The two of 'em are in bed together, y'know," he announced with a nod of his head and a slight smile.

"What?" cried Abigaile and the rock star's wife in unison.

"Really?" said Venus Maria, quite intrigued. Now that she thought about it, Cooper was probably right. He knew about such things.

"Who?" demanded Mickey.

"Andrew J. and Mona," Cooper said grinning.

"Don't be ridiculous!" exclaimed Abigaile.

"Abby, would *I* put you on?" Cooper teased. "They're making out. It's obvious."

Everybody started to talk at once.

Abigaile's dinner party was a success after all.

Lucky drove home slowly. "Home" was the rented hideout in the hills where she had only Boogie for company.

She missed Lennie. She missed Bobby. She missed Gino. She missed her life.

And then she remembered that Gino was in town, and it wasn't too late to call him. Maybe he'd come over. She couldn't risk being seen out anywhere in case she ran into someone who knew her and would report to Lennie that she'd been spotted hanging out in L.A. Too bad. She felt like visiting a club and listening to some good soul music—one of her passions in life.

What if she put on her disguise and sneaked into a club?

No way. She wasn't going to wear that godawful disguise any more than she had to. When all this was over—burn, baby, burn!

The house Boogie had rented for her was discreetly tucked away at the top of Doheny Drive. There was a drive-in garage with a door leading directly into the house. As she turned left and drew into the garage she had a sense of another car right behind her on the street, slowing down—probably because she was making a left. Unless Abe had had someone follow her home.

Why would he do a thing like that? Was she getting paranoid? Been reading too much Ed McBain, she thought with a laugh.

Boogie was in the kitchen flicking through car catalogs.

"Do me a favor, Boog. Drive down to Tower Records and buy me some sounds. I'm getting withdrawal symptoms!"

Boogie raised his lanky frame. "Sure. What do you want?"

"I'm in the mood for Luther, Bobby Womack, Teddy P., Marvin, and Isaac."

Boogie knew exactly who she meant. "No Billie Holiday?" he asked.

"Only when Lennie's around," she replied with a wry grin.

Boogie hurried off. Lucky picked up the phone and called Gino. There was no answer from his suite. She didn't leave a message.

Harry Browning sat in his car outside Lucky's rented house and waited. He didn't know what he was waiting for. In fact, he didn't know what he was doing at all. But whatever it was, he had a full charge of excitement coursing through his body. This was the best he'd felt in years.

He'd been following Luce all night. On impulse he'd trailed her from the studio. He'd always thought there was something odd about her and he was determined to find out more. Was he the only

one to notice that she wore a wig? And when he'd screened the
movie, she'd taken off her glasses and not replaced them with another pair. Also, her clothes were worth noting. They hung on her
as if she was trying to hide beneath them. And who these days wore
clothes like that? Especially at her age—because she was quite a
young woman, and if you looked closely, a good-looking woman.

Harry Browning had not sat in a projection booth for thirty-three
years screening every movie Panther had ever made without learning plenty about women's beauty.

And then there was the Sheila Hervey connection to consider.
Luce claimed to be Sheila Hervey's niece. But Sheila had no living
relatives other than her childless sister. She'd told him enough times
when she'd been after him to take her out on a date. Of course, that
had been quite a few years back, but Harry Browning did not forget.
He had an excellent memory.

If Luce had left him alone he probably would have left her alone.
But no. She'd invited him to dinner, and out of curiosity he'd gone,
and that's about all he remembered. He'd awoken in his own bed
the next morning with a dry, parched mouth, a throbbing head, and
an urge to wreak some kind of punishment on the woman who had
lured him to start drinking again.

Harry Browning had been dry for nineteen years. But he was an
alcoholic all the same—you never stopped being an alcoholic.

He thought about having a drink now—a cold beer, or a glass of
wine, maybe even a shot of scotch.

The thought tempted him, but he was determined never to give
in to temptation again. Never.

Following Luce had turned out to be quite an evening. First he'd
trailed her to this house—the same house he was parked outside
now. And when her car emerged, he'd followed her to Abe Panther's
mansion on Miller Drive. He knew it was Abe's residence for he'd
spent numerous evenings there screening movies in Abe's private
theater—many years ago, but he was sure Abe Panther still lived
there. Harry knew, because every year he sent the great Mr. Panther
a Christmas card signed "Harry Browning—Your Loyal Employee."

And he *was* loyal, for it was old Abe himself who'd stopped them
from firing him when he was caught drunk on the job one day. "Get

yourself over to A.A., Harry," Abe had told him. "Take a couple of weeks off and come back a new man."

Harry Browning would never forget Abe Panther's kindness.

Luce stayed inside the Panther residence for two hours. Harry had waited patiently on the street outside the fancy gates. When she left, he'd managed to catch a glimpse of her as she drove past his parked car.

Luce looked different, although he was sure it was her. The wig was gone. No glasses. Her mousy hair was now jet black and glossy.

That was all he could see.

He followed her back to the Doheny Drive house, and now he waited. Patiently. For Harry Browning was a patient man, and he knew he was on to something.

The only problem was—what?

Cooper Turner drove Venus Maria home. They laughed all the way.

Venus Maria: Did you *see* Abby's face when Andrew J. yelled the c word?

Cooper: Didja get a look at Ida when the wine hit?

Venus Maria: I thought she was going to come!

Cooper: First time in twenty years!

Venus Maria: Thirty!

Cooper: Forty!

Venus Maria: Fifty!

Cooper: A hundred!

Venus Maria: And Zeppo, when Abby threw the Brooklyn fish-cart shit at him?

Cooper: He turned red.

Venus Maria: Purple!

Cooper: Orange!

They were laughing so much he had to pull his black Mercedes over to the side of the street.

They were alone in the car. No entourage, no crew, no acquaintances, no paparazzi.

He was drawn to her, even though he knew instinctively she would turn him down.

Leaning across the seat, he kissed her, and for a moment she responded. Soft lips, wet lips, and a sweet pointed tongue that darted into his mouth for a second, and then withdrew as if she suddenly realized what she was doing.

"Cooper!" she scolded, cross with him and filled with guilt because she'd almost settled back to enjoy it.

"Can I help it?" he said, feeling an immediate hard-on in spite of her withdrawal.

"We're friends, remember?" she reminded him.

"Everybody *thinks* we're in bed together," he reasoned.

"Martin doesn't."

Oh, yeah, Martin. Why oh why had he ever introduced her to Martin Swanson?

26

O n Wednesday Olive called and said, "The job is yours."

"Fantastic!" exclaimed Lucky. "He's approved your trip?"

"He certainly has," Olive replied, sounding delighted. "Come over to our office after lunch and I'll introduce you to Mr. Stolli. After you've met him I can go over his daily routine with you. He's very particular."

"What did you tell him about me?"

"That you're discreet, trustworthy, and a fine worker. He says he'll take my word on it, so don't let me down, Luce."

"I won't, Olive."

"Are you sure this is going to be all right with Mr. Stone?" Olive fussed, hoping she was doing the right thing.

"Positive. He leaves on vacation tomorrow," Lucky assured her.

"Very well. You'll watch me all day tomorrow and take over on Friday. Does that suit you?"

"Yes, it suits me fine."

And indeed it did. In the heart of Mickey's office she would be able to find out everything there was to know.

"Herman, you're out of here," she said as soon as she put the phone down. "I just got promoted!"

Herman was impressed. He was also relieved. Now he could play

176

golf without interruptions and forget about Panther Studios for a while.

"I'll call you when it's time for you to come back," she told him. "In the meantime, why don't you put in an order to have this office painted? It's an absolute dump."

"You do it," he said. "You're my secretary."

A show of balls—albeit tired and old—but refreshing.

"I will," she said. "And I'll order a new air-conditioning unit. You're living in the Middle Ages over here. Have you *seen* Mickey Stolli's office?"

Herman shook his head. "No."

"You'd have a shit fit. It's a palace."

It bothered Herman that he was getting used to her language.

Olive greeted Lucky excitedly. "You'll use my desk. I'll explain the phone system to you. And then we'll have to go over Mr. Stolli's personal requirements."

Personal requirements? A blow job every hour, or two blondes for breakfast? Lucky couldn't help smiling.

Olive took this to be enthusiasm for the job. "Don't be too good at taking care of Mr. Stolli," she admonished, wagging a warning finger. "It's only for a few days, and then I'll be back."

Meeting Mickey Stolli for the first time was interesting. He sat behind his desk, king of his kingdom, bald, tan, and rude.

Proudly Olive led Lucky into his domain. "This is Luce, the assistant I told you about," she said in a reverent voice.

Mickey was going over some papers. He didn't bother looking up, merely waving a hand in the air. "Yeah, yeah," he said.

Lucky noticed an unruly clump of black hair growing wild on the back of his hand. If only it could be transplanted to the top of his head, it might be the start of something big.

"She'll be taking over on Friday," Olive said.

His private line rang and he picked it up. "Willya get outta here," he said, covering the mouthpiece of the phone.

"Thank you, Mr. Stolli." Olive almost curtsied.

Get outta here and she gave him a *thank you* and a bob? Something was wrong somewhere. Olive needed a refresher course in self-respect.

"Sometimes Mr. Stolli has too much work to cope with," Olive explained. "You'll get used to his moods. He doesn't mean any harm."

That night Lucky dined with Gino. She went to his hotel in full disguise and broke him up. "You're unbelievable, kid," he said, starting to laugh. "You shoulda been an actress."

"Would you have recognized me?" she challenged.

"I'm your father."

"That wasn't the question." She flopped into a chair, pulling her wig off and throwing it across the room.

He looked at her quizzically. "I guess I'd have to say no."

She laughed. "There's something very potent about changing one's identity. I'd probably have made an excellent spy."

"You'd have made an excellent whatever you wanted to."

"Thanks," she said, pleased.

They ordered room service. Thick juicy steaks, old-fashioned mashed potatoes, and buttery corn on the cob.

While they ate they talked. Gino told her all about his run-in with Paige's husband.

"I went over to the house an' met him. Funny thing—turns out he knows all about me and Paige."

Lucky leaned forward anxiously. "Yes? Does that mean I'm going to be a bridesmaid?"

"It don't mean nothin', kid. He tells me Paige can do what she wants. If she fancies a divorce, he'll give it to her. Only there's one problem."

"What's that?"

"She's never asked."

"Oh. Not so good."

"Then Paige comes home, sees me in her house an' nearly passes out. By this time Ryder an' me, we're gettin' along like old pals. The lady ain't thrilled."

"What happened then?"

"Ryder asks me to stay for dinner. I say no. Paige looks uncomfortable an' I split. Since then I haven't heard a whisper from either of 'em." He chewed on a corncob. "I'm on my way back to New York tomorrow. I'm gonna start datin' again."

"Dating! C'mon, Gino, I know you're a miracle—but you're also seventy-nine years old!"

"Do I look it?" he demanded.

"No."

"Do I act it?"

"Well . . . no," she admitted.

"So what the hell, kid. I wanna find me a wife."

They grinned at each other, Lucky and her old man. They were a matched pair.

Leslie Kane was too pretty and too fresh-looking to be an ex-hooker. But that's exactly what she was.

Leslie had long wavy red hair that hung below her creamy white shoulders, widely spaced eyes, a pert nose, and full, luscious lips. She was tall and willowy, with rounded breasts, a tiny waist, and extra-long legs.

She and Eddie had been married for one year. Before that she'd been a call girl for eleven months.

Leslie was crazy about Eddie, and Eddie was crazy about Leslie. They'd met at the car wash on Santa Monica Boulevard, and by the time they'd both followed the progress of their cars through the system, they'd decided it was love.

Leslie had told Eddie she was a secretary, which was true in a way, because she'd started out as a secretary, and some of the men she serviced liked her to dress up as one, although black leather and schoolgirl outfits were much more popular.

Eddie had told her he was head of distribution at Panther Studios, and Leslie, who had no ambition to be an actress, thought, "Hmmm, this is the guy for me."

And so true love blossomed.

Eddie gave up seeing a well-known television actress, who was not pleased.

Leslie gave up her apartment and her profession.

They were married in Marina Del Rey on a friend's boat.

Married life was good. They both enjoyed being in a formal relationship. It made a change. Eddie had always been a chaser. He liked women, they liked him. And being in the film business he'd found there was never a shortage of new talent. After meeting Leslie he had no desire to chase anymore. Not only was she gorgeous, she also kept him more than busy in the bedroom. "Where'd you learn all this stuff?" he'd asked her with a quizzical grin.

"*Cosmopolitan*," she'd replied, straight-faced. And he'd believed her.

Leslie had never been a street hooker. She'd arrived in L.A. at eighteen, found a job on Rodeo Drive in one of the fancy dress stores, and there she'd been discovered by a certain Madame Loretta, who'd set her up in an apartment.

Madame Loretta was a short, squat woman who'd come to America from her native Czechoslovakia many years earlier. She specialized in discovering beautiful, fresh young girls. She specialized in supplying top-of-the-line beauties to the Hollywood stars, executives, and moguls who came her way. She made her girls feel special and at all times beautiful. And they, in turn, made her clients very satisfied indeed. Leslie was no exception.

When Leslie told Madame Loretta she wished to get married, nobody could have been happier. The old madam invited her to tea in her hillside house and regaled her with a few facts of life. "There are three ways to keep a man," she informed Leslie, wagging a chubby finger in her face. "Three golden rules you must always remember. Rule one: Find something about your man that you think is the most wonderful thing in the world and tell him about it constantly. Maybe it's his eyes, his hair, his ass. Whatever it is, make sure he knows you love it. Rule two: When you're in bed together, tell him he's the most sensational lover you've ever had. And rule three: Whatever he says, be amazed at his knowledge. Look at him with adoration and assure him it's the cleverest thing you've ever heard anybody say." Madame Loretta nodded knowingly. "With these three rules," she said, "you'll never go wrong."

Leslie listened and learned well. She knew how to please in more ways than one, and Eddie was very receptive to her charms.

Leslie was happy—but the one fear she did have was that someday they would come across one of her previous clients and she would be exposed. She knew Eddie would never accept her past if he found out the truth, and it frightened her. At parties her wide eyes scanned the room, ever watchful. In restaurants she was always on the lookout. How many clients had she serviced in eleven months? It was impossible to remember.

Leslie knew her husband had a cocaine habit. She chose to ignore it. If a little snort of white powder made him feel good, who was she to argue?

She'd tried it once and hadn't liked it. Too comfortable. Too dangerous. She had a past to watch out for; it wouldn't do to put it at risk.

Lately Eddie had been jumpy and nervous. He snapped at her for no reason. He got up at four o'clock in the morning and wandered around the house. He took a double shot of vodka with his morning orange juice.

Leslie couldn't help worrying. Maybe he'd found out and was getting ready to tell her it was all over.

What would she do? What *could* she do? She had no desire to return to hooking. She couldn't go home to Florida, because she'd skipped with a thousand bucks of her stepfather's money. If Eddie wanted out of their marriage, her life was finished.

"Honey, is something bothering you?" she asked him one day, touching the back of his neck, ruffling his longish hair just the way she knew he liked it.

"Nothin', baby," he said, jumping up and pacing around the room. "Nothin' that a million bucks an' a little cooperation from Mickey Stolli can't fix."

Lucky started her position as Mickey Stolli's temporary assistant at seven-thirty on Friday morning. She knew he arrived in his office punctually at seven forty-five, and she wanted to be there waiting for him.

The faint smell of Olive lingered in the air: a crisp English toilet water, peppermint lozenges, and a small azalea plant.

Sitting behind Olive's desk, Lucky took a deep breath. She was prepared for action. Any action. She was not prepared for the first phone call to be from Lennie! She recognized his voice immediately.

"Olive," he said snappishly, "put me through to Mr. Stolli. This is an emergency."

Lennie! An emergency! She panicked—something she rarely did—and hung up. Whereupon Mickey Stolli made his entrance, clad in tennis clothes, sweating.

"Be in my office in ten minutes," Mickey said, and slammed the door to his private domain.

She figured Lennie would call right back, so she acted fast, buzzed Mickey, and said, "Lennie Golden is on the line. He says it's an emergency."

God was on her side. Just as Mickey grumbled a sharp "Put him through," the phone rang again and she quickly connected the call hoping it was Lennie ringing back. It was.

Lennie was a problem she had not considered. She could disguise herself physically, but she hadn't thought about her voice. Fortunately he had not called on Mickey's private line, so she was able to press a button and listen in on the conversation.

"I've had enough of this shit, Mickey. Either Grudge goes or I do," Lennie said angrily. "The man is an amateur."

Mickey stated a fact: "The man has been in the business longer than either of us."

"Perhaps that's his problem. He thinks he knows it all. And maybe he did twenty-five years ago. Things change, let's move with the times."

Mickey's soothing voice: "Don't worry. I'll deal with it."

"Your promises are crowding my ass. If nothing happens, I'm gonna walk."

"You wouldn't be threatening me, would you?"

"You can bet your wife's jewelry on it."

"I hate to remind you about something called a contract."

"Tell you what," said Lennie, sounding quite reasonable. "Take your contract, put it through a shredder, mix it with a bagful of cement, an' shove it up your ass. There'll still be room for a decent human being."

Bang! He hung up.

Bang! Mickey was out of his office bouncing with fury.

"Get me Lennie Golden's contract," he screamed. "I've had it with fuckin' actors." He threw a key at her and pointed to a file cabinet.

She kept her voice low and subservient, figuring that was what Mickey required from his staff. "Yes, Mr. Stolli."

"And don't put any fuckin' actors through to me in the mornin'. You got it?"

Shades of his native Brooklyn. Stay calm. Don't call him a rude prick—plenty of time for that when she took control.

"Yes, Mr. Stolli."

"An' get hold of Eddie Kane—cancel my ten o'clock appointment."

"Shall I give an excuse?"

"Fuck excuses. I'm head of this studio—no excuses. Remember that."

"Yes, Mr. Stolli."

He marched back into his office, slamming the door again.

Obviously working for Mickey was not going to be dull.

She went over to the contract-file cabinet, opened it with the key, and began investigating.

27

Martin Z. Swanson had his own private jet modestly named "Swanson." He had a crew of seven, and on his trip from New York to the West Coast, no other passengers.

Two flight attendants took care of his every need. They were pretty girls—a brunette and a redhead. Both twenty-five, five feet seven inches, and one hundred and twenty-five pounds.

The Swanson uniform was a short white skirt, a fitted white jacket, and a navy blue T-shirt with "Swanson" stenciled in white across the breast. The flight attendants' breasts measured thirty-six inches B cup. Martin was a stickler for detail.

The flight attendants called him "Mr. Swanson," and smiled a lot. Good teeth was another job requisite.

Martin never messed with the help, however attractive. In fact he hardly even noticed them. They were hired for a purpose, and that was to keep up the Swanson image. Martin did a lot of business entertaining, and if his guests cared to make time with his employees, that was their prerogative.

Martin demanded three things from the people who worked for him: loyalty, brains, and a decent appearance. If they didn't shape up, they were fired.

On the other hand, if they did things the Swanson way, they were richly rewarded.

At forty-five Martin had thought his life was more or less settled. From fairly modest beginnings he'd achieved more than he'd ever imagined. He was publicly known as a charismatic, dynamic wheeler-dealer who could make any dream come true. He had powerful, famous friends in politics, show business, sports, and the social go-round. Connections were his for the asking. And he had a beautiful wife who was obviously smart and intelligent.

But until four months ago, Martin had never truly known passion.

"Another glass of Evian, Mr. Swanson?" the redheaded flight attendant inquired solicitously.

He nodded, and a cut-crystal glass was in front of him in seconds. Pure Evian Water, one slice of fresh lime, and two ice cubes. Just the way he liked it.

"Are you ready to eat, Mr. Swanson?" asked the other flight attendant.

He noticed a dark spot on her tight white skirt and stared until she was forced to look down.

"Oops!" she exclaimed in an embarrassed voice.

He hated women who said things like "Oops!"—it made them sound as if they'd quit trying to better themselves after the sixth grade.

"Fix it," he said shortly.

"Yes, *sir*."

Deena had designed their uniforms. "Make them up-to-date, sexy, not too obvious," had been his instructions. Deena knew exactly what would please him.

Deena. His wife. A woman of steel. Not unlike him when it came to getting what she wanted.

When he'd first met her it was like looking in a mirror and seeing the female version of himself. A sharp woman, a worker. A woman who knew what she wanted and would do anything to get it.

Deena. He'd liked her a lot. He'd married her.

When he'd found out she'd lied to him about her age and background, something had clicked off. Martin did not appreciate being lied to.

Their marriage now was one of convenience. From the outside it appeared that the Swansons had it all. The truth was that Martin worked eighteen hours a day, while Deena tried to keep up. Perhaps children would have helped, but after two miscarriages Deena was informed she shouldn't try for more babies, and her tubes were tied to make sure it would never happen.

Although he had gallantly told Deena it didn't matter, Martin was a disappointed man. He would have loved a son. A small image of himself whom he could mold. Martin Z. Swanson, Junior. A boy he could take to ball games and teach the intricacies of real business.

Who was going to carry on the great Swanson name?

Who was going to inherit all his money?

Deena had let him down.

Sex was not particularly important to Martin. He'd been a virgin until he was seventeen, and his first experience was with a forty-three-year-old prostitute who'd sulkily told him to hurry up. She'd cost him ten dollars and an unfortunate dose of the clap.

An early lesson to be learned—you pay for what you get.

His second experience was with a five-hundred-dollar-a-night call girl who resided in a Park Avenue apartment. He'd used his Christmas-present money and, disappointingly, found the second time almost as unexciting as the first.

After that he settled for a series of young ladies who gave it away for free. He didn't exactly fuck his way through college, but he did O.K.

After college, business came first. Then Deena. Then the miscarriages. Then the mistresses.

Martin was not interested in mere physical beauty. He only pursued women who'd achieved something.

The chase excited him—targeting a woman he wanted, and then seeing how long it took to nail her. That was the best game. Sometimes he even stayed around for a month or two.

What he'd found out was they all had their price.

What he'd found out was that he could pay it.

Then along came Venus Maria, and finally, at age forty-five, Martin Z. Swanson discovered love and lust and living. And the passion engulfed him.

He leaned back in his seat and relived their first encounter.

Venus Maria.

Martin Z. Swanson.
A volcano waiting to erupt.

"Hi." Venus Maria smiled at him. She had small white teeth and a provocative smile.

"I'm an admirer," he replied with the charming, smooth Swanson look and a cavalier wink.

The smile did not leave her face. "You're full of shit. I bet you've never even seen anything I've done."

"Not true," he protested.

"So tell me."

"Tell you what exactly?"

"What you've seen me do?"

He paused. "You were on the cover of Time."

"That's not doing anything. That's publicity."

"I know that."

"So?"

"You're a singer."

"Wow! How astute."

"And an actress."

"But you've never actually seen me in anything, have you?"

He shrugged. "You've got me."

Still smiling she said, "You see, I was right, you're full of shit."

Martin was not used to people telling him he was full of shit. Especially a young woman, however famous she might be, with platinum hair, challenging eyes, and the strangest outfit he'd ever seen. She looked like some kind of traveling gypsy, strung with silver ethnic jewelry worn over a long multicolored skirt and a midriff-exposing gold blouse.

They were at a dinner party in New York given by the Websters. Effie Webster was an avant-garde fashion designer. And Yul, her husband, published books. Both of them were well known for their weird assortment of friends and their drug-taking proclivities. Although Deena was good friends with the Websters, Martin was there only because the party was for his old friend and former roommate, Cooper Turner. Deena had stayed home with a migraine. Her first mistake.

187

"Now we've established you're full of shit," Venus Maria said, enjoying herself as she plucked a shrimp cake from a passing waiter's tray and popped it between disturbingly full ruby-red lips, "what are we going to do about it?"

The "we" got his attention. He'd recently called it off with the feminist lawyer he was sleeping with—she was too demanding. So he was available for the next adventure. But this girl was something else—too young—too wild—too much. Warning signals told him to stay away.

"Do you know who I am?" he asked, fully confident she did.

"Nope," she replied nonchalantly. "Although I have to admit you do look a little familiar. Are you a politician? Like a Senator or something?"

"I'm Martin Swanson," he said, the way someone would say "This is the Empire State Building" or "Here stands the Eiffel Tower."

Venus Maria cocked her head on one side. He noticed her earrings did not match.

"No ringing bells," she said. "Zap me with a clue."

Now she was beginning to aggravate him, this strange-looking creature. Her eyebrows were too dark for her hair, and her eyes had a hooded quality—far too knowledgeable for the rest of her face. "Read Time, January 1984," he said abruptly. "You're not the only one who's been on the cover."

Cooper Turner walked over then. The handsome Cooper himself. Cooper, who was probably nailing this famous-for-fifteen-minutes bimbo into the ground. He had a reputation to maintain.

"I see you've met Venus," Cooper said with a grin. "Has she insulted you yet?"

"I'm not sure," Martin replied.

"Hang onto your balls, fellas. One day you might need 'em." Venus Maria laughed gaily and honored them with a jaunty wave. "I gotta go. Nice meeting you—uh . . . ."

"Martin."

"My memory stinks, but I give great head."

She left them with that line, sashaying across the room, attracting attention every step of the way.

"Ah, but I wish I knew," Cooper said wistfully. "Young Venus

Maria is what we used to call a prick tease. Remember them? Back in the good old sixties."

"You mean you're not in bed with her?" Martin asked curiously.

"Difficult to believe, isn't it?" Cooper said with a wry grin. "I finally seem to have struck out. She laughed when I suggested it. Do you think we're getting old, Martin?" Cooper said this last line with the confidence of a man who knew he'd never be too old for anyone.

Martin kept a watchful eye on Venus Maria for the rest of the night. She fluttered around the room like an inquisitive bird, never staying long in one place, all platinum hair and full red lips, her heady perfume trailing her wherever she went.

At one point their eyes met. Just once. She held his gaze like a cat, forcing him to look away first. Another small triumph for her. Martin was intrigued.

The next day he sent for her press file. His secretary handed him an avalanche of magazine and newspaper clippings. She was more famous than he'd thought.

He then asked for copies of her videos and the two movies she'd made. On screen she had a dynamic presence—a sexual siren with a solid dose of street smarts. She could dance, she could sing, she could even act.

By the end of the day Martin was in lust. He found out she was staying at the Chelsea Hotel and sent over three dozen "Sterling Silver" roses with a note. The note read: "So do I—Martin Swanson."

Not strictly true. He'd never given head to a woman in his life. Never had to.

She neither acknowledged nor thanked him for his flowers. He wondered if she'd even received them, for he discovered she'd returned to L.A. the next day.

Venus Maria.

Unfinished business.

Martin liked every deal sewn up tight.

Six weeks later Deena decided there was a party she wished to attend in L.A. It was for a big charity, and she quite fancied wearing her new sapphire-and-diamond necklace, which complemented her pale blue eyes and translucent skin.

"Let's go," Martin said agreeably, surprising Deena, because she knew he hated L.A.

He must have had an instinct about it. Venus Maria was at the event, standing out in black leather, while all around her there was a sea of Valentinos, Ungaros, and Adolfos. Her hair was dyed a harsh black—all the better to match her eyebrows—and her full lips were painted a strident purple. Under her black leather motorcycle jacket she wore a softer black leather bustier, studded with silver nails. Her breasts were creamy invitations to whatever else lay hidden beneath the leather.

"My God! That Venus Maria girl is just awful! Did you see her?" Deena asked.

Could he miss her?

No.

And this time he had no intention of doing so.

Cooper Turner was not anxious to part with her phone number. *"She's not the girl for you, Martin,"* he warned. *"This girl dances to a whole new step. Forget it."*

"Frightened of the competition?" Martin asked.

"I'm just trying to warn you. Venus is different. Say you did make out with her—which, I can tell you now, you won't. She's not the kind of woman who's going to sit at home while you run back and forth to Deena. Forget it, Martin. This is a tough kid."

"Do I get the number or do I go elsewhere?"

He got the number and called her, prepared for anything.

"I took my roses back to L.A.," she said casually. *"Oh, and I had my assistant get me* Time *magazine. I don't like the picture—you look like a self-satisfied asshole. I do a little photography myself—wanna pose in front of my lens?"*

He made an excuse to Deena and left her in the hotel while he hurried over to Venus Maria's house in the Hollywood Hills.

She made him a cup of herb tea and touched his face with long silky fingers. *"I won't sleep with you until I know you,"* she said softly. *"That might take a couple of years. Right?"*

Wrong.

It took five weeks, during which time he made six trips to the Coast and she visited New York twice.

It happened in a friend's house overlooking Big Sur in a four-poster bed with an incredible view of the ocean.

And Martin Z. Swanson—tycoon, sophisticate, billionaire, man of the world, forty-five years old—finally learned about love and sex and passion.

It was a revelation.

The first thing Martin did upon arriving in L.A. was to call Venus Maria from his limo. She was on the set, but he got through anyway, using their private code name—Mr. Wacko. He felt like a fool using such a name, but Venus Maria had insisted. "Only a stupid name like that will work," she'd assured him. And she was probably right. So Mr. Wacko it was.

"What time shall I come over?" he asked.

"You can't. My brother's still at my house."

"Goddamn it! I thought you were getting rid of him."

"I am. It takes time. I'd really prefer he doesn't go running to the *National Enquirer* to sell my secrets."

"He'll do that anyway."

"You think?"

"I know."

"I'll rent him an apartment."

"When?"

"Today."

"I've missed you."

"Good."

"Well?"

"What?"

"You *know* what. Have you missed me?"

"Martin, when you're here, you're here. When you're away, that's your other life. Missing you is negative energy. I don't have time for it."

She could be infuriating. Didn't she have any idea how much it took for him to say "I miss you"? He'd never said it to anyone in his life. And she dismissed it like it was nothing.

"I'm out here to do a takeover deal on a studio," he said, as if that would impress her.

"You told me on your last trip."

"That particular deal fell through."

"So what now?"

"New negotiations."

"I've gotta go, they're yelling for me."

"Make 'em wait."

"Martin! I'm surprised at you. I'm a professional."

"Get rid of your brother. I want to come to the house."

"I'll try."

"Don't try. Do."

"Later."

Later he would have her in his arms. That young vibrant body pulsating with energy. Pulsating all over him. Giving him the best hard-on he'd ever had.

And so to work. Martin Z. Swanson wanted to achieve a takeover. And when Martin Z. Swanson wanted something he always succeeded.

28

Lucky lit a cigarette. Once, long ago, she'd promised herself she'd give up smoking. Impossible. It was too intrusive a habit. And besides, she enjoyed the process. Lighting up, inhaling, allowing the smoke to drift lazily away.

Boogie didn't smoke. Boogie was into oat bran and wheat flakes and brown rice and other grains. He'd discovered health with a vengeance and kept on shooting disapproving looks at her when she gulped her coffee black, strong, and certainly not decaf, and settled into a thick, juicy steak for dinner.

It was Saturday morning and there was lots to do. No time to run off to London—maybe a day trip to Acapulco, if she wasn't supposed to be in Japan.

Goddammit! She needed to be with Lennie.

She called him, somewhat tentatively. From the sound of his voice on the phone when he'd talked to Mickey yesterday, he was not likely to be in the best of moods. She was right.

"Where are you?" was his first question, asked in a belligerent tone.

"Bowing a lot and drinking tea," she replied calmly.

He was getting more aggravated by the minute. "Are you aware you have moronic idiots working for you?"

"Don't we all?"

"C'mon, Lucky, I'm not screwing around. The people in your office are either slow-witted or totally obtuse."

Who had he spoken to? "Why do you say that?" she asked anxiously. It wouldn't do to blow it now.

"Because for the last twenty-four hours I've been trying to find out exactly where in Japan you are. A phone number. An address. Anything. 'We have no idea, Mr. Golden,' they tell me. Like I'm some kind of schmuck."

Two weeks, and she was already in deep shit.

"They don't know where I am," she answered blankly. "*I* don't know where I am. Mr. Tagaswaki is a strange and wonderful man who conducts his business in a somewhat eccentric way."

Lennie sounded disgusted. "What the fuck are you talking about?"

"It's difficult to explain," she answered quickly. "It's that kind of a deal. He's a little crazy. I'll be out of here soon."

Lennie was not to be placated. "Are you sleeping with this Japanese prick?" he asked tightly.

"Don't be ridiculous."

"No, Lucky, *you're* being ridiculous."

Now it was her turn to get angry. "*I'm* making a deal. Do I interfere with the way *you* do things?"

"All the time."

Oh, God! She didn't want this to develop into a fullfledged fight. "Please understand, Lennie," she said softly. "Just this once."

"I *don't* understand. Get your ass back here."

His accusing tone was beginning to grate. "Lennie," she said carefully, "I do what *I* want."

"Well, keep on doing it, honey, an' you'll be doing it on your own."

Honey! He was *really* mad.

"This deal is important to me. Why don't you just let me pull it off my way, and then I'm all yours. We won't move for the entire summer. We'll sit in Malibu and build sand castles." Her voice softened again. "O.K., baby?"

He calmed down. "I was going to surprise you this weekend. Just turn up. That's if there'd been anywhere to turn up at."

"What about the movie?"

"Screw the movie. I told Mickey Stolli if they're not prepared to dump Grudge, I'm walking."

"I'll have a big surprise for you soon."

"What?"

"Be patient."

He wasn't giving up. "Since when was I patient? What's your phone number?"

"There isn't one."

"Where are you speaking from, the street?"

"A hotel."

He sounded exasperated. "I don't know what game you're playing, Lucky. But do me and yourself a favor and get back here. I need you."

"I'll be with you sooner than you think."

Not the ideal phone conversation. How long was he going to believe her transparent excuses?

She tried Bobby in London next. He'd been to a James Bond movie and insisted on telling her the entire plot. She listened patiently, told her son she loved him, and hung up.

You're fucking up your life, Santangelo.

Only temporarily.

Monday morning, back at the studio, she knew a lot more than she'd known when she'd left on Friday carrying a briefcase full of papers and contracts from Mickey's locked file cabinet. She'd had plenty of time to study them over the weekend. It appeared Mickey was creaming money all over the place. The head of business affairs had to be in on it. Major collusion.

Mickey came running in late, snapping his fingers. "Get me Zeppo White on the phone. Cancel my nine o'clock with Eddie Kane. Tell Teddy Lauden to stay after the meeting. An' fix me fresh juice—grapefruit. Get your ass in here. Fast."

The man was unbelievable. Whatever happened to "Good morning" and a little common courtesy?

She followed him into his office. He was already throwing off his tennis shirt, revealing an extremely hairy chest. If the shorts came next she was out of there.

He trotted into his private bathroom, took a loud pee with the door open, and dictated a terse FAX to Grudge Freeport.

The FAX read:

> UNHAPPY ACTORS ARE A PAIN IN
> THE ASS. A PAIN THERE MAKES
> ME UNHAPPY. YOU ARE
> REPLACEABLE. THE STARS ARE
> NOT. DO SOMETHING NICE AND
> MAKE EVERYONE HAPPY.

He then dictated a similar FAX to Ned Magnus, the producer of Lennie's movie. Lucky added a terse

> ACCOMMODATE LENNIE GOLDEN IN
> EVERY WAY. ALLOW HIM TO
> MAKE ANY CHANGES HE WANTS.

Mickey then disappeared under the shower, while she hurried to make his phone calls.

He emerged screaming for his fresh juice.

Lucky darted into the stainless steel kitchen, sliced a grapefruit in half, nearly taking her finger along with it, and threw it on top of the juicer.

A fit of laughter almost overcame her. This was insane! What the hell was she doing this for?

Adventure.

A studio.

Lennie.

Eddie Kane was nervous. He had urgent matters to discuss with Mickey, and the prick was giving him a runaround.

Eddie Kane smoked a joint in the men's room ten minutes before the Monday morning meeting of the major players. He would have preferred a hit of coke, but he was all out, and Kathleen Le Paul never made her weekly visit until after lunch.

A joint took the edge off. Just about. Not really.

Fuck! He was wired to the hilt. He needed to sit down with Mickey and straighten out business.

Staring in the men's room mirror he noticed he'd developed a twitch. Almost imperceptible—only it was there, if you were looking.

Who's looking, for crissakes?

Eddie "The Twitch" Kane. Former child star. Still hot, with his "Miami Vice" attitude.

This is what Eddie was into.

Porno flicks.

Distributing them.

Hiding them along with Panther's legit products.

Making a tidy pile.

Scooping it in.

He stared at himself for a long while. Who else has a wife like Leslie? he thought. She was prettier than any movie star. Sexier, too.

Ah, what wouldn't he give to see her thigh-high in diamonds. She deserved every single one. Thigh-high and bare-assed. What a sight!

"Good morning, Eddie."

Zev Lorenzo, head of the recently formed television division, snuck up on him. Zev was an elegant man in his late forties with a pencil mustache, thinning hair, and a trim build. If he had to make a guess, Eddie would have said that Zev was the only executive at Panther who wasn't in business for himself in some way or other.

"Hiya, Zev."

The older man nodded and stood in the front of the urinals.

A *closet queen* zipped through Eddie's mind. Someone had told Eddie Zev was a closet queen. Although why, in 1985, anybody would bother staying in the closet was beyond Eddie.

"How's everything?" he mumbled, running a hand through his long hair.

197

"Excellent," replied Zev. He was into words like "supreme" and "primacy" and "surpass." Eddie had never heard him swear. Not even a simple "fuck."

"That's good, that's very good," Eddie said. "Hey—one of these days ya gotta meet my wife."

"I've heard she's a stunner." Zev zipped up and exited. Didn't even stay to wash his hands.

Eddie twitched again. He didn't feel good. He felt like shit. He looked like shit. He'd frightened Zev off.

"Do I accompany you to the meeting, Mr. Stolli?" Lucky asked.

"Yeah, yeah, yeah. Take notes. Get it all down. You do fast short-hand, right?"

She nodded.

"What's wrong with your hair?"

"Uh . . ."

"Forget it. Follow me an' don't open your mouth."

She trailed him into the conference room. Three steps behind. Like an obedient geisha.

The boys were gathered. No girls.

Shame.

That's Hollywood.

Quietly taking a backseat, notepad poised (shorthand was the one useful skill she'd learned at school in Switzerland), she looked around, silently identifying the players, matching them up to their photographs in the glossy Panther end-of-year financial report.

Ford Werne, Head of Production. Killer-sharp in an Armani suit and five-hundred-dollar tinted aviator shades. He was around fifty, but he'd kept his act very much together.

Teddy T. Lauden, Head of Business Affairs, was exactly the opposite. Thin, nondescript, precise.

Zev Lorenzo, the man who ran the Television Division, impeccable and charming.

While Eddie Kane, Mister Distribution, Mister Cokehead, looked like he was ready to fall apart. Seedy was too kind a description. He was handsome in a smarmy way. But definitely in trouble.

Which left only two other senior executives—Grant Wendell, Vice President of Worldwide Production—young and sharp-eyed, wearing baggy pants with a button-down Gap shirt.

And Buck Graham—Marketing. A plump, jovial man with ruddy cheeks and an "I'm-here-to-please" smile.

Average age of the group—early forties.

That's why there were no women execs. These guys had not experienced feminist mothers. What did they know?

Lucky grinned to herself. In her dowdy wig and glasses, her figure concealed by her baggy clothes, she was invisible to this group of—most likely—male chauvinists.

Two women appeared, ready to serve coffee and tea. One of them was Eddie Kane's black secretary, Brenda. She'd dressed for the occasion in a tight pink leather dress that ended somewhere mid-thigh. On her long legs she wore outrageous fishnet tights, more suitable for a lady of the night than an office meeting, and very high red patent heels.

Brenda fussed over the men, calling every one of them by name as she poured their coffee, gold-painted nails curling around the coffeepot handle.

The other woman was a ponytailed blonde, also in a miniskirt. She apparently belonged to Grant Wendell.

The men ignored the two females, although Lucky observed Eddie giving Grant's secretary a quick feel under her skimpy skirt as she passed by.

"O.K., girls. Outta here," said Mickey Stolli, Mr. Charm. "We're not runnin' a restaurant."

Brenda shot Lucky a mean look as if to say, What the hell are *you* doing here? Obviously this was a fill-in job most of the other secretaries would have been only too delighted to do.

And so the meeting started.

Mickey had a mind like a machine gun, firing questions, talking fast. He wanted to know every detail of what was happening around the studio, and around the world—if it was anything to do with Panther.

Ford Werne adjusted his aviator shades and talked about a million-dollar script he thought they should buy.

Grant Wendell discussed his desire to sign Madonna or Cher to a multipic deal.

Zev Lorenzo boasted about ratings on two of his television shows and claimed to be negotiating for the television rights to a Norman Mailer book. "We'll do it as a long-form miniseries—similar to Irwin Shaw's 'Rich Man, Poor Man.' "

"Too classy," Mickey interjected. "We need somethin' with jiggle. An' talkin' of jiggle—we gotta develop a property for that seventeen-year-old ex-porn star who's goin' straight. She's a natural."

"Natural what, Mickey?" asked Buck Graham with a barroom chuckle.

"I saw her in *Under Glass*," Teddy Lauden joined in, suddenly coming to life. "She was sixteen at the time. What a body!"

"Never mind the body, can she act?" asked Grant.

"Who gives a shit?" demanded Mickey. "She's gonna make us a fuckin' fortune. Fresh young snatch. It brings 'em into the box office every time. Cooper's givin' her a coupla lines in his movie."

Ah, to be in the company of real men, Lucky thought. *What a delightful bunch.*

Eddie cornered her after the meeting. He was a jumping time bomb. "Hey—hey—lady—you."

"The name is Luce."

"Okay, Luce. Ya gotta do me a big one."

"Yes?"

"Don't keep on canceling my goddamn appointments with Mickey. I havta see him—like today. Urgent biz."

She noticed he had a twitch. It was fascinating.

"*I'm* not canceling your appointments, Mr. Kane. Mr. Stolli does so himself. *I* merely do as I'm told."

Holy shit! She was beginning to sound like Olive!

"Sure. So when he tells you to cancel the next one—just forget. An' then, I'm there. Like in. Y'know what I'm sayin'?"

"Why would I do that, Mr. Kane?"

"You'll catch on. It's the only way to operate with Mickey. He flakes on everyone. Olive'll tell you. When's she comin' back?"

"Tomorrow."

"I gotta see him today. Arrange it."

"I'll try."

"Good girl."

"The name is Luce."

"I'd change it if I was you."

Back in the office there was a stack of messages. Mickey Stolli was a popular man.

She flicked through his appointment book. It was full for a month. Olive's neat script had jotted down every detail.

Knocking on the door to his office, she waited for him to call out his customary "Yeah," and went in.

"Mr. Kane would like to reschedule," she said, all business.

"I can't stand the sight of that bum," Mickey said.

"When shall I reschedule it for? He says it's urgent."

"Taking a dump is urgent. Eddie can wait."

"Are you sure?"

"Don't give me grief. Who's on next?"

"You have lunch with Frankie Lombardo and Arnie Blackwood, and then a three o'clock meeting at the Beverly Hills Hotel with Martin Swanson."

"Cancel lunch. I gotta go somewhere."

"May I ask where?"

"No."

"Thank you, Mr. Stolli."

Alerted by Lucky, Boogie was in place when Mickey Stolli left the studio. He followed him all the way to a modest West Hollywood apartment house, where he observed Mickey park his Porsche in a underground space reserved for apartment four.

Checking the listings on the front entrance, Boogie discovered apartment four belonged to a Warner Franklin.

Did Mickey Stolli have an afternoon boyfriend?

Obviously.

Boogie called Lucky from the car and gave her the information.

"Are you sure?" she asked.

"It certainly looks that way."

"Hang around. Maybe they'll come out together."

"I doubt it. They're not likely to be seen in public, are they?"

"Who knows? Mickey's hardly the smartest guy in the world."

"I'll see what I can find out."

"Nobody does it better."

Spurred by Lucky's praise, Boogie found out plenty. The mailman, an inquisitive neighbor, and a bored nine-year-old out of school with the flu supplied the story.

The facts. Warner Franklin. Black. Female. A cop.

Boogie smelled graft.

29

Martin Swanson had an army of lawyers. He called. They came running.

His lawyers had an army of top connections. They'd put the word out Martin Swanson was interested in acquiring a controlling interest in a major studio, and all possibilities fell into position.

Martin had examined every option, reading confidential reports on United Artists, Columbia, Fox, et cetera, and finally coming to the conclusion that Orpheus and Panther were the two most viable propositions.

Orpheus was ripe for a takeover. And Panther, still privately owned by the reclusive Abe Panther, was possibly available if the price was right. Or so his lawyers had led him to believe.

"If I want Panther, who do I talk to?" Martin had asked.

Mickey Stolli, he was told.

Martin had his people run an immediate check on Mickey, and while he might be chairman and chief executive officer of Panther, he was certainly not in a position to sell without his father-in-law's say-so.

Interesting. For Mickey had done an excellent job at Panther since taking over. The studio was turning a healthy profit.

Martin had been pursuing the idea of acquiring a large stake in a film studio long before Venus Maria entered his life. Hollywood was the lure. Money was the merry-go-round. And the film business as a potential money-maker was irresistible.

Orpheus Studios was in trouble. Owned by a parent company whose main concern was making airplane parts, it had been consistently losing money for the past three years. With Zeppo White, the former agent, in charge, things had gotten worse.

Right now they had five movies in production. Four were already millions of dollars over budget and had very little chance of showing a profit unless a miracle occurred.

Martin Swanson did not believe in miracles.

Orpheus could be bought. At a price.

Maybe Panther could—maybe not. But Martin was certain that Mickey Stolli was buyable. And if Martin's purchase turned out to be Orpheus, why not bring Mickey over to run things? He certainly had the right track record.

Hence Martin's planned meeting with Mickey. One way or the other they could do business.

Mickey had no idea what Martin Swanson wanted. He'd heard rumors that Martin was looking to gain control of a studio. But surely the guy was savvy enough to investigate? And if he did, he'd find out what everybody in town knew—that Mickey Stolli was just a paid employee, and could no more sell him Panther than take a flying dive in Macy's window.

It pissed Mickey off. It pissed Mickey off enough to trigger a twice-a-year furious fight with Abigaile, who didn't understand at all. She looked down at him like a mother who'd just caught her son jacking off over a naked picture of Hitler.

"My grandfather has been very good to you," she usually said, or words to that effect. "And when he goes, we'll get everything we deserve."

"Why do we have to wait?" was Mickey's argument. "How about the lawyers going in and declaring him senile?"

Abigaile would have none of it. She knew for a fact that her grandfather had constructed an extremely complicated and ironclad will, and any messing with it was going to cause nothing but unwanted complications.

She also knew that Abe Panther, in spite of his age, was certainly not senile. He was as smart as Mickey any day, and Mickey should think himself more than fortunate that Abe had not returned to run the studio and had allowed Mickey to do it his way.

Of course, there were financial restrictions put into place by Abe's lawyers. These restrictions infuriated Mickey. It meant that his salary could not exceed 1 million dollars a year. That sounded like a lot, but when some asshole actor could receive 5 or 6 million, plus gross points of a potential hit movie, it was hardly satisfactory.

Abigaile had her own trust fund of money inherited from her parents. But Mickey had to make do on a lousy million—and when tax was taken off . . .

It didn't bear thinking about, although Mickey thought about it quite a lot—not usually when he was humping Warner—but today was hot, and there was a fly buzzing in her apartment, and she'd just informed him she'd been promoted to Vice (*that* was a promotion?), and he was altogether not in the mood for their usual steamy sex session.

"What seems to be the matter, lover?" Warner asked.

He was on top of her at the time, exhibiting his lack of desire. It was hardly something he could hide.

"There's a fly in here," he said lamely.

Her voice rose in surprise. "A fly?"

"Maybe a wasp." That sounded better.

Warner couldn't help herself—after all, she'd grown up in a house where rats were an everyday occurrence. "Frightened it's gonna sting you on the ass, Mickey?" she teased, laughter in her voice.

That did it. No hiding the hot dog today. Lurching off her, he reached for his pants.

"Stop!" said Warner.

He continued to pull on his pants.

She sat up. "Stop! Or I'm gonna havta arrest and handcuff you."

His cock, searching for a life of its own, sprang to attention.

Mickey dropped his pants.

Warner reached for her handcuffs.

They were back in business.

The Polo Lounge was the perfect meeting place—at three o'clock in the afternoon relatively quiet, fairly discreet, and pleasantly air-conditioned.

Martin Z. Swanson and Mickey Stolli had never met before, although they were certainly well aware of each other.

They shook hands in front of the dimly lit, number one comfortable leather booth.

"We could've done this in my bungalow," Martin said.

"Or at the studio," Mickey offered.

"It's better here," they both agreed.

Mickey Stolli felt fucked. Literally.

Martin wondered what time he'd be able to meet with Venus Maria. "Let's talk business," he said.

"Show business," Mickey corrected with a sly smile.

"I want you to go," Venus Maria said in a not-to-be-argued-with voice. "I've rented you an apartment on Fountain Avenue. It has a swimming pool, television, and maid service. It's furnished nicely. I'll pay your rent for six months, and after that you're on your own. I'm sure you'll be able to manage."

Her brother Emilio stared at her. They possessed the same eyes, big and brown and soulful. Apart from that, they did not look at all alike.

"Why?" Emilio asked plaintively.

"Because . . . because I need my privacy."

"We're family," Emilio said, fixing her with a hurt expression, as if she'd let him down.

She was determined not to give in. "That's why I'm paying your rent for six months."

He sighed. A big sigh. A put-upon sigh. "I'll go," he said reluctantly. As if he had a choice.

Venus Maria nodded. "Good."

"When I'm ready," Emilio added.

He was pushing her. It was infuriating. But she had a temper too, and she refused to be pushed any further. "You go today," she said. "Within the hour. Or the deal is off and you can hustle your lazy ass on Santa Monica Boulevard for all I care."

"*Puttana!*" he muttered.

Her eyes narrowed. "What?"

"Do I get a car?"

She decided to ignore his insult. "You can borrow the station wagon," she said wearily.

Emilio scowled. Why should he drive a lowly station wagon while his sister sat in limos and Porsches? It wasn't the way things should be, but it looked like it was inevitable. Venus Maria meant business.

He slouched off to pack his belongings.

Venus Maria experienced a frisson of triumph. Small but satisfying. She sent her housekeeper out to buy fresh flowers and then hurried to her huge walk-in closet and tried to decide on the perfect outfit.

Martin liked her in white; he'd told her so. She preferred black. It was more sophisticated and more raunchy. It made her feel sexy.

How about white on the outside and black against her flesh?

How about nothing against her flesh?

Martin was not the greatest lover in the world. He was inhibited, fast, not into any real sensual pleasure.

She was teaching him.

Slowly . . .

Very, very slowly. . . .

Venus Maria was twenty-five, and she'd had four lovers, Martin being the fourth. The press would have a field day if they ever found out she'd only had four men. After all, she was a liberated woman— a high priestess of the sexual come-on. Everything she did radiated pure sex, from her videos to her acting performances. She touched herself in secret places publicly. And even with AIDS casting its giant shadow, she should have experienced more than four men.

Lover number one: Manuel. A killer in the sack. Black hair, black eyes, dark-olive skin. A cock to die for, and a dancer's flair for exquisite movement.

She met him a week after arriving in L.A. and he took her virginity with a sticky, hard passion she found breathtaking.

For three months they made love every day, and then he left her for a California beach bunny.

When she became famous he tried to insinuate himself back into her world.

Forget it.

Lover number two: Ryan. A sensualist. Rumpled blond hair, puppy-dog eyes, sunkissed skin. A cock to die for, and the best ass she'd ever seen.

He accompanied her on the ride, and got off when he fell in love with the bearded manager of an English rock group.

They'd remained friends.

Lover number three: Innes. A killer in the sack *and* a sensualist. What a lethal combination.

They stayed together nearly a year until her career became more than a threat.

Manuel, Ryan, and Innes were all in their twenties.

Martin was forty-five. He could have been their father. He could have been *her* father.

She loved him.

She didn't know why.

Choosing a virginal white dress, all layers and lace, she paired it with a short, tight brocade jacket, seventeen silver bracelets, dangling earrings—a different design for each ear—and skating boots without the blades. Then she called Martin at his hotel and left a message: "The Wacko family will be at home after six."

When Mickey entered his house, he was buzzing.

Thirteen-year-old Tabitha greeted him with a sulky glare. "Mommy says I can't go to Vegas with Lulu and her dad. I wanna go. Why can't I go?"

Tabitha had straight brown hair, a just-developing figure, and frightening braces on her teeth. She was hardly going to be jumped on by every guy in sight.

"If your mother says so—" he began.

"I wanna go, Daddy," Tabitha wailed. "*You* talk to her. You fix it. You're so smart you can fix anything!"

Had she been taking lessons from Warner?

"I'll try," he promised, without much enthusiasm.

Tabitha threw her arms around him, scraping his cheek with her braces.

Abigaile, as if sensing collusion, appeared in the front hallway. "Were you meeting with Martin Swanson in the Polo Lounge today?" she asked peevishly, ignoring her daughter, who was busy signaling Mickey behind her mother's back, urging him to say something.

Was nothing secret? The Beverly Hills Bush Telegraph worked like lightning, or maybe the new girl—what was her name?—Lucy, Luce—something stupid—had too big a mouth. Olive was smart enough to be aware that if he wanted Abigaile to know anything, he'd tell her himself.

"Who told you that?" he asked, automatically becoming defensive.

"Daddy!" complained Tabitha, panting for action.

"Does it matter who told me?" bristled Abigaile. "What matters is that you never let me know you were seeing Martin Swanson. I would have liked to have had a dinner party for the Swansons."

Ah, another cozy little dinner for fifty.

"Why? You don't even know them."

"I most certainly do," Abigaile countered indignantly. "I've met Deena on more than one occasion."

"She's not with him."

"Vegas, Daddy!" interjected Tabitha, hopping anxiously up and down.

"Uh . . . why can't Tabitha go to Vegas?"

Abigaile withered him with a look. She was good at reducing grown men to ashes. Raising an imperious eyebrow she said, "Are you serious?"

"Yes, I'm serious. She wants to go with her friend Lulu and Lulu's father. That sounds all right to me."

"Are you aware who Lulu's father is?"

"Uh . . . he's a singer. Right?"

"He's a *rock* singer." Abigaile spat the words out. "And not a very famous one at that—unless you count his time spent in A.A. and drug rehab. My daughter is not going anywhere with *that* family."

My daughter. It was always *my* this and *my* that. Sometimes Mickey felt Abigaile went out of her way to prove he didn't exist.

He was still buzzing, but now he decided to keep the buzz to himself.

Screw Abby. If things went the way he hoped they'd go, she'd find out soon enough.

30

Olive Watson broke her leg. As far as Lucky was concerned this was great news. Although she commiserated with Olive over the phone, she still felt guilty about being so pleased.

Mickey did not take it well. He summoned Lucky into his office screaming and yelling as if it was her fault.

"We'll manage, Mr. Stolli," she said calmly, the perfect secretary.

"*You'll* manage," he screamed. "My life is a fuck-up!"

It certainly is, she replied silently.

Eddie Kane arrived for his newly scheduled appointment. Mickey had attempted to cancel it, but Lucky told him she hadn't been able to reach Mr. Kane.

Eddie looked like a good night's sleep might be a fine idea. He winked at Lucky, whispered, "You're a good girl," patted her on the ass, and entered Mickey Stolli's lair.

Sitting outside, Lucky pressed the office intercom enabling her to listen in.

"What's going on, Eddie? I warned you if we went into this I wasn't to be bothered." Mickey sounded weary.

"Yeah," Eddie said. "Only I didn't reckon on a coupla bent-nose fuckheads breathin' down my pants for a bigger piece of the action."

"Whaddya mean?"

"It's simple. We take their porno product, bury it all the way outta

the country with the legit Panther stuff. Split the proceeds—an'
there ya go—they've got clean money. We've got us a nice healthy
score with no problems."

"So?"

"So they're claimin' we ain't splittin' fair."

Mickey's tone was ominous. "And are we?"

The lie was in Eddie's voice, plain to hear. "Would I try t'fuck the
big boys?"

"You'd try to fuck a skunk if it pissed in the right direction."

Lucky heard someone approaching. She slammed off the intercom, quickly picking up a pile of letters.

"Workin' hard, doll?"

It was the Sleazy Singles themselves. If they were a singing group,
Eddie Kane would have made a perfect third partner.

"Mr. Lombardo. Mr. Blackwood," Lucky said primly, emulating
Olive. "Can I help you?"

Arnie leaned across her desk, and before she could stop him he
flicked off her thick glasses. "Ya got nice eyes, babe. Get yourself
contacts."

She attempted to grab her glasses. He waved them at her, keeping
them just out of reach.

"Mr. Blackwood, I can't see," she said sternly.

"I get off on babes who can't see," leered Frankie.

"Yeah, all the better not to notice your one-and-a-half-inch dick!"
said Arnie.

This remark broke them both up. Lucky took the opportunity to
snatch her glasses and put them back on. What a couple of major
jerks!

"What's he doin'?" questioned Frankie, gesturing toward Mickey's
office.

"Mr. Stolli is in a meeting with Mr. Kane."

"Then I guess he's ready for the light relief brigade," Arnie said
with a hearty chuckle.

"You can't—"

Before she could finish, they were on their way into Mickey's
office.

She quickly buzzed Mickey. "Mr. Stolli. I'm sorry, they just barged past me. I—"

Mickey's familiar "Yeah, yeah, yeah. Order up coffee."

"And banana cake," yelled Frankie in the background.

All the better to enlarge your fat ass, Lucky thought.

The boys are having a meeting.

Let them eat cake.

Acapulco sunshine could be boring. Every day the same thing— blue skies, blazing sun, and a picture postcard setting.

Two friends of Lennie's arrived to stay for a few days—Jess and Matt Traynor. Jess was Lennie's oldest friend; they'd grown up together in Las Vegas, attended the same high school, and remained close ever since.

Only five feet tall, and very pretty, Jess was a supercharged package. She had wide eyes, a mop of orange hair, freckles, and a great body.

Matt, her second husband (the first was a drugged-out bum who'd run out on her) was, at sixty-something, almost thirty years older. He didn't look it, with his close-cropped silver hair and well-dressed, foxy style.

Lennie was happy to have visitors. How many nights could he spend with Joey Firello? Joey's continual pursuit of the female form was exhausting.

Nights spent alone were not much fun either, and he had no intention of socializing with either Grudge, Marisa, or Ned—the fun trio, he'd christened them.

Jess and Matt were a welcome relief. They arrived armed with photos of their sixteen-month-old twins, a boy and a girl.

"Your godchildren," Jess told Lennie proudly. "When are you going to have a few of your own?"

Trust Jess to come right out with it. She sounded like Gino, who was always dropping not-so-subtle hints.

"When Lucky decides to fit me in between deals," he said wryly.

"What does *that* mean?"

"She's busy."

"Ah, that's what happens when you marry a working woman."

"Tell me about it."

Jess had stopped work several months before her twins were born. She'd once been Lennie's personal manager. In fact, it was Jess who'd been responsible for getting his career off the ground in the first place. He owed her plenty. They'd certainly come a long way together.

"I miss you, monkey face," he said dejectedly.

"Don't call me that!" she shrieked; she still hated her nickname from their school days.

"Why not?"

"Because you know I hate it."

"But it suits you."

"Get fucked."

"I wish I could!"

"Very funny."

He flopped into a chair and stared at her. "Well, are you coming back to work with me or what? If you were still my manager I wouldn't be stuck in this piece of shit movie."

"When Matt divorces me," Jess replied matter-of-factly.

"What will that be?"

She grinned. "Never! I'm a very happy person!"

"Nice to know somebody is," he said ruefully.

Jess sat on the arm of his chair. "I may be slow, but do I detect a note of dissatisfaction here?"

He mugged for her. "Are you kidding? Why would I be dissatisfied? I'm making a movie I hate. I'm stuck in Mexico. And my wife is probably shacked up with Mr. Japan so she can add another million or four to her bank account. Things couldn't be better, Jess. Tell me about *your* life."

Jess ruffled the back of his hair. "Oooh, baby, baby. You want me to talk to Lucky?"

"If you can find her."

"Give me her number."

He sounded disgusted. "If I had it, I would."

"Where is she?"

"Who the fuck knows?"

Jess didn't question further. With Lennie you could only push so far.

Later she said to Matt, "A marriage counselor I'm not. But I have a feeling I should give this one a whirl. Lennie's about ready to blow."

"Don't interfere," warned Matt.

What did *he* know?

Mickey spent the week on the run, expecting Lucky to keep up with him at all times. He dodged from meeting to screening, and in between he stopped for another shower or fresh juice or a screaming fit about something or other.

Occasionally he had Lucky accompany him to the dailies on what he called his bread-and-soup movies, instructing her to take notes of everything he said while sitting in the darkened screening room. His comments ran from "Nice tits" to "Fat ass" to "She's too old" to "Get a close-up on her face when he sticks her with the knife."

He rarely had anything to say about the male actors, who all managed to stay fully dressed in spite of the gore and sex taking place around them.

Lucky discovered the Hollywood difference between hard-core pornography and so-called soft. In hard-core, the men took their clothes off too. In soft, as far as the women were concerned, anything seemed to go. They were forever stripping off their clothes, simulating orgasm, or getting their throats slit. Real classy stuff. With plenty of rape thrown in for good measure.

It was a sorry situation, and one that Lucky had no intention of continuing once she took control.

The three cheapo movies currently in production were all produced by the exciting team of Blackwood and Lombardo. It figures, Lucky thought grimly.

On perusing the books, to which she had free access now that she was ensconced in Mickey's quarters, she found out that the cheapo movies were the biggest money-makers Panther had: mostly abroad, where they scored on every level—theaters, cable, home video, and pay-as-you-view T.V.

The cheapos kept Panther in the black.

The big movies with the star names sometimes made money too. But only sometimes.

Any idiot knew the film business was a gamble. Sometimes you scored, and sometimes you crapped out. With his cheapos, Mickey had loaded the dice in his favor.

Lucky decided she had an interesting challenge ahead of her: How to make movies without exploiting women.

Hmmm . . . maybe she'd exploit men for a change. Not such a bad idea.

By the time she got home at night she was wiped out. Boogie was waiting for her with a strong drink. She ordered either pizza or Chinese, ate, made a few notes, and immediately fell asleep.

She'd called Lennie twice. His reception got cooler and cooler. Finally he informed her in an exasperated tone that he didn't care to hear from her unless she told him exactly where she was.

Fine. If that was the way he wanted it.

When he found out the truth he was going to be very sorry indeed.

Grudge Freeport's idea of doing something nice and making everyone happy was not to fart in public. Apart from that little concession to human dignity, he kept right on going.

Lennie took another week of it. He had Jess and Matt around to keep him calm. When they left, he blew.

"You know something, Grudge? You're an ass-licking, no-talent, drunken slob. And I'm out of here." He yelled this one day after Grudge had screwed up yet another scene.

Grudge took it like a true old-timer. "Fuck off," he said grandly. "All actors never should have left their mother's tit!"

Lennie didn't think about the consequences. He packed and flew back to L.A., spent two days alone at the Malibu house, and then took off for New York.

He did not go to the apartment he and Lucky shared. He vanished. She knew this because Mickey Stolli threw a fit searching for him.

"I'll sue the fucking son of a bitch for everything he's got. Everything! He's not getting away with this. I've got a crew and actors sitting in Acapulco slapping their dicks! It's costing this studio dearly, and that dumb cocksucker's gonna pay. Oh, is he gonna pay!"

Lucky was assigned the awkward task of tracking Lennie Golden down. She perfected a new voice and duly called his current agent and manager. Through secretaries she learned that nobody knew where he was.

"How about his wife?" Mickey screamed. "Isn't he married to some rich broad with a gangster father?"

So that's what it got down to. *Some rich broad with a gangster father.*

Not Lucky Santangelo, businesswoman supreme.

Not Lucky Santangelo, wife and mother.

Some rich broad with a gangster father. Charming!

"I don't know, Mr. Stolli," she said, attempting to remain cool.

"Find out an' tell 'em we're gonna sue."

Later in the day, Lucky took great pleasure in informing Mickey that she had indeed reached Lennie Golden's wife.

"And?" Mickey demanded.

"I can't repeat what she said, Mr. Stolli."

"What'd she say?"

"Uh . . . she said . . . uh . . ."

"Spit it out for crissakes."

"She said to tell you you're a pathetic asshole with cottonwool balls and a black heart."

Mickey was outraged. "Are you shittin' me?"

"I'm sorry, Mr. Stolli."

Mickey made a solemn vow. "As long as I'm here," he said, "Lennie Golden'll never work for this friggin' studio again."

"Quite right," Lucky agreed sympathetically.

That night she had Boogie install a sophisticated bugging system in Mickey's office. All the better to know exactly what was going on.

31

Venus Maria had rock-hard thighs on account of her daily work-outs with a personal trainer. Her stomach was flat and firm, her arms and shoulders lightly muscled since she'd been regularly using weights. She jogged every day and swam fifty lengths in her private pool. She treated her body as if it were a finely tuned instrument, never letting up on her vigorous schedule.

Martin Swanson appreciated every glowing inch. In bed with Venus Maria he felt as if the sex they enjoyed together couldn't get any better—except that every time it did.

Venus Maria had learned plenty from Manuel, Ryan, and Innes. She'd made it her business to find out the details that turned them on. Ryan had liked their taking showers together. Manuel had wanted her to massage his balls with a very expensive, highly scented body lotion. Innes was into being tied up with the lightest of silk scarves. The trick was, he'd told her, never to tear your binding.

Venus Maria had soon discovered what he meant. The exquisite torture of not breaking the silken bonds was excruciating ecstasy. She had saved that particular experience for Martin until she knew the moment was exactly right.

The night before he returned to New York she took him on a trip to heaven and back. First they dined on sushi and champagne. Then they frolicked in her open-air hot tub overlooking the spectacular

Hollywood view. And finally she led him into her bedroom, flicked off the towel around his waist, and instructed him to lie naked on her four-poster bed while she bound him with fine silk scarves.

She knotted the scarves lightly around his wrists, tying them to the bedposts. Then she did the same to his ankles.

"What are you doing?" he asked, putting up the semblance of a fight.

"Relax," she smiled. "Lie back and dream your favorite fantasy."

"I don't have fantasies."

"Unlucky you."

She sat back and admired her work. He was completely helpless as long as he didn't struggle, his excitement already evident.

Venus Maria smiled. What a turn-on! Martin Swanson—Mister New York—at her mercy.

"This is a challenge," she announced. "A game. You break the scarves and the game is over. If you're a good boy we'll play all night."

He fell right into it. "What's the penalty?"

"Ten thousand bucks a scarf," she said boldly.

"High stakes."

"Can you afford it?"

He laughed. "Can you?"

"I'm just the games mistress. I don't have to bet."

"Oh, yes, you do. Give me a time limit. If I don't break the ties— say in one hour—I win and you pay."

"Two hours an' you got a deal."

"One and a half."

"We're not negotiating on a building, Martin."

His hard-on stayed steady. Bartering was obviously another favorite sport.

"One hour and three quarters," he said.

"A deal," she replied. "Goodbye."

"Goodbye who?"

"Goodbye, you. I'll be back when I feel like it."

"Are you serious?"

"Never more."

"C'mon, Venus. What kind of a game is this?"

"A challenge. I told you that before. Let's see if you're up to it, Martin." She left the room.

Talk about a power trip! Little Virginia Venus Maria Sierra from Brooklyn had Martin Swanson—Mr. New York—trussed up and at her mercy.

With a secret smile she remembered the first time she'd set eyes on him. Ten years ago. 1975. She'd been fifteen years old.

Occasionally Virginia Venus Maria Sierra was able to get out of the house. It wasn't often, because with four brothers to look after and a demanding father, there was always work to be done. Oh, yeah, she got out of the house to attend school, but that wasn't the same as recreational fun. Ron, her next-door neighbor and confidante, was all for encouraging her to escape and accompany him on his many trips to Broadway and Times Square.

Ron was a few years older than she, and to her, he was incredibly exciting and daring. He was tall and gangly, and a laugh to be with, totally unlike her burly brothers, who were macho men, full of their own strength and only interested in scoring with any neighborhood girl they could get their hands on. Venus always had a strong suspicion they would try to score with her if given half a chance. She never gave them that chance.

Whenever she was able, she and Ron would wander around New York having fun. Sometimes they would lurk outside the stage door of one of the big Broadway shows waiting for the stars to emerge. Ron kept an autograph book and persuaded her to do the same. It was interesting to see which stars would stop and sign their names, and which celebrities would sweep past, climb into their limousines, and ride off into the night.

"Glamorous, isn't it?" Ron would say with a smile.

And Virginia Venus Maria would nod in total agreement.

"I'm going to be a dancer," Ron confided.

"How are you going to train for that?" she asked. "Who's going to put up the money?"

Ron said he was going to try for an audition at the School of Performing Arts.

"*How do you get to do that?*" Virginia Venus Maria asked curiously.

"*Talent,*" Ron replied.

One Saturday afternoon they were walking down Park Avenue when they saw a crowd gathered outside a church. "*It's a wedding!*" Ron said excitedly. "*I love weddings, don't you?*"

Virginia Venus Maria nodded vigorously.

"*Brides always look so gorgeous,*" Ron exclaimed.

Virginia Venus Maria nodded again, thinking that she never looked gorgeous. She had straight brown hair and a pretty face, but there was nothing special about her, much to her chagrin.

They joined the crowd outside the church, watched and waited. And when the happy couple emerged, Virginia Venus Maria set eyes on Martin Swanson for the first time.

She stood back in awe and watched him. He was handsome in a way she didn't believe. He was handsome straight off the pages of a glossy magazine. He had sandy-colored hair, full lips, and a ready smile for the photographers. He wore a morning suit and a bright red carnation.

Virginia Venus Maria glanced quickly at his bride, a pale and willowy redhead in an expensive white lace gown. They looked like a fairy-tale couple. They looked as if they came from another world.

"*Who are they?*" Virginia Venus Maria asked Ron.

"*Rich,*" Ron replied. "*And that's what we're gonna be some day.*"

The next morning she saw the bridegroom's picture in the paper, along with his new wife. His name was Martin Swanson. Property tycoon. Now married to the beautiful Deena Akveld, a Dutch society woman.

For some unknown reason Virginia Venus Maria clipped the newspaper photograph, stashing it beneath her underwear in her dresser drawer. The picture seemed to represent a fantasy world, and yet it was a world that one day she wanted to be part of. And why not? Virginia Venus Maria had ambition.

Martin Swanson's image stayed with her over the years. She read about him, followed his activities, watched him on television, and read even more about him in the gossip columns. Then one day she finally met him.

Of course, by the time she met him she was Venus Maria, the Venus Maria, and she pretended she had no idea who he was. Cooper Turner introduced them. The Cooper Turner.

Martin smiled that special bullshit smile of his and flirted outrageously. She looked around to see if his wife was present, but the coolly beautiful Deena appeared to have taken the night off.

When Martin sent her flowers the next day she was delighted. And when he turned up in Los Angeles a few weeks later, even more so.

By this time she'd found out more about him, having questioned Cooper relentlessly.

Cooper was amused. "Have you got a hot spot for Martin?" he asked, raising a quizzical eyebrow.

"Why? Would it bother you if I did?" she retorted.

"I don't know," Cooper said. "I thought I was going to be your golden boy."

Venus Maria laughed. "Cooper, you're everyone's golden boy!"

"And you think Martin is a virgin?"

"I just think he's . . . fascinating."

Cooper looked at her for a long moment. "I may as well tell you," he said, "Martin's had a lot of girlfriends. A lot of beautiful, talented girlfriends. And he always goes back to Deena. No question. Deena is in his life to stay."

"Only as long as he wants her to," Venus Maria pointed out.

"You're a determined little thing, huh?"

"Nobody ever accused me of being shy."

When Martin telephoned, Venus was not surprised. She invited him to her house. He arrived within the hour. "I'm not going to sleep with you until I know you," she warned him. "That might take a couple of years, right?"

"I feel I know you now," he said. "I've read every press clipping I could find. Why don't you look at my press file? Maybe we can save time that way."

"Are you interested in saving time?"

"I'm interested in being with a woman like you."

Five weeks later they consummated the deal. In the meantime he'd made three trips to the Coast and she'd visited New York twice.

The flirtation was hot, the anticipation almost better than the act.

*But the act wasn't bad either. Venus Maria staged a long weekend at
a friend's house in Big Sur. She made it a weekend to remember.
Scented candles, the best champagne, music, a four-poster bed, and
raunchy, unabandoned sex.*

*Their affair had been going on for several months and now she
wanted it to be more.*

*All she had to do was wait for Martin to leave his wife, get a
divorce, and marry her.*

Venus Maria had the uncanny knack of tapping into other people's
fantasies—hence the enormous success of her videos. She went for
the forbidden and dressed it up as entertainment. She could play
any role from little girl lost to voracious sexual superwoman. Her
strut was every bit as good as her soft gentle side. She could kick ass
or cuddle up with equal aplomb.

She could—if she so desired—tailor her act to fit any man's fantasy.

Martin Swanson said he didn't have fantasies.

Bull

Shit.

Martin Swanson was a man. He had fantasies all right. And Venus
Maria had figured out the one to really turn him on—that all-time
favorite, two girls together.

But Venus Maria had no plans to appear as one of the girls. Group
sex did not interest her. She liked her sexual experiences to be between two people. Private and personal and wildly sensuous.

Martin needed shaking up. He was too stiff-assed, more concerned about his next deal than his sensual pleasure, although,
Venus Maria had to admit, she'd already loosened him up considerably.

Late at night, alone in her bed, alone in Los Angeles, she often
wondered if Deena was receiving the benefit of Martin's new experience. He swore he never slept with his wife anymore, but he was a
man, and all men lied about sex. Especially married men.

Venus Maria loved Martin. She didn't know why. But she did
know she had to have him.

It wasn't his money, because she had plenty of her own.

It wasn't his appearance, because although he was an attractive man, he was no Mel Gibson.

It wasn't his personality, because even when he turned on the charm, he was not exactly Mr. Nice.

Love's a bitch, Venus Maria thought bitterly, and hurried to rendezvous with Ron, who had brought two expensive hookers to her house, supplied by his friend Madame Loretta (Ron collected weird friends—useful on this occasion).

The girls did not look like whores. One of them resembled a college cheerleader—in fact, she'd dressed the part. And the other was a five-foot-tall Oriental girl with shiny jet hair hanging below her ass.

Ron grinned. He adored intrigue. "Meet Tai and Lemon."

Venus Maria raised an eyebrow. "Lemon?"

"That's me!" squeaked the cheerleader. "My real name too! I love your records!"

That was the trouble with being famous. Everybody knew your business.

Trying to remain cool and uninvolved, Venus Maria told the girls exactly what she wished them to do, adding somewhat apologetically, "It's for a friend's birthday, y'know. A special treat."

"*Veree* special," interjected Ron, with a sly grin.

"Shut up!" whispered Venus Maria.

The girls were true professionals. They knew exactly what was expected of them. Stripping down to silky undergarments, they produced a lethal-looking vibrator and a bottle of scented oil, and entered the bedroom where Martin Swanson lay waiting.

Venus Maria estimated he'd been alone for twenty minutes. Long enough to drive him a little bit crazy.

She hurried to the two-way mirror she'd had specially installed.

"Can I watch too?" Ron begged, following her.

"No, you can't," she replied sternly. "Just wait and get these two girls out of here when I'm ready."

"Spoilsport!"

"Since when did *you* like watching girls?"

"Oh, I don't care about *them*. It's himself I wouldn't mind taking a peek at."

"Ron! Behave yourself!"

Martin was still tied up when the girls entered the bedroom. Determined not to lose the bet, he didn't move.

Tai and Lemon ignored him as they started in on each other. First they kissed. And then they touched nipples, delicately brushing silk against silk.

Breathlessly Venus Maria watched as Martin rose to the occasion.

Tai undid Lemon's bra, and the pretty blonde's breasts tumbled free, surprisingly large and firm.

Martin groaned.

Tai fixed her mouth onto a welcoming nipple.

Martin groaned louder.

Lemon divested herself of her panties. She had shaved her pubic area, and the skin there was very white.

Tai's long dark hair swept downward as she bent to kiss between Lemon's legs. Obligingly, Lemon spread wide.

"Oh, God, Venus!" Martin managed, desperately trying not to move.

Tai stopped attending to Lemon and unclipped her own bra before stepping out of her panties. Her black bush was forest-thick. All the better for Lemon to return the favor and bury her blond curls.

Venus Maria could see Martin was desperate for release. His penis stood erect and ready. But still he didn't break the bonds.

Tai stepped back from Lemon, took the bottle of oil, and squeezed it over the breasts of both.

Then Lemon reached for the vibrator, switched it on, and held it to Tai's pubic mound.

Martin reached orgasm, spurting all over himself.

"Goddamn it!" he muttered. "God*damn!*"

Time to do away with the entertainment. Venus Maria entered the room, waving the girls out.

They picked up their things and exited quickly.

"Hmmm." Venus Maria stared mesmerizingly at her prisoner. "You've been a bad boy. Look at the mess you've made."

"Come here," he said desperately.

"Wait!" she commanded.

"Come here!" he insisted.

She walked slowly into the bathroom, came back with a fluffy white towel and wiped him clean.

"Not such a big shot on campus, after all," she sighed.

"You're unbelievable!"

"I try to please."

"I want to fuck you."

"What else is new?"

"I want to—"

"What?"

"Spend more time with you."

"That's nice. How about your wife?"

"She's in New York."

"I know."

"Come here, Venus. Untie me. All bets are off."

She glanced at her Cartier tank watch, a present from Martin the last time he was in town. "You have another thirty-five minutes to go."

"I want out."

"Pay me."

"No way."

"Then . . . stay where you are and keep quiet. A bet is a bet is a bet is a—"

"I *know* what a bet is."

She had on denim cutoffs and a white T-shirt. Standing at the end of the bed she did a slow strip. Underneath she wore crotchless red lace panties and a cutout black leather bra—hooker gear designed to excite.

Stretching her arms into the air she grinned provocatively. "I think I'll go see Cooper," she said.

Martin broke the silk scarves in one bound and was on her like a randy New York tycoon.

"You're something else," he said.

"And so are you," she whispered softly. "So are you."

32

Harry Browning took his time deciding what he should do about Luce. He brooded about it on and off for a couple of weeks before approaching her. He couldn't help noticing her promotion. All of a sudden this strange woman who'd entered the studio as Sheila Hervey's niece was suddenly ensconced as Mickey Stolli's personal secretary. And where was Olive? The rumor was she'd broken her leg and was not coming back for a while. How convenient.

Harry waited until Luce was sitting alone in the commissary one lunchtime and approached her.

She glanced up at him. "Hello, Harry."

He sat down at her table without being invited. "What are you up to?" he demanded accusingly.

She started straight at him. Two more weeks to go and she was out of this charade. "I beg your pardon?" she said calmly.

He fiddled with his spectacles, took them off, cleaned them with a napkin, and put them on again. "What exactly are you up to?" he repeated excitedly. "I know it's something."

Lucky remained cool. "I'm not getting your drift."

"I'm no fool," Harry Browning said agitatedly. "You lured me to your apartment, got me drunk, and tried to wheedle information out of me."

This was unexpected. Lucky wasn't sure how to play it. "I've no idea what you're talking about," she said at last. "I never lured you anywhere. You asked me out and I offered to cook you dinner. It's not my fault you hit the booze."

Harry narrowed his eyes beneath his wire-rimmed spectacles. He was unhappy with the way this was going. He'd expected her to be more unsettled, not quite so in control. Determined to get to the point, he pressed on. "I know what you're up to," he said.

"If you know," she replied coolly, "how come you're asking *me?*"

This stumped Harry for a moment. He didn't like her attitude. He didn't like her. And he certainly didn't like the fact that she'd made him turn to the bottle again. "Does Mickey Stolli know who you are?" he demanded hotly.

"Who am I?" she replied, staring him down.

"Who are you?" he persisted. "Why don't *you* tell *me?* Or do I have to ask Mr. Stolli myself."

"What would you ask him exactly?"

"To investigate your background. I know that's a wig you're wearing. And you don't need glasses. I also know you visited Abe Panther the other night."

She stared him down. "Then perhaps you should ask Mr. Panther what this is all about."

Harry lapsed into silence. Spotting a mark on the tablecloth, he went to work, rubbing vigorously with his napkin.

Lucky took a slow beat. "Whose side are you on, Harry?" she asked, keeping an even tone.

"What do you mean?" he asked suspiciously.

"You're well aware of the kind of product this studio is turning out. You know how it used to be."

"It used to be great," he said vehemently.

Lucky nodded. "It can be great again, Harry. Just trust me."

He was indignant. "Why should I trust somebody who tried to get me drunk?"

"I had no idea you had a . . . problem."

He jumped on that one. "Did Mr. Panther tell you?"

"Abe Panther never mentioned you."

She wasn't sure whether he believed her or not. But she decided she wasn't hanging around to find out. She got up from the table and prepared to leave. "Harry," she said, "you'd be doing me an enormous favor if you didn't tell anybody what's going on."

"I'll do what I like," he said curtly.

"In two weeks' time," she said slowly, "everything will be clear."

"I'll do what I like," he repeated. "You'd better be careful. I'm watching you."

Hurrying back to the office, she thought about things. Another week working for Mickey Stolli. Another week closer to the end of this charade. And what had she discovered? That most people were stealing. That there were a lot of petty scams going on. And that men in the film business used women as commodities.

When she took over, Mickey Stolli was out, and so were most of his little band of merry men. She already had her lawyer, Morton Sharkey, preparing a list of suitable replacements.

"Let's bring some women executives aboard," she'd suggested, and Morton had agreed. Already he was coming up with suggestions, although there weren't that many women executives to choose from.

In the meantime, Lennie was still on the missing list. Nobody seemed to know his whereabouts.

She knew why he was doing it. Lennie had this childish habit of retaliating with more of the same. She'd done it to him, so he figured he'd pay her back.

She really couldn't blame him, because if the situation were reversed, she'd probably behave in exactly the same way.

Her conversation with Harry Browning had been disturbing. What exactly *did* he know? Maybe she should have stayed and talked to him some more. But the quickest way out of a difficult situation seemed to be retreat.

She made it back to the office five minutes before Mickey. He returned from his lunch early and shut himself away, telling Lucky that when Leslie Kane arrived she was to keep her waiting. "And if Eddie calls," he added, "don't let him know his wife's here."

Lucky had realized from Mickey's previous conversation and meeting with Eddie that they were indeed into some distribution scam with certain underworld figures. She'd instructed Boogie to investigate, and Boogie had come up with the news that Eddie Kane was dealing with Carlos Bonnatti.

It was a strange and unwelcome coincidence. Carlos, the scumbag brother of Santino, and son of Enzio. The Bonnattis had always been enemies of the Santangelos. Their feud went back to the good old Vegas days. And now that Santino and Enzio were deceased, it was Carlos who controlled the family drug and porno empire.

It's weird, Lucky thought, how the Bonnattis stayed connected to her life. She would be more than happy if she never had to hear the name again.

From what Boogie was able to find out, Eddie Kane had made an arrangement with the Bonnatti organization to distribute the Bonnatti porno films in Europe, hiding them along with legitimate Panther product. If Lucky read Mickey correctly, he was anxious to get out of the deal, and wisely so, for Lucky knew it was a big mistake to fuck with the Bonnattis.

Leslie Kane turned up promptly at three o'clock. She gave Lucky a friendly smile. "I'm here to see Mr. Stolli," she said brightly. "My name is Leslie Kane. I have an appointment."

Lucky was surprised. She hadn't realized Eddie was married to such a fresh-looking beauty. "He's expecting you. Take a seat, I'll let him know you're here."

Leslie sat down, picked up a copy of *People* magazine and leafed through it. After a moment she put the magazine down. "I'm not too early, am I?" she asked anxiously.

Lucky glanced up. "You're exactly on time. Your appointment is for three."

Leslie nodded thankfully. "That's right."

Mickey kept her waiting twenty-five minutes. He didn't come to his office door to greet her. Lucky had noticed he only made that meaningful move for major stars. As soon as Leslie entered his office, Lucky put on her miniature headphones, activated the tape machine, and began picking up every word.

. . .

"Sit down, sit down," Mickey said, gesturing at Leslie.

She sat in a chair opposite him, full of rapt attention. "You wanted to see me, Mr. Stolli?"

He cleared his throat and shuffled some papers around his desk. "Uh . . . y'can call me Mickey."

Leslie, the wide-eyed beauty, gazed at him. "Thank you."

Mickey wondered where Eddie had stumbled upon this Iowa beauty queen. She still had corn in her hair. "Honey," he said, "we got ourselves a problem."

"What's that, Mr. Stolli?" she asked, full of concern. "I mean . . . Mickey."

Oh, God! He'd found out about her past!

"Your husband is a jerk," Mickey said flatly. "I've tried to help him. God knows I've tried. Over the years I've given him jobs an' he's screwed up. I've given him help, an' he's thrown it back in my face. And now he's got us into a mess I refuse to take responsibility for."

Leslie lowered her eyes. She had long, sweeping lashes. "I'm sorry," she whispered, full of relief that this meeting wasn't about her.

"It's not your fault," said Mickey, wondering what she was like in bed.

"Then why am I here?" she asked, frowning slightly.

Mickey chewed the end of his pen. "You're here because Eddie's in trouble," he said. "And this time *I* can't help him."

"What kind of trouble?" she asked, sweeping lashes going into overdrive.

"A million big ones."

Leslie felt a flutter in the pit of her stomach. She hadn't taken Eddie seriously when a couple of weeks ago she'd asked him if something was bothering him and he'd replied, "Nothing that a million bucks and a little cooperation from Mickey Stolli can't fix."

"What can I do?" she asked earnestly, leaning forward.

"You'd better get Eddie to dig into his pockets and come up with the money," Mickey said harshly, " 'cause if he doesn't, he's gonna find himself wearing cement boots on the wrong end of Santa Monica Pier."

"Mr. Stolli . . . uh, Mickey . . . Eddie did mention this to me a couple of weeks ago. I thought he was joking."

"You go into business, you take the consequences. Eddie put together a deal. He brought it to me. And then he cheated me *and* his other partners, and now he's got to pay the price. He tells me he has no money. What's he done with it, Leslie, spent it on you?"

She sat up straighter in her chair. "No, certainly not."

"That's good, because he's going to need it and I can't help him. If he thinks I'm bailing him out yet again—I ain't doing it. He's on his own and he'd better pay up or he's in over the top." Mickey picked up a script and began to flip through it. "That's all," he said brusquely.

The meeting was over.

Leslie got up to leave. "I'll do what I can," she murmured.

She had a pair of legs on her that could strangle a giraffe! "You'd better," he said gruffly.

"I will," she assured him earnestly.

"Oh," Mickey added, "and do yourself another favor. Get that asshole husband of yours into drug rehab. He's snorting his life away. I hope he hasn't got you doing the same thing."

She was indignant. "I don't touch drugs."

"Make sure you stick to that."

Leslie rushed out of the office.

Lucky watched her on her way. Mickey Stolli was a mean bastard. What did he expect a young girl like Leslie to do about the mess Eddie had gotten them into?

Mickey left his office soon after. "I'm going out," he said, on his way to the door.

Lucky knew better than to ask where. When he wanted to reveal his destination he did so. She figured another visit to Warner was about to take place.

"What time can I expect you back, Mr. Stolli?" she asked politely. This perfect-secretary shit was driving her nuts!

"Expect me when you see me."

"And how shall I handle your afternoon appointments?"

"Cancel 'em."

Fuck you, asshole. "Yes, Mr. Stolli."

232

It was surprising that people were prepared to do business with Mickey at all. He cared about nobody except himself.

Twenty minutes after he left the building, Venus Maria appeared in the office. She wandered in wearing torn jeans, an oversize T-shirt, sneakers, and a Lakers baseball cap.

At first Lucky thought she was a messenger. "Can I help you?" she asked.

"I need five minutes of Mickey's time," Venus Maria said. "A mere five minutes so I can tell him what I think, an' then I'm outta here."

Lucky recognized her voice. "I'm sorry, he's not in his office."

"Shit!" Venus Maria exclaimed. "I really needed to talk to him today."

"Is there something I can tell him?"

Venus Maria threw a script onto Lucky's desk. "Yeah. Tell Mr. S. this script stinks. He promised me a strong woman, and naturally he's come up with the usual dumb bimbo victim. There's no way I'm playing this sexist crap."

Lucky picked up the offending script. It was *Bombshell*, Mickey's pet project.

"I'll be happy to tell him," she said.

Venus Maria threw herself into a chair. "It's not your fault. Jesus! When are these dumb jerks ever gonna learn?"

Here was a woman after Lucky's own heart. "Are you not doing it because of the way it's written?" she ventured.

"You can bet your ass I'm not," Venus Maria replied vehemently. "I only do things I believe in."

"That's the right attitude," Lucky encouraged, forgetting her role for a moment.

Venus Maria glanced at her. "It's nice to know you agree. All girls together, huh?"

"It's about time somebody stood up to these . . . producers."

"Hey, you'd better not let your boss hear you talk that way." She looked around. "Where's the English angel?"

"Olive's on sick leave. She broke her leg."

Venus Maria stifled a laugh. "What did Mickey do, kick her out of the office?"

Not wanting to blow her cover, Lucky didn't respond, although she realized here was a woman she could get along with just fine.

Venus Maria stood up, yawned, and stretched. "Well, I guess it's back to the grind. I'm on the set if he dares talk to me. He can call me in my dressing room or at home later. Just tell him this is *not* the story line we discussed. The woman in this script is a victim, and this baby ain't playing no victims."

Lucky was delighted. Venus Maria had a big future at Panther. She would make sure of that.

33

Eddie was pacing restlessly around the house when Leslie arrived home. He hadn't been to the studio for three days. He looked haggard, there were bags under his eyes, and the beginnings of a full beard. "Where have you been?" he demanded, staring at her accusingly.

Leslie wasn't sure whether she was supposed to tell him she'd been summoned to visit Mickey or not. She decided honesty was the best way to handle this. "Um . . . I went to see Mickey Stolli," she said, taking off her jacket.

Eddie immediately exploded. "What the fuck did you go see him for?"

"Because he asked me to," she explained patiently.

"And if he asked you to give him a blow job, you'd do that, too, huh?"

She walked into the kitchen. "Eddie, don't be silly."

"Quit talkin' to me like I'm a schmuck, O.K.? You go see Mickey an' you don't even tell me about it. Then you come back here an' try to put me down. What's the game, Leslie?"

She looked at him with wide eyes. "We're in trouble, Eddie, aren't we?"

"Trouble?" he snorted. "What kind of *trouble* are we in, honey?"

She picked up the kettle and began filling it with water. "Mickey says we're in trouble. He says you owe a lot of money."

Eddie paced up and down. "Oh, he says *I* owe money, does he? Well let me tell you this, baby. The studio owes money. They're responsible. He's in this as much as I am. And there's no way he's getting out."

"Mickey says you owe a million dollars."

Eddie snapped. "Why is he bringing *you* into it?"

Leslie shook her head. "Maybe he thinks I can help."

Eddie laughed mirthlessly. "Help? *You?* Who's he kidding?"

Leslie looked at him with a hurt expression. "Maybe I can," she said defensively.

"Come on, baby, it's a million bucks we're talkin' here, not ten cents. Wise up."

"What are you going to do?"

Eddie shook his head. "I haven't figured it out yet. But whatever it is, Mickey's gonna to be on for the ride. Panther can pay without blinkin'—why should *I* take the fall?"

"Eddie," Leslie said tentatively, "Mickey says you've got a drug problem. He says you should do something about it."

Eddie exploded. "What's his friggin' game? It's none of his goddamn business what I've got. So I do a little coke occasionally. Big fucking deal."

"More than occasionally."

"Hey, hey, hey, who am I married to, Mother Teresa?"

"I only want to help you."

"I'll tell you how to help me, baby. Just shut the fuck up and leave me alone, O.K.?"

Leslie nodded miserably. "O.K."

Warner was not at home. Mickey couldn't believe he'd driven all the way to her apartment to find she wasn't there. They'd arranged the rendezvous on the phone the previous day, and it wasn't like Warner to break a date. He rang the doorbell, and then in frustration kicked the door a few times before angrily making his way down to the underground garage. Climbing into his Porsche, he revved the engine.

Mickey Stolli liked to get laid on a regular basis. Warner satisfied him, but she had to be there when he needed her.

Sitting in his car he made a call to Ford Werne. Ford had often mentioned in passing that he did not believe in having affairs, he believed in paying for it. Mickey had laughed in his face. "Paying for pussy? In this town?" he'd exclaimed. "L.A. is free pussy heaven!"

Ford had responded in a calm and sensible way. "You pay for it, Mickey, you know exactly what you're getting. They don't want a part in your movie. They don't want a piece of your life. They don't want you to take them to Hawaii, give them head, and buy them dresses. They do what *you* want. It's the perfect situation. Sex without guilt, served up exactly as you like it."

Mickey had visions of a Chicano hooker on the corner of Vermont and Sunset in a fake leather miniskirt, fluorescent tube top and ten-inch heels.

As if reading his mind, Ford had said, "And let me tell you something else. The girls I sleep with are far more beautiful than any transient date."

"Where do you find them?" Mickey had asked curiously.

"That's the great thing," Ford had replied. "I don't find them, Loretta does."

"Who's Loretta?"

"She's the greatest little madam in town. She has a house in the hills and she hand-picks all her girls. They're only in action for a few months, and let me tell you this, they're gorgeous."

It sounded like a great deal for those who were interested. After Ford had told him about it, Mickey heard the name Madame Loretta from a couple of other guys. He'd never given it a whirl because he'd always had Warner standing by. But today he needed action, and he needed it immediately.

When Ford came on the line he requested Madame Loretta's number.

Ford chuckled softly. "Coming around to my way of thinking?" he asked.

Mickey lowered his voice, even though he was sitting in his car where nobody could possibly hear him. "Is this woman discreet?"

Ford reassured him. "She gives the word 'discreet' a whole new meaning. I'll call her and tell her you're on your way."

"Do that," Mickey said. He didn't like asking anybody for a favor, but today he had no choice.

Madame Loretta greeted him like an oversolicitous Jewish mother. She was a plump woman with glowing skin and a warm smile. "Welcome, welcome," she beamed, leading him into a large living room overlooking the city view. "Can I get you a refreshment? Coffee, tea, a drink?"

"You know what I'm here for," Mickey said, getting right to the point.

Loretta smiled warmly. "Oh, yes, and you won't be disappointed. Now tell me, what are your preferences?"

Mickey cleared his throat. "Do you have any black girls?"

"I have a lovely black girl," Madame Loretta replied. "She's a college graduate, clean, works hard. You'll be very happy."

"Can I see her now?" Mickey asked.

Madame Loretta was not put out. "Give me five minutes," she said and left the room.

Mickey gazed out over the view. How simple it would be if he could have great sex with his wife. But there were too many hurdles to overcome with Abigaile. Too many conversations to survive before one could even think about sex, and in the end it was too much of a hassle.

Madame Loretta returned to the room and smiled reassuringly. "Yvette will be here shortly."

"I'd like to see her first," Mickey said. "Before I make a decision."

Madame Loretta nodded knowingly. "I can assure you, you'll be very happy. I never make a mistake."

Every evening Lucky tried to work out the tangled web of business deals going down at Panther Studios. She knew about the scam with the distribution overseas of the porno movies, but apparently Mickey had decided to make this Eddie's problem, not the studio's. His position was, Eddie had got them in, it was up to him to get them out.

It was quite obvious Eddie had been stealing all over, and that Mickey didn't care to bail him out.

Then there was Harry Browning to deal with. What was he going to do? Was he planning to blow her cover before she was ready? She just had to wait and see.

Boogie had hired a secretary to come to the house each night, sit in a room, and type out the transcripts of Mickey's taped conversations. They made interesting reading.

Working nine to five was an exhausting business. Kissing Mickey Stolli's ass every day for hours on end was depressing to say the least. Lucky wasn't used to being in a subservient position, and it didn't suit her.

It was also depressing not to know where Lennie was. Boogie was working on tracking him down.

In London, Bobby whined on the phone. It was unlike him. "Mommy, Mommy, when are you coming? I haven't seen you for ages. Where are you?"

"Don't worry, we'll all be together soon, sweetheart," she assured him, feeling full of guilt.

And then she remembered she hadn't called Brigette since she'd started this caper. Quickly she placed a call to the boarding school Brigette attended.

A secretary informed her the school was closed for the summer and Brigette had returned to New York and her grandmother.

"Freedom," Lucky whispered to herself. "I need my freedom."

34

Nona Webster belonged to a crazy family. Brigette had never met anybody quite like them before. Effie, Nona's mother, was an extraordinary-looking woman. No more than five feet tall, and bone-thin, she had hair even redder than her daughter's, worn in a strange cockatoo style with a renegade clump of brilliant green at the front. Her makeup was bright and unusual, and her clothes reflected the image of a woman who'd never accepted convention.

On the other hand, Yul Webster, Effie's husband, was a very proper-looking man. Tall and imposing, he wore Savile Row suits, silk shirts, and handmade shoes, and his only concessions to his wife's outlandish taste were his ties, which were designed by Effie and made up specially for him. Yul's ties featured hand-painted naked women, birds in flight, airplanes landing—any subject that took Effie's fancy. And he wore them with panache.

"My parents are slightly weird," Nona warned her before they arrived in New York—an understatement to say the least.

Weird they might be, but warm and friendly they certainly were. They welcomed Brigette into their home as if she were a member of the family.

"They take drugs," Nona confessed rather sheepishly. "I've learned to ignore it. Actually, it's only a little snort of recreational coke here and there, and they're into grass. You know what it is, they're kind of bogged down in that whole sixties thing. Just pretend you don't notice, and if they offer you anything, say no."

Brigette understood. "I went through my drug stage when I was fourteen," she explained.

Nona nodded. "Another coincidence. So did I."

"Karma."

"Definitely." Warmly Nona took her friend's arm. "Y'know, I really feel comfortable with you," she confided. "We're so alike."

"Alike—but different."

"You know what I mean," Nona said.

The Websters' New York penthouse was a splash of color from the moment you entered. They'd settled on a startling array of modern furniture. The walls were painted black and covered with contemporary art. Their paintings made a striking statement.

Every week they threw an enormous party attended by an army of beautiful and talented people.

"A few months ago Venus Maria was here," Nona confided. "She's the best. I got to stare at her all night!"

Brigette was impressed. "Amazing!" she said.

"Absolutely," agreed Nona. "I love meeting interesting people, don't you?"

"Where's your brother?" Brigette asked curiously.

"Don't worry, he'll turn up. Whenever he needs money he's here." Nona nodded wisely. "That's his thing—getting money out of anyone he can."

"What's his name?"

"Paul," Nona replied. "They must have been having a normal day when they named him."

Brigette picked up a framed photo from the piano and studied it. "Is this him?" she asked.

"Handsome, isn't he?" Nona said.

"Not bad," Brigette lied. She thought he was gorgeous. "What does he do?"

"He's an artist. Unsuccessful. Paints bloody great canvases of naked people. If he asks you to pose for him, say no."

"Right—like I'd say yes!"

"We're going to have a terrific summer." Nona sighed happily. "I have a feeling, don't you?"

Brigette nodded.

Deena Swanson and Effie Webster were best friends. An odd coupling, but one that seemed to work. They'd actually been friends for many years since Deena first came to America. They'd met when Effie had visited the showroom where Deena worked and picked out several pieces of furniture.

When Deena began dating Martin Swanson, Effie had immediately suggested she should think very seriously about marrying him. "Darling, the man is going places," Effie had assured her. "And methinks you should go right along with him."

Deena didn't need much persuading. She thought Martin was attractive and killer-sharp. Definitely a man on his way to the top.

Martin and Yul did not get along quite so well. Yul found Martin boring. "The man has an ego the size of the Empire State Building," he told Effie.

"As long as it's only his ego, darling!" she replied gaily.

When Martin started to sleep around, the first person Deena confided in was Effie. "What shall I do?" she'd wailed.

"Ignore it," Effie had advised. "Most men play—it's their damn libido! If you take no notice they soon get bored and come home to Momma. After all, a lay is a lay, but a wife is a lifetime commitment. The very thought of the alimony involved drives them straight back into your arms."

"How about Yul?" Deena wanted to know.

"I couldn't care less," Effie had replied briskly. "As long as he comes home."

"But you would care if it interfered with your marriage."

Quite firmly Effie had said, "*Nothing* will ever interfere with my marriage."

Effie Webster obviously adored her only daughter. She took both Brigette and Nona to Saks, and then on to Trump Tower, where they shopped until they couldn't carry any more bags.

Anything Nona asked for, her mother bought her. "I told you," Nona whispered to Brigette. "They spend everything they make. My parents are crazy!"

After shopping, Effie took them to lunch at the Russian Tea Room, where they spotted Rudolf Nureyev and Paul Newman lunching at different tables.

"What do you get up to when you're in town with your grandmother?" Nona asked, wolfing delicious blinis.

Brigette grimaced. "Charlotte's really boring. She never takes me anywhere."

"What was your mother like when she was alive?"

"Well," Brigette replied slowly, thinking about it. "She was kind of fun. At least we did things. We were always flying off to stay with my grandfather on his island. Or to the fashion shows in Paris. We used to travel all over the world. It was exciting."

"You must miss her," Nona said sympathetically, touching her friend's arm.

Brigette nodded sadly. "Yes, I do," she replied, realizing for the first time that she did miss Olympia very much indeed.

Nona's brother, Paul, turned up on Sunday wearing dirty jeans, scuffed cowboy boots, a black T-shirt, and a distressed-leather motorcycle jacket. He was thin and intense looking, and he did not have the family red hair. His hair was long and dark, and worn in a tight ponytail. His eyes were covered by dark shades.

Nona greeted him brightly.

"I'm here for money," he announced.

"The story of your life." Nona sighed. "Don't I at least get a greeting? A kiss? A hug? Anything?"

"You got bucks, you get a greeting."

"Thanks a lot! It's so nice to find all this brotherly love flowing in my direction."

Paul threw himself into a chair, removed his dark shades, and stared straight at Brigette. "Who's this?" he asked rudely.

"The one girl you can't resist," Nona replied.

"Too young," said Paul.

"Uh-uh." Nona shook her head. "Wait until you hear what she's got that you want."

"Too young," Paul repeated.

Brigette was not sure she was enjoying this conversation. Who did this idiot think he was?

"This is my new best friend, Brigette," Nona said, introducing her at last.

"Hiya, Brigette," Paul said casually.

"Stanislopoulos," Nona added.

Paul raised an eyebrow. "As in *the?*" he questioned, brightening considerably.

Nona grinned triumphantly, "You've got it."

Paul's stare intensified. "I'd like to ask for your hand in marriage," he said, staring at Brigette.

She went along with the game. "Too late. You're much too old for me."

Nona laughed delightedly.

"How about a second chance?" Paul begged.

"I told you, didn't I?" Nona said. "Money. That's all this stinker cares about. He doesn't have a heart, he has a cash register!"

"Is there anything else?" Paul asked, checking Brigette out.

Effie entered the room dressed from head to toe in flaming orange.

"You look like a mynah bird who just got a nasty shock," Paul remarked. "What *is* that outfit?"

Effie smiled. Obviously the Websters were used to Paul and took no notice of his rudeness. "That's no way to ask for money," she admonished, shaking a finger at him. "Naughty, naughty."

"How come everybody is under the impression I only come here for money?" Paul complained.

"Because it's true," Nona said.

Watching this family scene, Brigette decided that even though he was exceptionally rude, Paul Webster was perhaps the best-looking man she'd ever seen.

But Brigette knew what handsome meant. It meant danger, excitement, and then even more danger.

She was wise enough to steer clear.

There were times in life to get away, and this was one of them. Lennie rented a loft in the Village and holed up. As long as he had instant coffee, a bottle of scotch, and plenty of yellow legal pads, he was happy.

Walking out on the movie was the best move he'd ever made. Compromise and Lennie Golden did not mix. He needed to be creative, and sometimes the pressures of stardom stifled the creative spirit.

Not to mention Lucky's pissing off to Japan.

He'd had the "movie-star-in-a-bad-film" trip, and now it was time to get back to work.

It occurred to him if he wanted a successful movie he'd better sit down and write it himself. And being alone was exactly what he needed.

He was well aware that his agent and manager were probably frantically searching for him. But he also knew he was not in the mood to be bothered, so he covered his tracks, making a large cash withdrawal at his bank and not writing any more checks.

The only person he phoned was Jess.

"Listen," he told her, "I've got to be by myself for a while. If Lucky calls, tell her you've heard from me and I'm fine, nothing else."

Jess replied they were both playing games and should grow up.

"This isn't a revenge move," he explained patiently. "Lucky's in Japan. When she gets back, I'll see her. Right now she doesn't want me to contact her. So I won't. That's not playing games."

"Oh, c'mon," Jess said disgustedly. "You're worse than a couple of kids."

"Whatever," he replied. "I'll call you in a week." He hung up.

Lennie enjoyed solitary confinement. It gave him the freedom he required. From early in the morning until late at night he sat at a large table by the window and wrote. Writing made him feel good. It released the pressure.

When he wasn't writing he thought about Lucky and tried to figure out what was really going on between them. She worked in

New York. He worked in L.A. And in between they saw each other for brief spells.

Oh, yes. The sex was great. Sure. Why not? But great sex wasn't enough. He wanted more.

The thoughts he'd had about taking a year off were getting stronger. If they didn't do it, he had a bad feeling their marriage was going to fall apart. It wasn't what he wanted.

He kept on writing and found his script turning into the story of their life together.

Right now he didn't know the ending. He only hoped it would be a happy one.

35

When Martin Swanson arrived back in New York from the Coast, Deena greeted him like a dutiful wife, even though she feared the worst. Each time he went away she feared the worst. Was Martin getting ready to tell her their marriage was over?

"How was L.A.?" she asked, as soon as he walked into their bedroom.

"Hot," he replied, loosening his tie.

"And business? Did we get a studio?"

Using the word "we" was an important part of the strategy she'd decided to employ. Martin wasn't getting any help from her. If he wanted a divorce he was going to have to tell her himself.

"Still negotiating," he said. "But it looks like we're going to take over Orpheus."

"Weren't you interested in Panther?"

Martin sat down on the edge of the bed. "I met with Mickey Stolli. He doesn't seem to have any say in the matter. The studio still belongs to Abe Panther, and apparently he doesn't want to sell. Although Mickey promised he'd have his wife talk to the old man— she's Abe's granddaughter."

"What's Mickey Stolli like?" Deena asked, moving on to the interested wife role.

"A Hollywood type," Martin replied, yawning. "Full of ideas. He's made Panther into a money-making machine. They produce a lot of movies nobody's ever heard of."

"What kind of movies?"

"You know the sort of thing," Martin replied offhandedly. "Tits and ass."

"That's nice," Deena said, thinking to herself—*your girlfriend would fit nicely into that kind of film.* "Who else did you see while you were out there?"

"The usual."

Deena imagined The Bitch must be putting on the pressure by now. Martin didn't give a hint of trouble.

"The Websters are throwing a party in your honor next week," she said.

"Why?" he asked, shrugging off his jacket.

"Because it's your birthday," she said. "Had you forgotten?"

As a matter of fact he had. There was so much on his mind that the last thing he wanted to think about was getting a year older. He got off the bed and walked over to the mirror, peering at himself. "I guess I don't look too bad for nearly forty-six," he said, waiting for the compliment.

"You're a handsome man, Martin," Deena replied, coming up behind him. He'd always thrived on flattery.

He turned around and kissed her lightly on the cheek. "I've a few calls to make," he said. "I'll be in my study."

He left their bedroom and went downstairs. It was quite clear Deena had no idea anything was amiss. She obviously did not suspect this latest infidelity. He wondered how he was going to broach the subject of divorce if it ever came to that. Venus Maria had told him if he wanted to be with her he was going to have to think about being with her permanently. Otherwise it was goodbye.

Martin hadn't made up his mind yet. But it was a thought.

"One, two, three, four. One, two, three, four."

Venus Maria's personal trainer was a son of a bitch. He worked her like a dog.

"One, two, three, four. One, two, three, four."

Sweat was pouring off her, yet he didn't quit. He kept making her do the excruciating exercises. Arms, legs, buttocks, stomach—everything had to be toned.

"I've had enough!" she gasped.

"You've had enough when *I* say you've had enough," replied her trainer. He was young and vigorous, with sleek muscles and an enthusiastic attitude. Had she not been involved with Martin she might have considered a fling.

At last he allowed her to stop. "You'll thank me when you're in the middle of your tour," he said.

"Thanks," she replied breathlessly.

As soon as he left, she threw herself into the shower, washing her hair, watching the water trickle down her body. Her firm, hard body. The famous Venus Maria body that turned so many people on.

Martin had flown off to New York the night before. She knew she had him hooked. All she had to do now was reel him in.

Ron appeared at her house for lunch. Her business manager had taken care of separating their financial interests. Ron had accepted it well. Now he could buy his boyfriend Rodeo Drive if he so desired, and it wouldn't bother her one bit.

"Where's the Ken Doll?" she asked mockingly. "I was under the distinct impression he never let you out of his sight."

"Now, now. Don't get bitchy," Ron retorted, heading straight for the kitchen. "Has Major Mogul returned to New York?"

"Yes, he has," she said, dancing along behind him, humming her latest recording.

"Did we have fun while he was here?" Ron asked, opening up the fridge and removing a bowl of tuna salad.

"We had a great time," Venus Maria replied, reaching for the lettuce and tomatoes, while Ron grabbed a fresh loaf of bread. Companionably they began to put together large sandwiches filled with tuna salad, lettuce, tomato, and avocado.

"This is a riot," Ron said slicing tomatoes like an expert. "We don't get to do this enough. I adore behaving like a normal person!"

Venus Maria agreed. "I sent the maid to the market. I wanted to thank you for helping me out the other night."

"My pleasure," Ron replied, "I enjoyed every delicious minute. Oh, and I have *the* most scandalous gossip."

"What?" she asked, stuffing a wedge of lettuce into her mouth.

"Your boss."

"I don't have a boss."

"Does the name Mickey Stolli mean anything to you?"

She laughed. "I don't regard Mickey as my boss."

"Well, anyway, my dear, Mr. Stolli himself turned up at the house of a certain very close friend of mine. All bushy-tailed and eager for action."

"Who would that be?"

"Who do you *think*?"

Venus Maria almost choked. "Not Loretta?" she gasped.

"The very same. And guess what his preference is?"

"I can't wait to hear!"

"Ladies of a darker hue."

"Oh come *on*, you're kidding me."

"Would *I* kid the greatest kidder of all time?"

Venus Maria grinned. She loved gossip as long as it wasn't about her. "How do you know this?"

"Madame Loretta tells me everything," Ron said proudly. "I am her confidant and friend."

"Obviously she doesn't know about your big mouth," Venus Maria teased.

"Mmm . . . look who's talking about a big mouth."

"Abigaile would skin Mickey if she ever found out."

"Can you imagine what Abigaile must be like between the sheets?" Ron mused. "A laugh a minute, no doubt. The poor man probably has to get his R and R elsewhere. Not to mention a blow job." He strolled over to the fridge and took out a can of 7-Up. "By the way, have you heard from Emilio since you chucked him out?"

"Why?" Venus Maria frowned. "Should I have?"

"He wasn't exactly thrilled about you forcing him to leave. I have a feeling we might be reading your secrets somewhere."

Venus didn't care to be reminded of her erstwhile houseguest. Her brother was a big boy. He could look after himself. She refused to feel responsible for him. "Don't start that again," she groaned. "Emilio wouldn't do that to me. I'm paying his rent, for God's sake."

"Hmm . . . if they offered him enough money, Emilio would probably do anything."

Venus Maria placed her hands on her hips. "What could he possibly tell them that the great unwashed doesn't already know?"

"About Major Mogul."

"He doesn't know about Martin."

"Are you sure?"

"Positive." She grinned confidently. "Anyway, I'm not exactly shivering waiting to find out what Emilio has to say about me. He's a deadhead. A loser."

"Emilio is your brother, dear. Speak kindly."

"He's still a loser, *and* you know it."

"Is Mr. New York hooked?" Ron inquired, raising an eyebrow.

She smiled. "Martin's a very special man, and we have a very special relationship."

"Ah, yes," agreed Ron. "And thank God the newspapers don't know about it, or even Emilio. Because if they did, Martin would really be in deep shit, and he'd take it out on you."

"I was very careful when Emilio was around," she assured him. "He knows nothing."

Ron nodded wisely. "Keep it that way."

Emilio Sierra and one of the editors of *Truth and Fact* met at Café Roma on Canon Drive. Emilio had dressed for the part. He wore an off-white jacket, white chinos, a cream shirt, and several heavy fake gold chains around his thick neck. His hair was slicked back. Unfortunately he was thirty pounds overweight, which rather spoiled the effect.

Dennis Walla, the Australian reporter sent to meet him, slumped at a corner table slurping beer. He was a big man, also overweight, in his early forties, with bloodshot eyes, bags under them, and a ruddy complexion.

Emilio stood at the door to the restaurant and surveyed the room.

Dennis spotted him, thought he might be the so-called brother, and waved a copy of *Truth and Fact* in the air.

Emilio swaggered over to his table.

"Hello, mate," Dennis said with a strong Australian accent.

Emilio sat down. *"Truth and Fact?"* he questioned.

"The very same," Dennis replied, thinking to himself this guy must be a real dolt if he had to ask. "And you're Emilio Sierra?"

Emilio's brown eyes darted around the restaurant. He spotted two women he fancied. They were expensively dressed and obviously out on a shopping spree. Dennis caught him watching. "Nice class of tarts in here," he said. "Wouldn't mind zipping up the back skirt of that one, eh?"

Emilio licked his lips. "I got a hot story to sell," he announced.

"Well, mate, that's exactly why we're here," Dennis said cheerfully, downing another healthy slug of beer. He peered across the table at Emilio. "You don't look like your sister, do you?"

"There's a certain family resemblance," Emilio replied proudly, almost preening but managing to control himself.

"Are the two of you friendly?" Dennis probed.

"Of course we are," Emilio snapped. He hadn't planned on enduring a third degree. "Why wouldn't we be?"

"Don't get shirty with me, mate. You're here to sell her dirty little secrets, aren't you?"

"I'm here to make money," Emilio corrected, as if that made everything all right.

"Aren't we all," replied Dennis sagely.

One of the expensive-looking women got up and walked outside.

Emilio whistled softly as she passed his table. "These Beverly Hills women," he mumbled under his breath.

"I know what y'mean, mate," agreed Dennis. "They'll get you hotter than a hamburger on a barbecue."

Two bikers swaggered into the restaurant. Emilio thought he recognized one of them as being a famous actor. He decided he should get himself some biker gear; it would look good on him. He should also lose a few pounds. But who had the time? And who could make the effort? Venus Maria had her own personal trainer; it was all right for her, she could afford those kinds of luxuries. Besides, she had an investment in her body. She made money from it.

He decided she wasn't so different from a hooker, in a way. They were both hawking sex.

There was nothing wrong with his selling her secrets, he thought self-righteously. Why shouldn't he? He was her brother, after all, and she treated him like a leper. Putting him out of her house. Sticking him in some crummy apartment while she lived in luxury. Giving him a station wagon to drive. A station wagon! He should be sitting proud in the latest Porsche, or a Ferrari at least. As her brother he had a certain standard to adhere to. People expected things.

"Well," Dennis said, leaning back and belching not so discreetly, "what have you got to tell me about your sister that we don't already know?"

Emilio glanced around. He wasn't sure he liked this man with the exceptionally loud mouth. Couldn't he be a little more discreet and talk in a quieter tone?

Emilio leaned close. "I don't think this is the place."

"Listen, we're not taking it any further than this until you tell me what you got for me," Dennis said loudly. "How do I even know you're her brother? Do you have any proof?"

Emilio had been expecting questions. He fished out his driving license and handed it over.

Dennis checked it out. "O.K., so your name is Sierra. Big pickings. What does that prove?"

Emilio dived into his pocket again and came up with a picture of him and Venus Maria taken in Brooklyn in the early days. He thrust it at Dennis. "See?"

Dennis glanced at the photo and then at Emilio. "O.K., O.K., I believe you."

"If I tell you what I know," Emilio said craftily, "how much will you pay me?"

Dennis sighed wearily. It always got down to money. He was used to dealing with relatives of the stars. They all thought they'd been given a bad deal. This one was no different, and he'd get his bucks as long as he had something worthwhile to sell.

"It depends on what you got," Dennis said.

"She's sleeping with a married man," Emilio blurted out. "How much is *that* worth?"

"Who?" Dennis asked.

"Big time," Emilio said, lowering his voice. "Real big time. When I tell you it'll blow you away. You'll sell more copies of your magazine than you've ever sold before."

"Sounds good t'me," Dennis said, picking his teeth with the corner of a pack of book matches.

Emilio was getting into it. "More than good," he promised.

Dennis was intrigued. "So who is it?"

Emilio backed off. "I'm not givin' out his name till we fix a price an' I get a check."

"We'll have to work this one out," Dennis said. "No name, no loot."

Emilio scowled.

"Come up with a name that means something, an' if it's worth anything to us we'll give you a fair amount of moola. But you have to substantiate whatever you tell us. Do you understand what that means?"

Emilio glared at him. "What do you think I am, an idiot?"

Yes, Dennis wanted to reply, but he kept quiet. This had the smell of a good story. And there was nothing *Truth and Fact* liked better than a headline-busting, sex-filled, superstar-and-married-man good story.

Scandal. That was the name of the game. And nobody capitalized on scandal better than *Truth and Fact*.

36

Lucky called Abe and told him that Harry Browning had been to see her and had his suspicions.

Abe was silent for a moment before saying, "Sure, I remember Harry. The man's a drunk. You be careful of him."

"Thanks a *lot*. What shall I do? We don't want news of our deal leaking, do we?"

"You're not throwin' him out of a job when you take over, are you?" Abe asked.

"There's a lot of people I'll fire," she replied. "So far he's not one of them."

"Good," Abe said. "Leave it to me, girlie. I'll handle it."

"Thanks."

"I've got t'go now. My granddaughter's payin' me a duty visit."

Lucky knew what the visit was all about. Listening in on Mickey's conversations, she'd discovered the reason he'd met with Martin Swanson. The New York tycoon was interested in buying or gaining control of a movie studio, and from Mickey's conversation with Ford Werne, whom he'd later confided in, it seemed one of the studios Martin was interested in was Panther.

"I'm gonna get Abigaile to sit down with her grandfather. See if the old man shows any interest in selling out," Mickey had said to Ford. "When she speaks to him, she won't tell him what they're willing to pay. She'll suggest he makes an agreement with me, then *I'll* sell the studio. That way I can get myself a cushy management deal and I'll be here forever. And so will you, Ford. You and I work well together."

"What if he doesn't want to sell?" Ford had asked.

"Then I got a new plan. There's another studio my connection is considering. If he buys, I'm there."

"What about Panther? You'd walk away?"

"Hey," Mickey had said, "a deal is a deal is a deal. I treat the old man as good as he treats me, an' he's not treating me so good."

"You'd really go?"

"Do rabbits fuck? But only if the deal is right, Ford. It all comes down to the deal."

The more Lucky listened to Mickey, the more she realized that here was a man with no conscience. His life consisted of business, his mistress, and brief trips home—although in the last couple of days he seemed to have added Madame Loretta to that list.

Boogie had found out Madame Loretta was the biggest madam in town, running a high class brothel high in the Hollywood Hills, supplying beautiful young girls to the rich executives who could afford the exorbitant prices. Obviously Warner was not doing her job. Mickey was restless.

Olive returned to Los Angeles and managed to hobble into the studio on crutches.

Mickey, ever sympathetic, emerged from his office, glared at her, and said accusingly, "How could you do this to me?"

"I'm so sorry, Mr. Stolli," Olive apologized, as if she could have helped it. She would have kissed his feet if she'd felt it would do any good.

Mickey merely continued to glare at her and stomped back into his office.

"What happened with your fiancé? Did everything work out?" Lucky felt obliged to ask.

Sadly Olive shook her head. "It's not to be," she said, crestfallen. "I shouldn't have gone."

"Bad break," Lucky said, trying to look suitably sympathetic.

"These things happen." Olive glanced around the office, checking to make sure everything was in place. "How are you managing?"

"Fine," Lucky said carefully.

"Hmmm . . ." Olive didn't seem pleased. She'd rather hoped things would fall to pieces without her conscientious touch. "Mr. Stolli isn't an easy man."

"I'm glad to say you taught me well. I seem to be making him happy."

Olive looked even more displeased. "I should be back in about six weeks," she said waspishly. "When my cast is off."

"Excellent." Lucky tried to make her feel good. "Everyone misses you."

Olive brightened. "What about Mr. Stone? Aren't you supposed to be working for him again?"

"I discussed it with Mr. Stolli. He thought it best if I stayed here. Mr. Stone doesn't mind. He's extending his vacation."

After more small talk, Olive finally left the office. Later, Lucky observed her having lunch in the commissary with Harry Browning. She hoped Abe had already talked to Harry and warned him not to open his mouth.

With only another week to go, Lucky felt she was coming to the end of a long-term prison sentence. It seemed amazing to her that some people actually led their lives like this. Day in, day out, being bossed around by a crude, irascible boss. Taking shit from all the people who visited his office. Putting up with rude sexist comments from the men. And this was while she'd made herself look as unattractive as possible. God knows what the other girls had to put up with—the secretaries in their miniskirts and low-cut blouses and long blond hair.

Hmm . . . maybe they loved it. Maybe they'd been brainwashed into thinking getting hit on by randy married men was a compliment.

Eddie Kane hadn't been in for over a week. Lucky decided to pay a visit to Brenda and Talon Nails, his two faithful secretaries who stood guard downstairs, and find out what was going on.

Now that she was officially known as Mickey Stolli's personal assistant, most of the other secretaries in the building knew who she was.

Brenda, as usual, was perusing magazines, while Talon Nails sat in the corner making personal phone calls.

"Is Mr. Kane around?" Lucky asked. "We haven't seen him in a while. Mr. Stolli was asking."

"He's sick," Brenda volunteered.

"Flu," Talon Nails added, covering the mouthpiece of the phone with her hand.

Lucky wondered if he'd had the crap beaten out of him by Carlos Bonnatti's boys or if this was merely an interim period while he struggled to get his act together and come up with a million bucks.

"Perhaps you can let our office know when he returns," Lucky said, all business.

Brenda put down her magazine. She had a snippy expression on her face. "May I ask you something?"

Talon Nails hung up the phone and shot Brenda a warning look.

"What?" asked Lucky.

"We were wondering," said Brenda belligerently.

"*She* was wondering," interjected Talon Nails.

"Bull!" Brenda said sharply. "*You* were wondering just as much as I was."

"Can we get to the point?" Lucky asked politely.

"How come you snuck in out of nowhere an' grabbed the key job around here?" Brenda stared at her accusingly.

What the hell, Lucky thought, would it hurt if she jumped out of character—just this once? The temptation was too much. "I slept with the boss," she answered, straight-faced. And made her exit.

Brenda and Talon Nails were speechless.

As usual, Abigaile insisted that Tabitha accompany her when she went to visit her grandfather. Naturally Tabitha complained. But Abigaile was having none of it. "You'll come with me and like it," she insisted firmly.

"I'll come with you, but I won't like it," Tabitha retorted with a sulky glare.

"Young lady," Abigaile said grandly, "it's about time you learned to treat me with respect. I do not appreciate your attitude."

"Please!" Tabitha said in disgust. "Don't start playing Mommy with me now. It's a little late."

Abigaile glared at the girl. Thirteen years old, and with a smarter mouth than her father.

Inga was as pleased to see them as they were to be there. "Come in," she said haughtily and stalked away, leaving them to fend for themselves.

They found old Abe out on the patio, surrounded by newspapers, magazines, and a blaring television.

Dutifully Abigaile kissed him on the cheek. Dutifully Tabitha followed suit.

"Another month zip by already?" Abe asked, squinting against the bright sun.

"I beg your pardon," said Abigaile.

"Another month," repeated Abe. "You only come every four weeks. I bet Mickey says the same thing!" He cackled at his own ribald joke.

Tabitha sneaked a smile. The thought of her mother coming was ludicrous. In fact, the thought of either of her parents having sex was the funniest notion she'd ever heard of.

Abigaile dusted off a patio chair with a tissue and sat down. "How are you feeling, Grandpa?" she asked solicitously.

Abe's canny old eyes crinkled. "Why? Whattaya care?" he asked suspiciously.

"Don't be silly, Grandpa. How come you're always so abrasive with me?"

" 'Cause I calls it the way I sees it, girlie."

"I'm sorry you feel that way," Abigaile replied primly, smoothing down the skirt of her Adolfo suit. "Now, Grandfather, there's something I wish to discuss with you."

"Go on," Abe said. "Shoot." He winked at Tabitha, who giggled.

"Well—" Abigaile plunged ahead, deciding to ignore his irascible attitude—"you're not getting any younger."

Abe chortled with laughter. "Zippo—the girl's developin' brains. I'm not gettin' any younger. Eighty-eight years old and she finally realizes it!"

Abigaile took a deep breath. This was going to be difficult. She'd told Mickey he should come with her. Selfish as usual, he'd refused. Gamely she pressed on. "Um, what would you say if I told you that Mickey could possibly sell the studio?"

Tabitha picked up on that. "What do you wanna sell the studio for? It's Daddy's," she said sulkily. "He's gotta keep it. I wanna have my sweet sixteen there."

"Shhhh," scolded Abigaile.

"I'm not gonna shhhh," Tabitha retorted. "You told me I had to come with you, so why do I have to shhhh?"

Abigaile fixed her daughter with a look. "Will you kindly be quiet." Her tone would have quieted the Russian army.

Abe cackled again. "Why would I wanna sell my studio?"

"Because," Abigaile replied in a cool, reasonable voice, "we can get an excellent price for it."

"Who's the 'we'?"

"Inga and you," Abigaile replied quickly. "And me. And of course, Tabitha."

Abe rose from his chair. "Big fat news," he said. "I could've had a hundred buyers for Panther if I'd've wanted to sell it."

"Then why didn't you?" Abigaile asked tartly.

" 'Cause I didn't want to. An' if I did, it'd be none of *your* business, girlie." Without a backward glance he marched into the house.

Abigaile didn't feel like following him. She'd always been in awe of her grandfather, and now that he was a very old man she still felt uncomfortable in his presence.

"Can we go home now?" whined Tabitha.

Abigaile stood up. "Yes," she said tightly. "Let's do that."

Venus Maria strolled into Mickey's office at four o'clock. As she passed by Lucky's desk, she smiled and said, "Hi, howya doing?"

As soon as Mickey's door closed Lucky put on her earphones to listen in.

Venus Maria didn't play polite games. She got straight to the point. "I hate this script, Mickey," she said. "I hate it with a passion, and there's no way I'm doing it unless it's completely rewritten. Right now the script tells the story from a man's point of view. You promised me this was about a strong woman. A survivor. In this piece of crap she's just another victim. And I'm not playing victims."

"Aw, c'mon, baby, this is a great role for any actress," Mickey said in his most charming voice. "An Oscar-winning role."

"Don't snow me with that tired old bullshit you hand to all the other actresses around here, and I use the word loosely," Venus Maria said sharply. "A rewrite or I'm out of this project. And another thing—"

Cunt! "What?"

"The only way I'll take my clothes off is when the actor playing opposite me strips off too."

Mickey sounded disgusted. "Wake up, baby. Broads don't want to see naked guys on the screen. They're not interested in seeing some poor schmuck with his *schnickel* hanging out."

"That's where you're wrong," Venus said forcefully. "That's exactly what they want to see."

He looked offended. "Maybe *you* do."

"No, not just me. Women get off on seeing guys with it all hanging out. And the reason we don't see it is because men run the film industry, and men can't handle the competition, so they don't want us getting an eyeful. I'm telling you, Mickey, I'm not walking around the screen bare-assed if my leading man is clothed. No fucking way."

"You're a demanding broad," Mickey griped.

"Yeah," Venus Maria agreed. "And I'm in the fortunate position of being able to demand whatever I want. Are we making contact here?"

He stood up from behind his desk. "You need a rewrite, you got a rewrite, O.K.?"

"Good. And if I do decide to sign for this movie, I also want co-star and director approval."

This broad was driving him crazy with her demands. "You got it. It's in your contract already."

"I haven't signed a contract for this film yet."

"It's in your old contract."

"That doesn't mean anything, and you know it. It has to be in *this* contract. In writing. And I'm not signing until I've seen the rewrite. Am I coming across loud and clear?"

"Yeah, yeah, yeah," he said disgustedly.

Venus Maria left his office without another word. She stopped at Lucky's desk. "Tell me," she said, "how can you work for such a jerk and stay sane?"

Lucky laughed. "It's not easy."

As soon as Venus Maria left, Mickey came running out, screaming and yelling.

"Who the fuck does that dumb broad think she is? Actresses! They're all the same. You make 'em a star, an' they think they did it on their own without any goddamn help. If that bimbo didn't have a studio behind her, *and* a good director, *and* a great lighting cameraman, she'd be checking out dog meat in Safeway. Actresses!"

He didn't like actresses. He didn't like actors. Who did he like?

"I'm out of here," he said gruffly.

She knew better than to ask where he was going.

Ten minutes after Mickey left, Johnny Romano made an unscheduled entrance, swaggering his way into the office, macho to the core.

"Hello, beautiful," he said. "Is the big man around?"

Johnny's faithful entourage hovered two steps behind him.

"Mr. Stolli had to go out," Lucky said.

"Shame," exclaimed Johnny. "I thought I'd visit him. Celebrate."

"What are you celebrating, Mr. Romano?" she asked politely.

"My movie, sweet stuff. It opens this week. Don't you keep up around here? *Motherfaker*'s gonna make this studio the biggest bucks it's ever seen." He leaned across her desk, his handsome, arrogant face insolently close to hers. "You know what a motherfaker is, beautiful?"

Yeah, you, asshole, she replied silently.

"Well, do you?" he demanded.

She shook her head.

Johnny Romano laughed.

His entourage laughed.

They waited for her to laugh.

Lucky stared at him blankly.

"Hey, lady," Johnny said, leaning even closer. "Lighten up. You're way too serious. Working for Mickey is a tough business, huh? You want my autograph?"

On my butt, Lucky thought.

Without waiting for a reply, Johnny snapped his fingers. One of his entourage stepped forward with a signed photo.

"Hey, I'm gonna make your day an' personalize it," Johnny said magnanimously. "Gimme your name, baby."

"Luce," she muttered.

"Lucy. To Lucy. I'm gonna write 'To Lucy,'" Johnny said, scrawling an illegible "To Lucy" on the picture. "Love and heart, Johnny Romano" was already stamped on.

He handed her the signed picture with a flourish. "Tell the man I was here," he said. "An' enjoy yourself, you hear? Johnny Romano, he say so."

Big fucking deal!

Suddenly Lucky knew what Mickey meant. Actors! You could have 'em!

When she took over, things were going to be different around here.

37

The telephone woke Gino at three in the morning.

"We're having a baby," Steven said urgently. "Can you get over to the hospital?"

Gino groped for his clothes. "We're having a baby," he repeated delightedly.

"Mary Lou's in the delivery room now," Steven said, sounding stressed.

"I'm on my way," Gino assured him.

"Where's Lucky?

"I'll try and contact her."

"She should be here with us," Steven said. "Mary Lou's asking for her."

Gino was elated. Much to his aggravation, Bobby lived in England and he hardly ever saw him. Now Steven and Mary Lou were presenting him with another grandchild. It was an exciting moment.

Hurriedly pulling on his clothes, he called down to the doorman and ordered a cab. Then he rushed out of his apartment.

Steven was pacing the floor of the hospital when he arrived.

Gino patted him on the shoulder. "You gotta calm down. Take a seat. This happens every day, y'know."

"Not to me," Steven said grimly.

"Shouldn't you be in there with her?"

"She doesn't want me," Steven said with a shrug. "Threw me out."

"How come?"

"Her mother's with her. You know what mothers are like. She's an old-fashioned lady, doesn't want the husband there. Hey—I don't mind. Who *wants* to be there? It's a frightening business."

Gino laughed. "I went through it twice," he said. "When Lucky was born. And Dario. I wish I'd been there for you, Steven."

It was a moment. Their eyes met and then they moved on.

"Did you get hold of Lucky?" Steven asked.

"I'm trying," Gino replied. "Don't worry. She's not gonna miss being an aunt."

Mary Lou gave birth to a seven-pound ten-ounce little girl at eight o'clock in the morning. They named her Carioca Jade.

When Gino got back to his apartment he called Lucky in California and told her.

"Oh, no!" she exclaimed. "The baby was early and I missed it! Are they both all right?"

"They're fine," he assured her. "Mary Lou came through it like a veteran!"

"I'll send flowers. I'm so sorry I wasn't there. The good news is I'll be back next week."

"What makes you think that?" he said. "You're takin' over the studio. That's when you're really gonna have to spend time in L.A."

"I guess you're right. But at least I'll be free to do what I want. I can fly into New York every weekend. I'll get Panther running smoothly and then . . ." Realization sunk in. "Oh, God, it'll take me a while, won't it?"

"Yup."

"Lennie will help me. He'll be ecstatic when he hears!"

Gino wasn't so sure. "Where is he?" he asked.

"I'll worry about that when I take over."

"If you're certain," Gino said.

"I'm certain," she replied.

. . .

265

Warner was trembling by the time Mickey finished making love to her. It gave him a great sense of power to have a six-foot black vice cop trembling because he made love to her with such finesse. "Mickey, you're truly the best lover I've ever had," she told him ecstatically.

Funny, one of Madame Loretta's hookers had said the very same thing to him two days earlier. A man couldn't ask for any further proof than that. First the hooker, now Warner. He really must be something between the sheets. It was a shame Abigaile never told him so.

He tried to remember the last time he and Abigaile had made love. It had something to do with her birthday and a diamond bracelet. And it wasn't making love, it was a blow job. But don't knock a blow job when you're married. It was better than nothing. Actually, in a town where blow jobs had been elevated to a fine art, Abigaile was way up there.

He wondered where she'd learned. They'd really never discussed their past lives. To this day Abigaile had no idea that he had an illegitimate son who lived with his ex-girlfriend just outside of Chicago.

Abigaile would not be pleased if she found out.

Mickey had no intention of ever telling her, although, to his credit, over the years he'd supported his son with a healthy monthly check. He'd promised his ex-girlfriend that the money would keep on flowing as long as she kept her mouth shut.

He'd never seen his son. It was a part of his past he kept locked away. He never wanted it to interfere with his future.

When he got up to take a shower, Warner remained spread-eagled on the bed like an impressive ebony carving. "I can't move," she gasped. "You're too much man for me."

If he were smothering her with furs and jewels, he would have been suspicious of her words of praise. But Warner wanted nothing from him, so he was inclined to believe her.

He hurried into her small bathroom to take a shower. Unfortunately she didn't have a shower, just an attachment above the tub, which really pissed him off.

"You know somethin', honey," he yelled. "I gotta get you a new bathroom, I don't care what you say." ·

"No way, Mickey. You're not spending that kind of money on me."

She walked into the bathroom stark naked. She had breasts the like of which he'd never seen on anyone else. They were jutting and angular, with enormous black nipples. Edible tits.

The black girl at Madame Lorretta's had small breasts, nothing like this. Warner's were straight out of a proud African tribe.

"Did your parents come from Africa?" he asked.

Warner laughed. "No, Watts! Why?"

He reached out to touch one more time before struggling with the shower, nearly tripping. Then he wrapped himself in a too-small bath sheet, pummeled himself dry, dressed, and left.

At home Abigaile was on red alert. She glared at him. "Why do *I* have to do all the dirty work?"

He sighed. "What's the matter now?"

"I saw my grandfather today. He's definitely not interested in selling. What made you think he would be? He's perfectly happy the way he is, and quite frankly, Mickey, we should be happy too. Because when he dies, Panther is ours. And we can do exactly as we please."

"Says you," Mickey said sourly.

Abigaile was ready for battle. "What's *that* supposed to mean?"

"Who knows what the old guy's gonna do."

"Well, exactly. That's why I have to talk to you about it. You mentioned the other day you were considering accepting a job elsewhere. If you do, who's going to run Panther? And more important —who will inherit Panther?"

"*You'll* inherit, there's no question. You and your charming sister."

"Yes, I know, Mickey, but if somebody else is running the studio, it could create problems." She shook her head, making the decision for both of them. "You're going to have to turn Martin Swanson down."

"Abigaile, I am *not* saying no to Martin Swanson if it means more money."

"Why? You're making a million dollars a year, plus whatever you can steal. Isn't that enough?"

He looked at her with disgust. "Thanks a lot. It's great to have a really supportive wife. I thrive on the support you give me, Abigaile."

She took his sarcasm and swallowed it. "Thank you, Mickey. I aim to please."

38

Effie Webster loved giving parties. They were an important part of her life. She couldn't imagine not giving them. After all, Effie and Yul Webster were famous for their parties.

Half the fun was putting together an eclectic mix. Anyone from starving actors and artists to successful Broadway producers. Or maybe not-so-starving actors and artists.

Effie knew everyone. Planning a party for Martin Swanson's birthday was not difficult, because Martin and Deena knew everyone, too. The hard part was who not to invite.

Effie decided a theme party would be fun. She sent out black invitations with gold printing: COME AS YOUR FAVORITE FANTASY. What a charming way to delve into the psyches of the rich and the famous. Come as your favorite fantasy was an invitation to reveal your very secret self—an invitation most people couldn't resist.

Effie decided she was going to dress up as Queen Nefertiti. "Darling," she informed Deena on the phone, "I've always wanted to be a queen, and this is a perfect opportunity. What are you coming as?"

Deena had given it a lot of consideration. "I've decided on Marlene Dietrich. The way she looked in *The Blue Angel.*"

"Wonderful idea!" Effie exclaimed, wishing she'd thought of it. "With *your* legs you'll be a sensation! But I suppose that's the whole point, isn't it?"

"Yes," Deena agreed. "I suppose it is."

She put down the phone and thought about Martin. He hadn't said a word about divorce. In fact, since he'd been back from L.A., he'd thrown himself into business, concentrating on his Swanson Sports Stadium, where he planned to stage the next world-heavyweight championship fight if he could arrange it. And the new luxury automobile soon to be launched: the Swanson.

Martin was very excited about the Swanson. It was a sleek and powerful car. A car that represented everything he wanted the public to know about him.

Martin planned to present the Swanson at a big media publicity launch in Detroit.

Deena felt sure her errant husband wasn't going to jeopardize the anticipated publicity on the Swanson for a tawdry little slut like Venus Maria.

She tried to imagine what hold the girl had over him. It was sexual, of course.

But why? Martin wasn't particularly interested in sex.

Deena shook her head. She couldn't figure it out. She could only stand by, wait, and see what happened.

And if the worst happened, she had her solution.

Brigette was excited about the party, although she didn't let on to Nona, who appeared to take it all very casually. To Brigette it was a return to the real world. She'd been shut up in boarding school for so long, and when she *was* allowed out, it was always with Charlotte, who never took her anywhere. Now here she was, part of an exciting life again, back in the big city.

"I can't make up my mind whether we should go or not," Nona vacillated. "How about taking in a movie instead and skipping the party?"

"I vote for the party." Brigette was full of enthusiasm and dying to go. "It'll be a blast."

"My idea of a blast is *not* attending my parents' crazy parties."

Finally Brigette got her to agree that it might be a laugh. The next question was, Who would they go as?

"I'll be Janet Jackson," Nona decided.

"That's not exactly easy to put together," Brigette pointed out.

Nona thought about it. "Why not? I'll do an incredible black makeup. And I'll wear a Janet Jackson wig, tight jeans, and a motorcycle jacket. I can borrow Paul's. He's coming to the party, you know."

"What's *his* favorite fantasy?" Brigette inquired, trying not to sound too interested.

"Probably Picasso mixed with Donald Trump's money," Nona replied dryly.

Eventually they decided it would be fun if they both dressed up as Venus Maria.

Nona giggled. "We'll blow everybody's mind!"

"She's not going to be here, is she?" Brigette asked anxiously, thinking it wouldn't be too cool if she was.

"You never know *who's* going to turn up at my parents' parties," Nona answered.

They went on a wild shopping spree in the Village, running into places Effie would never dream of visiting. They arrived home with a selection of outlandish clothes, everything from long army-surplus overcoats to frilled miniskirts, leather bustiers, and midriff-exposing tops.

"Venus Maria always puts together such a fantastic look," Nona said, poring over an interview with Venus in one of the latest magazines. "I think she's great. It's obvious she doesn't give a damn about anybody."

Brigette laughed. "Just like you, huh?"

"What's so bad about *that? My* opinion is that women do what men *think* they should do. I'm not going to be like that when I'm old."

"What's old?"

"It says here Venus Maria is twenty-five. I guess she's sort of old."

Brigette laughed again. "Don't let your mother hear you say that!"

"Effie is forever young," Nona said with a wicked grin. "She'll be young when she's eighty. I bet she'll still have that crazy streak of green hair, and wear outlandish clothes. Mom's quite a character."

"You're fortunate to have her," Brigette said wistfully.

"I know," Nona agreed. "Oh, and by the way, have you spoken to your stepfather? When are we going to Malibu? Effie needs to know. It's not that she's dying to get rid of us, but she's got this little side trip planned to Bangkok, and she doesn't want us tagging along."

"I've left a message with Lennie's agent to call me here," Brigette said. "I heard he walked off the movie, and nobody seems to know where he is. He'll come through. Lennie won't let me down. He promised me Malibu, and Lennie always keeps his promises."

"Great!" exclaimed Nona. "I don't know about you, but I can't wait."

Emilio Sierra and Dennis Walla formed an uneasy alliance. It was a relationship based on greed rather than trust. They had a couple of meetings bickering about money back and forth. Emilio flatly refused to say who Venus Maria's married lover was until a price was settled. Dennis, on the other hand, insisted there could be no price until Emilio revealed his information.

After their initial meeting in Café Roma, they got together in a seedy coffee shop on Pico and tried to hammer it out. Finally they met at the office of *Truth and Fact* in Hollywood.

Emilio said he wanted fifty thousand dollars. *Truth and Fact* agreed to pay if the name he gave them was worth it. Now they were meeting to finalize the deal.

" 'Morning, mate," greeted Dennis, sitting behind a littered desk, smoking a cheap, foul-smelling cigar. "Today's the day, huh?" A mangy cat strolled by.

Emilio nodded uneasily. He wasn't sure if he should be here. Appearing at the offices of *Truth and Fact* was really blowing his cover. When he'd walked through the main room he'd noticed people at desks, behind typewriters, glancing in his direction. He felt like a traitor. And yet, why shouldn't he do what he had to if it made him money?

Dennis introduced him to one of his colleagues, a short, squat Englishman with a rat face, scraggly eyebrows, and a droopy little mustache.

"Who's he?" Emilio asked suspiciously.

"We gotta have a witness," Dennis explained. "Can't hand over a check without a witness. You gotta give us the facts, Emilio. Times, places, names. The lot."

Emilio nodded. "I know all that," he said somewhat ill-temperedly. *God, you would think it would be easier than this. Why couldn't he just tell them who she was sleeping with, take his money, and go?*

"Sit down," said Dennis. "Want a beer?"

Emilio shook his head. For the last week he'd been working on his gut. This meant cutting out beer. A real drag.

When he had his fifty thousand dollars he wanted to be in better shape. He'd buy a decent car, new clothes, and move to a luxurious apartment. Emilio Sierra was going places.

"Let's get this show on the road," Dennis said, switching on a tape recorder.

"Why are you doing that?" Emilio asked, alarmed.

"I keep telling you," Dennis replied patiently, "we need the proof. Don't plan on getting sued, do we?"

Emilio thought about that one. "How can you be sued if it all happened?" he asked.

"You'd be surprised who tries it on. Sinatra, Romano, Reynolds, the biggies. They're stupid, 'cause they never win. It ends up costing them big money. But we don't want to be dragged through the courts for years, do we?"

"No," agreed Emilio, wondering if Venus Maria would sue.

"O.K., shoot," said Dennis, releasing the pause button.

Emilio felt hot. A thin sliver of sweat trickled down his neck. He had an ache in his gut. He didn't feel well. "It's like this," he said, sitting down. "Uh . . . where's my check?"

Dennis opened his desk drawer and took out a check for five thousand dollars. He waved it under Emilio's nose. "You get this now, the rest when the story's ready for press."

Emilio tried to grab it.

Dennis snatched it out of reach. "Not so fast. I'm only showing it to you. Before you get it we need the name. If it's worth something to us, an' you've got proof, it's yours, an' plenty more to come."

Shit, Emilio thought, *better get this over and done with.* "The boyfriend's name is Martin Swanson." He blurted it quickly, savoring the shock and amazement on both men's faces.

Dennis let out a long, low whistle. "Martin Swanson! The New York biggie?"

"Martin Swanson?" repeated the Englishman. "This is juicy stuff."

"Shit!" exclaimed Dennis happily. "If you can back this one up, you've given us a good one, mate."

"Oh, I can back it up," Emilio boasted. "I even have a picture of them together." His trump card.

"A picture?" Dennis said, getting more excited. "You never mentioned you had photos."

Emilio thought quickly. "Yeah, well, if you want the picture, it's extra."

"Oh," said Dennis. "The picture is extra?"

"If you want it," Emilio said.

"We want it," Dennis said.

Martin Swanson stood in his dressing room and examined his face in a magnifying mirror. He reached for the tweezers and plucked a few offending hairs from beneath his eyebrows. Then he stood back and admired himself in a full-length mirror. He was dressed as a Confederate soldier. Deena had thought it an original costume. He had to admit the outfit suited him.

Birthdays usually sank him into a deep depression, but today he felt particularly good. It seemed he had lots of friends. Presents had been arriving at the house all day, along with flowers, balloons, and birthday-greeting telegrams.

Deena had presented him with a solid-gold picture frame. In it she had placed their wedding picture. There they were, Deena and Martin Swanson, standing outside the church, the happy couple.

Was it only ten years ago? It seemed like a lifetime. When he married Deena he had been ready to settle down. Who knew he'd ever find a woman like Venus Maria?

Venus had called him at his office earlier. "Happy birthday, Martin," she'd said, long distance. "I'm disappointed you couldn't get out here to celebrate with me."

"It's been difficult," he replied. "Business."

"You shouldn't let business run your life," she'd chided. "All work and no play makes Martin a very dull boy indeed."

He'd laughed. "I'm never dull when I'm around you, am I?"

"Baby, *I* make sure of that."

They'd talked a few minutes more. She hadn't said, "When am I going to see you?" She didn't have to. He knew it was on her mind. It was on his mind, too. Their relationship had reached the point where she required more than promises.

It wasn't easy. Sure, he could divorce Deena. It would probably cost him a bundle, even though he'd made her sign a prenuptial, and they'd suffer through a wave of bad publicity. But after that he'd be free to do whatever he wanted.

O.K., so right now they were the Swansons. They owned New York. But Martin Swanson on his own could still own New York.

It was a difficult decision and one he wasn't quite ready to make. He'd ended the phone conversation with Venus Maria by promising to fly to L.A. the following week. The thought excited him. She really knew how to turn him on. Her little tricks and surprises were something else. For a moment he allowed his thoughts to linger on the two hookers and the silk scarves. Quite an event. Venus Maria knew how to keep a man interested.

One final glance and he strolled out of his dressing room satisfied with his appearance.

Deena was downstairs, her full-length sable coat covering her outfit for the evening.

"Let's have a look at you," Martin said easily.

She swung around, dropping her coat.

"Wow!" Martin was impressed. He'd married a beautiful woman.

Deena had on *some* outfit. Her long legs were encased in sleek black stockings. And the rest of her getup was a carbon copy of the famous Marlene Dietrich costume in *The Blue Angel*. Deena, when she wanted to, could turn herself into a real stunner.

"You're very handsome tonight, Martin," she said, reaching out to smooth the back of his hair.

"And you, well, what can I tell you? You've really done it, haven't you?" He laughed. "Effie will be a jealous wreck."

Deena smiled triumphantly. "Why is that?"

"Because, my dear—" he held out his arm—"tonight, everyone is going to be looking at you. Including me."

Deena felt her triumph grow. She raised an eyebrow. "Really?" she said.

"Really," he said.

39

There was not much spare time in Venus Maria's life. From the moment she got up in the morning until the moment she went to bed at night, she was always busy doing something. If it wasn't her workouts, it was rehearsals for her videos. If it wasn't rehearsals, she was in the studio, recording. Or she was sitting with the two song-writers she liked to work with, making suggestions as far as lyrics were concerned. Several times a week she worked with Ron. He still choreographed all her routines, and they were still best friends—in spite of the Ken Doll.

Then there was her acting. She tried to read every script sent to her. And if she didn't have time, she depended on a reader she employed.

Frankly, she was annoyed that Martin hadn't flown back for his birthday as he'd promised. She confided in Ron while they sweated their way through a new dance routine in his rehearsal room.

"What do you want from the man?" Ron asked, straight to the point as usual.

"To be with me all the time," she said.

"That's a ridiculous suggestion," Ron blasted truthfully. "Martin Swanson is based in New York. You're here. What kind of life would the two of you have together? He'd be out screwing around and so would you. I *know* you, Venus."

"Maybe you don't know me as well as you think you do," she replied indignantly.

"Come off it," Ron said. "I know you better than anybody. I knew you when—before all the big-deal star stuff. I knew you when Venus Maria was just a twitch in your fanny."

"And don't you forget, Ron," she retaliated. "I knew *you* before you were the gay prince of Hollywood."

"The what?"

"You heard," she replied tartly.

"Oh, thank you *so* much, madame. I always wanted to be a gay prince."

"And may I be the first to tell you you're doing a marvelous job? You and the Ken Doll are the talk of boys' town."

Ron was irritated. "Don't call him the Ken Doll. I've told you a million times."

She brushed a hand through her platinum hair. "That's what he is."

"Listen, honey, don't talk about *my* lover and I won't talk about yours, O.K.?"

They glared at each other and continued the rehearsal.

Ron was a hard taskmaster. When he choreographed a routine it had to be perfect. And he made sure Venus Maria practiced every move before he put her with the other dancers. She was his star pupil.

Secretly she knew Ron considered he was totally responsible for her success. It didn't bother her. If he wished to take credit, let him do so. She knew she would have gotten to the top with or without Ron. He'd been a great help, especially in the early days. Now she didn't need him.

She didn't need anybody.

Except Martin.

Effie greeted all her guests personally. Not for her an army of servants, although there were plenty around. Effie considered the personal touch important to make any party successful.

When Deena and Martin arrived, Effie was at the door to welcome them.

Deena slid her sable coat off her shoulders.

"My God!" Yul said, hovering behind Effie. "I never realized you had such incredible legs."

Deena smiled her cool smile. Tonight she was going to make every man in the room hot, and she knew it.

"You look divine, darling," enthused Effie. "And Martin, the handsome-soldier look suits you. You should do it more often. I simply adore a uniform."

"I feel like a fool," Martin said, perfectly at ease.

Yul, who was dressed as a caveman, said, "*You* feel like a fool? Try this outfit for ten minutes."

Martin laughed and got lost in a sea of greetings. Everyone wanted to wish him a happy birthday. He was Mr. Popular.

Gathered in a corner, Brigette, Nona, and Paul watched the activities.

"Martin Swanson is such a corny old smoothie," Nona proclaimed. "Just watch him work a room. What an operator!"

"Wow," Paul said. "Get a load of his old lady's legs."

"She's too ancient for you, *and* she's married," Nona said snappishly.

"But she's rich," Paul remarked.

"Will you get off it? She's not as rich as Brigette."

"Oh, well, we all know it's impossible for anyone to be as rich as Brigette. And while we're on the subject, since she's so rich, how come you two didn't come up with decent outfits? You look like a couple of tarts."

Nona narrowed her eyes. "We're supposed to be Venus Maria, can't you tell?"

"Nope," replied Paul. "You still look like two little tramps."

"Honestly!" Nona said crossly. "You're so full of b.s."

"Takes one to know one."

"Do you two fight all the time?" Brigette asked curiously.

"This isn't fighting," said Paul.

"Oh, no!" agreed Nona. "You should see us when we *really* go at it!"

Paul had decided not to play dress-up, refusing to change his all-black outfit. Nobody seemed to notice except Brigette, who couldn't keep her eyes off him, much as she tried.

She remembered the first time she'd spotted her first boyfriend, Tim Wealth. It seemed such a long time ago, and yet it couldn't be more than two years. Tim had been tall and gangly, with a thin face, a nice smile, and longish hair. The first time she'd seen him at the opening of Lucky's hotel, it had been love at first sight. Later that same night he'd invited her to his hotel suite, made her snort coke, and instructed her to undress. He'd had no idea who she was or that she was only fourteen. And then he'd made love to her. Fast and furious.

Memories of Tim were making her uncomfortably warm. She took off her short brocade jacket. Underneath she wore a skimpy white bra and a minuscule skirt.

Paul second-glanced her. "Not bad," he said. "It's a shame you're still a baby."

I was even more of a baby when I met Tim Wealth, she thought. *It didn't bother him.*

Paul's eyes followed Deena's seductive legs across the room. "She sure looks good tonight," he sighed lustfully.

"She's old enough to be your mother," Nona said disapprovingly.

"Not quite."

"Almost," Nona countered.

He got up. "I'm leaving you two nymphets to fend for yourselves. I'll be back in a minute."

"I don't believe it!" Nona exclaimed. "He's planning to hit on Deena Swanson. Can you imagine? He's going to hit on Mommy's best friend!"

Brigette forced a laugh. She was jealous. But she was determined not to let anybody see it, because falling in love meant heartbreak, and Brigette knew heartbreak only too well.

"Howya doin', Mrs. S.?"

Deena turned to look at the thin young man with the intense stare. "Have we met?" she asked coolly.

His eyes clashed with hers. He had a very direct gaze. "It's me, Paul. Effie's son."

She was genuinely surprised. "Oh, my God, Paul. How you've changed. It's been so long since I've seen you."

"It has been a while," he agreed. "I was traveling around Europe. Backpacking. Not quite your style, huh?"

"You were a little boy last time we uh . . . we were together," she said.

He gave her the intense stare. "That sounds sexy, Deena."

Was he coming on to her? No. Impossible. He was just a kid— albeit a very attractive one. "I beg your pardon?"

"Well, y'know . . . like 'when we were together' sounds sort of sexy. Don'tcha think?"

"Paul, are you flirting with me?"

Now came the charming smile. "I hope so. If not, I'm doing a lousy job."

Deena couldn't help smiling back. "It's nice to see you, dear," she said. "And I can tell you've inherited your mother's sense of fun."

He moved on to the brooding look. "Enough with the dear. Don't try and put me down, Deena."

"I wouldn't dream of it."

Time to challenge her. "You wouldn't dream of what?"

"I wouldn't dream of trying to put you down, Paul. Where *is* your mother?"

"She's around. Why? Do you need her to get you out of this?"

Deena shook her head.

Paul switched moods and grinned. "Feeling threatened?"

"By you? I don't think so, dear." She turned her back and walked briskly away.

"Nice legs," he said to her retreating back.

He felt it was a victory. Satisfied, he returned to Nona and Brigette.

"She totally wants my body," he said. "I had to say no."

"Really," said Nona sarcastically. "How nice for you. I always knew you were the biggest liar in the world."

"Don't believe me. See if I care." Nonchalantly he turned his attention to Brigette. "Can I bug you for a loan? Like maybe a hundred thousand big ones? I'll pay you back when I'm rich and famous."

"Ha!" snorted Nona.

"I don't control my money," Brigette muttered. "It's all in various trusts."

"And even if she did," Nona interrupted, "you'd be the last person to get any. *I'd* be the first, wouldn't I?"

Brigette would never admit it, but she thought Paul was even more attractive than Tim Wealth.

Emilio signed the contract. He probably should have taken it to some high-powered Hollywood lawyer and had him look it over. But Emilio knew what he was doing. His business instincts were good. After all, he'd negotiated himself a fat fifty thousand dollars without any help from some sharp lawyer. Now all he had to do was give them the exclusive story of Venus Maria and her married lover.

The first thing he did was open up a bank account. Then he promptly withdrew three thousand dollars in cash, and hit the town, taking in all the clubs.

Everyone who knew him was surprised. "Where'd you score the bucks, man?" they asked. They were all aware that Emilio was an expert at using his sister's name, joining peoples' tables, and getting his drinks put on other peoples' tabs.

"My sister gave it to me," Emilio replied with a jaunty wink.

In a way it was true. Without Venus Maria, he certainly wouldn't have fifty thousand stashed away. Well, only five for now, but he'd get the balance when the story was written and checked out.

Several Margaritas later he picked up a hooker at one of the bars. He didn't realize she was a hooker. She said she was an actress. They all said they were actresses or models. It was the Hollywood game.

She had long dyed-blond hair and even longer skinny legs. She wore a very short red dress cut low in the back and even lower in the front. There was not much left to anybody's imagination.

Emilio wasn't into imagining; he was into celebrating.

He took the girl back to his apartment and made love to her for a fast five minutes.

"Is that it?" she asked indignantly when he was through. "I came here for a good time. I coulda had more action with a jackrabbit!"

"I gave you a good time," Emilio mumbled, wishing she'd get the hell out.

She demanded fifty bucks for a cab home.

He was outraged. "Fifty bucks for a cab?"

"Honey, I didn't come here for your smile."

Grumbling, Emili gave her a twenty and shoved her out.

When she was gone he switched on the television and fantasized about Gloria Estefan. Now *she* was a real woman. He bet Gloria Estefan wouldn't start asking him for fifty bucks.

Eventually he fell asleep. Tomorrow he had another session with Dennis and his tape recorder. They were progressing on the story.

Soon he would be headline news. It was some kind of kick.

Emilio Sierra was going to be famous too.

40

Eddie Kane thought he might be going crazy, totally freaking out. And nobody wanted to help him, there wasn't one person he could trust.

He roamed around his house like a man possessed. Goddamn it! Ten days ago he'd had everything. Plenty of money, a gorgeous wife; things were running smoothly. And he'd had his coke to keep him warm. A little snort of cocaine and everything looked rosy. Now it took more than a little snort to get him out of bed in the morning.

He'd known he was in trouble when Mickey stopped talking to him. Mickey, whom he'd depended on over the years and had always turned to.

So he'd got them into a jam. Jesus Christ, it wasn't like they were standing at gunpoint in front of the fucking Mexican army. It was a mess a million bucks could solve. And Mickey Stolli and Panther Studios were going to have to come up with the money. Fast.

But no, Mickey was trying to act like a big man and pretend it wasn't his responsibility. Mickey was full of crap.

The calls had started nicely enough. "Hey, Eddie, you owe us money. When's it coming?" Then they'd progressed to "Hey, Eddie, ya better get the bucks soon. Mr. Bonnatti ain't a patient man." And now it was "Eddie, your time is up. Mr. Bonnatti don't appreciate bein' kept waiting."

At first it seemed like such a sweet, irresistible deal. Eddie had been introduced to Carlos Bonnatti in New York at Le Club. Actually he'd known one of the women Bonnatti was with, his L.A. cocaine connection, Kathleen Le Paul.

After Kathleen introduced him to Carlos, they'd got to talking. "Panther Pictures, huh?" Carlos had said. "I'm in the picture business myself."

"You are?" Eddie had asked, surprised that he'd never heard of him.

"Yeah." Carlos had laughed. "We don't make quite your style of movies."

Eddie had been accused of a lot of things in his time—being slow was not one of them. "You're into the other side of the tennis net, huh?" he'd said smoothly.

"There's plenty of money in it," Bonnatti had replied. "Plenty. My brother Santino started the business. When he, uh, unfortunately passed away, I took over. I got a guy running it out on the West Coast. An' my own people in New York. Our only real problem is abroad."

It went on from there. Bonnatti was looking for a way to get his porno product into Europe. There were certain countries such as Spain and Italy that had a block on importing pornographic material.

Eddie came up with the perfect solution: Smuggle it in with legitimate product. Who was going to question Panther Studios when they shipped in their big movies?

Bonnatti was easy to convince. When Eddie smelled a deal he went all the way. "Maybe I can help you," he'd said. And they'd worked out a tentative arrangement.

All Eddie had to do was run it by Mickey, guaranteeing him a big chunk of the action.

He'd thought about it long and hard before going to Mickey. First he'd formed his own shell company in Liechtenstein, reckoning he could shift the European funds through the company without becoming personally involved.

Mickey was immediately receptive to the idea. "Just money, no risk?" he'd asked.

"That's the deal," Eddie had said. "A fifty-fifty split with Bonnatti. An' I hand you half my action. It's as easy as that."

Mickey had agreed.

Screw Mickey. For three years he'd been happy to take the money when things were running smooth. Now that there was trouble—he didn't want to know.

Eddie wondered how everybody had found out he was creaming off the top. Fuck it, he was the one doing all the work, setting up the deals in the various countries, funneling the money through. If anybody was going to get busted, it was him. So why shouldn't he take more than his share?

Now he was busted. Carlos Bonnatti had discovered he was stealing, and Bonnatti wanted what was his.

Leslie followed Eddie around the house looking mournful. "How can I help?" she asked for the tenth time.

He was in no mood for the caring-wife bit. "By shutting up."

It occurred to him that the fastest way he could raise the money in a hurry was by selling their only real asset.

"We gotta put the house on the market," he announced. "Call a realtor an' tell 'em we need a cash sale, an' we need it like yesterday."

Leslie looked dismayed, but she did as he told her, even though they both knew it wasn't going to be fast enough.

Now that he had the threat of Bonnatti breathing in his face, he didn't know what else to do.

Eddie had sensed it was going to be a bad day the moment he'd awakened. It was Friday. There was a thick smog hanging over the beach. There was a a thick smog hanging over his head. He felt more than depressed. Rolling across the bed he reached for the phone and called Kathleen Le Paul. "Come by my house," he ordered. "I need medication."

"I don't make house calls," she replied testily, not exactly thrilled to hear from him.

His head was exploding. "I'm out of the office."

"I noticed. If you'd let me know, I could have saved myself a trip."

"Listen, honey, I've got the flu. Whaddya want from me? Come to my house. Bring the goods."

"Cash?"

"Yeah."

"You're into me for fifteen hundred from last week."

"It's waitin' for you."

Reluctantly she agreed, and they arranged a noon rendezvous.

Leslie was in the kitchen frying eggs and bacon. The smell made him sick. "I'm cooking breakfast for you," she sang out, too goddamn cheerful for her own good.

"Take off your clothes," he said.

She spun around, startled. "What?"

"Take off your clothes," he repeated. "How about cooking my breakfast bare-assed naked?"

There was pain in her voice but he failed to hear it. "Eddie, don't be like this."

"Aw, forget it." He stomped back into the bedroom. And then he felt bad. Poor kid, he was taking it out on her, but who else did he have to take it out on?

Five minutes later Leslie surprised him. She walked into the bedroom wearing nothing but high heels and a frilly bib apron.

What a body! For the first time in weeks he felt the old juices begin to flow. "Hey," he said, "come to Poppa!"

"It's what you wanted, isn't it?" she asked stiffly.

"I wasn't serious," he said, tweaking her breasts. "Only now that you're here . . ."

He lay back and let her do all the work. She was very good at performing. For a girl from Iowa she sure knew plenty.

Later he wolfed breakfast, downed a couple of vodkas, smoked a joint, and went for a long walk along the beach.

When he got back to his house, Carlos Bonnatti was sitting in his living room.

A white-faced Leslie said, "I didn't know you were expecting company."

Eddie stared at Carlos. He felt his skin crawl. "Neither did I."

Carlos Bonnatti was a stockily built man in his mid-forties, with tightly curled hair, drooped eyelids, sallow skin, and an indolent expression.

"I was in the neighborhood," he said easily. "Thought I'd drop by."

"Since when was your neighborhood the beach?" Eddie brooded, glaring at him.

Carlos waved a vague hand in the air. "Since you owe me a million bucks," he said. "An' since I don't seem to be getting no answers to my questions, I figured I'd make a side trip, see what's goin' on. You have anythin' to say for yourself, Eddie?"

Leslie hovered at the back of the room, paralyzed with fear. She'd known something was up the moment the long black limousine had deposited Carlos Bonnatti at her door with two heavies stationed right behind him. When she'd opened the door, he hadn't even asked if he could come in, merely pushed past her with a terse "I'm here to see Eddie," as if that was explanation enough.

"You shouldn't have come here," Eddie said tightly. "I don't need this shit. You'll get your money, I told you that last week."

"Last week was then," Carlos said. "Now is now. I want my money by Monday morning or you know what you can expect."

"Are you threatening me?" Eddie demanded, full of false bravado.

"Call it a threat if you want," Carlos replied mildly. "You should know one thing—Carlos Bonnatti don't make threats. He makes things happen. Either I get what's owed me by Monday or you an' I are outta business. In fact—" Carlos rose to his feet—"you're likely to find you won't be doing business with nobody." He walked toward the door, stopping to touch Leslie on her bare shoulder. "Pretty wife," he said. "Very pretty." And then he was gone.

Eddie rushed into the bathroom and threw up. When he emerged, Leslie was waiting, gazing at him expectantly, those damn big eyes staring at him, trusting him to come up with an answer to all of this.

"I'll go see Mickey," he said quickly. "Don't worry, babe, I'll have this worked out today."

"You will?"

"This is a promise."

He hugged her and hurried outside to his car.

Now it was Leslie's turn to pace around the house. She didn't know what to do. She only knew Eddie was in trouble, and there had to be some way she could help.

Picking up the phone she dialed Madame Loretta's number.

When the older woman got on the line, Leslie sobbed out her story. "Can you help me?" she begged.

"Leave him," Madame Loretta cautioned. "You're still young and beautiful. There's plenty of other men. Come back to work. I'll find you another one."

Leslie was shocked. "But I don't want anyone else," she protested. "I love Eddie."

"Love's no good," Madame Loretta warned her. "He'll bring you down with him. I've seen this happen before. Leave him, Leslie, before it's too late."

"No," Leslie replied gravely. "I could never leave Eddie. I love him."

"Then I can't help you," Madame Loretta said brusquely, and put the phone down.

41

Eddie Kane allowed his white Maserati to rip on the Pacific Coast Highway. When he hit the freeway he really let loose.

Five minutes later he was pulled over by a motorcycle cop.

The cop was movie-star handsome as he swaggered toward Eddie's window. "Hey, bud, you going for a world record or what?" the cop said, pulling out his notebook.

Eddie sensed this was somebody he could deal with. "Listen, uh, I got a hot date, you know how it is."

The cop grinned. He certainly knew how it was.

"Nice car," he remarked, pen poised for action.

"I worked hard to get it," Eddie said, trying to sound humble.

"You been drinking?" the cop asked.

Eddie laughed mirthlessly. He knew he looked like a bum. Only the car gave him credibility. "Who, me?" he said. "Are you serious?"

The cop rocked back and forth on the heels of his boots. "Yes, I'm serious. Have you been drinking?"

Eddie forced a friendly smile. "Let me introduce myself. Eddie Kane. Head of distribution at Panther Studios. Hey—did you ever think about being an actor?"

"Yeah, I've thought about it," the cop said. "Who hasn't, in this town?"

"Tell you what," Eddie said in his most persuasive voice. "I'll give you my card an' you can call me at the studio. I'll see if I can get you an audition."

The cop laughed.

Eddie fished out one of his cards and handed it over. "I'm serious. What are you laughing at?"

The cop laughed again. "I've heard of being discovered, but this is ridiculous!"

"You've got charisma," Eddie said, rising to the occasion. "You've got the look. And a sense of humor. So come on, I'll try to help you, an' you can help me. Let me go, huh? I'm late for an appointment."

It was the one good thing that happened to Eddie that day. The cop pocketed his card and waved him on his way.

Undaunted, Eddie did not slow down. He hit the gas all the way to Panther.

Mickey was in a meeting with a writer on one of his pet projects. When Eddie burst into the office Mickey was taken by surprise.

Lucky let him through without question. This was her last day at the studio and she didn't care what happened.

The writer, an earnest young man, leaped to his feet as soon as Eddie entered. Eddie looked like a madman with his ten days' growth of beard, crumpled clothes, and wild, bloodshot eyes.

"I'm through takin' shit," Eddie yelled, placing both hands on Mickey's desk and glaring at him. "Carlos Bonnatti came to my house. My fucking *house*, for crissakes! No more, Mickey. You're in this with me, an' there's no way you're backin' out. Panther's gotta pay him."

Mickey's eyes narrowed. This was what happened when you tried to assist a friend? "Luce," he shouted.

No acknowledgment.

"Get the guards up here," he screamed.

"You get the fucking guards an' you got more trouble than you ever believed possible," Eddie yelled, grabbing Mickey by the lapels of his sports jacket. "I'll go to Abe Panther. I'll spill the works. Your fat ass won't be worth a dime."

The writer slowly and carefully backed his way toward the door.

He'd heard about these scenes where unhinged maniacs went on a rampage. Sometimes they had a gun. This could get nasty. "I'll come back later, Mr. Stolli," he said.

"Get your hands off my jacket," Mickey growled at Eddie.

"Fuck you," replied Eddie.

They began to scuffle.

The writer scuttled out of the office, slamming the door behind him.

Lucky glanced up from her desk.

"Did you call the guards?" the writer asked urgently.

"I think they'll be able to work it out between them, don't you?" she said sweetly.

Shaking his head, the writer ran out. He was paid to write, not to get involved in grudge battles.

Just as Leslie was recovering from Madame Loretta's callous attitude, the doorbell rang.

Tentatively she peered through the peephole. A woman stood on the other side of the door—a well-dressed, heavily-made-up woman. "Yes," Leslie called out. "Can I help you?"

"Where's Eddie?" the woman said irritably.

"He's not here."

"Shit! We had an appointment."

"I'm Mrs. Kane," Leslie said, attempting to assert herself. "And who are you?"

"Kathleen Le Paul. Open up this goddamn door."

Tentatively Leslie opened it an inch, keeping the security chain firmly in place. "What do you want?" she asked.

"Eddie told me to meet him at noon," Kathleen said. "I haven't driven all the way here for nothing. Did he leave me the money?"

"What money?"

"The money for his . . . delivery. I have a package for him."

"How much does he owe you?" Leslie asked curiously.

"Fifteen hundred dollars, cash," Kathleen replied, thinking to herself she was getting too old for this kind of thing. If Umberto Castelli would only divorce his fat Colombian wife and move to Los Angeles, she could live in luxury instead of being a runner.

"He didn't mention you or any money," Leslie said.

Kathleen impatiently tapped a Chanel-clad toe on the sidewalk. "Take a look," she said abruptly. "Maybe you'll find he left something for me."

Leslie shut the door in her face and scurried into the bedroom. Sure enough there was a pile of cash on top of Eddie's dresser.

For a moment she was unsure about what to do. If she refused to accept this package, Eddie could be angry. And yet, if she took it and gave the woman money, he could also be angry. Thinking fast, she tried to reach him on his car phone. There was no reply.

By this time Kathleen Le Paul was banging on the door again.

Leslie hurried back to the door.

"I'm not standing out here all day," Kathleen Le Paul complained. "Do you have the money or don't you?"

Leslie took a deep breath and decided to pay. She went back to his dresser, counted out fifteen hundred dollars and took it out to the woman.

In return Kathleen handed over the package and left.

When she was gone, Leslie carried the small wrapped package into the kitchen, put it on the table and opened it with a kitchen knife.

Inside was a small glassine bag filled with white powder.

Carefully Leslie slit the bag and tipped the powder onto the table. Cocaine.

It was ruining their lives.

It was taking all their money and screwing up their marriage.

She knew what she had to do.

42

It was incredibly great knowing this was her last day of purgatory. After today she was a free person. No longer Luce, quiet, obedient little secretary. Within hours she was returning to her true identity: Lucky Santangelo. Winner takes all.

It was Friday noon, and at the end of the day she'd be out of there.

She knew the first thing she'd do. Burn the goddamn wig and the dreadful clothes. Smash the vile glasses. And dance around a bonfire chanting thanks like a crazy woman.

After that she'd get on the next plane to New York and be with Lennie. She'd found out from Jess that he was in New York, and Boogie was tracking down exactly where.

Ah . . . she couldn't wait. A long weekend with her husband was just what they both needed. A very long weekend in bed, catching up on all the time they'd been apart. And during the weekend she'd give him the news.

Dear husband, I've brought you a present. I hope you like it.

Naturally they'd run Panther Studios together. What a trip!

Soon Bobby would be out of school for summer break. He'd travel with his nanny straight to California. And Lennie had mentioned something about Brigette joining them. It was going to be the most wonderful summer. A real family affair. Maybe she'd even persuade Gino to come out for a week or two.

When Eddie Kane came racing through her office like a deranged maniac, she didn't take much notice. Eddie Kane was Mickey's problem, not hers. In fact, Mickey was going to have a lot of problems to deal with after today—not the least being that on Monday morning he was going to find himself out of a job.

This was the plan: Today, she was out of there. At six o'clock there would be a meeting at Abe's house to sign the final papers, with both sets of lawyers present. And when all was signed, sealed, and delivered, Panther Studios would be officially hers.

Monday morning Abe had requested the pleasure of announcing the sale himself. He'd already sent an urgent telegram to his other granddaughter, Primrose, and her husband, Ben Harrison, in London, summoning them to the meeting.

Abe had decided to visit the studio personally for the first time in ten years. "Can't wait to see their faces," he'd told Lucky excitedly. "Can't wait to present 'em with you, girlie." As long as she had the weekend to spend with Lennie, she was ready for anything.

The noises coming from Mickey Stolli's office were becoming violent. Idly she wondered who was getting beat up. In a fight she would put her money on Mickey. He was shorter than Eddie, and older, but he had the real strength. Mickey was a street fighter. She'd recognized that quality in him the first time she'd seen him.

Her intercom was buzzing out of control. "Call security," yelled Mickey. "Get 'em up here *now*."

Clearly she heard Eddie's raised voice. "Don't fuck with me, Mickey, 'cause you're fucking with the wrong guy."

"*I'm* fucking with the wrong guy?" screamed Mickey. "Me? Clean up your act, shithead, and get the fuck out of my sight."

Lucky called the front gate. "Can you send a security guard to Mr. Stolli's office, please?" she requested.

"Sure, ma'am," one of the guards replied. "Is it urgent?"

"It depends what you call urgent," she said calmly.

"Life-threatening?"

"Hardly."

Before the guard had a chance to arrive, Eddie stormed out with a bloodied nose.

Hmm, Lucky thought, she was right. In a fight it was always the street fighter who came out on top. Eddie was a little too weak around the edges. Too many late nights and too much cocaine.

Mickey emerged from his office in a black fury. "You dumb cunt!" he yelled. "Don't you ever let anybody in here unless I tell you to. Even if you have to throw yourself in front of my office door and they have to trample over your body, you *do not* let anybody in here. Am I makin' myself clear?"

"No," she said blankly, trying to ignore the fact that he'd screamed "dumb cunt" at her. Nobody called Lucky Santangelo a dumb cunt and lived.

"What?" he bellowed.

"No, I don't understand you," she said evenly. "I'm not allowing people to trample over my body. And I'm certainly not putting myself at risk for you."

He stared back at her in disbelief. A secretary? Answering back?

"Are you tryin' to get yourself fired?" he said angrily, practically hopping up and down.

She shrugged. "Whatever you want to do. It's up to you."

He could hardly believe what he was hearing. Until now, this one had been the perfect secretary. She'd fended his calls, taken care of his appointments, made him coffee, squeezed his juice. She'd even squeeze his balls if he told her to. Now she was developing lip. Jesus Christ!

He stormed back into his office and slammed the door. When the fuck was Olive coming back?

Lucky took a final leisurely lunch in the commissary as Luce.

When she was finished, she strolled over to Harry Browning's table and said, "Do you mind if I join you?"

He glanced up, not pleased to see her. "Yes, I do," he said shortly.

"I'd like to explain something," she said. She felt ever so slightly guilty about Harry. If she'd known he was an alcoholic she'd never have plied him with liquor that fateful salmon mousse night. She sat down. "Harry—" she began.

"Mr. Browning to you," he interrupted.

"I'm sure you imagine I'm playing some kind of strange game."

"I *know* what you're doing," Harry said forcefully. "The whole studio knows what you are."

She raised an eyebrow. "What am I?"

"You're Abe Panther's spy. He sent you in to sleep with Mickey Stolli."

She began to laugh. "Huh?"

"You told Brenda in Eddie Kane's office you were sleeping with Mickey Stolli," Harry said furiously. "Now the whole studio knows."

Lucky almost choked—the thought of shacking up with Mickey did that to a person. "Are you kidding me? I was joking when I said that to Brenda."

Harry drummed his fingers on the table. "A sick joke," he said grimly.

"Oh, you bet it is," she agreed. "And anyway, what do you mean, the whole studio knows?"

"Brenda told everybody. All the secretaries, messengers, assistants. And they in turn told everybody else."

Oh, wonderful! She sighed. What a reputation to have. Sleeping with Mickey Stolli, the man of my dreams! "And does everybody at the studio think I'm Abe's spy?" she asked.

"No," Harry replied shortly. "Only *I* know. I suppose that's why you're sleeping with Mickey Stolli. Mr. Panther told you to."

Now she was getting irritated. "Cut it out, Harry. I am *not* sleeping with Mickey. Everything's going to become clear on Monday."

"Yes?" He looked at her suspiciously.

"Yes." She nodded her head and got up from the table. "Don't forget. Monday morning. Things are going to happen around here."

Abigaile Stolli called at three o'clock. She had an annoying voice, sharp and imperious, as if everybody should jump the moment they heard it. "Who's this?" she asked.

"Luce," Lucky replied. "And who's this?"

"Mrs. Stolli," Abigaile said haughtily. "Are you the new girl?"

"I've been here a few weeks," Lucky answered.

"When is Olive coming back?" Abigaile demanded, as if it was a great imposition for her to have to talk to Lucky at all.

"Soon," Lucky replied.

"Have you ordered our car?"

"What car is that, Mrs. Stolli?"

"Our limousine for the premiere tonight. Surely you know?"

"I wasn't aware you needed a car."

Abigaile exploded. "My God! Do I have to take care of everything myself? Didn't Mr. Stolli tell you? We need a studio limousine. My usual driver. And the car must be stocked with Cristal champagne and Perrier water. Oh, and have it at my house at six-thirty. Not six twenty-five or six thirty-five. Six-thirty. Arrange it."

Lucky decided Abigaile and Mickey made the perfect couple. Both of them dripped with charm.

"I'll see to it, Mrs. Stolli," she said, the perfect secretary.

"Where's my husband?" Abigaile asked irritably.

For a moment Lucky was tempted to say "Why don't you try Warner's apartment? You know, the black vice cop he's been screwing twice a week for God knows how long." Instead she replied, "I have no idea, Mrs. Stolli. But I'll be sure to leave a message you phoned."

"Do that," snapped Abigaile, banging the phone down.

Lucky called up dispatch. "Marty," she said, "Mrs. Stolli needs a car for tonight—not her usual limousine. She's requested one of the small sedans, O.K.? Have it at her house at six forty-five. Thank you."

While Mickey was safely out of the office, she called Boogie. "Did you charter a plane for tonight?"

"All set," he replied.

"And you've found out where Lennie is?"

"Yes."

"What would I do without you, Boogie?"

"You'd get into a lot of trouble."

She smiled to herself. He was probably right.

43

"Mickey," Warner asked, "are you seeing other women?"

Mickey looked at her in surprise. "What kind of a stupid remark is that? Why would I want to see other women?"

"I'm just asking," Warner said. "I can ask, can't I?"

He didn't like the tone of her voice. "You can do what you want, but it's a goddamn stupid question."

Warner stared at him. He'd been in a bad mood all day. Usually she respected his moods and tiptoed around them, but today she'd heard some disturbing gossip and it was on her mind. Some of the cops in vice had a sting going on concerning a brothel in the Hollywood Hills. The high class whorehouse was run by a woman called Madame Loretta. And according to the word around the locker room, many important and influential people in the film industry frequented this place. One of the names she'd heard mentioned today was Mickey Stolli.

Mickey got up from Warner's bed. The sex had not been good. Maybe it was time to move on.

"It really pisses me off when you ask questions like that," he said. "For those kind of questions I may as well stay home with my wife. What do I need to come here for?"

Warner wondered if Mickey's guilt was making him even angrier.

She clenched her teeth and didn't say anything. Instead she walked briskly into her tiny kitchen and plugged in the kettle.

"How about a cup of coffee?" she called out. *Bastard!* If he was playing games with other women—especially hookers—she wasn't going to take it. No way.

"What are you trying to do, kill me?" he complained, following her into the kitchen. "All that caffeine they put in coffee. I have to watch my diet."

She bit back a sharp retort. Mickey watched his diet only when it suited him. Who was he kidding? "Did you remember to get my tickets for tonight?" she asked tightly.

"Huh?" Mickey looked guilty.

She strode out of the kitchen. "You promised me four tickets for the premiere of *Motherfaker*, remember?"

"Oh, Christ," he mumbled, right behind her. Naturally he'd forgotten, and she'd made the request months ago, Johnny Romano being one of her favorite movie stars and all. Shit! He'd gotten her an autographed picture of Johnny, wasn't that enough? Now she had to have tickets for the goddamn premiere too.

He reached for the phone. "Luce," he said, when his dumb secretary picked up. First thing Monday morning he was firing her. He'd bring in Brenda, the pretty black girl from Eddie Kane's office. At least he'd have someone decent to look at.

"Yes, Mr. Stolli?"

"Get me four extra tickets for the premiere tonight. They don't have to be great seats. And I want them . . . uh . . . shit, you'd better messenger them to . . . uh . . ." He held his hand over the mouthpiece. "Warner, I can't give them your address. Where shall I have the tickets sent?"

"Why can't you give them my address?" Warner asked belligerently.

She was definitely beginning to needle him. " 'Cause it's not a smart thing to do."

"I'll pick them up," she said. "I'm going to be out that way today."

The thought of Warner appearing at his office to pick up tickets for *Motherfaker* was a sight he didn't even wish to contemplate. "The best thing is to have them left at the box office," he said quickly, "under your name."

"If that suits you."

"Leave 'em at the box office under the name of Franklin," he mumbled into the phone, hanging up and turning back to Warner.

"Who are you taking anyway?"

She glared at him. "Don't worry, Mickey. I won't come near you or your wife."

He didn't like the way she said that, or the way their relationship was going. He'd thought Warner was different, making no demands. But all women turned out to be the same. They all ended up nagging and wanting more than any sane man was prepared to give.

"O.K., O.K.," he said, reaching for his clothes. "I've got to get dressed an' out of here."

The scene with Eddie had unsettled him. He hated scenes, let alone a fistfight. God knows what Eddie would do next; he was hardly a stable character. If Leslie wasn't such a stupid piece of ass she'd have gotten him into drug rehab long before now.

Driving back to the studio Mickey felt dissatisfied and restless. Making a sudden detour, he headed for Madame Loretta's. Finally he realized Ford Werne had spoken the truth. *Pay for it and you don't get any grief. Pay for it and your life is your own.*

Madame Loretta greeted him warmly. No hassles. No ticket requests. No questions.

"Who've you got for me today?" he asked, as if he was chatting to a butcher in the supermarket selecting a better cut of meat.

"A beautiful Oriental girl," Madame Loretta offered soothingly. "Very nice. Very sweet. Very talented. You'll like her."

"Yes," Mickey said, looking forward to being pampered. "I will."

Eddie called Kathleen Le Paul from his car phone. "I'm sorry," he mumbled. "I forgot."

"Perfectly all right," Kathleen replied calmly. "Your wife gave me the money."

Eddie was shocked. "She did?"

"You left it for me, didn't you?"

"Yeah, yeah, sure. I had to run to the studio. Unexpected."

Kathleen gave a deep sigh. "One of these days you'll clean your life up, Eddie."

"No thanks to you."

"What do you mean by that?"

"You introduced me to Carlos Bonnatti. Now I'm in deep trouble."

"What kind of trouble?"

"Don't give me the 'you haven't heard' bit. It's all over town."

Kathleen's voice had a steely edge. "What did you do, steal from him?"

"I tried to make a living. That's all, a living," he said defensively. "What is it, a crime? The studio'll pay."

"Eddie, Eddie, you'll never learn, will you? You don't fuck with a man like Carlos. If you do, you could end up dead."

Jesus Christ! Eddie Kane had no desire to end up dead. Maybe the only answer was to get out of town. He'd thought about running to Hawaii, where he'd once had such a good time. Plenty of cheap dope and gorgeous girlfriends.

But wait a minute, wasn't he forgetting about Leslie? What was he going to do about her?

Christ! Why had he allowed himself to get into this mess?

Why had he allowed his perfect existence to fall apart?

The call from her sister took Abigaile by surprise.

"What's this all about?" Primrose shrieked all the way from London.

Abigaile quivered with aggravation. Primrose managed to make everything seem like it was her fault. Whatever happened to the niceties of life such as, "How are you?" "Are your children well?" No, Primrose jumped right to it as though Abigaile owed her an explanation.

"I have no idea what you're talking about," she snapped.

"The telegram," Primrose replied impatiently.

"What telegram?"

"Oh, for God's sake! Don't tell me you're going to pretend you don't know anything about it. Ben's furious."

Abigaile spoke slowly and evenly to make sure her sister understood every word. "Primrose, I have absolutely no clue what your problem is."

"Ben and I received a telegram from Grandfather today," Primrose said in an accusing voice, as if Abigaile should know.

Abigaile was surprised. "You did? Saying what?"

"Saying that he wishes us to be at the studio for an urgent meeting on Monday morning."

Abigaile frowned. Did this have something to do with her recent visit to old Abe? Was he readying himself to inform Primrose and Ben that Mickey was trying to sell the studio without his knowledge?

She sighed. "I really don't know what it's about."

"Inconvenient. That's all I can say," Primrose snorted. "Do you realize we've got to get on a plane tomorrow morning? That hardly gives me time to pack. *And* I have to make arrangements for the children. It's simply disgraceful."

"Why don't I get back to you?" Abigaile suggested, anxious to get off the phone. "I'll call Mickey and see what he knows."

"Fine," Primrose said snappishly.

Abigaile put down the phone. The easiest thing would have been to immediately contact her grandfather. Unfortunately she didn't have the courage. Abe, in his feisty old way, would say something rude and insulting, like "Butt out, girlie, it's none of your goddamn business."

She placed another call to Mickey and got his new secretary again. "Is he back yet?" she asked impatiently.

"He's not, Mrs. Stolli."

"Are you sure you don't know where he is? This is urgent."

Irresistible, thought Lucky. "Well . . . I do have a number you might try."

"Give it to me," Abigaile said, brooking no argument.

"One moment, please."

Lucky scooted into Mickey's office, dashed over to his private phone book and looked up Warner's number.

You're being a real bitch, Santangelo.

So what? The guy called me a cunt. This is his punishment.

She returned to the phone and gave Abigaile Warner Franklin's number.

Abigaile called, expecting to reach an office. "Is Mr. Stolli there?" she demanded imperiously when a female answered.

"Who's this?" asked Warner.

"This is his wife."

"Are you calling *me?*" said Warner.

"I beg your pardon?" said Abigaile.

"Is it me you're calling?"

Abigaile was having the most confusing day. "No, I'm not calling you," she said crossly. "Whose secretary are you?"

"I'm nobody's secretary. I'm Warner Franklin." She said her name as if Abigaile was supposed to know who she was.

"Are you an actress?" Abigaile asked, sniffing instant danger.

"No, I'm not an actress, I'm a cop."

"A cop?"

"That's right."

Abigaile was confused.

Warner took a slow beat. "I'm also your husband's mistress," she added, thinking it was about time Mickey's wife realized she existed.

44

Twenty thousand dollars' worth of IBM stock made out in her name was delivered to Venus Maria's house on Friday afternoon. She arrived home from the studio early to find a large, hand-delivered envelope waiting for her. Inside was a Tiffany card from Martin. His name was hand-engraved on the top, and on it he had written, "Don't say I never pay my bets!"

Venus Maria grinned. Obviously Martin could afford it, but it was nice to know he'd remembered. It was also a clever way to settle his bet without involving cash.

How should she respond? It had to be something original. Ron was always full of great ideas, so she called him.

Naturally he was out. He and the Ken Doll had gone shopping at Fred Segal on Melrose. They were not expected back for a couple of hours.

Hmmmm, Ron was probably making more purchases for his live-in lover. He certainly knew how to spend money.

She thought about who else she could call. Unfortunately she didn't have any close women friends. It was difficult in her position. She was rich, young, and famous. She had everything most other females in Hollywood wanted. The envy factor was high.

Oh, of course there were the executives' wives, but she was hardly going to become bosom buddies with Abigaile Stolli and the like. All they seemed to be interested in was giving great charity parties, buying designer dresses, and having long, leisurely lunches where they trashed everybody in town.

It would have been nice to have one special close girlfriend to confide in. Growing up in Brooklyn she'd always been different from the other girls. While they were hanging out at the corner drugstore, going to movies and rock concerts, and sitting around drinking sodas and flirting with boys, Venus Maria had always been obliged to rush home from school to take care of her many chores. Looking after her father and four brothers was extremely demanding. Sometimes she'd felt like a modern-day Cinderella.

None of them appreciated it. They took her completely for granted.

And then she'd met Ron, the boy next door. *The fag next door,* she thought with a hysterical giggle.

They'd hit it off right from the beginning. Two soul mates who had found each other in Brooklyn, of all places.

Ron had encouraged her to cut loose, taking her on wild trips to Times Square, and then down Broadway, where they'd enjoyed hanging out. Ron and she spoke each other's language—Show Biz. They both knew exactly what they wanted and were determined to get it: Stardom and fame. And staying in Brooklyn was not going to do it for them, so eventually they'd taken off.

Both were prepared to work hard. Venus Maria's big turn-on had always been singing, dancing, and acting. It was a thrill, a major charge. She strived to do everything to the best of her ability and usually succeeded.

Ron loved dancing and putting together fantastic routines. Hard work and tenacity had brought them both the recognition they craved.

Venus Maria's father and three other brothers still lived in the same house in Brooklyn. She'd offered to buy them something better. They hadn't accepted the offer, although her father had said he wouldn't mind a new car, and her brothers had mentioned they could do with some extra cash. Two were married. Venus Maria imagined the wives were doing all the work now.

She'd bought her father a brand-new Chevrolet and given her brothers ten thousand dollars each. Nobody bothered to thank her. Nice family.

And then there was Emilio, following her out to Hollywood, installing himself in her house, moaning when she'd asked him to leave. Since then she hadn't heard a word from him. Not so much as a "Thanks, it's nice of you to pay my rent. It's nice of you to lend me a car."

O.K., so she was rich—but she'd worked hard to get where she was. Nobody had ever given her anything for nothing.

She took the envelope containing the stock certificates up to her bedroom—a bright, spacious room overlooking the obligatory Hollywood swimming pool. Off to one side was her bathroom, and on the other her mirrored gym.

On the wall in her closet hung a giant blowup photograph of her taken by Helmut Newton. It was an interesting photo. She was sitting on a stool, wearing a flesh-colored leotard. Her legs were bent under her, her body arched, and her head was thrown back in profile. She looked sexy and innocent, wanton and prim, all at the same time. It was her favorite photograph. Taken before Martin.

With a wry grimace she realized her life fell into two categories: Before Martin, and after.

Maybe she'd been better off before. Who needed a man to obsess on?

She pressed a hidden button and the photograph slid aside to reveal a medium-sized safe. Clicking the knob, she hit the right combination and the safe opened. In it she kept her passport, stock certificates, letters from old lovers, and a photograph of herself with Martin. Cooper had taken the photo one night at her house. It was the only picture she had of them together, and she loved it. They were sitting on the couch in her living room. Martin had his arm around her, while she gazed up at him. It was definitely an intimate photograph. Anyone seeing it would know immediately they were lovers—which is why she couldn't put it in a frame and display it. Too risky. It would be like telling the world, "Hey, this is my boyfriend." And she didn't want to be the one to reveal their relationship. Martin had to make his own decision.

Johnny Romano's voice was on her private answering machine. "Hey, baby," he crooned. "You promised to call me back. This is Johnny. You were s'posed to let me know if you were comin' to my premiere with me tonight." A plaintive cry from a superstar.

Oh, sure, Johnny would love her to arrive on his arm. Let the media salivate over Johnny Romano and Venus Maria together at last. What a picture! What a break! Not to mention sensational publicity for his movie.

Word around the studio was that the film was a bomb. But this was Hollywood—land of hype. The movie would make a fortune, whatever it was like. Johnny Romano could take a piss on Rodeo Drive and still make money!

Why was he calling her anyway? She'd never said she would even consider going with him.

The man obviously got off on rejection. He was always calling her, and she was always saying no. Why did he bother? He could have any girl he wanted. How come he was so intent on having her?

She put away her IBM stock certificates and closed the safe. Then, feeling just a tad guilty, although she didn't know why, she picked up the phone and dialed Emilio's apartment.

He'd moved with the times and bought himself an answering machine. "Emilio Sierra is out," his message said. "But Emilio Sierra would love to know who is calling him, so you call back and I'll call back. Don't forget now—leave your number."

She waited for the beep and said a crisp "Emilio, this is Venus. Just checking in to see if you're settled."

Duty call. It was done. Not that she owed him anything. But still . . .

While she was on a family kick she decided to call her father in New York. He'd never acknowledged her success. He was happy to accept the monthly check she sent him, but he wouldn't give her one word of praise. To her chagrin, she couldn't help herself from still seeking his approval. It was a losing battle.

She was sure he was home, sitting in front of the television, with his beer belly, a can of Heineken, a large pepperoni pizza, and two bags of salted potato chips.

"Hi, Dad, it's Venus," she said when he picked up.

"Virginia?" He refused to use her professional name.

"Yeah. How ya doin', Dad? Just thought I'd check in."

"Can't complain," her father replied gruffly. "Why're you calling?"

Why *was* she calling? He had her number, but he'd never bothered to use it, except once when he'd wanted to complain about one of her videos. "Ya look like a cheap little whore," he'd exploded. "Whaddaya think it's like for me at work? I got guys ribbin' me all over."

That was at the beginning. When the money started to pour in, the ribbing hadn't seemed to matter so much.

"I'm calling to see how you all are," she said flatly, feeling rejected as usual. "Nothing important."

"We're O.K.," he said gruffly. "Could do with some extra money."

So what else was new? "I'll talk to my business manager," she said with a sigh. And that was the extent of their conversation.

If Martin Swanson left Deena and married her, the wedding would be a riot! She could just see her father and brothers mixing with New York high society and the cream of Hollywood.

God, she was hungry. Sometimes fame was a drag. If she wasn't so famous she could jump in her Jeep, race down to Fred Segal, find Ron and the Ken Doll, and they could sit in the restaurant and pig out on delicious club sandwiches. But God forbid she wasn't looking her best, didn't have makeup on, and her hair styled. People would say, "Oh, look, there's Venus Maria, she doesn't look as good as she does on her videos or in the movies, does she?" And then others would come over and start asking for her autograph. She was always polite to them, but it soon became too much of a hassle. And she lived in fear of that one maniac fan coming at her from out of nowhere, screaming, "Whore!" and stabbing her to death.

Only another famous person could understand her fears. Cooper for instance. Cooper understood everything. In fact, he was the only one she could really talk to.

Strut was winding down. She'd finished all her scenes. It was funny—when they were in the midst of shooting, she and Cooper fought all the time. Now she found that she missed him.

The end of filming was always difficult. During the shoot, everyone became part of a large family, all working toward the same goal. And when it was over, you were suddenly cast adrift and no longer had that family to depend on. It was a wrench.

She decided to call him.

He was in his office at the studio. "What's up?" he said cheerfully.

"I was wondering, will you be going to the premiere tonight?"

"Are you certifiable?" He laughed. "I wouldn't see *Motherfaker* if you paid me. Mucho bucks."

"Then why don't we get a bite to eat?"

He sounded amused. "Are we talking Spago here?"

"If you like."

"That means we'll be photographed together," he warned. "What will Martin have to say about that?"

"I don't tell him everything I do," she replied defensively.

"I'm glad to hear it. We'll dine at Spago and enjoy ourselves."

She was pleased, but she hoped he hadn't got the wrong impression. "Cooper, I need somebody to talk to. I'm not calling so you can jump my bones."

"When did I ever try to jump your bones?" he asked indignantly.

"You know . . ."

"Sweetheart," he said firmly, "don't worry. We'll have a quiet dinner. We'll talk. I'll take you to your house, leave you at the door, and then I'll go home and jerk off. Does that suit you?"

She couldn't help laughing. "The day *you* have to jerk off is a day indeed."

"Don't be too sure. With AIDS creeping around every corner I'm not that interested anymore."

She didn't believe a word. "Oh, Cooper, please! It's me you're talking to."

He laughed ruefully. "Yeah, I suppose so. You don't buy my lines, do you?"

She smiled. "No."

"What time shall I pick you up?"

"Eight o'clock."

"I'll be there."

She put down the phone and felt quite pleased. An evening with Cooper. He was a friend. He was also Martin's friend, which meant if she wanted to she could talk about Martin all night long.

And that was just what she felt like doing.

45

Eddie wiped the back of his hand across his nose. There was dried blood there, he could feel it. The humiliation of allowing Mickey Stolli to beat up on him was too much. He'd gone into Mickey's office expecting action, but certainly not the violent kind. Mickey Stolli was a son of a bitch.

The Maserati got him home in record time. He barged into the house, wound up and ready to kick ass.

Leslie was waiting for him. "I was worried about you," she said, full of wifely concern.

He knew he was treating her badly, but he couldn't help himself. "Where's my delivery?" were the first words out of his mouth.

Leslie faced him, wide-eyed and sincere. "I paid the woman who came here," she said tremulously. "Your debt is clear."

"O.K., O.K., where's the stuff?" He wasn't in the mood for a lecture. He needed to get high. And fast.

She faced him. His lovely wife.

"I threw it away, Eddie," she said quietly. "We're starting a new life."

Abigaile hyperventilated all the way to Warner Franklin's apartment. When she reached the street, she drove around the block twice, unsure about where to park. Abigaile had used valet parking for so many years she didn't know how to manage without it. Finally she left her Mercedes on a red line, walked up to the front of the building and pressed the buzzer marked "Franklin."

A disembodied voice instructed her to come to the third floor.

Heart beating, Abigaile took the elevator. What was she doing here? This was madness.

One look at Warner and her heart almost stopped altogether. *This* was Mickey's girlfriend? *This* was the woman he was having an affair with? This six-foot black giant of a female?

Abigaile experienced serious palpitations. Was this a sick joke?

"Come in," Warner said, facing Mickey's wife for the first time.

Abigaile was sure she'd made some kind of insane mistake. Clearly she was about to be kidnapped, bundled into the trunk of a Ford Taurus, and driven to a deserted spot. They would call Mickey for the ransom and he'd refuse to pay. She'd be raped, shot, and thrown over the edge of Mulholland.

"I don't think so," she said, shrinking away. "I've made a mistake."

"What mistake?" asked Warner, towering over her.

"You and my husband. It's not possible."

"Oh, honey, it's possible all right."

Abigaile took two steps backward. "No."

"Trust me."

Abigaile never trusted anybody who said "Trust me." Quickly she turned around and scurried back to the elevator. Pressing the call button, she prayed for its imminent arrival before she was brutally attacked.

"We should talk," Warner called out after her.

"No," Abigaile said, controlling hysteria. "No, we shouldn't."

She got in the elevator and pressed the button. When Mickey heard about this he was going to be furious. Anything could have happened.

Reaching the safety of her Mercedes, she slumped weakly over the wheel. Oh, God! At least she was safe.

After a few moments of deep breathing she remembered she had to go to the beauty shop. Tonight was the premiere of *Motherfaker*, followed by a big charity dinner.

In her panic she forgot about phoning Primrose back. She forgot about Abe summoning her sister and brother-in-law to an urgent meeting on Monday morning. She drove straight to Ivana's and surrendered herself into Saxon's tender, loving hands.

"You look a little pale, Mrs. S.," Saxon commented, tossing his mane of blond hair, strutting around, snug in indecently tight white chinos.

"I had a nasty experience," she confessed.

He caught his reflection in the mirror and checked himself out. "Yeah?"

"*Very* nasty."

"You've got to watch yourself, Mrs. S.," he said vaguely.

"I know."

She did look upset. "You want me to call your husband for you?" he asked casually.

That was the last thing she wanted. "No, no, I'll be fine," she assured him.

He stepped back and narrowed his eyes, viewing her in the mirror. "So, how do we want to look tonight?"

"I don't care."

Saxon went to work.

When Mickey arrived back at the studio, refreshed after a relaxing session with a Chinese hooker, Lucky couldn't wait to give him the good news. "Mr. Panther has called a meeting for ten o'clock on Monday morning," she informed him. "He'll be here personally, and he's requested that you and Mrs. Stolli attend. He's also contacted your brother-in-law, Ben Harrison, and his wife. They'll be flying in from England. Oh, and Miss Franklin has called twice. She says it's urgent."

Mickey stared at his secretary. Luce. This mousy woman. This harridan. "Fuck!" he snarled, before slamming his way into his office.

Mickey Stolli was not having a good day.

46

The photographers gathered outside Spago went into a feeding frenzy when they spotted Cooper Turner arriving with Venus Maria. This was the break they'd been waiting for. The magic couple. A picture capable of making them thousands of dollars.

Venus and Cooper refused to pose. On the other hand, they didn't duck in the back way. Holding hands, they walked down the little hill to the entrance, giving the photographers plenty of excellent photo opportunities.

At the front desk, Bernard greeted them with a friendly handshake, and Jannis ushered them to a window table.

Venus immediately ordered a frozen Margarita and one of Wolfgang's famous smoked salmon pizzas with cream cheese.

Cooper was amused. "I thought you were one of those strong-willed women. Y'know, the kind who never puts anything between her lips if it's fattening."

"Tonight, I'm doing exactly what pleases me," she replied recklessly.

He nodded agreeably. "Does that mean we'll have sex?"

She burst out laughing. "Cooper! You're Martin's best friend. Behave like it. Anyway, you promised."

"You know I'm only joking," he said, waving at Ida and Zeppo White, who were dining with Susie Rush and her husband.

She smiled. "Yeah, sure."

Cooper was forty-six years old, the same age as Martin, and yet he had a little-boy quality she loved. He might be the famous Cooper Turner, but to her he was a friend, and a good one.

"How well do you know Martin's wife?" she asked, trying to sound casual.

"Deena? I've known her as long as Martin has. I met her before they were married."

"What's she like?"

"Deena's an interesting woman."

"In what way?"

"She's got balls."

"Like me?"

"*Nobody's* got your balls."

The pizza arrived, and Venus Maria dug in. "Does she know about me?" she asked, chewing ravenously.

"Look, Martin's never been the faithful husband type. I told you before. A lot of beautiful women have passed through his life. I'm sure Deena knows what goes on. She chooses to ignore it."

"I'm not just another woman," Venus Maria stated vehemently.

"I know that."

"Are you sure you know it? Has he told you?" she pressed, gulping her Margarita.

"No. But you couldn't be just another woman in anybody's life. You're special, kiddo."

Cooper made her feel good. "You think so, huh?"

"I know so." He picked up his glass and toasted her. "You're an original."

"Thank you, Cooper. Coming from you I appreciate it."

Their waiter interrupted to recite the specials. Venus Maria ordered duck with a rich plum sauce, while Cooper settled for thinly sliced steak.

"By the way," he said, once they'd both ordered, "I've been meaning to tell you."

"What?" she asked eagerly.

"I have to admit it—you're really something in the dailies. I know I tried to tone down your performance, but whatever you were doing up there, it works. You've got it, kiddo. Whatever *it* might be."

His praise delighted her. "That's because I was in the hands of a good director."

"You sure know how to flatter a guy, huh?"

"I know how to do a lot of things," she replied provocatively.

He nodded knowingly. "Yup."

She leaned across the table, an intent expression on her face. "Cooper?"

"What?"

"Do you think Martin will ever leave Deena?"

He looked at her quizzically. "Are we back to that?"

"Sorry."

He sighed. "Do you want him to?"

She looked unsure. "Sometimes I think it's what I want more than anything else in the world, and other times I'm not so sure."

"You'd better make up your mind, because whatever *he* does depends on what *you* do."

He was telling her what she already knew. "I guess you're right."

"But I'll tell you this," he added. "If he does decide to leave Deena, it won't be easy. She's a tough lady."

Venus Maria sat up straighter. "I'm tough, too."

"Sweetheart, next to Deena, you're a cupcake."

Across town, Emilio sat in a small, cramped office with Dennis Walla, putting the finishing touches to his tape-recorded story. He'd come up with everything he could think of. Everything from what color panties Venus Maria wore to how she looked when she got up in the morning.

Dennis was satisfied they had a good story, but he still pushed for more. "When are you going to show me the photo you talked about?" he asked. "We need it on the double."

"I'm getting it."

"I thought you already had it," Dennis countered.

"Yes, I do, it's somewhere safe," Emilio replied, slouching in his chair. "You don't expect me to keep a valuable picture like that hanging around, do you? My apartment could be broken into. Anyone could get hold of it. Besides, we haven't agreed on a price."

Dennis picked up a can of beer and took a hearty swig. "The price depends on the photo. If it's worth it, you'll get your money."

Emilio scratched his head. "I'll have it for you soon," he promised.

Dennis rocked back and forth impatiently. "Yeah, well, soon better be within the next twenty-four hours if we're gonna run it."

"Don't worry, I'll have it for you tomorrow," Emilio replied, thinking to himself, what the hell was he promising here? He knew there was a photograph, he'd seen it one day when Venus Maria had left her house in a hurry, forgetting to close her safe. When he was staying with her he'd enjoyed taking little exploration trips around the house while she was out. That had been a bonus day. He'd inspected the safe's contents and spotted the picture of Venus with Martin Swanson. What he should have done was taken it then and there, and had it copied. But he hadn't thought about it at the time.

Now it was a question of getting back into her house, opening the safe, and stealing the photograph.

Clever as he was, Emilio wasn't quite sure how he was going to manage such a feat.

Dennis stood up, yawned, and stretched. "That's it for tonight, mate. I've had it," he said, scrunching his empty beer can and tossing it into a trash basket.

Emilio nodded thankfully. He had a hot date. It was amazing how women's attitudes changed toward him once they discovered he had money. He'd already leased a decent car and bought himself some new clothes.

His date was a hot little dancer who wouldn't have second-glanced him two weeks ago. Now she purred, "Sure, Emilio honey. Love to," when he'd called and asked her out. Her name was Rita and she was a bundle of dynamite. Half Puerto Rican, half American, she was the girl of Emilio's dreams. She looked a little like Venus Maria, but so did half the other would-be video stars in L.A.

Dennis and he shook hands. "Tomorrow, mate," Dennis said, slapping him on the shoulder. "I'll be waiting for your call."

"Right," agreed Emilio. And they parted company.

Cooper Turner was a good listener. His advice was always construc-
tive. "I understand what you're going through," he said sympathetically. "You're in love with the guy. There's no way to explain why
we fall in love with certain people. You and Martin make a strange
couple. You must admit the two of you have absolutely nothing in
common. But you love him, and I understand."

Venus Maria nodded wistfully. "I wish I knew why."

Cooper looked wise. "Maybe you're searching for a father figure.
He *is* twenty years older than you."

"So are you, Cooper. And I wouldn't regard *you* as a father figure."

He reached across the table and took her hand. "What would you
regard me as?"

She smiled. "A very attractive man, who, if I wasn't involved, I
could quite easily think about being with. Even though your reputation goes before you."

"What reputation?" he asked casually.

She began to laugh. "There's no way you can hide it, Coop, you're
a real tomcat. You've been around this town so long there's not a
woman over thirty-five you haven't had, including the married
ones."

Cooper had a glint in his eye. "That was when I was young and
didn't know any better."

"What are you now, senile?"

"Do you want me to talk to Martin?" he asked, briskly changing
the subject. "Find out how he really feels?"

Venus tossed her platinum curls. "I know he's crazy about me.
But I guess I wouldn't mind knowing if he sees a future for us."

"I'll do it."

"You will?"

"For you—anything."

"Not a hint that we've spoken about him, O.K.? Can you be cool?"
she asked anxiously.

"Can *I* be cool?"

"Well, can you?" she demanded.

318

"Sweetheart, I can do whatever you want me to."

She was suddenly very serious. "I trust you, Cooper."

He returned her big brown-eyed gaze. "And so you should."

They drove back to her house. She couldn't help thinking how simple it would be if it was Cooper she was in love with. But no, it had to be Martin. It had to be Mr. New York himself.

"Am I coming in?" Cooper asked when they pulled up outside.

"It depends on what you expect."

He gave her a wry smile. "I expect a cup of coffee."

"Then you'd better come in."

Inside the house she activated her answering machine. There were several messages. Two were business-related, and the third was from Martin. "Did you get my payoff?" his voice said. "I always settle my debts."

The fourth message was from Emilio. "Hey, little sis, nice of you to call me, I 'preciate it. I bin workin' pretty hard. Scored myself some cash. Is it O.K. if I come by in the morning and put it in your safe? Thanks. I don't like to leave it lying around the apartment. See you tomorrow."

"Who was that?" Cooper asked.

"My brother," she replied. "God knows what he's done to get himself a stash of cash. And why does he have to bring it here? Why can't he rent a safe-deposit box?" She sighed. "I tell you—family."

Cooper nodded sympathetically. "I know what you mean." He watched her as she flitted around the room. She was making him uncomfortably hot.

"How about a brandy?" she asked. "I can't be bothered making coffee."

Abruptly he stood up. "I've changed my mind. I'm going home. Early call in the morning."

"Are you sure?"

"Listen, if I stay I'm likely to attack you. So I may as well get out of here while we're still on good terms. Agreed?"

She laughed. "The man is honest."

"The man is horny!"

"I'm sorry I can't do anything about it."

He looked at her ruefully. "No, you're not."

"You're right."

She walked him to the door, stood on tiptoe and kissed him on the cheek. "Thanks, Cooper. You've been a real friend tonight."

When she was alone she thought about Martin. The trouble with sleeping with a married man was that you couldn't pick up the phone and call him when you felt like it.

Restlessly she opened the freezer, helped herself to a carton of chocolate chip ice cream and curled up in front of the television.

Soon she fell asleep.

The hottest young superstar in America slept alone.

47

Abe Panther had dressed up for the meeting. He looked dapper for an eighty-eight-year-old man, in white pants and shirt, a blue blazer, a jaunty red scarf tossed casually around his scrawny neck.

Lucky arrived with Morton Sharkey. She'd rushed back to her rented house from the studio, showered, washed her hair, put on makeup, and piled the wig, glasses, and clothes in a bundle on the bathroom floor ready for the burning ceremony she planned to perform before leaving for New York.

Abe greeted her with a hug and a rascally wink. "This is it, girlie! This is it!" he said exuberantly.

She grinned back at him. "It sure is, Abe. You look wonderful."

"I'm lookin' forward to Monday mornin'," he said. "It's gonna be a real killer!"

Inga appeared. There was actually a pleasant expression on her face. "Good evening, Lucky," she said.

Good evening, Lucky! Inga acknowledged her existence! Abe must have promised her a bundle.

"Well, girlie, you ready to take over?" Abe asked. "You got all your plans in place?"

"I can tell you this, Abe. I'm going to be changing the way Panther does things. No more exploitation films. No more using women. Panther Studios is about to become the equal opportunity studio."

He cackled. "An' you really think you'll make money that way?"

She took a beat. "Sometimes," she replied slowly, "standing up for principles is more important than making money."

Abe cocked his head to one side. "You know somethin', girlie? I wouldn't mind meetin' that father of yours. He taught you good."

She nodded. "He certainly did. We'll all have dinner next time he's out here."

"If I'm around."

"Don't give me that. You're going to be around forever."

The lawyers were lined up and waiting. Morton had two assistants with him, while Abe's lawyers consisted of two businesslike men in three-piece suits.

Abe made quite a ceremony over signing the final papers. He'd had Inga put out the best glassware, all the better to serve vintage champagne.

Just before signing he handed Lucky a Cartier box. "Got you this, girlie," he said, pleased with himself. "Wanted you to have a souvenir of today."

Lucky was quite touched. She opened the box. Inside was an exquisite gold panther pin. On the back was inscribed "To Lucky, from Abe Panther. Kill 'em, girlie!"

She leaned over and kissed him. "This is beautiful, Abe. I'll wear it proudly. And I'll look after your studio." Her black eyes gleamed. "Bet on it!"

Abe signed the papers with a flourish, and the champagne flowed. "Here's to the end of an era," he said, toasting her. "The start of somethin' new."

"It'll be something new all right," Lucky said. "I made you a promise and I'll keep it. Panther Studios will be great again."

They locked eyes. Lucky Santangelo and Abe Panther: nearly sixty years separated them, but they were perfectly in tune.

An hour later Boogie drove her to the airport. She was elated beyond her wildest expectations. Lucky Santangelo. Owner and President of Panther Studios. Goddamn it! Who would ever have believed it? She couldn't wait to see Lennie's face. *And* the rest of him.

Triumphantly she boarded the chartered plane.

Boogie made sure the luggage was aboard, then joined her.

It was a clear L.A. night. Lucky gazed out the window as the smooth jet zoomed down the runway and took off into the star-studded night sky.

She ordered champagne from the steward and toasted the sea of lights spread out like a shimmering blanket beneath her.

"Here's to you, L.A.," she said. "And here's to Panther."

A new adventure was just beginning.

48

The white triple-stretch limo snaked its way through the crowds to the front of Grauman's Chinese Theater on Hollywood Boulevard. A red carpet led from the sidewalk into the theater. Lining the sides of the carpet were various members of the press and camera crews from many different countries. The huge crowds spilled over into the road. When they saw the white limo approaching, a chant went up from the crowd. "Johnny! Johnny! Johnny!" screamed the masses. "We want Johnny! We want Johnny Romano!"

Safely ensconced in his limo, Johnny Romano could hear the tribal yell. He grinned at his date, a pretty young actress with large breasts and a twinkling smile. He'd called her at the last moment because the woman he'd really wanted on his arm was Venus Maria. But since Venus wouldn't honor him with her presence, he'd settled for this one.

Also in the car were his two faithful bodyguards and his manager.

When the limo pulled to a halt, they all stayed put for a couple of minutes, allowing the excitement to build outside on the sidewalk.

"What's going on?" the actress asked. "Why are we waiting?"

"Foreplay," Johnny replied with a suggestive wink.

First the manager got out of the car, followed by the bodyguards, followed by Johnny's date, and finally the great Johnny Romano himself.

A hysterical scream went up from the crowd.

Johnny acknowledged his fans with a kingly wave, pausing by the limo for a few seconds before strutting down the red carpet, his bodyguards flanking him on either side, his date trailing behind, his manager bringing up the rear. Reporters and camera crews pleaded for a moment of his time.

He ignored them all until he reached "Entertainment Tonight." "E.T." was his favorite TV program. He watched it every night.

Jeannie Wolf was there with a microphone and a welcoming smile. "Johnny, are you pleased about the movie?" she asked.

"Hey, Jeannie. Good to see you. Howya doin'?" he said, playing Mr. Humble Movie Star to the hilt. "Yeah, I guess I'm kinda pleased. *Motherfaker*'s gonna surprise a lot of people. I put mucho heavy work into it. My fans are gonna like it. My mother's gonna like it. My father's gonna be ecstatic!"

The crowd roared its approval. They wanted Johnny to be a hit. They rooted for him.

Jeannie laughed politely.

Johnny threw a long, lingering look straight to camera. "All you folks out there, go buy your tickets for *Motherfaker*. You'll have a good time. Johnny—he promises you that."

"Thank you, Johnny," said Jeannie.

"Thank *you*, Jeannie," said Johnny, waving to his fans as he strode manfully into the theater.

Crawling along Hollywood Boulevard, caught in a horrendous traffic jam, trapped in a small sedan, were Abigaile and Mickey Stolli. They'd bickered all the way from their house. First of all, the car had arrived late, and when it finally did get there, Abigaile had freaked out when she realized she was expected to ride to the premiere in a small sedan. She'd thrown an absolute fit, screaming at the driver, an out-of-work actor, who almost walked off the job.

"I never ordered a car like this," she'd yelled. "I've never been in a car like this in my life. Where's my stretch limo?"

"It's down on the sheet, ma'am," the driver had replied politely. "This is the car you requested."

Abigaile narrowed her eyes, naturally blaming Mickey. "I'll murder that secretary of yours. She's an idiot. And it's *your* fault."

"Don't worry about it," Mickey had replied calmly. "I'm firing her first thing Monday."

"Monday isn't soon enough," Abigaile said ominously before turning her attention back to the driver. "Why are you so late?"

"Six forty-five, ma'am. That's the time I was told to be here."

"I expected the car to be here at six-thirty," Abigaile had said through clenched teeth. "This is simply not good enough."

Mickey had shrugged. There were enough things on his mind. He didn't need Abigaile screaming, too.

She'd wanted him to send the car back and get a limousine, but he'd pointed out there wasn't time. "I'll have the driver arrange everything while we're in the theater," he assured her. "There'll be a limousine to meet us when we leave."

She finally agreed and got in the car reluctantly. Image was all-important to Abigaile, and this just wouldn't do.

Even earlier than that, when Mickey had arrived home from the studio, they'd discussed Abe Panther's calling a Monday morning meeting without consulting either of them.

"I don't understand what's going on," Abigaile worried. "Why would he contact Primrose and Ben without first telling me? I saw him this week. It would have been easy for him to mention something."

"Why is he coming to the studio at all?" Mickey had growled. "There's something out of line going on."

Abigaile had muttered her agreement, wondering if now was the right moment to tell him about Warner.

Eventually she'd decided against it. Mickey would accuse her of being insane if she admitted she'd called a number and gone to see a woman who claimed to be having an affair with him.

Mickey had not returned Warner's urgent phone calls. Why should he? He'd finally decided it was time to ease out of the relationship, and the fact that she'd called his office twice really annoyed him.

They were the last to arrive at the theater. The television camera crews were packing up. Only the stragglers remained. Mickey hustled Abigaile inside.

"Sorry," said an officious usher. "The doors are closed."

"Do you know who I am?" demanded Mickey in a rage.

"I'm sorry, the doors are closed," the usher repeated firmly.

"I'm Mickey Stolli, President of Panther Studios. You'd better let us in right now if you plan to keep your job."

The usher snapped to attention. "Certainly, sir," he said, changing his tune in a hurry.

To get to their seats they had to squeeze past Johnny Romano, who was not pleased. "You're late," he hissed at Mickey. Like they didn't already know.

Finally they were settled. Abigaile gazed at the screen, her mind elsewhere.

Mickey settled back and tried to concentrate on the film.

"You motherfuckers," sneered Johnny Romano in full close-up, his handsome face filling the screen.

"Who you callin' motherfucker?" answered the actor playing opposite him.

"Don't fuck with me, man," said Johnny menacingly. "Don't do it."

"Listen, motherfucker, I fuck with anyone I want," replied the other actor.

Oh, nice, Abigaile thought to herself. Another one of Mickey's classy productions. She leaned over to her husband and whispered sarcastically in his ear, "Are there going to be any normal words in this picture?"

Mickey grunted. "It's a money-maker," he replied gruffly.

At the party afterward, everybody told Johnny Romano he was wonderful, the movie was a surefire hit, and how creative and clever he was to have starred, written, and directed.

Johnny Romano accepted their praise modestly, with a shrug here, a smile there.

Privately the buzz was, "How come this asshole gets away with making a piece of shit like this? And how come it's going to score a fucking fortune?"

Johnny strutted around the party giving interviews, greeting friends, playing superstar to the hilt.

Some of the early reviews on the movie had been less than positive. In fact, there'd been some killers. Johnny didn't care. He knew he could do whatever he wanted and the public would accept it— because he was Johnny Romano, and they loved him, and they'd take anything he cared to dish out.

Abigaile and Mickey sat at a table with several Panther executives. Mickey knew something deadly was up when Ford Werne leaned across the table and said, "What's all this about a meeting on Monday morning?"

"Huh?" Mickey feigned ignorance.

"I received a communiqué from Abe Panther," Ford said. "Apparently he's coming to the studio on Monday, and has requested a meeting with all the senior executives at noon."

"Really?" Mickey was aware of a sinking feeling in the pit of his stomach. Crafty old Abe Panther was finally emerging, and he was up to something serious. Maybe he was coming back to take over.

Mickey decided he'd better call Martin Swanson and find out what was happening with the other deal, because if Abe Panther came back to work, Mickey Stolli was getting the hell out. There was no way he was answering to a decrepit, senile old man. No way at all.

As he was thinking all this, he happened to glance up, and there was Warner, all six feet of her, wearing a short spangly dress, talking to Johnny Romano. Jesus Christ! She was actually talking to Johnny Romano!

Mickey did a double take. What the hell was Warner doing here? He'd gotten her tickets for the movie, certainly not an invitation to the party.

No doubt that stupid secretary of his had fucked up again and left a party invitation along with the tickets. From the perfect replacement, Luce had turned into dumb cunt of the year. He couldn't wait to fire her.

"Oh, my God!" exclaimed Abigaile, spotting Warner a few moments later. "It's that dreadful woman."

"What woman? Where?" spat Mickey, knowing she couldn't possibly mean Warner.

"Over there," Abigaile pointed straight at Warner. "Talking to Johnny Romano. It's her."

Mickey looked blank. "She's just another one of Johnny's dates," he said. "What are you getting so bothered about?"

"Something happened today," Abigaile said excitedly, her face flushing.

"What?" Mickey was in no mood to hear about Abigaile's day.

"I . . . I called your office," she said, "to find out where you were so I could tell you about Primrose and Ben and the cable."

He had a dull feeling he wasn't going to like what came next. "Yes?"

"And your secretary gave me a phone number. I called, and this woman answered."

"What woman?"

"The one talking to Johnny."

"Get to the point, Abigaile. Make sense, for crissakes."

"A woman answered the phone and told me she was a cop, and she was your girlfriend. Can you believe such nonsense? Anyway, I didn't know what to do." Abigaile hesitated before plunging on. "You're going to kill me for this, Mickey, but I was so confused, I got in my car and I went to see her. She lives in a tacky little apartment. She tried to threaten me. I'm sure it was some sort of kidnapping plan. Of course, I got out of there as fast as I could."

Mickey scratched his head. "I don't fucking believe what I'm hearing. Some woman says on the phone she's my girlfriend, and you buy that? And you go over to a strange apartment?" He shook his head wearily. "Abby, Abby, you've gone too far this time."

Abigaile cast her eyes down. "I know, Mickey, it was a foolish thing to do. I'm fortunate to have escaped."

While Abigaile was talking, Mickey was thinking fast. Once Abigaile got to consider what had taken place, she would realize all was not as it seemed. He had to come up with some explanation as to why his stupid secretary had given her Warner's number. And then he had to explain who Warner was.

"Listen," he said quickly. "I didn't want you involved in this, but now I guess I'll have to tell you what it's all about."

Abigaile looked alarmed. "What, Mickey?"

"Johnny Romano is heavily into drugs."

"Oh, dear," cried Abigaile.

"Uh . . . I've had this uh . . . private cop following him and uh . . . obviously Luce got confused and gave you the wrong number. The woman must have thought it was Johnny's girlfriend calling him."

"Why would she think that?" asked Abigaile. "I told her my name."

"What am I, a thought reader?" he snapped. "All I know is you should never have gone over there. Don't you realize your position?"

"Why is that woman here tonight? Is she watching Johnny?"

"Yeah, yeah. That's it. She's an undercover drug cop. I have to protect Johnny."

"I didn't realize you got involved in this kind of thing."

"Honey, when you run a studio, you get to watch over everybody and everything."

Mickey figured he'd covered his tracks, for now, anyway. He shot a quick glance at Warner. She was still all over Johnny Romano, and was it his imagination, or did Johnny seem to be responding?

In all the time they'd been together, Mickey had never seen Warner dressed up before. She didn't look bad. She certainly had the longest legs in town, and although she wasn't pretty, she had a certain style of her own. Come to think of it, he'd only seen her in her cop's uniform or in the nude. This was a new, exciting Warner. He experienced a sharp twinge of jealousy.

"When can we go home?" Abigaile whispered. "I hated the movie. I hate this party. I hate the fact we don't know what's going to happen at the meeting on Monday morning. Let's go now."

"You're right," Mickey agreed. "Give me five minutes and we're out of here."

"Where are you going?"

"I gotta go stroke ego, tell Johnny he's the greatest thing since banana yogurt. It'll take me two seconds."

"Shall I come with you?"

"No, stay here. You'll send him over a gift from Cartier's tomorrow."

Mickey walked toward Johnny just in time to hear him say to

Warner, "Hey, baby, baby, you got the longest legs I ever put my eyes on. They about measure up to the height of my date. Bet you can do things with those legs I've never even imagined."

Warner, the six-foot, seen-everything-done-everything, hard-knuckled cop, gazed at Johnny Romano as if he were God.

"How about you an' me gettin' together later?" Johnny suggested, bored with his actress girlfriend, who was busy scanning the room.

Mickey made his presence felt. "Hey, Johnny, we've got another big money-maker here. Congratulations."

"The biggest," Johnny replied modestly.

Mickey kissed ass. He knew how to do it when he had to. "No doubt about it."

Johnny stroked Warner's arm. "Have you met . . . um . . . what did you say your name was, babe?"

Warner threw Mickey a filthy look.

He was infuriated. What had *he* done. *She* was the one at fault, talking to Abigaile on the phone and telling her to come to her apartment. He couldn't wait to have it out with her. But not now, not while Abigaile was present and probably tracking his every move.

"Warner Franklin," she said, cool as you like.

"That's a pretty name, baby," said Johnny with a sexy leer. "Warner, huh?"

Mickey shook her hand.

She squeezed too hard, favoring him with a real bone-crusher.

"Hey, baby, this here's Mickey Stolli, the head of the studio." Johnny nudged her and winked. "This guy's an important man to know. What do you do, honey? You an actress?"

"No." Warner loved to shock. "I'm a cop."

Johnny thought this was the funniest thing he'd ever heard. "A *cop? You?* Oh baby, baby, I wouldn't mind gettin' myself arrested by you."

She shot Mickey a triumphant look. "Maybe you will be. Later."

Seething, Mickey returned to Abigaile, yanked her by the arm, and said, "Let's go."

The Stollis made their exit. Head of a studio and his Hollywood princess wife.

Who knew what Monday morning would bring?

49

It was three o'clock in the morning when Lucky, accompanied by
Boogie, finally arrived on the sidewalk outside Lennie's rented New
York loft. She looked around. "God, Boogie, this is a real dump.
Why didn't he stay at our apartment?"

Boogie shook his head. "Beats me. I suppose he felt he could hide
away here."

"He did a pretty good job," she replied, feeling nervous and excited at the same time. Tracking Lennie was an adventure, and this
little caper had her adrenaline pumping. She took a deep breath.
"O.K., Boog, exhibit your skills, and let's break in here without
anybody knowing."

"You're going to surprise him in bed?" Boogie asked.

"That's *exactly* what I plan to do."

It was unlike Boogie to offer a comment, but he did so anyway.
"You're pretty confident."

"Oh, you *know* I'm confident."

Boogie shot her a look.

Hmmmm, she thought. Did he honestly imagine she was going to
find Lennie shacked up with a woman? Her husband might be mad
at her, but he certainly wasn't that mad. Their relationship was
based on trust, and the last thing she expected was for Lennie to
break that trust. Not that she imagined he wasn't attracted to other

women. But being attracted and doing something about it were two different things.

The loft he'd chosen was on the eighth floor of a rundown building. Boogie sprang the street door with ease, and the two of them entered the lobby, where they were confronted by a row of mailboxes. Lennie's was marked with a cryptic L.G.

The elevator didn't appear to be in great shape. "We'll take the fire stairs," Lucky decided.

"You feeling energetic?" Boogie said. "It's eight floors up."

"You're full of questions tonight, Boog. What's with you?"

"I don't approve of this," he said dourly.

She sighed. All she needed was an uptight Boogie. Why couldn't he get into the spirit of the adventure and enjoy it? "How come?" she asked lightly.

"It's not your style."

"That's where you're wrong. It's *exactly* my style." And it was. Vanish for six weeks. Come back with a bang. What was wrong with that?

They traipsed upstairs, Lucky making better time than Boogie. When they reached the top and let themselves through the fire door to Lennie's floor, they were faced with a steel front door.

Boogie frowned. "I can get through a lot of things, but this looks like a no go."

"How about the back door?" Lucky suggested brightly. "There must be an easier way to get in."

"I don't know." Boogie shook his head uncertainly. "What if he's not living here? What if a new tenant's moved in? A new tenant with a gun?"

"Are you frightened?" Lucky teased. "I always considered you such a macho man."

"I'm protecting your ass," Boogie reminded her tightly.

"*I'll* worry about *my* ass, *you* worry about *yours*."

The back door turned out to be an easier proposition. It took Boogie about five minutes, but eventually he clicked it open.

"Shhhh." Lucky held a finger to her lips as they stealthily made their way into a small, dark kitchen.

Once inside she turned around and whispered to Boogie, "You can go now. I'm fine."

"I can't leave you here," he objected.

"Sure you can," she whispered. "Wait downstairs in the car. If I'm not out in ten minutes, take off."

"I shouldn't go," he repeated stubbornly.

"Will you get out of here?" she said impatiently. "You'll spoil the surprise."

He didn't budge.

"Split," she hissed, "or you're fired."

Reluctantly he departed.

She closed the kitchen door behind him and made her way into a huge studio. In the middle of the open space was a winding flight of stairs leading to a gallery. Since this appeared to be the extent of the apartment, she imagined the bedroom must be at the top of the stairs. Pulling off her sneakers, she stealthily made her way upstairs.

In the center of the gallery there was an enormous circular bed, and in the middle of the bed was Lennie, fast asleep on his stomach, a sheet half covering him.

Lucky couldn't remove the smile from her face. She stood there for a moment just staring at him. Her husband! Her gorgeous husband!

Quietly she began to remove her clothes until she was naked. And then, without a sound, she edged her way into bed next to him.

Lennie groaned in his sleep and threw an arm across her.

She snaked closer, wrapping her body around him.

In his sleep he started to become aroused.

She smiled, trying to decide whether to be insulted or pleased. Was he getting hard because he knew it was she? Or was he merely in the middle of a wonderful dream?

It didn't matter, because she was just as horny as he was. "Lennie," she whispered, rubbing against his back. "Wake up."

He let out a groan and slowly opened his eyes. "What the—" he began.

"Shhh." She held her finger to his lips, attempting to silence him.

"Hey—I don't believe this," he mumbled, still half asleep.

"Believe it, baby. It's me. I'm back!" she exclaimed delightedly.

He rolled over. "How the hell did you find me?"

She laughed softly. "Who did you think you were dealing with here, a wife?"

He propped himself up on one elbow. "You're too much, you know that?"

"Uh-huh."

"Jess told you where to find me, huh? I always knew she had a big mouth."

"My sources are secret. I'm here. Isn't that enough?" As she spoke, her hands caressed his body.

He attempted to push her away with very little real intent. He was mad, but losing the battle. "Jesus, Lucky. What happens next? Another great sex scene so you can take off again when it's over?"

"No way," she replied indignantly. "I never repeat myself. You should know that by now."

"The only thing I know about you is that you're crazy."

"I know I'm crazy, too. Six weeks away from you is the longest I can take."

He sat up, brushing his hands through his hair. "Was it worth it? Did you make your deal?"

She put her arms around him from behind. "I'll tell you all about it tomorrow."

He shook his head. "How did you get in here?"

She grinned. "I used to be a burglar. Didn't I tell you?"

"Oh, baby, you're something else, you really are. I should be mad at you."

She scratched the back of his neck, a place she knew he loved to be touched. "Are you, Lennie?"

He shook his head again. "What am I supposed to do?"

"You're supposed to kiss me—make love to me. And we're supposed to have incredible sex." She took a beat, continuing to stroke the nape of his neck. "I'm ready," she whispered tantalizingly. "How about you?"

He didn't fight it. What could he do? He loved her.

He turned her over until she was flat on her back. And then he bent to kiss her. Slow, burning kisses, his lips scorching hers, making up for six weeks of pent-up passion.

She sighed voluptuously. It was like the first time she'd ever been kissed. It was like going off a diet and having chocolate for the first time in months. It was like a hot summer day after rain. It was like the time they'd made out on a raft in the South of France with nobody around to bother them.

He kissed her long and hard until they both fell into the slow fast buildup to the wild roller-coaster trip they knew awaited them.

His hands moved ravenously down her body, touching her as only he could. "Oh, Christ," he groaned. "I still love you. You know that, don't you?"

"Did you think it was over?" she murmured, winding her body around his, touching him wherever she could.

"I never know what to think when it comes to you."

"You've got to learn to trust me, Lennie."

And so they made love, long and leisurely, slow and even slower, their bodies fusing together as if nothing else in the world mattered. And at that very moment nothing else did.

She gave herself up to ecstasy, luxuriating in the thought of a wild, throbbing release. And as it drew close, she whispered in his ear. "I want to come with you," she whispered urgently. "I want us to come together."

"You got it, lady. There's no way I'm goin' anywhere without you."

"I love you, Lennie," she sighed happily. "I love you so much."

And they made it happen.

And they made it last.

And they ended up wrapped into each other's arms, sleeping soundly until the morning light.

50

Eddie Kane paced up and down Kathleen Le Paul's living room, talking fast. "My life's a fuck-up. I got no idea what I'm gonna do. You can't help me. Leslie can't. And Mickey doesn't give a fuck. I'm a failure. An' on top of everything else I hit my wife." He slapped his forehead with the palm of his hand—a gesture of self-hatred. "I've never hit a woman before. Do you understand what I'm saying? I've never hit a woman, and I hit Leslie, who's the sweetest person in the world."

Kathleen was really not interested in hearing Eddie's stream of consciousness. She was interested in getting him out of her house. "How did you get my address?" she asked edgily, her calculator brain figuring out how much he owed her.

"You think I've dealt with you all this time and haven't found out a thing or two?" Eddie replied heatedly. "I tried to call you from my car, but I couldn't get through." His facial twitch went into overdrive. "I gotta have some stuff, an' I gotta have it like now."

"Eddie," Kathleen said patiently, although she didn't feel patient at all—she felt like throwing the bum out—"I made a delivery to you today. Another fifteen hundred dollars' worth, which, I might remind you, is currently on your tab."

"Yeah, well, you wanna know why I laid one on my wife? You wanna know?" Now he smashed his fist into the palm of his hand. "She threw my stash down the friggin' garbage disposal."

Other people's problems bored Kathleen. She had enough of her own. What Leslie did was not her concern.

Eddie was on a roll. "How was I supposed to handle that? Say, 'Thank you dear for saving my soul'? No way. I'll get fuckin' straight when *I* wanna get straight." He walked over to the window and stared out. "I can stop any time. Right now I don't need crap." He turned back to her. "So you're gonna help me out."

"If you think I keep a supply in my house, you're not as smart as I imagined," she said, hoping to get rid of him.

There was no getting rid of Eddie. "Kathleen, don't talk to me like I'm a schmuck. Go to the safe or wherever the fuck you keep it an' get me somethin'."

"Eddie, I can't encourage this kind of behavior. If you ever come to my house I'll be forced to put a bullet through your ass. I can always say I thought you were an intruder."

Now he was getting really edgy. "Fine, fine, whatever makes your day. Do I get the stuff or not?"

"Cash only."

This broad was getting on his nerves. "I gave you cash this morning."

"You owed me. Now you owe me more. You haven't even paid for the stuff your wife dumped."

He was truly surprised. "Shit! Am I supposed to pay for that?"

"Am *I?*" she answered coldly.

"So I owe you. Don't get your balls in an uproar."

It was quite obvious there was only one way to get him to leave. "Wait here," she said brusquely. "Don't touch anything."

While she was away, he rifled his pockets. All he could find were a few credit cards, his driver's license, and maybe two hundred and fifty bucks. That was it.

Painfully he relived the scene with Leslie.

"I threw it away, Eddie," she'd said, all sweetness and light. "We're going to start a new life."

"You did what?" he'd shouted, unable to believe anyone could be that stupid.

"I threw it away, Eddie," she'd repeated. "You're addicted."

What was she all of a sudden, a nurse? "I hope you're kidding me," he'd said ominously.

"No," she'd replied, as if it was her right to do what she liked.

He'd slapped her so suddenly it surprised even him. One good whack across the face, and Leslie went down like a bowling pin. Oh, Christ, he hadn't even felt bad about it then. He'd gone on a rampage through the house, searching everywhere, throwing clothes out of drawers, dishes from kitchen cabinets. And then he'd walked back into the room where she still lay on the floor. "Tell me where the fuck it is," he'd screamed.

By that time she was crying. Her eye already beginning to puff up where his pinkie ring had caught it.

"I threw it away," she sobbed.

"Bitch!" he yelled. "You *know* what I'm suffering. A little coke helps get me through the day. You're nothin' but a bloodsucking bitch! All you want is my money, an' now I don't have any, you're drivin' me nuts."

"Eddie, I'm only trying to help you," she'd said miserably, tears running down her cheeks.

"If this is the kind of help you give, get out of here. This is *my* house, an' I want you gone when I get back."

He'd stormed out, climbed in his Maserati, and now he was at Kathleen's.

When Kathleen came back into the room he handed her four fifty-dollar bills. "This'll hold you, unless you'd sooner have a check."

"I don't take checks," she said icily.

He hunched his shoulders. "What's the matter, you're not into trustin' me?"

"I don't trust anybody," Kathleen Le Paul replied flatly. "And what am I supposed to do with a lousy two hundred dollars?"

She could stuff it up her snatch for all he cared. He needed a snort more than he needed anything. "Come on, baby," he wheedled. "I'm good for the money." Maybe he should throw a fuck into her. Kathleen looked like the kind of woman who could do with it.

"What are you doing about your debt to Bonnatti?" she asked curiously.

He picked up a gold table lighter and studied it. This broad must be doing pretty well for herself. "I put my house on the market. Monday I'll get a bank loan. He'll get paid, don't worry about it, and so will you."

She tried to control her underlying anger. "Eddie, I'm strictly a cash business. This is the last time." She handed him the package. "I mean it."

"You want to do some together? Be sociable?" he suggested.

Was he crazy? She wouldn't touch the stuff. "No, just get out of my house."

Outside in the car he snorted the white powder from the back of his hand. And once the effect took hold, he immediately felt like a calmer, saner man.

In fact, he felt as if he could accomplish anything.

Leslie was stunned. Never in her wildest dreams had she imagined Eddie would ever strike her. It brought back every bad memory. When she was a little girl, her stepfather had knocked the hell out of her. When she was a big girl, her first boyfriend had done the same thing. And when she'd run away to California with a thousand dollars of her stepfather's money, which she reckoned he owed her, she'd vowed that no man was ever going to get away with hitting her again. Now this.

Leslie had really thought she loved Eddie. But Leslie was no victim. One blow, and he didn't have to tell her to go—she was out of there.

Hurrying into the bedroom, she threw some clothes into a suitcase. Then she went outside to her Jeep, got in, and drove directly to Madame Loretta's.

When the friendly old madam saw her, she was immediately sympathetic and took her upstairs.

"Can I stay here until I figure out what to do?" Leslie asked mournfully.

Madame Loretta nodded. "Are you coming back to work?"

Leslie shook her head. "It's not what I want to do."

"No pressure," replied Madame Loretta. "We'll talk tomorrow. Why don't you take a hot bath and get a good night's sleep?"

Leslie nodded. At least she'd had somewhere to run to.

51

Saturday morning in New York dawned crisp and clear. The sun filtered through the flimsy blinds in Lennie's loft and woke Lucky. For a moment she was disoriented, and then she remembered where she was and smiled to herself. Lennie was asleep next to her, exactly where he should be.

Trying not to disturb him, she crept from bed, dashed into the bathroom, and switched on the shower. It was old and rusty and didn't have much pressure, but she stood under it anyway, allowing the warm water to sting her into a state of awareness.

Emerging from the shower, she wrapped herself in Lennie's white terry-cloth robe. It swamped her. Barefoot, she padded downstairs to the kitchen and inspected the contents of the fridge. There wasn't much there: a couple of eggs, some moldy tomatoes, a stale loaf of bread, and half a pint of sour milk. Hardly ingredients for a feast.

Cooking was not one of her greatest talents, but she could rustle up scrambled eggs and toast if the mood took her. "Hmmm," she murmured, surveying what was available. It didn't look very promising.

Quietly she padded back upstairs, slipped into her clothes, grabbed her purse, found the keys to the loft lying on a table next to the bed, and let herself out.

Down on the street it was New York crazy, hustle and bustle, and the smells, sights, and sounds she'd missed, having been in California for six weeks.

In the neighborhood grocery store she picked up fresh rolls, juice, eggs, fruit, butter, and milk. Then she had the old man behind the counter slice her half a pound of fresh ham.

Satisfied, she hurried back. Lennie was still asleep, and who could blame him? It had been some wonderful night!

Busying herself in the kitchen, she mixed the eggs and heated the rolls. Then she squeezed fresh orange juice, made coffee, and set everything out on the kitchen table After that she scrambled the eggs, and then yelled out, "Hey, Lennie, get your sexy ass down here for breakfast."

No response.

Noticing a stereo, she slotted in a Stevie Wonder tape and "Isn't She Lovely" blasted out.

Finally Lennie staggered downstairs with rumpled hair and a half-asleep look.

"Good morning," she sang out cheerfully.

"I had this wild dream," he mumbled. "Who're you?"

"Your wife. Remember?"

"A wife who cooks?" he said blankly, shaking his head. "I don't have a wife who cooks."

She offered him a spoonful of eggs. "Try it and live!"

Gingerly he tasted the eggs. "Hmm . . . not bad."

"Not bad, my ass. They're fuckin' great! Admit it."

"You're back."

"Oh, yeah!"

"Still as crazy as ever, huh?" he said, sitting at the table.

She grinned. "Would you have it any other way?"

"It'd be nice if you stayed home occasionally."

"Stop nagging!" She stood back and surveyed him. "Hey—look at you in the daylight. Is that the very same beard that was scratching the hell out of me all night long?"

"The very same."

"Hmm . . ."

"You like?"

"I hate."

"It's gone."

She put her arms around his shoulders, anticipating the surprise she had for him, but not wanting to reveal it yet. "I'm really back."

"I noticed. For how long this time?"

"No more trips, Lennie. We'll be together all summer long. That's a Santangelo promise."

"A Golden promise," he corrected.

She smiled. "Right!"

He surveyed the table. "So . . . what made you turn into housewife of the year?"

"I thought you might be hungry." She bent down and kissed his neck. "Did I make you hungry, Lennie?"

"Ravenous!"

"Really?"

He twisted around and his hands began to stray beneath her T-shirt.

She backed away. "Later. I want to see you eat."

He ate like a starving man, grabbing everything in sight. "This is great," he said with his mouth full. "Best meal you've ever cooked me."

She laughed. "The *only* meal I've ever cooked you, right?"

"You made me soup once."

"Was it good?"

"Passable."

"Thanks a lot!" She glanced around the loft. "This place is a mess. Who's been looking after you?"

"Nobody."

"I can see that. What have you been doing?"

"What I should have done a long time ago. Writing a script. A movie I might direct."

"Oh, we're a director now, are we?" she teased.

"Why not? If Grudge Freeport can do it, anyone can."

"You're talking to the right person," she encouraged. "Will you star in it too?"

He laughed. "Hey—you think I'd let anyone else do it? It's a terrific role."

"When can I read it?"

"Not until it's finished." He paused. "So, I guess you heard I walked off the film?"

"It's not exactly a secret."

"I warned everyone it had to happen. They'll probably sue, but who cares? It was something I had to do."

She almost told him about Panther, but held back just in time. It was too important to blurt out.

"Don't worry, they won't sue," she said reassuringly.

"What makes you say that? I hear Mickey Stolli is so crazed he nearly blew a blood vessel."

"Listen to me, Lennie. I *know* they won't sue."

"Why?" he joked. "Are you getting Gino to put a hit on them?"

She laughed. "Gino doesn't do that kind of thing."

"But he could arrange it if he wanted to, huh?"

"Why do you always imagine my father was such a major gangster?"

"Wasn't he?"

"He shipped booze in during Prohibition. And then he ran a speakeasy. After that he got into Vegas and became respectable."

"Sure."

"Really. Have you seen him?"

"I haven't seen anybody. I've been holed up here."

"We must call him."

"Later." He pushed his chair away from the table and got up. Then he reached out his arms for her. "C'mere, cook."

"Why?"

"Because I want to try to knock you up."

She grinned. "Sweet-talker."

"And don't you love it!"

52

Saturday morning in Los Angeles was smoggy. Emilio Sierra couldn't help but notice that Rita had stayed the night. Her clothes made a trail from the living room to the bedroom, and she herself was asleep in his bed. Score one for Emilio. He was some stud!

Nudging her roughly, he urged her to wake up.

"What time is it?" Rita mumbled, hugging the pillow.

"I told you—it's late, an' I gotta go out."

Rita buried her face in the pillow. "I'll stay here."

"You won't stay anywhere," Emilio replied, agitated. "I gotta lock the apartment."

"Whaddaya think? I'm gonna rip you off?" Rita accused.

"Naw. My mother's comin' over," he lied. "I better drop you off."

She dressed, unabashed about strutting naked in front of him. She was a hot little number all right. Although not quite so hot in the harsh light of morning with the sun streaming through the windows, hitting her unmade-up face.

"Come on," Emilio urged, forcing her to dress in a hurry.

She did so, complaining all the way.

Then he hustled her out to his car, drove her to her apartment, and said a fast goodbye.

"When am I gonna see you again?" she asked, stalling.

"Soon." He winked. "I'll call you."

She wasn't thrilled with his reply, but she sashayed into the entrance of her apartment building as if she didn't have a care in the world.

Women, Emilio thought to himself, *the worse you treat 'em, the more they like it.*

Once rid of Rita, he drove directly to Venus Maria's house. He knew it was too early for her to be up, and as it was a weekend, the housekeeper had the day off—which was exactly what he was counting on. Her housekeeper was too protective by far, always spying on him. With just himself and Venus Maria in the house, he'd have a better chance of getting what he needed from her safe.

He didn't bother ringing the doorbell. There was a window in the back that allowed him easy access. Why disturb her if she was alseep? All the better to surprise little sis.

Venus Maria was asleep, all right, curled up in front of the television, an empty ice-cream carton on the floor beside her, a jacket thrown casually across her body.

This was too good to be true.

Stealthily Emilio made his way through the living room, up the stairs to her bedroom, straight to her hidden safe. He knew where she'd jotted down the combination in some kind of code. Quickly he found her private phone book, located the coded combination, hurried to the safe, opened it, slid out the picture of Venus Maria with Martin Swanson, and placed it safely in his pocket.

All this took only a few minutes. It was far easier than he'd expected. Now he could skip, and she wouldn't even know he'd been there.

Unknown to Emilio, when he'd opened the window he'd triggered a silent alarm connected directly to the police. As he started to make his way downstairs he was shocked to hear the screaming siren of a police car. It sounded like it was right outside the house.

Venus Maria awoke with a start. "Oh, God!" she exclaimed, realizing she'd fallen asleep in front of the television. The police were already urgently pressing her front-door buzzer.

Groggily she rushed to the door.

Two uniformed cops stood at attention. One of them had a hand hovering near his gun. "Your alarm went off, miss," he said. "You all right?" And then realization hit. He nudged his partner. "Excuse me, aren't you—?"

She nodded. "Yes, I am, and I'm not looking my best. What do you mean, my alarm went off?"

"There's an intruder in your home."

Oh, God! The crazed fan she'd always dreaded was somewhere in her house. She shivered. "I'm here by myself."

"Don't worry. We'll check everything out. Do you mind if we come in?"

"Mind? I'd be delighted."

Emilio lurked at the top of the stairs, listening. How was he going to get out of this one?

His mind raced with possibilities. He could always say the back door was open and he'd gone up to her bedroom to see if she was awake. Venus Maria wouldn't be pleased, but what could she do? He *was* her brother.

Before he could make any move at all, the two cops were crouched at the bottom of the stairs, guns drawn. "Hit the floor, sucker," one of them yelled. "Don't even think about going for a weapon."

Dennis Walla groped for the ringing phone. "Yeah," he muttered into the receiver. "Wassa matter?"

"Dennis?"

"Who's this?"

" 'Ere, Dennis, it's yer New York connection, Bert. You got a short memory or wot?"

With a weary sigh Dennis recognized the rough cockney accent of Bert Slocombe, one of his colleagues in New York. Just for a lark, they'd put a man on Swanson watch.

Dennis yawned and scratched his balls. "Find anything out, mate?"

"Only that they go out a lot," replied Bert sourly. "Bleedin' 'ell, they're never at 'ome."

"Yeah? Where'd they go?"

"Try just about every party in town. An' every club. It's bloody well not easy following 'em."

"Do they seem like a happy, loving couple?"

" 'Ere, you ever seen a husband and wife out in public who don't seem lovey-dovey? They're all over each other. It's bleedin' sickenin'."

"Hmmm." Dennis groped for a cigarette, lit up, and inhaled deeply. "I don't suppose he'll be so cheerful come Monday."

"Yer think the bugger'll sue us?"

"Talk sense, mate. Nobody's that stupid. Four or five years with lawyers swarmin' all over you, an' then finally sloggin' it out in court. No. He won't sue."

"Yeah, but Martin Swanson's a tough one."

"Don't worry about him being so tough. Today I'm getting my hands on a photograph of him with Venus Maria. A very telling photograph. When our story runs we'll have plenty to back it up."

"O.K. Am I off duty now?"

"Stick with 'em another twenty-four hours."

"It's a useless waste of my time," Bert complained.

"Waste it. You're gettin' paid," Dennis said. He took another drag of his cigarette, stubbed it out in an overflowing ashtray, turned over, and went back to sleep.

At seven o'clock on Saturday morning Martin Swanson played racquetball for two hours. He got off on the challenge of beating the hell out of his opponent, and since most of his opponents worked for him, he managed to win every time.

Afterward he took a shower, toweled himself dry, dressed, and jogged up the stairs to the top floor of the Swanson Building, where his penthouse office gave him an overall view of the city.

It was too early to call Venus Maria in California. He wondered what her reaction had been to his gift. Well, it wasn't a gift, really. He'd lost a bet. And what a beautiful way to lose!

Gertrude, his personal assistant, greeted him with a triumphant smile. She'd been with him eleven years and knew more about his business than anyone. "Good morning, Mr. Swanson, and how are we today?"

He nodded.

"I'm sure you'll be delighted with these," she said, handing him a sheaf of FAXes. "Yes, Mr. Swanson, it looks as if we'll be taking over a studio. Shall I alert your pilot and have him ready the plane?"

He read the first FAX quickly. And the second one. And the third.

A smile played around his lips. "Do that," he said. "I'll leave first thing tomorrow."

Mickey was awakened by a troop of Mexican gardeners using their illegal leaf blowers right outside his bedroom window. The smell of gas pervaded his nostrils. Furiously he turned over to prod Abigaile, but she was already up and gone from the room.

"Goddamn it," he muttered under his breath. How many times had he told her that under no circumstances were the gardeners to come anywhere near his house on a Saturday. He groped for his watch. Was it ten o'clock already?

Rolling from his comfortable bed, he stalked into his bathroom, glared at himself in the mirror, filled his sink with ice-cold water, and plunged his face into the icy bowl. It woke him in a hurry.

When his head cleared he called Warner. "What the fuck kind of game are you playing?" he demanded in a low voice, just in case Abigaile was listening.

"It's over, Mickey," hissed Warner, not pleased to hear from him.

"What do you mean, it's over?"

"I've had enough."

"Enough of what?"

"Your bad moods, your wife, and the way you use me for sex. Besides, I'm in love with somebody else now."

He nearly choked. "You're *what?*"

"Yes, I'm in love with somebody else." She confirmed the ego-busting news.

"And who might that be?" he asked tightly.

"Johnny Romano," she replied, and promptly hung up on him.

And Leslie Kane awoke in L.A. and shivered when she realized where she was and what she'd done. She'd run out on Eddie, straight back to her old life. On reflection, it probably wasn't the smartest move in the world.

Tearfully she thought about her husband. Eddie wasn't so bad. He had his problems. Didn't everyone? And she'd deserted him just when he'd needed her most. What kind of wife did that make her?

Madame Loretta's house was very still. Saturday mornings and sex for sale did not mix. Most men were busy with their families.

She lay in bed and tried to decide what to do. One thing was sure, and that was she had to teach Eddie some kind of lesson. He had to be made aware that he could not treat her like dirt.

Twenty-four hours should do it.

Twenty-four hours and then she'd go home.

In New York, Deena opened her eyes at ten o'clock, removed her black satin sleep mask, and summoned her maid, who served her tea in bed and brought her the morning papers. She skipped straight to the gossip columns, anxious to know who was doing what to whom and if there were any parties she might have missed. Satisfied that there weren't, she immediately turned to the fashion pages. Not for Deena world events and crime news. She wasn't interested.

Her houseman buzzed the bedroom to tell her there was a call for her.

"Who is it?" she asked.

"Mr. Paul Webster," he replied.

Hmm . . . what was Effie's son calling her for?

She picked up the phone. "Paul?" she questioned. "*Little* Paul?"

"Do you get your kicks trying to make me feel small?" he asked.

Nice voice. Very low. Very sexy. In spite of herself, Deena felt a tingle. "I don't think your mother would enjoy it if she knew you were flirting with me," she said.

He came right back at her. "What makes you think I'm flirting?"

"Either that or you're calling to ask after my health. Which is it, Paul?"

"You're a turn-on, Deena."

She couldn't help being amused. "Paul, I'm old enough to be your . . . your . . ."

"Older sister?" he offered helpfully.

"Something like that."

"Can I take you to lunch?"

Why not? she thought to herself. Effie would have a thousand fits. But Effie didn't have to find out, did she? "Where did you have in mind?"

"The park," he said easily.

She thought he meant Tavern on the Green. "What time?"

"I'll pick you up at noon." He paused, waiting for her response.

"I'm not sure. I—"

"Twelve o'clock," he interrupted forcefully. "See you."

She smiled. There'd been nobody since the soul singer. Just because Martin said she wasn't supposed to . . .

Why should she listen to Martin when he did exactly as he pleased?

But Paul Webster . . . a boy . . . Effie's son.

Deena Swanson, she scolded herself, you ought to be ashamed.

And Eddie Kane didn't sleep at all. He went to a party at the beach house shared by Arnie Blackwood and Frankie Lombardo. He got well and truly bombed. He snorted as much cocaine as he could manage because he knew Arnie and Frankie kept a generous supply for their friends, and it would cost him nothing. At one point he'd asked Arnie for a loan. Arnie had laughed in his face.

There were plenty of girls around, but Eddie didn't feel like getting laid. He knew how badly he'd treated Leslie. He'd hurt her, and he didn't know how she'd react. What was he going to do about it?

First of all, he had no idea where she'd gone. And second, he wasn't sure how long it would take her to return.

Talk about screwing up a perfect relationship. The story of his life.

Saturday morning he came to, only to find himself slumped on the living-room floor of Arnie and Frankie's house in Trancas, along with half a dozen other bums who'd spent the night.

Fortunately he'd managed to score enough coke at the party to give himself a jump start. After visiting the bathroom and doing just that, he felt considerably better. He made his way outside to his car.

Home sweet home.

He could only hope Leslie was waiting.

53

"**D**on't shoot! I'm her brother," Emilio shrieked, his voice filled with panic.

"Hit the ground *now*, or you ain't gonna be nobody's brother," one of the cops yelled.

Venus Maria hovered behind them.

"Get back, miss," said the other cop.

She'd recognized Emilio's voice. Damn! What the hell was Emilio doing sneaking around her house without permission? She hid in the kitchen trying to decide what to do.

Warily one of the cops climbed the stairs, while the other one stayed behind and covered him.

Cop number one reached Emilio, twisted his arms behind him and roughly handcuffed his wrists.

"You're making a big mistake," Emilio managed. "I'm tellin' you, man, I'm Venus Maria's brother. I'm no trespasser."

"We'll see about that," said the first cop. "On your feet."

"You bet we'll see about it," Emilio shouted, gaining confidence. "I'll sue you."

"You'll sue us, huh?" said the cop in a bored voice. He'd heard it many times before. It was the Beverly Hills battle cry.

Once downstairs, they frog-marched him outside to the police car.

"Get her to identify me," Emilio screamed, suddenly panicked. "I'm telling you, I'm her brother."

One of the cops walked back to the house and found her in the kitchen. "Can I have your autograph?" he asked. "For my little girl. It'd really make her day."

"Sure," Venus Maria said, signing the piece of paper he thrust at her.

"Uh, I don't know if we've got a deranged fan or what, but this guy claims he's your brother. You have a brother?"

She nodded glumly. "Four of 'em. All bums."

"How about takin' a look before we haul him in an' book him."

For a moment she was tempted to say no, but then she thought about the headlines and reluctantly agreed.

Outside, Emilio slouched against the side of the police car looking guilty.

Shit! It *was* him. "I'm sorry, guys," she said. "This *is* my brother. I have no idea what he's doing in my house; he doesn't live here."

The cops exchanged glances. "Should we let him go?"

She had no choice. Locking Emilio up for being a pain in the ass was just not on.

Reluctantly she nodded. "I guess so." A night in jail would've done Emilio a world of good. Paid him back for all the bullying he'd inflicted on her when she was growing up.

They removed the handcuffs. Emilio rubbed his wrists, glaring at both cops. "There'll be a court case about this," he said, puffing himself up. "Count on it, man."

"Shut up and get inside," Venus Maria interrupted. "Why are you breaking into my house anyway?"

"Breaking in?" replied Emilio, aghast. "You think *I* would break in? Your own brother? I came to bring the money you said I could leave in your safe. I was looking for you in the bedroom when the cops arrived."

"How did you get in?" she asked suspiciously.

"Through the back window. It's always open."

"You set off the silent alarm. There's a beam across it."

He tried to look contrite. "Sorry, little sis, didn't mean to cause no trouble."

Venus Maria glanced helplessly at the officers and ran a hand through her platinum hair. "I'm sorry you've been bothered, guys. Seems like it was a mistake."

"No bother," they both agreed. "Any time. Love your records. Love your videos."

She smiled. "Thanks. Hey, why don't you leave me your names? I'll see you get tickets for my next concert."

The cops looked pleased.

Emilio slunk back into the house. All he had to do now was get out. He didn't want Venus opening her safe and finding her precious photo missing. He had the photograph safely stashed inside his jacket. Best to make a speedy getaway.

Venus Maria followed him in. "When you come to my house," she said clearly, "you will ring the front doorbell. Can you do that?"

He nodded sulkily.

"Give me the money you want me to put away. And Emilio, next time, telephone before you come here."

He hit his forehead. "I'm stupid!" he exclaimed. "I rushed over here so fast I forgot the money. Left it in my apartment. Y'know, maybe I should put it in a bank anyway."

"Yes, maybe you should," she agreed, wondering what he was up to.

He prepared for a fast exit. "I'll see you, little sis."

Of all her brothers, Emilio was the most devious. She didn't trust him. She never had, and he was far too anxious to get out of there. He ran like a rat.

Maybe the police had unnerved him.

Or maybe not.

Venus Maria's gut instinct told her Emilio was up to something.

The trouble was, she couldn't figure out what that something was.

54

"**W**hat do you want to do today?"

"I don't know. What do you want to do today?"

"*I* dunno, Marty. What do *you* wanna do today?"

Lennie laughed. "Hey, you're too young to have seen that movie."

"So are you," she retorted affectionately, happy to be in her husband's company.

"I'm not as young as I used to be."

"Who is?"

They bantered back and forth, delighted to be together. It was a hot New York day. They'd had breakfast, made love again, and now it was time for decisions.

"What I'd really like to do," Lucky decided, "is visit Mary Lou and the baby. How does that grab you?"

"It would grab me great if I even knew she'd given birth. What am I—the poor relation?"

"No. You're the rich movie star relation who—if you hadn't vanished out of everyone's life—would have certainly been told."

"Enlighten me—is it a boy or girl?"

"A girl," she said excitedly. "I haven't spoken to Steven yet. He must be out of his mind!"

"Let's call 'em."

"Yes, and then I've got a great idea. We'll raid Zabar's, pick up a whole load of food, and go over to see the baby."

"Is that all you have on your mind, food?" he chided. "What is it with you lately?"

"I'm building up my strength."

"For what?"

"A surprise."

He groaned. "Not another one."

"This one you're going to like."

"Does it involve travel?"

"Not without you by my side."

"Does it involve sex?"

She looked at him quizzically. "Hmm . . . do you find power sexy?"

"It depends who's got it."

"You'll see," she answered mysteriously.

He shook his head. "You're a tough act to handle, kid."

She laughed. "And you're beginning to sound just like Gino."

"Poor old Gino. It must have been some struggle bringing you up."

"Yeah, that's why he married me off at sixteen."

"He really did that, huh?"

"You'd better believe it. I was the perfect little Washington wife. Craven and I lived with the Richmonds in their tasteful mansion while I played good little wifey-pie at all the fancy functions. And guess what? Peter Richmond is going to run for President one of these days. Ain't *that* the laugh of the century?"

"Whatever happened to husband number one?"

"Ah, Craven. He met a girl who liked horses. And I can assure you, a horse is about the only thing she'll ever find between *her* legs!"

Lennie burst out laughing. "Hey, lady—I love it when you talk dirty."

She grinned. "Why do you think I do it?"

"To turn me on."

"You got it!"

He pulled her to him. "Come here, wife."

She pushed him gently away. "Not now."

"How come?"

" 'Cause we gotta go out like normal people. We can't make out the entire weekend."

"Why not?"

"No, Lennie," she said firmly, trying not to give in.

He sighed with disappointment. "O.K., so what are we going to do?"

"Visit my brother. Unless you want to work. That, I'll understand."

"I've been locked up here so long I'm stir-crazy."

"Can I read the script soon?" she asked eagerly.

"I told you—not until it's finished."

"When will that be?"

"I'm heading toward a rough draft."

"I can read it then, huh?"

"We'll see."

"Bullshit! I'm reading it, Lennie!"

"That's what I love about you—Little Miss Reticent!"

She called Gino, who sounded pleased to hear from her. "So you're back. It's about time," he said good-naturedly.

"I sure am."

"Everything go according to plan?"

"It sure did."

"Hey—you broken the news to Lennie?"

"I sure haven't." She made a quick change of subject. "How about lunch today? I'd like to see Steven and Mary Lou. Is she at home? How's the baby?"

"Hey, hey, one question at a time. Yeah, they're all at home. It's a good idea. Steven's been missing you."

"We thought we'd pick up lunch and come over. Will you call Steven and warn him?"

"You got it, kid. Family reunion, huh?"

"Can't wait, Gino."

Boogie drove them to Zabar's and then Lucky decided she needed to pick up gifts at Bloomingdale's, where she ran riot in the baby department, selecting hundreds of dollars' worth of toys and clothes.

"What's Mary Lou going to do with all this stuff?" Lennie asked, exasperated.

"Use it."

"Very funny. Can we leave?"

"Let's go."

Loaded down with packages, they made it to the elevator, where Lennie was recognized and a crowd began to surround him. They had to run to get out of there.

Laughing and giggling, they piled into the car.

"I'm glad to see you're still a star," Lucky joked. "I thought you might have lost it."

"Yeah. I really get off on being mobbed in good old Bloomie's," he said wryly.

"I love you." Gently she touched the side of his face. "And I missed you more than you can imagine."

"Don't get sloppy on me, I can't take the pressure."

Giggling, she stuck her tongue out.

"Nice tongue!" he said admiringly.

"Keep this up an' you ain't never gonna know just how nice!"

Boogie sat impassively in the driving seat. "Where to?" he asked.

"Steven's house," Lucky said. "And fast." She turned to Lennie. "Have you spoken to Brigette?"

"Not lately. I promised she could stay with us in Malibu."

"Great. Maybe we'll all fly back together on Sunday night."

"What's your hurry?"

"We don't want to hang around here, do we? It's hot and muggy, and we've got that great beach house sitting empty."

He shrugged. "Whatever you like. I can pack in five minutes."

"So . . . what are we waiting for? You'll finish your script at the beach. It'll be sensational. A real family summer, right?"

"Yeah, all the better to deal with the lawyers," he said grimly.

"I keep telling you, relax. They're not going to sue."

"Don't bet on it, Lucky."

"Oh, I'm betting. And I'm right."

Steven greeted her with a big hug and a kiss. "Where have you been?"

"Japan," she lied. "I learned to give a great back rub. Can I see the baby?"

Mary Lou smiled proudly. "Come on, we'll take you up to her room."

"What did you name her?" Lucky asked.

"Carioca Jade," Steven replied.

Lennie nodded wisely. "That'll get her through school with no problems."

"It's a beautiful name," Lucky enthused.

Carioca Jade was a cute little bundle, small, helpless, and appealing. Steven picked her up and handed her to Lucky. "Say hello to Auntie," he said.

"Auntie?" Lucky exclaimed. "That makes me feel ancient!"

"Well, you're not exactly a kid anymore," Lennie pointed out.

"Thanks!" She peered at the baby. "I'll be picking up my old age pension next week! Steven, Mary Lou—this child is gorgeous!"

"I did my best," Steven said modestly.

"You did *your* best!" Mary Lou objected.

"It wasn't easy," Steven joked.

Mary Lou picked up a cushion and threw it at him. "Get outta here!"

Gino turned up shortly after. Once more he asked Lucky if she'd told Lennie about Panther.

"I will," she said. "Quit bugging me."

"When?"

"What's the big deal? I'll tell him tonight. I want to savor the moment."

"Are you sure he likes surprises?"

"Don't worry about it, Gino. He'll be delighted."

They spent a couple of hours at the house and then wandered off on their own. She'd given Boogie the rest of the weekend free.

"What do you want to do?" Lennie said, as they strolled along the street hand in hand.

Lucky smiled. "You're always asking me that. More important, what do *you* want to do?"

"Whatever makes you happy."

"Can we walk around like normal people, or will you be recognized again?"

"We can walk around like normal people. I'll avoid eye contact. I've discovered being recognized is a state of mind. If you want them to recognize you, they do, and if you don't, they don't. It's that simple."

"This is what I'd like to do," she decided. "Go to a movie. Eat popcorn and spill it all over myself. Feel sick, have one of those horrible fizzy orange drinks. And then I want to go home and make love all night long. Can we do that?"

"You know something? That's why I'm crazy about you. We have exactly the same tastes." He took a beat. "Woody Allen?"

She answered instantly. "But of course."

They lined up for a Woody Allen film. Saw it. Loved it. And talked about it all the way home.

It wasn't until they were back in his rented loft that Lucky looked at him, started to laugh and said, "Hey, wait a minute, we own a luxury apartment in New York. What are we doing in this dump?"

"It's romantic," Lennie replied. "Nobody knows we're here. No phone calls. No nothing. We'll stay tonight and take off for L.A. tomorrow."

"Suits me."

"And now what do you want?"

She couldn't help thinking to herself how much she loved him. And how much she'd missed him. "I want Chinese food, Marvin Gaye music, and great sex. What do *you* want?"

"Indian food, Billie Holiday, and great sex."

"I guess if we can't make up our mind about the food, it'll have to wait."

"I guess so."

She shrugged. "And if we can't make up our mind about Marvin or Billie, same thing, huh?"

He shrugged too.

"Well . . ." she said slowly, "it looks like there's nothing else left to do except . . ."

Together they shouted it out: "Great sex!"

And then, laughing, they fell into each other's arms.

55

Paul Webster's idea of the park was certainly not Tavern on the Green. Deena, clad from head to toe in Chanel, discovered this when he arrived to pick her up.

"We're going on a picnic," he informed her.

She raised an imperious eyebrow. "Really?"

"Why not?" he asked. "It'll be a blast."

She didn't want to reveal that grown women with rich husbands, dressed in Chanel, did not picnic in the park. "I'm hardly dressed for it," she pointed out.

"Go change."

"I don't think so," she said.

He stared at her with his intense eyes. "Do I make you nervous?"

She gave an amused laugh. "How could *you* possibly make *me* nervous? I've known you since you were a baby."

"Go change, Deena," he said.

He seemed determined, so she capitulated, hurried upstairs, took off Chanel and put on a Christian Dior track suit and jogging shoes.

Paul waited in the front hall. Deena wondered what her house-man thought. What *could* he think? After all, Paul was young enough to be her . . . younger brother.

Martin was safely at the office. He always left early on Saturday mornings, never returning until six or seven at night. He did the same on Sundays. Sometimes they spent the weekend at their Connecticut house. When they did, Martin usually spent his entire time on the phone or receiving FAXes. Martin was a true workaholic. He found it difficult to relax.

Did The Bitch make him relax?

Did The Bitch make him forget business for more than five minutes at a time?

Deena tried to put the thought from her mind. It wasn't healthy to ponder about Martin and Venus Maria. If she shut it out, maybe that relationship would fade away and Martin would be all hers again.

And if that failed to happen . . . if The Bitch tried to take it further . . .

Deena sighed. She had her solution.

Paul greeted her when she reappeared. "You're a real sport," he said, looking her up and down. "Now we can relax and enjoy ourselves."

"How are we going to get there?" she asked when they hit the street, already regretting her decision to go with him.

He took her hand. "We're walking."

She quickly pulled her hand away. "I don't walk."

He stared at her quizzically. "You don't walk? That's funny—seems to me your legs look like they're moving one in front of the other."

"Don't be facetious, Paul. We'll take a cab."

He was intent on asserting his manhood. "We'll walk."

Deena hid behind a pair of large black sunglasses and hoped she wouldn't bump into any of her friends. Not that there was anything wrong with strolling through the city with Effie's young son. But still . . .

She entered Central Park as if she were taking a trip on the wild side. She couldn't remember the last time she'd been in such close proximity to so many people. Deena led her life in a rarefied atmosphere, and she wasn't comfortable getting down among the people. But she had to admit it made a change. And the attentive Paul Webster was certainly an intriguing young man. Besides, she needed

someone to tell her she was beautiful, intelligent, and attractive—
all the things Martin usually forgot to mention.

"Guess where Paul's gone today?" Nona said, struggling into a pair
of too-tight jeans.

"Where?" replied Brigette, biting into an apple.

"He's taking old lady Deena Swanson to lunch. Are you ready for
that?"

Brigette almost choked. No, she was not ready for that. Swallow-
ing her hurt feelings she said, "Why?" Then added, "How do you
know?"

"I know everything," Nona replied confidently, finally closing the
zipper on her jeans. "I listened in on the phone when he called her."

"Does he like her?" Brigette asked casually.

"Do *you* like *him*?" Nona asked, not so casually.

"Don't be crazy," Brigette replied, trying to look cool.

"I think you do," Nona said, very sure of herself.

Before Brigette could reply, Effie swept into the room. "There's a
phone call for you, Brigette, dear. It's your stepfather, Lennie
Golden. We'd love to meet him sometime. Ask him over for drinks."

Brigette was pleased. She thought Lennie had forgotten her.
"What shall I tell him?" she asked Nona.

"Tell him he's got us whenever he wants," Nona said. "You *have*
mentioned *I'm* coming, haven't you?"

Brigette looked vague. "Sure."

Nona made a face. "Bet you haven't—do so now."

"I will," said Brigette, rushing to the phone.

Lennie sounded like his old self. He said the Malibu trip was on,
and, yes, she could bring a friend. They agreed that she and Nona
would fly out in a week.

Nona was delighted. "Can't wait to meet your stepfather," she said
excitedly. "Is he as hot as he looks on the screen?"

"Lennie? Hot?" Brigette almost laughed aloud. She'd never
thought of him in that way, although of course he did have quite a
following.

On reflection she considered he probably was hot. "You don't fancy him, do you?" she teased Nona.

"Not as much as I fancy Tom Cruise," Nona replied, grabbing her jacket. "Come on. Let's go shopping. I can't wait to buy the smallest bikini anybody's ever seen in their entire life!"

Bert Slocombe figured he was the smartest reporter in town. Well, reporter-photographer really, because he never went anywhere without his little camera cleverly concealed on his person. Bert was known to be the best at getting the goods on the rich and famous—which was exactly why they'd put him on Swanson watch.

That morning he'd considered following Martin Swanson, but a hunch had made him decide to concentrate on Deena instead. And sure enough, his hunch paid off. The stylish Mrs. Swanson emerged from her house just after noon, all togged out in a fancy jogging outfit. She was accompanied by some young geezer who kept giving her lustful looks. Bert recognized a lustful look from five hundred yards.

Happily he settled in behind them as they made their way to the park. He'd known something good was up the moment she'd left her house and didn't immediately climb into a chauffeured limousine.

Deena Swanson walking to the park was picture enough. But add some young stud, and it really made a front page scandal shot. Nothing like a well-known married woman playing around to sell magazines. Especially with a younger man.

Bert wondered who the kid was. He was good-looking enough with his long hair and one small gold earring in his earlobe. Maybe he was a rock star. Those rock-and-rollers managed to get in everywhere.

No, Bert decided. He didn't recognize him, and he was familiar with most of the long-haired brigade.

When they arrived at the park, the young guy pulled out a blanket from the bag he carried and laid it out on the grass.

Bert thought he'd died and gone to heaven.

He could see Deena arguing—she obviously wasn't used to this kind of outing—but she sat on the grass anyway, making it an easy job for Bert to scoot around behind a tree and shoot some great pictures.

The two of them stayed in the park for over an hour. Bert was hoping the guy would make a move on her. No such luck. A lot of talk, and that was it.

He wished he could hear what they were saying. Impossible, couldn't make himself too obvious. As it was he was flitting around behind trees like a secret jerk-off artist.

He managed to get one picture he knew was going to be special. Deena had a wasp or something trapped in her hair and the kid leaned forward to brush it out. Of course, the gullible public wouldn't know what he was doing. It looked like he was about to give her a hot, wet one full on the lips.

Bert followed them back to Deena's house and lingered for a moment. Sure enough, the young guy emerged almost immediately, and Bert fell into step a discreet distance behind him. May as well put a name to the kid.

He chuckled to himself. This story, combined with the Venus Maria stuff, was going to be bigger than ever. He couldn't wait to give Dennis the good news in L.A.

56

Once she was rid of Emilio, Venus Maria spoke to Ron on the phone.

"And where were *you* last night?" he asked crisply. Ron always liked to know everyone's business.

"At Spago."

"Hitting the town, are we? Who was your fortunate escort?"

"Cooper."

"Hmm . . ." Ron was intrigued. "And did we finally do the deed?"

She sighed. "No, Ron. We did *not* do the deed. Cooper and I are just friends. Why even ask a question like that?"

"Because I know you. You're not exactly a patient wench, and if you can't have Martin all the way, you're hardly going to wait forever."

She twirled the cord of the phone. "What makes you so certain I can't have Martin all the way?"

"He's not gettable," Ron said firmly. "He's taken."

"I can get any man I want," Venus Maria replied, full of bravado.

"Show me," Ron taunted.

It infuriated her that Ron always thought he had to challenge her. "I'll show you all right," she snapped, hoping to shut him up. "Talk to you later." She hung up without giving him a chance to say another word.

In a couple of weeks they were supposed to begin serious rehearsals for her upcoming "Soft Seduction" tour. She planned to hit twenty-two cities. A grueling prospect but one she looked forward to. The "Soft Seduction" album would be released at the same time, along with her video of the title track. She was filming the video next week. It was to be directed by the famous Italian photographer Antonio, a good friend of hers.

Ron was pissed off because he'd wanted to direct it. She'd tried to explain that sometimes a change was good for everyone, but Ron was in a sulk about it, even though he'd done all the choreography.

In the video she was to play three roles: a beautiful, seductive woman; a handsome gigolo-type man; and a half woman-half man creature. As usual, it would create controversy and criticism. That was the whole point. Her fans would love it, they'd go "Soft Seduction" crazy. She was going to give them the Venus Maria they *really* craved.

As far as her fans were concerned, Venus Maria could do no wrong. She was their video queen. Their princess. She was everything they aspired to be. Dangerous. Stylish. A woman unafraid in a world run by men. A fuck-you woman.

The thought of the upcoming tour excited her. She'd only been out on the road once before, and that was right before her career took off, just after her first hit record. At the time she'd been too inexperienced to understand the intricate interaction between audience and artist. Now she knew it was going to be a sensational blast —some kind of heady exchange of energy and power between star and fans. And after the tour, if the script was changed to her liking, she was to star in Mickey Stolli's big movie *Bombshell*—a role coveted by every young actress in Hollywood.

First the video, then the tour, next the movie. The rest of her year was well taken care of.

She'd heard that all the tickets were sold out in record time as soon as the box offices opened.

Maybe she shouldn't even worry about Martin until she got back, although she knew if she didn't cement their relationship with a definite commitment from him before she went, by the time the tour was finished it would be over.

His phone call came at just the right moment.

"I'm going to be in L.A. tomorrow," he informed her, all business. "I'm planning a takeover at one of the studios. I'll pick you up at noon and we'll fly to San Francisco for the day."

She didn't like it when he took her for granted. "What if I'm busy?"

"Are you?" he asked abruptly.

She took a moment before replying. "No."

"Why do you always try to give me a hard time?"

"Because nobody else does."

He laughed. "Good reason. Did you get the shares?"

"Oh, those little things," she said casually. "I added them to my collection."

"That's what I like about you."

She held the phone tightly to her ear. "What?"

"You're totally independent."

Sure, Martin. But not when it comes to you. "Isn't everyone?" she said coolly.

"No. Definitely not."

As soon as she hung up, she couldn't wait to call Ron back. "We'll have to cancel the video rehearsal tomorrow. I'm flying to San Francisco for the day."

"With whom?"

"Martin."

"Mmm . . ." Ron said in a bitchy tone. "Mr. Big calls—little Virginia runs."

"Don't call me that."

"Why not?"

" 'Cause you *know* it pisses me off."

"Well, now, I'm *so* sorry, miss. However, some of us do feel we can still talk to you as if you're a mere mortal."

Ron was in his definite pain-in-the-ass mood. "Cut it out," she said crossly.

He changed his tune, suddenly becoming overly solicitous. "Shall I pop over and help you select outfits for tomorrow? You have to look your best."

"I can manage."

"How about Madame Loretta's girls? I could arrange to have them waiting at the hotel."

Trust him to bring up the hookers. She should never have let Ron in on that little game. "The girls were a one-time experience. O.K.?"

"Just checking. What are you doing the rest of the day?"

She relented. After all, he was her best friend. "Nothing. Come over if you want."

"Can I bring Ken?" he asked anxiously, still dying for her and the Ken Doll to become close buddies.

No way, José. "Another time, Ron."

"You're such a bitch."

"Thank you. I love you, too."

"Have fun tomorrow."

"I plan to."

Putting the phone down on Ron, she immediately called Cooper.

"What are you doing tonight?" she asked, getting straight to the point.

He sounded cautious. "I have a date with a seventeen-year-old ex-porn queen. Why?"

"Can I come too?"

Now he sounded amused. "Are you suggesting a threesome?"

"No! I am not! I'd like to go out for dinner. Martin's arriving tomorrow and I don't feel like being alone tonight. Can I join you or not?"

"I'm sure my date will be thrilled," Cooper said dryly. "We're going to a Mexican restaurant."

"Will you pick me up?"

He sighed. "Venus, I'll do anything you want."

"Just pick me up. That'll be fine."

Martin arrived home from the office early to attend a dinner party. Since he planned to tell Deena he was leaving the next morning for Los Angeles, he didn't care to experience her wrath by walking in late.

Deena seemed particularly restless.

"I'm off to L.A. in the morning," he announced. "That studio deal is coming through."

She didn't hesitate. "I'll come with you."

"No," he said quickly.

"Why not?" she asked, narrowing her eyes.

"Because this is a complicated takeover. And when I'm this involved I can't have outside influences."

She glared at him. "Is that what I am? An outside influence? I was under the impression I'm your wife."

"You know what I mean," he said.

She felt a sickness in the pit of her stomach. This was it. He was going back to Los Angeles sooner than anticipated. All this talk about the studio takeover coming to fruition was merely a smoke screen. The Bitch beckoned, and he came running.

Deena knew the time was drawing close to put her master plan into operation.

57

Eventually the moment of truth had to come, and Lucky was excited beyond belief. She waited until late Saturday night. They'd made love again, sent out for pizza, and now Lennie was settling down to watch "Saturday Night Live."

"Hey—you coming in?" he called out.

She was in the bathroom brushing her long, dark hair. Clad in one of Lennie's oversized shirts and nothing else, she wandered back into the bedroom.

"Are you really going to watch TV?" she teased.

He was stretched out on the bed. "Sweetheart, I don't have the strength to do anything else."

"Doesn't take much to tire you out, huh?"

"Right!" he joked. "Nonstop sex'll do it every time!"

She curled up beside him. "Complaining?"

"Are you kidding? C'mere, wife."

He kissed her, putting his tongue in her mouth and sliding it across her teeth.

She shivered. "Don't do that unless you mean it."

"Oh, I mean it, lady." His hands began to explore beneath her shirt.

She felt herself responding. Lennie always had that effect on her. "I thought you were tired."

"I made a rapid recovery."

"You're turning into Superman, Lennie."

He smiled lazily. "Hey, give me a break. I've been seriously deprived."

Gently she pushed him away. She wanted to make love again, but not until after she'd told him her news.

"It's time to break open the champagne," she said softly.

"How come?"

She took a deep breath. "Remember that surprise I mentioned?"

"Yeah."

"Now's the time."

He stared at his wildly beautiful wife and it came to him in a flash. She was about to tell him she was pregnant. *That* was her surprise. And he was going to be the happiest expectant father in the world!

"Hold everything," he said. "Don't move. I'll get the champagne, you light the candles, and I'll be right back. Then you can give me the good news."

"You'll be crazy with happiness," she promised him, kneeling on the bed.

He couldn't stop himself from grinning like an idiot. "You're probably right. You're always right."

She grinned back. "Oh, yeah, I'm always right!"

He rushed downstairs, grabbed the bottle of champagne she'd put in the fridge earlier, balanced two glasses, and raced back upstairs.

Lucky sat cross-legged in the center of the bed.

He popped the cork on the champagne, poured the golden liquid into two glasses, and handed her one.

Solemnly she toasted him. "Lennie Golden," she said, controlling her exhilaration, "I know it's not your birthday, but . . . I have something for you."

He reached out and touched her face. "Did I ever tell you how much I—"

"Quiet!" she interrupted. "This is *my* surprise."

He settled back on the bed. "O.K., go for it."

In his mind he thought about a name for the baby. Maria for a girl, after Lucky's mother. And if it was a boy, how about Lennie Junior? Or was it too difficult for a kid to grow up with Junior attached to his name? Yeah, it probably was. Hmm . . . How about Nick? A real gangster's name. Nick Golden—sounded good. A killer name for a killer kid.

"Lennie," Lucky said quietly, savoring every word, "I bought you Panther Studios."

He stared at her blankly. "Huh?"

She repeated the words as slowly as she could. "I said, I bought you Panther Studios."

There was a long moment of silence while he digested this incredible information. "You've done what?" he managed at last.

"How many times do I have to tell you?" she yelled happily. "*I* bought Panther Studios. *We* bought Panther Studios. It's ours, Lennie, it's ours!"

"What about the baby?" he couldn't help blurting out.

She looked puzzled. "What baby?"

Her news sank in. "Jesus, you're serious, aren't you?"

"Of course I'm serious. Where do you think I've been for the last six weeks? I made a deal to buy the studio from old Abe Panther, and he wouldn't sell to me unless I went in there undercover for six weeks. What a trip! Can you believe it? Me, undercover—pretending to be Luce, the obedient little secretary. And Lennie, get this. I've been kissing Mickey Stolli's ass! In fact, I even talked to *you* on the phone one day."

He was in a severe state of shock. "You talked to me on the phone one day," he repeated blankly.

"That's right." She grinned. "Isn't it incredible! We're movie moguls. We're gonna kick butt and make great movies!"

This wasn't exactly the news he'd imagined. This was a bombshell. "You're serious, aren't you? You've bought a goddamn studio."

"You bet your ass I have," she said excitedly. "That's why we have to fly back to L.A. tomorrow. I've arranged a meeting on Monday morning I think you should come to. It'll be great. The lawyers will be there, and old Abe Panther himself. He's quite a character. I can't wait to see Mickey's face when they tell him. Not to mention his wife, the delightful Abigaile."

"How much did it cost you?" he asked blankly.

"A lot. Trust me, *a lot*. But you know me when it comes to business, and Panther is worth every penny. There's land to be sold off, and a wonderful library of old films. Plus, the television department is really successful. Of course, when we stop making these dumb tits-and-ass films, the revenues will go down. But only temporarily." Her black eyes gleamed with excitement. "I plan to make really good movies, Lennie. I want to show women as real people. I mean, come on, what do we see on the screen today? We see women as men's fantasies. The guys making movies are a bunch of jerks—and it seems to me they all hate women. They've either got some slasher chasing them around cutting their heads off or they've got them taking off their clothes while adolescent boys jerk off through holes in the wall. I mean, movies don't celebrate the human condition— they degrade it."

He stood up, shaking his head. "Lucky, you don't know the first thing about filmmaking."

"You hardly have to be a fucking genius to put together a movie," she pointed out. "Have you *seen* the guys running the industry? Anyway—" she continued, racing on at full tilt—"let's discuss what we can do about *your* movie. I've taken a look at the dailies and there's some terrific stuff in there. If we leave Marisa on the cutting-room floor, recast, reshoot, and you'll rewrite, then we can hire a new director and put it together again. It's salvageable if we take control." She paused for a breath. "Hey—maybe you'd even like to direct it yourself? How about that for a great idea?"

"Would I be working for you?"

She missed the tightness in his voice. "Lennie, aren't you listening to me? I bought the studio for *us*. We're in this together."

Agitatedly he ran a hand through his hair. "Did you use my money?"

"I don't have your money, do I?" she replied patiently. "I used *my* money."

"The money you inherited from Dimitri?"

Was his problem whose money she used? "O.K., so I had a rich husband; I inherited part of the Stanislopoulos fortune. But now it's my money, and I can spend it any way I like."

He began pacing up and down the room. "So you weren't in Japan?"

Was Lennie being obtuse on purpose? "Hardly."

"Let me get this straight. You were in L.A. impersonating a secretary at Panther Studios, while I was getting my balls busted in Acapulco. Is that right?"

"I was securing our future," she corrected. "You want to be a movie star—let's be in control. It's the only way."

"*You'll* be in control, Lucky. I'll be working for *you*."

She was exasperated. "Will you quit saying that? How many times do I have to tell you? It's our studio. *Ours.* Hey—Lennie—I'm beginning to feel like a broken record."

"Why didn't you at least mention what you planned to do?"

She reached for a cigarette. "Because it would have spoiled the surprise."

"You know what I thought, Lucky?"

"No, what?"

"I thought you were going to tell me we were having a baby."

She stared at him. His negative reaction was so totally unexpected and hurtful. She struck back. "I'm so sorry," she said sarcastically. "Maybe you'd be happier if I was in the kitchen, barefoot and pregnant."

"Is that such a terrible thing?" he retorted angrily.

She leaped off the bed. "I don't *believe* this. I've been stuck at the studio imitating a secretary for six weeks for *us*. And now I tell you, thinking you'll be knocked out, and what do you do? Goddamn it, you start nagging."

He glared at her. "Nagging? Oh, so that's what I'm doing, is it? You blatantly lied to me for six weeks. Then you break into my apartment, we have nonstop sex for twenty-four hours, and finally you spring this on me. And *I'm* nagging. Do you really think the world has to revolve around you, Lucky?"

She couldn't understand his attitude. "What have I done that's so terrible?" she demanded. "Tell me that."

"You did it without me," he said flatly. "We should have discussed it. I do not appreciate being shut out."

"And I don't appreciate being told what to do. I'm not a child, Lennie."

"Sometimes you act like one."

"Fuck you!" she exploded. "If this situation was reversed, you'd expect *me* to be jumping up and down with delight."

"And would you?"

"Yes."

He stared at her for a long time before saying, "You know what I feel like?"

She dragged on her cigarette. "What?"

"Like a kept man. It's as if you said to yourself, 'Oh, poor Lennie's not happy at the studio, I'll buy it for him.' You've made me feel like nothing."

"That's the most ridiculous thing I've ever heard," she said abruptly.

"It's how I feel."

"You're not being fair."

"I'm not, huh? Can't you see what you've done?"

"I can see very clearly what's going on around here. I'm not pregnant, so you're pissed off. That's what it really gets down to, isn't it?"

He didn't reply.

She stubbed out her cigarette and walked into the bathroom. From sheer exhilaration she was now reduced to frustrated anger. Men! They pretended they liked women with balls, and when they found one, they just couldn't handle it. She'd thought Lennie was different. It seemed she was wrong.

Quickly she threw on some clothes and emerged. "I'm getting out of here," she said curtly. "There's no need for this to escalate into a bigger fight than it already is."

Her words made him even more furious. "What are you saying? That you're going to walk?"

"I don't want to be around you anymore tonight."

Now it was his turn to explode. "*You* don't want to be around *me?* Hey, Lucky—you walk out of here and you walk out of my life."

Her black eyes were deadly as she turned to him. "Are you threatening me?"

"Can't you listen to what I have to say?" he yelled. "Has it always got to be your way?"

She felt tears sting the back of her eyelids and quickly turned

378

away. "Like you said, Lennie, I'm not the little woman at home. I never will be, and I never pretended I was. I've got nothing against having a baby one of these days, but right now there's so much I want to do."

"Then maybe you'd better do it by yourself," he said bitterly.

She couldn't believe how wrong this was all going. Lennie's reaction, her disappointment. This was supposed to have been the most wonderful moment for both of them. And yet it was turning out to be the worst. Maybe he was right—maybe they weren't destined to be together. After all, what did they really have in common? A sense of humor, great sex, Chinese food, and walking on the beach—it wasn't enough.

She picked up the phone and called a cab. "I'm going to the apartment," she said. "We both need time apart. Think about it, Lennie. And remember—I did this for you. I didn't do it for selfish reasons."

He couldn't look at her. "You can't buy me, Lucky," he said tightly. "There's no sales tag."

"That wasn't my intention. I'm flying back to L.A. tomorrow. If you decide to come I'll be delighted. Let me know."

With a sick feeling she walked to the front door, waiting for him to call her back. Longing for him to say he was only joking, that everything was O.K., and he was thrilled.

He said none of those things.

Outside on the street she was accosted by a stoned teenage girl, eyes as big as saucers, long, matted hair. "Spare a coupla bucks?" the girl whined.

Lucky handed her a fifty. "Get yourself a life. Throw away the drugs and straighten out."

"Hey, man—what else is there?" the girl said blankly as she wandered off down the street.

Lucky's cab zoomed up to the doorway. The Puerto Rican driver was busy muttering to himself.

She opened the door and climbed in. Leaning from the window she could see the lights in Lennie's apartment. He hadn't even bothered to follow her down.

"Goodbye," she whispered. "Don't write, don't call. I can make it without you."

"Huh?" the cab driver said.

"Just drive," she replied dully. "And while you're at it, try not to kill us both."

58

Emilio Sierra delivered the goods, much to Dennis Walla's satisfaction. The photograph of Venus Maria with Martin Swanson was worth every penny they'd had to pay. It was sexy and intimate. Two people entwined. A real front-pager.

Dennis congratulated Emilio. "You really came through, mate," he said, clapping him on the shoulder.

Emilio was pleased. He'd decided to spend a week in Hawaii and take his newfound love, Rita the firecracker. She was a wildcat between the sheets, and pretty too. It was best to get out of town before the shit hit. And that was exactly what would happen when *Truth and Fact* arrived on the stands. Venus Maria was going to freak out.

Too bad. He didn't need little sis anymore. With his newfound notoriety he would soon become a famous actor. Now he'd be able to call important agents and producers and say, "Hey—this is Emilio Sierra." And they'd reply, "Emilio, good of you to call, my friend. Come in and see us."

Yes, it was all going to happen for him. It was about time he was discovered.

Shortly after Dennis received the photograph from Emilio, Bert Slocombe telephoned from New York.

"Hold the front page," Bert crowed triumphantly. "We're about t'make a bloody great splash."

"What's up?" Dennis asked.

"Sit still an' listen."

When Dennis heard the story Bert had to relate, he was only too happy to hold the front page.

This issue of *Truth and Fact* was going to be a total sellout.

And Dennis Walla was planning on taking full credit.

Warner had been in his life too long for Mickey to allow her to walk when she felt like it. The fact that he was visiting Madame Loretta's on a regular basis had nothing to do with their relationship. Warner couldn't break up with him. He had to be the one to say it was over.

On Saturday morning he played a vicious game of tennis with an ambitious director. And instead of staying for lunch at the club he drove directly to Warner's apartment. She was not home. Deflated, he continued on to his house. Abigaile was also out.

"Where's Mrs. Stolli?" he asked Consuela.

"She's shopping, mister." Consuela replied, rolling her eyes as if she, too, disapproved of Abigaile's shopping mania.

Shopping, Mickey thought. Not at the market, that was for sure. To Abigaile shopping meant Saks and Neiman Marcus, with a side trip down Rodeo Drive.

Tabitha appeared. "Daddy, can I have a Porsche when I'm sixteen?" she whined.

Why was it that every time he came into contact with Tabitha she wanted something? "We'll talk about it when you reach that age," he replied as calmly as he could manage.

"Why can't we talk now?" she nagged. "Why can't you promise me?"

The girl was just like her mother. Relentless.

"Because now is not the time," he said patiently.

"Mommy said I could."

Trust Abigaile. "She did?"

"Yes," Tabitha said triumphantly. "She promised me if I got good grades and if she never caught me doing dope or sleeping with boys —then I could have a Porsche. So I've decided not to smoke anymore."

He stared at his thirteen-year-old daughter. "You smoke?"

"Everybody at school does," she answered defensively.

He wondered what else she did. She was turning into a well-developed girl. Too well developed for her age.

"We'll see," he said vaguely, bored with all this father-daughter crap. He had other things on his mind.

"Some man phoned you," Tabitha announced. "He asked for our address."

Mickey was immediately alarmed. "What do you mean—he asked for our address?"

"What is it, a state secret or something?"

"I don't like people having our home address, Tabitha. You know that," he said sternly.

"Like I *don't* know that, Daddy," she replied smartly. "Like you never told me."

"Yes, I did."

"I can't do anything right in this house," Tabitha said. "Maybe I'll run away," she added, flouncing from the room.

Ha! Mickey thought. No chance.

Saturday was supposed to be a day of rest, and all he was getting was stress. Fuck! Stress at his age was no good.

Not that he was old. He was in perfect physical shape, and his bedroom prowess only improved with age.

But still, stress was the enemy. And if he had to contend with Abe Panther on Monday morning *and* his brother-in-law, there was plenty of added stress headed in his direction. Plenty.

Across town in Johnny Romano's Hancock Park mansion, Warner thought she'd died and gone to movie-star heaven. Warner Franklin, vice cop, cavorting with Johnny Romano—too much!

He'd called her that morning right after she'd put the phone down on Mickey.

"Come on over, baby," Johnny had crooned. "We'll read my reviews together."

And that's exactly what they'd done.

It would have helped if the reviews had been good. As it was, they were terrible.

It didn't seem to bother Johnny. He'd shrugged nonchalantly. "So what, baby," he'd said. "My public loves me. I belong to 'em. They don't give no friggin' power to nothin' these uptight critics gotta say. You think they got knowledge what's goin' on in the world today? No way, baby. Johnny knows what's goin' on in the world. Johnny's givin' the people exactly what they wanna see."

It was slightly disconcerting when Johnny referred to himself in the third person, but Warner went along with it. She wasn't too sure about his confidence in the movie. After all, she'd seen *Motherfaker* the previous evening, and while Johnny was tall and sexy and certainly handsome, he was not a great actor. He was everything she'd ever dreamed of in a man, but he was also a sexist pig. And his movie celebrated that fact.

The Romano entourage milled around the house. There were bodyguards, managers, agents, friends, well-wishers. And yet he'd chosen to be with her. She was immensely flattered.

"Come on, baby, let's go get us some private time," he'd finally said. And they'd retired to his bedroom where at last they were alone.

Sexually he was a raging bull. He made Mickey Stolli seem like a nonstarter.

Being with a younger man was a revelation. Warner had forgotten how energetic and fun sex could be. With Mickey, sex was not fun, although of course she'd always assured him it was. Mickey never really relaxed. He approached the sexual act as if it were a game of strenuous tennis and he had to perform well or there would be a punishment.

Sex with Johnny Romano was exactly the opposite. He laughed a lot and crooned "Baby, baby, baby" nonstop in her ear.

As far as she was concerned, he could call her anything he wanted. He was her favorite movie star, and this was her fantasy come true. Skinny Warner Franklin from Watts was just about to get it on for the second time with Johnny Romano. She loved Hollywood!

Johnny lay spread-eagled on the bed, erect and ready.

"You really a cop, baby?" he asked, absentmindedly stroking his own erection.

"I really am," she replied, admiring every inch of him.

"Well, baby, baby, cop this," he drawled, pushing his hard-on toward her.

She mounted him because he obviously liked it that way. And then she squeezed him all the way to heaven.

When they were through, she began to dress, ready to go to work.

"Come back soon, baby, baby," Johnny mumbled before falling into a deep sleep.

Oh, he could count on that.

Cooper was alone when he arrived to pick up Venus Maria for dinner.

"Where's your seventeen-year-old ex-porn star?" she asked, looking around.

He shrugged. "Why share you?"

"If we dine by ourselves again, people will talk."

He watched her carefully. "Does it bother you?"

She shook her head. "Nope. I'm used to it. Does it bother *you*?"

"Not at all." He didn't want to mention that he'd had to put up with the press longer than she could remember.

"Let's go," she sang out. "I'm starving!"

On the way to the restaurant she told him about Martin flying in and their plans to spend the day in San Francisco. "I've got a great idea. Why don't you come with us?" she suggested brightly.

Cooper burst out laughing. "Oh, yeah. That would *really* go down well with Martin. He'd be thrilled."

"*I'm* inviting you," she insisted. "You're one of Martin's best friends. Why shouldn't you come? It'll be great. And if we're spotted or anything, people will think *we're* the big romance. You don't mind people thinking that, do you?"

"Ah, if only it was true," he said wistfully.

There was a challenge in her big brown eyes. "Come on, Cooper. Live dangerously."

"What'll Martin say?"

"He'll say what I tell him to."

"Oh, Miss Ballsy."

"You bet. It'll be great, and it'll also give you a chance to talk to Martin. You know I really want you to do that for me."

He nodded. "If it pleases you, I'll come."

She smiled and took his hand. "You're the best."

By late Saturday afternoon, bored and almost addicted, Mickey decided he wasn't in the mood to hang around the house waiting for Abigaile to get home or for Warner to contact him. So he called up his addiction, Madame Loretta, and informed her he was on his way over and that she should have the Chinese girl ready for him.

When he arrived, he was discreetly taken upstairs and ushered into a private bedroom.

Lemon, the beautiful Oriental girl he'd had before, greeted him with a shy smile, her long, black hair flowing down her back. "And how may I pleasure you today?" she asked dutifully.

There was nothing like an obedient woman. He unzipped his pants and flopped down on the bed. "Gimme a blow job."

The nice thing about going to a whorehouse was that you could actually come right out with it. No flowers. No sweet talk. Just action. Every man's dream.

Lemon nodded and reached for a bottle of aromatic oil.

Mickey allowed his mind to go blank as she began to gently massage his balls, her delicate fingers doing marvelous things.

Forget everything. Go with the moment. Relax.

He closed his eyes.

When he felt the insistent tip of her talented tongue he couldn't help groaning aloud. The pleasure was overwhelming.

Unfortunately for Mickey, just as he was about to reach ecstasy, the door was flung open, and Warner and another plainclothes vice cop burst into the room.

"O.K., buddy, get your pants on. This is a raid. We're vice," said the male cop.

"Mickey?" cried a surprised Warner.

Mickey's hard-on deflated like a pricked balloon.

59

"What the fuck is going on?" demanded Carlos Bonnatti.

"Whaddya mean, Big C?" asked Link, his bodyguard and right-hand man.

"I mean, what the fuck is going on?" repeated Carlos flatly.

Link shrugged. He was a tall, thin-faced man with slit eyes and a lethal scar curving down his left cheek. "Ya talked to Eddie Kane yourself," Link pointed out.

"I know that," Carlos said impatiently. "And I also know he don't have the money. The asshole snorted it. All my goddamn money up his goddamn nose."

Link came up with a good suggestion. "Do ya want me to break his legs?"

"If I thought broken legs would get me my money, I'd go for the idea. But let's get realistic here. The prick don't have the money. So I gotta go to the studio. Panther Studios, Mickey Stolli. Set me up a meet."

Link nodded. "It's arranged. When d'ya want it?"

"Monday," Carlos said broodingly. "Set it up."

He walked to the window of the Century City penthouse he used when he was in Los Angeles and stared at the view. He liked visiting L.A. Maybe he should think about spending more time on the

Coast. Get out of New York with the dirt and the crime and the homeless roaming the streets.

Now that he was a free man, it didn't seem like such a bad idea. After ten years of marriage his wife had left him. Her loss. The dumb broad had run off with some fag interior designer.

He'd decided to let her learn a lesson the hard way. After a few months she'd come crawling back, begging for what she was missing. When she did, he'd take great pleasure in slamming the door in her face.

Fortunately there were no kids to consider. Carlos had always wanted a son, but his wife had never delivered.

He was not fond of people who didn't deliver.

He was not fond of Eddie Kane.

Nobody stole from Carlos Bonnatti and got away with it.

60

"I've got to make a phone call," Mickey said urgently, zipping up his pants.

"I told you, bud, you make your phone call down at the station," replied the male cop, who couldn't care less.

Warner stood back and stared at him in disgust, shaking her head as if he was the lowest of the low.

"Do you know who I am?" Mickey persisted, concentrating on the male cop because he knew he was getting no help from Warner.

"Yeah, we know who you are," replied Warner sharply, joining in for both of them. "Just another pathetic john."

He was hustled downstairs along with everybody else. Madame Loretta was trying to put up a good front as she assured customers and girls alike that everything would be all right. Surrounding her were the girls in various stages of undress. Among them, Mickey thought he saw Leslie Kane. But it was just a glimpse, and he knew he must be mistaken.

Mickey was in shock. He could not afford to be arrested in a whorehouse and carted off to jail like a common criminal. This was somebody's idea of a bad joke.

"Who's in charge here?" he demanded, looking around for an authority figure.

Although there were police everywhere, plainclothes and otherwise, he couldn't seem to find the captain of this operation.

Warner threw him another filthy glare. "Do yourself a favor and shut up," she said, vitriol accompanying every word. "*Mr.* Stolli."

He glared back. "Why don't you get me out of this stinkin' mess?"

"You got yourself into it, work it out," she retorted sharply, adding under her breath, "Asshole." If looks could kill, he'd be ten feet under.

This was the woman he'd been sleeping with for over a year? The woman who'd gone out of her way to constantly tell him how wonderful he was? Whatever they'd had together, it was definitely over.

Eventually everybody was herded outside and bundled into a police van.

Mickey shielded his face and huddled by the window, wondering if he could sue. He'd certainly like to sue the son of a bitches for harassment.

By the time they reached the holding jail, there were television-news crews and photographers milling around, waiting to greet them.

Charming! A fucking circus! How could this be happening to him?

He considered what Abigaile's reaction would be and knew he was a dead man.

Locked in the police van, Leslie Kane shivered at the injustice of it all. In vain she'd tried to explain to the cops she was merely an overnight guest. "Right, honey," they'd said, ignoring her protestations of innocence, and bundled her into the van with everyone else.

Her heart was beating wildly. When Eddie found out he would surely investigate further, and her past would be revealed.

Oh, the shame! Eddie was going to discover he'd married a prostitute.

She tried to calm herself. Not so bad, really. After all, *she'd* married a cocaine addict. Maybe it was time they both cleaned up their acts.

She spotted Mickey Stolli outside. Mickey Stolli, head of Panther

Studios, pillar of Hollywood society. Married to Abigaile, the Hollywood princess. What was *he* doing there?

Men! When she'd been a working girl she'd always been surprised at the types that came in for a little action. Why should Mickey Stolli surprise her? He was typical.

Men went to whores for two things—conversation and sex. The conversation always came first.

She hoped he hadn't seen her, and turned away.

Arriving from London, Primrose and Ben Harrison checked into the Beverly Hills Hotel. Abigaile felt obliged to invite them over for dinner on Saturday night.

"We're tired," Primrose warned her over the phone, agreeing to come anyway.

It was most inconvenient. Jeffries, the butler, and his wife usually had Saturdays off. Now Abigaile realized she would have to try to find them and summon them back. They would not be pleased. And neither was she.

"Where's Mr. Stolli?" Abigaile asked Consuela, after instructing the cook to prepare lightly grilled chicken with broccoli and fresh corn on the cob.

Consuela shrugged. Why did the Stollis always imagine she knew where everybody was? "Don' know, missus," she answered vaguely. "Mr. Stolli, he out. You shopping."

"I know, I know," Abilgaile said irritably, "I went shopping and now I'm back. Did Mr. Stolli leave me a message?"

"No." Consuela shook her head and wondered why she couldn't have weekends off like most of the other maids in Beverly Hills.

After locating Jeffries, Abigaile went to find Tabitha. Flinging open the door to her daughter's room, she was assailed by the ear-splitting sounds of Van Halen blaring from the stereo.

"Tabitha," she shouted above the din.

Tabitha, lying in the middle of a messy bed surrounded by teen magazines, did not hear her. She was too busy speaking on her pink Princess phone.

"Tabitha," Abigaile yelled crossly, marching across the room and switching off the stereo.

Tabitha sprang to attention as though she'd been mortally wounded. "Whacha do that for?"

"Because I wish to speak to you," Abigaile replied haughtily. "How can you hear yourself? How can you speak with all this noise going on? You'll damage your hearing."

"Don't be so old-fashioned." Tabitha muttered something into the phone and hung up. "By the way, did Daddy tell you? He said I can have a Porsche when I'm sixteen."

"Don't be ridiculous," snorted Abigaile.

"He did. He said so."

"Where *is* your father?"

"Dunno."

"Didn't he say where he was going?"

"Dunno."

Getting information out of her daughter was like persuading the pope to have sex.

Abigaile stalked from the room.

Before she was one step out the door, Van Halen blasted from the stereo, twice as loud as ever.

Down at the police station, Mickey made a lot of noise and was finally allowed his one phone call. He called Ford Werne.

Unfortunately Ford was not home.

Leslie used her one call to telephone the beach house, hoping Eddie was there. Indeed he was.

"Eddie," she exclaimed thankfully.

"Sweetheart! Where are you? I'm glad you phoned. I want you to come home, baby. I'm sorry, I'm so sorry. I'll never hit you again. I don't know what came over me."

"I'm in trouble," Leslie whispered.

"Just tell me where you are and I'll come get you," he promised.

"I'm in jail, Eddie. I've been arrested. You need to bail me out."

He was shocked. "What?"

"It's a mistake. I'll explain everything when I see you."

"What've you been arrested for?"

"It doesn't matter. Just come and get me."

"I'm on my way."

61

Abigaile and Primrose greeted each other with a stiff embrace. Primrose was taller than her sister, with fine golden hair and china-blue eyes. Her husband, Ben Harrison, was a heavily built man, youthful-looking for his fifty years in spite of crinkled gray hair and a stern expression. He treated Primrose with a certain amount of deference.

"Where's Mickey?" was his first question.

"He'll be home soon," Abigaile replied agitatedly. "He's out on a business meeting."

"We have to talk," Ben said curtly. "I have no clue what this is about. I only know we're not happy being summoned here at the last moment. Has anybody contacted Abe?"

"I saw him last week," Abigaile said. "He never mentioned anything. I've tried to call him. Inga insists he can't be disturbed."

"Can't be disturbed?" Ben repeated, frowning darkly. "What kind of excuse is that?"

"We'll find out on Monday morning," Abigaile replied stiffly, wondering where Mickey was.

They were in the middle of dinner by the time Mickey finally showed up. Abigaile heard him sneaking into the house, trying to slide past the dining room and vanish upstairs.

"Excuse me a minute," she said with a sweet smile to Ben and

Primrose. She rushed into the hall. "Mickey! Where the hell have you been?"

He looked disheveled. "I was in a car accident," he lied.

"A car accident? Is the car all right?"

Is the car all right? A typical Abigaile question.

"Yeah," he said sourly. "The car is fine. I'm dead, but the car is fine."

"Primrose and Ben are here," she announced, ignoring his sarcasm. "Hurry up and join us. I am not entertaining them on my own."

"Gimme a break," he protested. "I nearly got myself killed."

"Mickey." The warning in her voice spoke volumes.

What did she care? "O.K., O.K., five minutes."

He hurried upstairs. Jesus! This was his worst nightmare come true. Arrested while a Chinese hooker was giving him a blow job. Was nothing sacred anymore? Thank God Madame Loretta had gathered her wits about her and contacted her lawyer. The man had arrived in record time and bailed everyone out.

Now Mickey had a date to appear in court.

If Abigaile ever found out he was visiting a whorehouse . . .

The ride back to the beach seemed longer than usual. Eddie was silent for a while, driving with one hand on the steering wheel, drumming his fingers on the dashboard with the other.

Finally he spoke. "What were you doing in a whorehouse, Leslie?"

"I met Madame Loretta when I first came to Los Angeles," Leslie explained, telling him the story she'd decided to use. "She seemed like a nice woman. In fact, she helped me out. I used to go up to her house for tea."

"Tea?" Eddie yelled excitedly. "What did you think she was running? An English tea parlor?" He paused to make a point. "She runs a whorehouse, Leslie. You were sleeping there last night. What's goin' on here? *How* did she help you out?"

Leslie stared straight ahead. "I can explain."

The Maserati roared down the highway. "The facts speak for themselves, huh?" Eddie said edgily.

"How many times do I have to tell you? I was sleeping over. By myself. I had nowhere else to go."

Eddie slapped the side of his head. "Jesus!" he said sarcastically, "I can't figure out why I'm suspicious, can you?"

"Will I have to appear in court?" she asked anxiously.

"Naw," he replied. "I'll havta fix it."

"Can you?"

"If I say I can do it, I can do it."

Her voice was almost a whisper. "Thank you, Eddie."

The car swerved along the highway. Eddie's driving was erratic, to say the least.

He pressed on. "How come you never told me about Madame Loretta before?"

"You never asked," she replied quietly.

He glanced in his rearview mirror. "Oh, I'm supposed to ask, am I? Hey, Leslie, babe, you friendly with a whoremonger? Is that what I'm supposed to ask? That kind of shit?"

Her eyes filled with tears. It wasn't like she'd done anything wrong. She was just sleeping over. It was his fault in the first place. This wasn't fair. "Eddie, please. Don't be mad at me. I'm very tired."

"*You're* tired," he said, outraged by her selfishness. "What the fuck do you think *I* am? I've got this hood Bonnatti crawling all over me. It's a responsibility I don't need."

She sighed. "How did you find yourself in this position? If you and Mickey are partners, why doesn't the studio pay?"

"It's not exactly Mickey who owes the money," he grumbled. "The fact is we had an arrangement, and, uh, I guess I sliced a little too much off the end. I didn't think anybody would notice. Trouble is, they did."

She was relieved to have steered the conversation away from Madame Loretta. "We're talking about a million dollars, Eddie."

"I know, I know. I had some debts to pay. Gotta face it, cocaine ain't cheap."

"What you should do," she said firmly, "is forget about the debt and check yourself into a detox center. I'll support you, Eddie. I'll be by your side."

"You don't seem to understand," he said urgently. "Carlos Bonnatti is threatening to break more than my balls if I don't pay."

"That's ridiculous," Leslie gasped. "Things like that only happen in gangster movies."

"Honey," he said dryly. "Welcome to the real world."

Mickey joined his sister and brother-in-law for dinner. His mind was in fast forward. He had so much to take care of and yet he had to sit there and suffer through polite bullshit. The main topic of conversation concerned Abe Panther. What could the meeting on Monday morning possibly be about?

Mickey shrugged. "I got no idea. We're making money, the studio's doing well. The old man should stay home an' stay happy. We don't need his interference."

Ben Harrison didn't seem to agree. "You know, Mickey," he said thoughtfully, "maybe Abe doesn't like the films the studio is producing. I have to tell you, I saw *Motherfaker* and it's a disaster. It's a movie I wouldn't want my mother to see, or, come to think of it, my sisters either."

"Yeah, well, everybody else in the country's going to love it," Mickey said defensively. "This is the kind of movie they're clamoring for today."

"I don't know." Ben shook his head dubiously. "It'll do a big weekend gross and then fall down. There'll be no word of mouth. In fact the word of mouth will be to stay away."

"Johnny Romano's a big star," Mickey pointed out. "The public is crazy about him."

"He loves himself," Ben replied evenly. "That much is obvious. Who had control over him? Didn't anybody try to pull in the reins?" He lowered his voice. "You know how many times he says 'motherfucker'? Not to mention the other actors."

Primrose heard him anyway. "Ben!" she admonished. "Kindly don't use language like that."

Mickey raised an eyebrow. Primrose lived in England for a few years and suddenly she became the Queen Mother!

Jeffries, the butler, entered the room. "There is a phone call for you, Mr. Stolli," he said, looking down his long, thin nose.

"Who is it?" Mickey replied rudely. "I'm eating dinner."

"He said it was most important. A Mr. Bonnatti."

"Bonnatti?"

"That is correct, sir."

This was not turning out to be a good day.

62

Sitting in the Swanson private jet, Venus Maria felt a million miles away from the scrawny little kid who'd lingered on Fifth Avenue and watched from afar as Martin Swanson married Deena Akveld. It was unbelievable, really. Here she was with Cooper Turner, famous movie star, on one side, and Martin Swanson, billionaire, on the other. And she had them both under her spell.

Venus Maria smiled. It was kind of a kick. In a way, she wished Ron were there to witness it. He'd love every minute.

Cooper wandered off to visit the pilot, and Martin leaned over to speak to her. "Why did you ask Cooper?" he said in a low voice. "What do we need him for?"

"Cooper's your best friend," she replied guilelessly. "I thought you'd be pleased."

"I'm not pleased," he said irritably. "A romantic day for two in San Francisco hardly works when it's for three."

She laughed softly. Was Martin jealous? "Don't be silly. Cooper's hardly a drag. He'll find plenty to do."

"He'll go off and leave us alone, will he?" Martin asked sarcastically.

"No," she replied firmly. "The three of us are going to have a fantastic time together." She kissed him on the cheek, flicking her tongue into his ear just to give him a little taste of things to come. "I'm going to freshen up," she added, excusing herself.

As she wandered off down the plane she winked at Cooper on his way back. Now was the time for him to have a serious talk with Martin and find out his intentions.

The Swanson jet was luxurious to say the least. It was set up like an expensive apartment, with a living room, a functional stainless-steel space age kitchen, a glamorous bedroom, and two marble bathrooms.

She shut herself in the bedroom, closed the door and threw herself on the circular bed. *Hey, this is great*, she thought. *Maybe he'll lend it to me for the tour.*

Not exactly subtle. They still had to keep their relationship quiet.

In San Francisco they were met by a limousine and taken straight to the penthouse suite of the Fairmont. Martin had a short business meeting to attend, so Venus Maria and Cooper admired the panoramic view and ordered a bottle of champagne.

"So?" she demanded anxiously. "Did you talk to him? What did he have to say?"

Cooper considered his reply. In his opinion Martin didn't have the balls to leave Deena. He was enjoying his affair with Venus, and indeed, who wouldn't? But he wasn't prepared to screw up his marriage. Deena represented stability. She was his wife, and they'd achieved a certain social standing Martin was not ready to give up.

But Cooper's opinion was not what Venus wanted to hear.

"Hey," he said, "you know Martin—Mr. Closed Mouth."

She was disappointed. "Do you mean to tell me you couldn't get *anything* out of him?"

"He thinks you're fantastic."

"Yes?"

"Oh, yes."

"Is that all?"

"Just that I agree with him."

She laughed, not taking him seriously at all. "You would!"

Later the three of them dined out, creating quite a sensation.

"You see," Venus Maria whispered to Martin, "it's good that

Cooper's with us. Now everybody will think he and I are an item. Can you imagine if we were spotted in San Francisco alone together?"

He agreed. "It was a wise decision."

She hammered the point home. "There's only one way we can be seen out in public, and that's if you split with your wife."

It was not the first time she'd said something like that to him.

He didn't reply.

After dinner they drove down to the bay and drank strong cappuccinos in a small, crowded café. Women appeared from nowhere, strutting their stuff in the hope of getting noticed. Cooper Turner and Martin Swanson in the same place at the same time—what an irresistible challenge! Men eyed Venus Maria up and down, and so did the women—while Martin and Cooper gave her their full attention.

"Don't you feel like getting laid?" Venus teased, flirting with Cooper, a mischievous twinkle in her eye.

"Getting laid today is a perilous business," he replied, perfectly serious. "I need to know their sexual history for the past seven years. It takes time and energy. Not like the old days. I'm too tired."

Martin shot him a look. "I never thought I'd hear *you* say that."

Venus Maria shook her platinum curls. "Oh, he's always saying that. Take no notice."

Cooper smiled. "I'm saving myself."

"Who for?" she asked curiously.

"I'll let you know when she comes along."

He held her gaze.

She looked away.

Later they boarded Martin's plane and flew back to L.A.

"Do you want to stay at my house?" she asked Martin.

"I'm desperate to stay at your house," he replied. "I didn't fly in early for my health."

"Just the two of us this time," she promised.

"No more games?" Was it her imagination, or did he sound just the tiniest bit disappointed?

"Yes, Martin. Just the two of us."

They said goodbye to Cooper in the limo.

"I'll call you tomorrow," she said. Cooper was rapidly turning into her best friend.

"Tomorrow," he said.

"Good night." She kissed him lightly on the cheek.

And then she was alone with Martin.

Dennis Walla stared at the current edition of *Truth and Fact*. Even now it was being delivered all over the country. The front page was the strongest layout he'd seen in a long time. It made the latest headlines in the *Enquirer* and the *Star* look sick.

First of all there were the headings in blazing red letters:

MARTIN SWANSON—BILLIONAIRE LOVER!

VENUS MARIA AND COOPER TURNER!

THE HEIRESS AND THE WIFE!

Surrounding these headings were five photographs. In the center was the large picture of Venus Maria with Martin Swanson. On the left, a small shot of Venus entering Spago with Cooper Turner. Beneath that, another photo of Venus and Cooper, taken on the set. And the two smaller photographs on the right were of Deena Swanson and Paul Webster in Central Park and of Paul strolling along the street with Brigette Stanislopoulos.

Dennis was more than delighted. He'd never expected this to turn out to be such an important story. At first it was merely going to be Emilio's revelations about Venus Maria. Now they'd held that part of the story for the following week; this week they'd concentrated on the various romantic entanglements of the main players. Excellent coverage!

Bert Slocombe had really come up trumps when he'd discovered Deena stepping out. But he'd doubled Dennis's pleasure when he'd managed to catch a photo of Deena's toyboy with Brigette Stanislopoulos, the teenage shipping heiress. What a coup!

There was more copy above the photographs:

LADY BOSS

BILLIONAIRE'S MISTRESS IS VENUS MARIA!

BROKEN WIFE DEENA SEES YOUNGER MAN!

DOES SWANSON KNOW SHE'S CHEATING?

Dennis Walla threw the magazine down on his coffee table. He was well pleased. As far as he was concerned every editor in town was going to be after him.

Dennis Walla was about to become the hottest tabloid journalist in the world.

Without the silken bindings and the two exotic hookers to excite him, sex with Martin seemed a little pedestrian. He was too fast in every way.

Much to Venus Maria's chagrin, foreplay seemed to have gone by the board, and all he could give her was a cursory going over. Sex by numbers. Touch the breasts for twenty-five seconds, move the hands down, spread the legs and go for it.

Venus Maria was disappointed. This wasn't the way she liked to make love at all. He had no stamina either. It was all over in minutes.

"What's the matter with you tonight?" she asked edgily, feeling totally unsatisfied.

Obviously he wasn't aware anything was amiss. "Aren't you happy?"

She frowned. "No, I'm not particularly happy. It was so quick."

Martin seemed unconcerned. "What did you expect?" he said, yawning. "It seems like I've been on planes for the last twenty-four hours. I'm not Superman."

You can say that again, she thought bitterly.

Venus Maria hated bad sex. It made her feel dirty and used. Sex was supposed to be long and leisurely and satisfying.

Bad sex reminded her of the sort of behavior her brothers used to dish out to the neighborhood girls who'd come to the old house in Brooklyn whining and crying about their treatment.

It was quite obvious her brothers considered women were put on this earth to clean, cook, fuck, and shut up.

Charming monsters.

Observing them had given Venus Maria a great deal of determination to make it as a strong woman, capable of anything. And she'd done it. She'd really done it!

Now that she was a modern-day sex symbol, it had to drive her brothers crazy.

She jumped out of bed and marched into her bathroom, slamming the door behind her. Damn Martin. Did he expect silken ties and two hookers every time they did it?

She imagined Cooper Turner didn't need any props. He was probably a master between the sheets. Well, he'd had enough experience over the years, hadn't he? Mr. Casanova. The Don Juan of Hollywood.

She wouldn't care to go to bed with him. God, no! The comparisons! He'd had some of the most beautiful women in the world.

Ah . . . the Cooper Turner Hall of Fame. Venus Maria never planned to be part of *that* long parade.

Martin was asleep when she returned to the bedroom. He lay on his side, snoring loudly.

Maybe she wasn't being fair. He'd had a long journey and was probably exhausted.

She snuggled into bed beside him and closed her eyes. It took forty-five minutes before she was able to fall asleep.

63

Lucky flew back to Los Angeles with only Boogie for company. Lennie hadn't called, and she had too much pride to call him. If this was the way he wanted things to end—so be it.

Face facts, she told herself. She'd bought the studio for Lennie, and he didn't give a damn. He felt it was a blow to his ego or some such masculine crap. Why the hell couldn't he just relax and enjoy it?

When she arrived back at her apartment in New York, she'd phoned Gino and told him of Lennie's reaction.

"I tried to warn you, kid," he'd sighed. "I had an idea this was the way he'd feel."

"Why do you say that?"

" 'Cause it's a man's thing. You can buy him a sweater or a tie, but a studio . . . Jeez! What can I tell you?"

"His attitude is totally old-fashioned. I'm not putting up with it," she'd said stubbornly. "I'm excited about owning Panther. He should be, too."

"So what are you gonna do, kid?"

"Leave Lennie in New York until he gets over his sulks."

"Big solution."

"What else *can* I do?"

"How about tryin' to work it out?" he'd suggested.

"Too late. The next move is his."

The truth was, she felt hurt and frustrated by Lennie's macho attitude. He, above all people, should understand her. She'd never pretended to be the perfect little wife prepared to sit home and have babies. He'd always known she was a woman who liked to take chances. That's why he'd fallen in love with her.

Now he was acting like "You—woman. Me—man." It was almost as if he were saying, "Get knocked up or it's over." They had Bobby and Brigette. Wasn't that enough of a family for now?

Screw Lennie Golden.

She had a life to live.

From LAX, Boogie drove her straight to the Malibu house.

Miko greeted her with a polite bow. "So good to have you back, madame."

It was good to be back. She felt strong. She felt invincible. She was ready to accomplish anything.

On Sunday evening Morton Sharkey came over and they spent the evening going over Panther business. She had so many plans to put in place. New people to hire. Decisions on all the various productions. Who stayed and who did she dump.

Later, when Morton left, she walked out onto the deck and stared at the sea. *Everything's going to be all right, Santangelo,* she promised herself, breathing in the crisp night air.

All her life she'd had to make it on her own, prove she could do it. And Panther Studios was no different from anything else. She'd show everyone. And if Lennie didn't want to come along for the ride, she'd do it by herself.

Lucky Santangelo was a true survivor.

Nothing and nobody stopped her.

Abe Panther had decided they should all arrive at the studio together. So on Monday morning Lucky reported to Abe's Miller Drive home, along with Morton Sharkey.

Abe greeted her with a feisty grin. "Morning, girlie. Are we ready to kick us some ass?"

"I'm always ready to kick ass," she replied, confirming what he'd suspected.

She looked particularly beautiful with her mass of wild jet hair, olive skin, and dark eyes full of drama.

She wore a cream leather Claude Montana suit and very high heels, diamond hoops in her ears, and a large diamond ring on her finger. She was all business in a classy, sexy, stylish way.

What a difference from drab little Luce! That was the whole idea.

Abe seemed full of high spirits, and so did Inga, for once. He'd promised she could come to the meeting, and she'd dressed up for the occasion.

Lucky wondered what the old man was planning to do with all his money. Probably sit on it until he dropped!

"Are we meeting in Mickey's office?" she asked.

"Naw, we'll settle in the conference room," Abe decided. "I want to be there before any of 'em arrive."

"Mickey usually gets in early," Lucky pointed out.

"Maybe not today," Abe replied with a wicked laugh. "Here's a little something for you to feast your eyes on, girlie."

He handed her a copy of the *L.A. Times.* On the bottom of the front page there was a picture of Mickey being led out of a police van. The caption read:

STUDIO HEAD ARRESTED IN RAID ON HOLLYWOOD
HOUSE OF SHAME

"Oh, my God!" she exclaimed. "He's getting it from all sides today. Do you think he'll turn up?"

"Of course he will," snapped Abe.

They set off in convoy, Abe and Lucky in the first car, Inga following behind with Morton Sharkey and Abe's lawyer.

All the way Lucky could feel Abe's excitement building. And when they approached the studio gates he really started to buzz.

"This is like coming home, girlie," he said rubbing his hands together. "Can't think why I ever left."

"Why *did* you leave?" she asked.

He shrugged. "Don't know. We were entering a new decade. I didn't like what was goin' on in the movies anymore. The public wanted to see things I wasn't prepared to show 'em."

She could understand that. Abe came from a different era. "How does it feel to be coming back?" she asked.

He bobbed his head happily. "Pretty damned good!"

Up in the conference room, nervous secretaries were flitting all over the place.

"Good morning, Mr. Panther."

"Welcome back, Mr. Panther."

"Is there anything I can get you, Mr. Panther?"

Abe took his place at the head of the table and indicated to Lucky she should sit on his right.

She did so. Although the studio was officially hers, she wouldn't dream of cheating him out of his moment of glory.

At ten o'clock precisely Mickey Stolli marched in. He was followed by Abigaile, Primrose, and Ben.

Abe waved his hand in the air. "Take a seat everybody. Make yourselves at home."

Mickey glanced around the room. His eyes passed Lucky without a flicker of recognition.

"You're looking well, Grandfather," said Primrose, rushing over to kiss him.

"How come you never write or call?" Abe demanded, clicking his false teeth in and out.

Primrose sighed, as if he had no right to ask such a question. "We're all so busy, Grandfather. The children send you their love."

"Sit down," instructed Mickey sharply. He didn't need Primrose kissing the old man's ass.

When everybody was settled, Abe got right to it. "I've been outta here ten years," he said roughly, "an' I let you all do whatever the hell you wanted. Now I've made other arrangements. I've sold the studio."

There was a stunned silence. And four shocked faces.

Mickey was the first on his feet. "You've done *what?*" he asked incredulously.

"I've sold the studio," Abe repeated with a crafty cackle. "It's mine to sell, eh?"

"Grandfather, you can't do that without consulting us," Abigaile protested, a flush spreading across her face.

"Certainly not,' agreed a distressed Primrose.

"Girlies, I can do what I damn well please. I'm old enough and ugly enough."

"What you're saying is you've sold the studio. Is that it?" Mickey said harshly.

"This is good," joked Abe. "The man understands English."

Ben joined in. "Who've you sold it to?"

"Ladies and gentlemen—" Abe savored the words—"I'd like you to meet the new owner of Panther Studios." He turned to Lucky. "Allow me to introduce Lucky Santangelo."

There was another long silence. Once again Mickey was the first to break it. "What is this? Some kind of joke?"

"You can't do this, Grandfather," shrieked Abigaile.

Morton Sharkey rose to his feet. "Miss Santangelo will be taking over, effective today," he said. "In the future you will report to her."

"If you think I'm staying to be told what to do by some dumb broad—you're wrong," spat Mickey. "I'm out of here."

Good, Lucky thought.

"Now wait a minute," interrupted Ben. He knew who Lucky Santangelo was. He was well aware of her reputation. She'd taken over the Stanislopoulos shipping empire when Dimitri Stanislopoulos passed away, and today, under her management, it was more successful than ever. Lucky Santangelo knew what she was doing. "We're going to have to discuss this unexpected situation."

"Who gets the money?" asked Abigaile furiously, unable to control herself. "It's *our* money."

"Grandfather," Primrose said, the voice of reason, "we have to sit down and talk privately. Not in front of all these people."

"I feel like I'm at my own funeral," Abe cackled, enjoying every minute. "What? You think I'm dead already? I can do what I want with my money. It's not *your* money, It's *my* money."

Lucky spoke. "Gentlemen, there'll be a meeting of all department heads at noon today. Right here."

"What do *you* know about the movie business?" Mickey asked rudely, turning to glare at her.

"Let's just say, as much as you," she replied coolly.

He recognized something in her voice. Had he met her before? Lucky Santangelo. Lucky Santangelo . . . Christ! Wasn't she the broad with the gangster father? Wasn't she the one married to Lennie Golden?

Of course! Now it began to make sense. Her husband got pissed off with the studio and the broad bought it to keep him happy. Son of a bitch!

He couldn't look at Abigaile. His dear wife wasn't speaking to him on account of the story of his arrest making the front page of the *L.A. Times.* When Abigaile had seen it, she'd turned into a hysterical shrew. "Out of this house," she'd screamed. "Out of my life. I'll sue you for every penny you've got. How *dare* you disgrace me and Tabitha! This is the biggest humiliation of my life."

"It was a mistake," he'd replied lamely. "I was visiting the place with a director. The guy was researching a movie. I told him a scene he wanted to shoot wouldn't work. He took me up there to prove it would. It was business, Abby."

"Mickey Stolli, you've lied to me for the last time," Abigaile had shouted, narrowing her eyes. "We'll meet with my grandfather and behave like human beings. And then you'll pack your bags and get out of *my* house. We're through."

He wondered how she felt now. Abigaile wasn't going to continue to ignore him after *this* little shocker. He shot her a look.

She was destroyed.

He glanced over at Ben and Primrose. Ben was all but foaming at the mouth, and Primrose seemed about to burst into tears.

Abe was loving every minute of the confusion he'd caused. Crafty little shithead, Mickey thought sourly. He stood up. He didn't have to take this crap. He could get a job anywhere in town. He'd made Panther the success it was today.

"I resign," he said sharply. "Find yourself another schmuck."

64

Venus Maria slept in the nude. When she was a little girl she'd read an article about Marilyn Monroe.

What do you wear in bed, Miss Monroe?

Chanel Number Five.

Venus Maria wore nothing except her favorite scent, Poison, and a delicate tattoo of two white doves on the inside of her left thigh—a souvenir of a two-day visit to Bangkok.

She awoke early, stretched languidly, and reached out for Martin. He was not there.

She jumped out of bed and checked the bathroom. No note. No nothing.

Who the hell did he think he was dealing with here? Some Hollywood bimbo he could visit when he came into town, bang, and then take off? No way. She was Venus Maria. She deserved better than this. Goddamn it! Martin Swanson had to be taught a lesson.

Jumping under a cold shower, she thought things over.

Martin Swanson . . . Martin Swanson . . . Why this obsession? What was wrong with her for God's sake? He was just another man, after all.

Once out of the shower she wrapped herself in a terry-cloth robe and vigorously shook her wet hair. Today she was supposed to rehearse for the video. She loved it when she had nothing else to do except rehearse. It meant she didn't have to bother with makeup and putting on the Venus Maria persona. She could just be herself, bundle her hair into a ponytail, not bother with makeup, wear exercise clothes, and relax.

Ron made sure it was hard work. But he also made it fun. Long ago she'd decided she was a gypsy at heart. Her work was everything. And the recognition an added bonus.

She decided Martin Swanson wasn't going to spoil her day. Screw him.

Downstairs, Hannah, her housekeeper, greeted her with the usual large glass of freshly squeezed orange juice, and a glass dish filled with chopped apples, melon, bananas, and oranges, covered with a healthful sprinkling of bran.

"Good morning," Venus sang out, feeling surprisingly good in spite of mediocre sex and Martin's early exit. "How was your weekend?"

Hannah didn't mention that her two days of rest were nonstop drudgery while she caught up on household chores in her downtown two-room apartment. With four children and a husband to look after, it wasn't easy. "Fine, Miss Venus," she said, clearing up the dishes.

After the juice and fruit, Venus Maria indulged in a couple of pieces of toast liberally spread with chunky English marmalade.

Just as she was in the middle of the second piece, Ron arrived.

She looked up, pleased to see him. "What are you doing here? Aren't we supposed to meet at rehearsal in an hour?"

He carried a magazine, which he placed carefully on the table. "I thought you should hear it from me first," he announced dramatically. Ron always liked to make the most of everything.

"Hear what?" she asked brightly.

His voice rose. "You mean nobody's told you? You haven't *seen* it?"

"What are you talking about?"

He was making a three-course meal out of this one.

"Remember I warned you about Emilio when you chucked him out?"

She had a nasty feeling she wasn't going to like what she was about to hear. "Yes?" she said slowly.

Ron picked up a piece of toast and took a bite. "I never trusted him."

"Ha!" she said. "You think *I* trusted him? He broke into my house on Saturday."

"Yeah? I wonder what he was after? Take a look at this." He picked up the copy of *Truth and Fact* and waved it in front of her face.

She stared at it in horror. There, on the front page, was a photograph of her with Martin. It was *her* photograph. It was the two of them together taken by Cooper.

"Oh, no!" she cried.

"Oh, yes!" stated Ron firmly. "He probably dropped by to rip off the photo. Where did you keep it?"

She jumped up. "In my safe."

He sighed. "Let's go check it out."

"I can't believe he'd do this to me," she said angrily. "I'm paying his goddamn rent. I let him stay here for months! Ron, oh, God! Look what it says: 'Next week Venus Maria's brother is going to reveal all!' What the hell is all?"

"When you're famous you can't even take a crap in peace," Ron said succinctly.

Venus headed upstairs, with Ron close behind her.

She stormed over to her safe, opened it, and frantically searched for her picture.

It wasn't there.

"He stole it!" she yelled. "That lousy low-life rat-faced piece of shit!"

"Don't hold back," encouraged Ron.

"Oh, my God," she wailed. "What does the story say? Martin's going to have a fit. Oh, Jesus!"

"It's not such a bad thing," Ron said, trying to calm her. "At least Deena will know you exist now. You won't have to creep around in hiding every time you get together with Martin."

Venus Maria snatched the magazine from him, eyes racing over the story.

Billionaire Martin Swanson's phone calls and secret visits to rav-
ishing superstar Venus Maria are driving his beautiful society wife,
Deena, into the arms of young Paul Webster, son of Deena's best
friend, interior designer to the rich and famous, Effie Webster.

Sexy superstar Venus Maria can teach billionaire tycoon Martin
Swanson a thing or two about getting to the top. Heartbroken Deena
moved in on Paul after hearing about her husband's fascination with
video superstar Venus Maria. Deena is making a last-ditch effort to
get Martin back. In the meantime, Martin Swanson has been show-
ering Venus Maria with gifts. According to a close friend, Venus
Maria and Martin Swanson met casually at a party in New York
several months ago. But after a chance second meeting in Los An-
geles, they couldn't resist each other any longer. All of Venus Mar-
ia's close friends were soon telling Swanson, "She likes you," "She
wants you." Within a week the two got together at a hideaway in Big
Sur. According to another close friend, Martin told Venus he was
not happy in his marriage. "From the beginning," an acquaintance
said, "Venus Maria and Martin Swanson were magic together. Mar-
tin finds her extremely erotic, and Venus Maria is fascinated with
his power and wealth.

Venus threw the magazine down in a fury. "Where do they get all this garbage?" she yelled.

"Let's call Emilio," Ron suggested. "It's quite obvious he's been paid for this."

She made a face. "How can people *do* these things? If he needed money so desperately I would have given it to him. Doesn't he have any pride?"

"Emilio, pride?" Ron said, raising a skeptical eyebrow.

She was determined. "Gimme the phone."

Ron did so, and she dialed Emilio's number. His answering machine picked up.

"Fuck you!" she screamed into the receiver and slammed the phone down.

"That'll do you a lot of good, dear," remarked Ron.

Venus snatched the magazine again. "Oh, and get this bit— Cooper's going to be really thrilled." She read aloud from the magazine. " 'While Venus Maria plays house with Martin Swanson, Cooper Turner thinks he's her only lover.' Can you believe this crap? I'm calling my lawyer."

"What can *he* do?"

"I'll sue 'em."

"How can you? Most of it's true."

She hadn't thought about that. "I'd better warn Martin."

"Where is he?"

"He left early. He's involved in some kind of takeover bid. He's gaining control of a studio."

"Oh, just like that. The very rich *are* different."

"Ron, do me a favor. Call his office in New York and find out where I can reach him."

"What do you think he'll say?"

She shrugged. "I don't know. He's not used to this kind of publicity. At least *I* know what to expect. I've been everything from a lesbian alien to a woman with three breasts! And that's just this year! The shit comes with the territory."

"Don't kid yourself, dear," Ron said mildly. "Martin will probably love every minute of it."

Martin Swanson was in a board meeting when a secretary discreetly entered the room, tapped him on the shoulder, and said, "Your assistant in New York has to speak to you urgently, Mr. Swanson."

Martin couldn't possibly imagine what was so urgent that they had to interrupt him in the middle of a meeting. "Excuse me, gentlemen," he said standing up.

He walked outside. The secretary hovered behind him. "I'm sorry to disturb you, Mr. Swanson," she apologized. "However, your assistant did say it was imperative that she speak to you at once."

"Don't worry about it." He waved a vague hand in her direction and picked up the phone. "What is it, Gertrude?" he asked abruptly.

"Mr. Swanson, Venus Maria is trying to reach you. She says it's extremely urgent and that she must talk to you immediately."

"Very well, Gertrude."

"Mr. Swanson?"

"Yes? What now?"

"I do believe I know what it's about."

"Do you want to tell me? Or would you prefer to keep it a secret?" he said sarcastically, not feeling particularly patient.

Gertrude plunged right in. "There's a magazine called *Truth and Fact*, it's similar to the *Enquirer*."

"So?"

"On the cover of the issue out today there's a front page story concerning you and Venus Maria. Of course, I'm certain it's all lies." She hesitated, and then rushed on, "Mr. Swanson, it's not a very nice story. Mrs. Swanson will not be pleased."

Martin turned to the secretary hovering nearby. "Is there a newsstand downstairs?"

She nodded.

"Be a good girl, run down and get me a copy of *Truth and Fact*."

"Certainly, Mr. Swanson, at once."

He replaced the receiver and immediately phoned Venus Maria. "Have you seen *Truth and Fact*?" he demanded.

"I just read it," she replied.

"Do you want to tell me about it?" he said curtly. "What have they got? San Francisco? Is Cooper in the picture?"

"It's worse than that, Martin. Remember that photo Cooper took of us one night at my house? Well, I had it in my safe, and I suspect my brother must have stolen it and sold it to *Truth and Fact*."

"Your brother?"

"Emilio. He was staying with me. A real loser."

"So what you're telling me is that they've printed this picture of us together?"

"Yes, and it's pretty intimate. We're kind of sitting on the couch with our arms all over each other."

"Didn't you destroy it?"

She resented his tone. "Obviously not. I had it in my safe. That seemed like a pretty secure place to me."

"Christ!" he exclaimed, thinking of Deena's reaction.

Venus, too, could get uppity. "Don't get pissed with *me*, it's not my fault."

"Whose fault is it?" he asked coldly.

"I don't know, and quite frankly I don't give a fuck." She slammed the phone down. It was about time Martin learned to treat her with a little respect.

"Trouble in Lifestyles-of-the-Rich-and-Famous land?" Ron ventured, pretending not to be enjoying every minute.

"Let's go rehearse," she said. "I've had it with that ego-inflated asshole."

65

The news spread like an out-of-control brushfire. This was Hollywood after all, capital of innuendo, gossip, and scandal. Already everyone was talking about Mickey Stolli's arrest at Madame Loretta's. What a delicious item to start the day! Now the rumor was that Lucky Santangelo had purchased Panther Studios, with Abe Panther's full cooperation.

The word was out of the room before they finished the meeting. The word spread from person to person. Phones were picked up. Calls were made. The news was passed on. The news spread across Hollywood.

At Panther everyone was abuzz with Mickey Stolli's arrest. Ford Werne couldn't understand it. The rule was, if you go to a prostitute, never get caught. Mickey had spoiled it for all of them.

It was hardly another Monday morning at the studio.

When Arnie Blackwood and Frankie Lombardo had finished sniggering about Mickey's misfortune, they heard about Lucky Santangelo's purchase of the studio and her call for a noon meeting with all the department heads. They immediately placed a call to Eddie Kane.

Eddie picked up his own phone. "Yeah?"

"Don't you come in anymore?" Arnie demanded.

Eddie was in no mood to be harassed. "Only when it suits me."

"So I guess you've got no idea what's going on," Frankie said, speaking on a conference call so Arnie could join in.

"You got something to tell me?" Eddie asked impatiently, knowing that Arnie and Frankie would never call just to inquire about his health. Maybe they were about to complain he'd scored too much coke at their party. Well, fuck 'em. Don't have the party if you can't part with the goods.

"Yeah," Arnie replied, drawing the words out slowly. "Some rich broad from New York walked in with Abe this morning and bought the fuckin' studio."

"What?" Eddie wasn't sure he'd heard correctly.

"Yeah, old Abe sold the studio from right under Mickey. Didn't you know?"

"If I knew, do you think I'd be sitting here?" Eddie replied agitatedly. "I got problems of my own."

"Get your stoned ass down here," ordered Frankie sharply. "There's a meeting of all department heads at noon. We need someone in there."

Eddie's mind was racing. He wondered if Mickey had known about this beforehand. Maybe that was why he'd been so cold and uptight.

Christ! Yes, Arnie and Frankie were right; he should be there. "I'm on my way," he said.

Leslie was puttering around in the kitchen. She looked beautiful. Eddie still hadn't figured out what she'd been doing in a whorehouse. Eventually he was going to have to investigate.

"Gotta go to the studio, babe," he said, like this was the start of another normal day.

She looked dismayed. "Oh, no, Eddie. I thought we were going to find a counselor and talk about getting you to a detox center. Do you have to go?"

"Yeah," Eddie said, his twitching in full swing. "Too bad about that counselor thing. We'll do it next week. O.K., babe?"

It wasn't O.K., but Leslie didn't say a word.

. . .

Lucky had an advantage. She knew who the players were, and they didn't know her.

At twelve o'clock precisely, they all trooped into the conference room.

Abe had taken off, followed by Inga, followed by Abigaile, followed by Primrose and Ben, both complaining bitterly. No doubt she would hear from them later.

The contingent of department heads was led by Ford Werne, still looking as if he'd stepped from the front page of G.Q. magazine, impeccable in another Armani suit, the same five-hundred-dollar tinted aviator shades covering his eyes. He was an attractive man—if you liked killers.

Zev Lorenzo followed Ford into the room and walked straight over to Lucky, offering his hand. "Welcome aboard," he said in a friendly fashion.

Then came Grant Wendell Junior, vice president of worldwide production, looking like a reject from the mail room in his baggy pants and Dodgers baseball cap. He gave her a casual half-wave. "Hiya."

Lucky wondered if Mickey was going to put in a final appearance, or if his resignation was it. He must be in shock. Good. Mickey deserved a little shock in his life.

Teddy T. Lauden hurried into the room—a thin, precise man, constantly glancing at his watch. "Good afternoon, Miss Santangelo," he said, opting for a more formal relationship. "A pleasure to meet you. I do hope I'm not too late. I had another meeting to attend. Unfortunately I wasn't allowed enough time to cancel it. As you must understand, this has been a big shock for all of us."

Lucky nodded. "Yes, I do understand," she said quietly. "I'm sure it has been."

"You could say that," Ford Werne agreed, taking off his aviator shades and immediately putting them on again.

"I *am* saying it, Mr. Werne."

He was obviously surprised she knew who he was since he hadn't bothered to introduce himself. "Where's Mickey?" he asked.

"He won't be joining us," Morton Sharkey said, from his position beside Lucky.

Glancing around, she observed that Buck Graham and Eddie Kane were the only two still missing. "Will Mr. Graham and Mr. Kane be joining us?"

Grant Wendell shrugged. "Ummm, I talked to Eddie this morning. He's on his way in. And, uh, Buck had another meeting he's trying to break out of."

Lucky was cool and in control. "Why don't we give it ten minutes?" she said pleasantly.

"Suits me." Ford adjusted his expensive shades yet again, and stood up. "I have a phone call to make. Will you excuse me."

"What a group!" Lucky murmured to Morton.

"They all want to keep their jobs," he answered in a low voice, "unless a better offer comes along."

"I understand what goes on in this town very well," she replied. "It's no different from any other business. Naturally, if there's something better around the corner—go for it. If not, stand firm. The rules of the game."

"I hardly think any of them are thrilled to find themselves working for a woman."

"I guess not. After all, this is Hollywood, and women are not exactly power figures here. Ford is probably on the phone right now trying to get another job. Right?"

Morton agreed. "I wouldn't be surprised."

Buck Graham burst into the room, red in the face. Buck was head of marketing. His specialty was getting right down to the common denominator. Whatever the content of the film, Buck sold it with a strong dose of tits and ass. As far as he was concerned, America had a permanent hard-on.

He'd used a body double on the poster for Susie Rush's last movie —Susie's face atop an outrageously overdeveloped body. She was furious, and threatened to sue unless the poster was immediately withdrawn. Buck had given in—reluctantly.

Finally Eddie Kane came bouncing in, making the meeting complete.

Eddie looked like he'd slept in his clothes. His growing beard was a serious mistake, and his eyes were bloodshot and more spacy than ever.

"Where's Mickey?" were the first words out of his mouth.

"Not here," Buck said, shaking his head.

Eddie twitched. "Is he coming?"

"Didja see the *L.A. Times?*" Grant asked. " 'Cause if you did, you know there's no way he'll be in today."

"What's happened?"

"He got caught buyin' pussy."

Before Eddie could get into it, Ford returned from his phone call and Lucky got straight down to business.

"Well, gentlemen," she said, rising to her feet. "I'm sure you've all heard the news. My name is Lucky Santangelo and I'm the new owner of Panther Studios." She paused while a buzz went around the room. "I'm also new to the film industry. But I do know what I want. And that is to make good movies—films Panther can be proud of. I'm interested in hearing what you feel hasn't been accomplished here in the last few years." She paused again. At least they were listening. When she'd first taken over Stanislopoulos shipping, it had taken months to get the male executives' attention. "Trust me when I say this—Panther's been putting out garbage, and those days are over. I'm leading this studio on to great things." She stared at them, black eyes ablaze. "Gentlemen," she said forcefully, "you can bet on it."

66

Deena Swanson did not enjoy exercise. She was not some crazed Californian who thought an hour of aerobics and two hours of Jane Fonda were exciting stuff. No. Deena hated exerting herself. However, the trend was to do it. And nobody had ever accused Deena of being behind the trends. So, eventually, like all chic New Yorkers, she'd hired her own personal trainer, who came to the house. His name was Sven, and fortunately he didn't speak much English, which suited Deena fine, because it was not conversation she was after.

Sven certainly knew how to get the best out of her in fifteen minutes of pure torture. Three times a week she started her day with him. When he left she usually luxuriated in the tub for fifteen minutes before dressing to go to her office for an hour or so before lunch.

Lunch was the most important part of Deena's day. She dressed for lunch. She accessorized for lunch. She made sure her makeup, nails, and hair were always perfect. Deena knew maintenance was a woman's best defense.

Most of Deena's women friends worked for their husbands. It was the new chic thing to do. They gave their opinions on style, fabrics, perfumes, cosmetics, and in return they were paid a fat director's fee for their input. But all of them found time to lunch.

Deena belonged to that exclusive group of rich New York women

423

who wore only designer clothes, real jewelry, and fur coats if they were sure they weren't going to get a can of paint thrown over them by animal rights activists.

Today, Deena was lunching at Le Cirque. Effie and she had a standing appointment for Mondays.

Deena dressed carefully in a lime green Adolfo suit, Chanel shoes and bag. She then added Bulgari earrings and a choker, plus a huge diamond ring Martin had presented her with last Christmas.

Outside her apartment on Park Avenue, her car and driver waited to take her the few blocks to her office in the Swanson Building, a gleaming tower of modern architecture.

She loved her office. Effie had decorated it in cool pastels—a tranquil haven away from home.

Deena was proud of the fact that her fashion and perfume business was successful. When she'd embarked on it, she'd surrounded herself with the best executives money could buy. Martin had advised her. But that couldn't change the fact that it was *her* name on the products the public bought. Deena Swanson: her name sold.

One of her secretaries greeted her with the news that Effie Webster had called and canceled lunch.

"Why?" Deena asked, disappointed.

The girl shrugged. "I don't know, Mrs. Swanson."

"Get her on the phone for me," Deena said, quite put out. For as long as she could remember, Effie and she had always lunched on Mondays.

"Mrs. Webster is not at her office," the secretary informed her.

"Try her at home," Deena ordered.

"I already did. An answering machine picks up," the girl said.

Deena frowned. Was Effie sick?

She sat behind her bleached-wood desk and counted ten perfectly sharpened pencils in a Lucite holder. The pristine legal-sized pad of white paper with "Deena Swanson" printed in pink on the top awaited her attention. A silver-framed photograph of her and Martin faced her. There was really nothing for Deena to do at the office; everything was taken care of.

She called Martin in California. He was not at the hotel. Then she called another friend of hers, a sleek redhead who made exorbitantly priced belts and other fine accessories.

"Lunch, darling?" she asked.

"Isn't Monday your day with Effie?" her friend replied.

"She's sick," Deena explained.

"Ah, well, so I'm the substitute."

"If you like. Le Cirque at one o'clock?"

"Why not?" her friend said.

It was arranged. Deena replaced the phone.

"Send Mrs. Webster some flowers," she told her secretary. "A hundred dollars' worth. Make sure it's a beautiful arrangement."

"I can't wait to get out of here," Nona whispered. "My mother is in an absolute fury. I warned Paul."

Brigette wasn't exactly delighted herself. She'd managed to stay out of the supermarket rags for quite some time, and now they'd sneaked a picture of her and Paul taken with a hidden camera. Not so bad, but above that picture, there was Paul, practically kissing Mrs. Swanson. It was disgusting!

Effie Webster had taken it personally: her son photographed in what looked like a compromising position with her best friend. Really!

She summoned Paul to the house immediately. "What's this?" she demanded, thrusting a copy of *Truth and Fact* at him.

"Oh, that," he said casually, as if it didn't matter. "I took Deena out to lunch, big deal."

"It doesn't look like you're lunching here," replied Effie furiously. "You're all over her."

"So?" Paul said. "What's wrong with that? She's a woman. I'm a man."

"You're a *child*," Effie emphasized. "And how dare you take one of my friends out! Deena is married."

"I told you, we were lunching—not fucking," Paul retorted sharply. "And may I remind you, I'm nearly twenty-four years old. I'm hardly a child."

Effie didn't take this well. "Stop asking us for money, and get out of here. You will not speak to me like that."

Paul slouched from the room.

Nona caught him at the front door. "Where are you going?" she asked.

"I don't have to put up with her talking to me like I'm nothing. It's not like I live here. There's no way I have to answer to anyone."

"Stop asking for money and maybe she'll leave you alone," Nona said, wise beyond her years.

"Butt out. You've no idea what's going on."

"Oh, yes I do. You're trying to score with her best friend. No wonder she's pissed with you."

"I can do what I like."

"Do you want to see Brigette while you're here?"

"She's a kid. Quit pushing her at me."

Brigette overheard. Her stomach knotted. Why had she ever set eyes on Nona's stupid brother?

Casually Nona tried to gloss over things. "Take no notice of Paul," she said airily when her brother had departed. "He's a jerk. All men are. That should be our new credo. All men are pigs, don't you agree?"

Brigette couldn't help laughing. "You're right."

"Let's get the hell outta here," Nona decided. "Call Lennie and see if we can fly to Malibu tomorrow."

Deena was sitting at her desk wondering what to do next when her secretary informed her that Adam Bobo Grant was on the line.

Deena was always delighted to hear from Adam Bobo Grant. Apart from being entertaining, gay, and independently rich, he was also one of the premier gossip columnists in New York.

She grabbed the phone. "Bobo, darling! What can I do for you?"

"You can call me Adam for a start, it's so much more macho, don't you think?"

"But, darling," Deena protested, "everyone calls you Bobo."

"Not during business hours, Deena."

"Is this a business call?"

"I need your confirmation on something."

"My confirmation about what, darling?"

"About the story."

"What story?"

Bobo paused for a moment, sucking on a silver Cartier pen. "You *have* seen it, haven't you?" he asked at last.

Deena didn't want to appear slow. She racked her brains going over all the items she'd read in the papers that morning. Nothing of great interest. "Clue me in, Bobo, um . . . Adam, and I'll give you a quote."

On the other end of the line, Adam Bobo Grant came to the swift conclusion that Deena Swanson had no idea what he was talking about. The woman had not seen *Truth and Fact*. Nobody had dared show it to her.

He made a quick decision. "Are you free for lunch, Deena?"

Lunch with Adam Bobo Grant was considerably better than lunch with another woman. "Why, yes, as a matter of fact I am," Deena said, mentally canceling her other date.

"We'll have an early lunch," he decided. "I'll meet you there. Does half an hour suit you?"

"Wonderful," she replied. "Shall I keep my table at Le Cirque?"

"Unless you prefer Mortimer's?"

She considered where she wanted to be seen with Bobo, and decided Le Cirque was where she'd be most visible. "On a Monday? I don't think so."

"Then Le Cirque it is."

Deena was happy. She'd hear all the latest gossip—everything he couldn't write about because it was too outrageous and scandalous. The real dirt.

She buzzed her secretary. "Cancel my other lunch," she said coolly. "I shall be lunching with Adam Bobo Grant today."

As soon as Adam Bobo Grant put the phone down, he checked with one of his minions. "Did you manage to locate Martin Swanson?" he asked brusquely.

"He's in Los Angeles. Right now he's in a meeting at Orpheus Studios. The rumor is there's a takeover going on."

"And Venus Maria?" asked Bobo.

"I spoke to her publicist. She's in rehearsal for the 'Soft Seduction' video."

Adam Bobo Grant nodded knowingly. "Place calls to both of them. Leave my name and home phone number. Tell them I'd like them to call me back as soon as possible. And warn Mack in the news room to make space for me on the front page. If I judge people correctly, we're going to have a new exclusive on the Swanson-Venus Maria affair."

67

While Lucky Santangelo was conducting a gathering of department heads at Panther Studios, Mickey Stolli was meeting with Carlos Bonnatti in a high-rise Century City penthouse.

Mickey would have been only too delighted to see what the dumb broad had to say. What did Lucky Santangelo know about running a studio and making movies? Absolutely nothing.

The morning announcement had taken him by surprise. He'd imagined Abe Panther was coming in to tell everybody he was returning to work. No way. The crafty old fart had sold the goddamn studio!

Abigaile's face! It was almost worth it to observe her stunned expression.

When they left the meeting, Mickey had given her a brusque "Gotta go to another meeting."

"We have things to discuss," Ben objected, pushing his long nose in where it wasn't wanted.

"Impossible," Mickey replied with a certain amount of satisfaction.

"Your resignation was premature," Ben said.

"But satisfying," Mickey replied.

Abigaile glared at him. It wasn't bad enough he'd been arrested with a hooker; now he was walking away from the most important moment of their lives.

"We must consult our lawyers immediately," she said grimly, turning to her brother-in-law for support. "Isn't that right, Ben?"

Ben and Primrose both agreed.

Mickey shrugged. "Sorry," he said, not sorry at all.

Abigaile continued to glare at him.

Ben took her arm. "I'm sure Mickey will catch up with us later," he said soothingly.

Abigaile's voice took on a high, feverish pitch. "Later is not good enough," she cried. "Mickey, why are you doing this to me?"

Abigaile Stolli, queen of the "me" generation. Mickey didn't care. He'd spent his life worrying what Abby would think. Now it was over.

When he was rid of them he stopped by his office. No Olive. No Luce. Where was his stupid temporary secretary? He was in the mood to fire her before he did anything else.

His office was strangely quiet. He picked up the phone, deciding to call Warner so he could tell her exactly what he thought of her. Then he changed his mind and banged it down.

He'd had it with Warner. As far as he was concerned she'd never hear from him again.

He'd already placed a call to his lawyer, who'd assured him they would find some way to get around the necessity for him to appear in court.

Carlos Bonnatti had reached him at home and requested his presence. Mickey didn't usually jump, but he knew enough about the ways of the world to realize that if Carlos Bonnatti called, he'd better be there. Eddie Kane had really fucked up. Now it was up to Mickey to straighten things out. As usual.

Driving over to Century City he arrived at a smart conclusion: Maybe the million dollars was Panther's problem after all. Maybe it was Lucky Santangelo's inheritance. . . .

He tried to reach Eddie on the car phone.

A subdued Leslie told him he wasn't there.

For a moment Mickey was tempted to say, "Didn't I see you at Madame Loretta's?" Then he thought better of it and hung up.

Carlos Bonnatti greeted him with a menacing smile and a limp handshake. He had a low, grating voice. A dangerous voice. "Mr.

Stolli," he said slowly, "nice of you to come. It's about time we talked. I don't seem to be getting anywhere with your associate, Mr. Kane, and it's good that you and I are meeting like this."

Mickey decided the setting was exactly right. Flashy apartment, a couple of goons hanging around in the front hall. Where was the obligatory blonde?

"You're right, Mr. Bonnatti," he said smoothly. "How can I help you?"

"I got a little problem," Carlos said, rubbing his fingers together. "You may have heard 'bout it. You run a big studio, maybe you don't hear everything."

"What's your problem?" asked Mickey, knowing perfectly well what it was.

The oil in Carlos's hair glistened. His smile was snakelike. "Well, we entered into a business deal, no contracts, but a handshake is a handshake," he said in his low, dangerous voice. "I mostly dealt with your colleague Eddie Kane. We put our product in with your product. It was sent over to Europe an' the money came through. This all went fluently for a time." He paused.

Mickey stared at him. Carlos was wearing a dark blue suit, a black silk shirt, and a white tie. The hood look. You could spot New Yorkers a mile away. They always overdressed when in California.

"So," Carlos continued, "the money flowed good for a while, and then the amounts comin' to us got smaller and smaller, and I knew somethin' wasn't right." He threw his arms up in a gesture of surrender. "But what am I gonna do? Panther's a big outfit—so I trusted you."

"I'm getting the message," Mickey said. "You didn't receive all the money you were expecting."

"Let's just say there's a shortfall of a million bucks," Carlos said, nodding to himself. "Yeah, an' who owes the money? That's the question. The big question."

"You want to know whose pocket it ended up in," Mickey said.

"I refuse to point a finger." Carlos smoothed the cuffs of his silk shirt. "But Eddie Kane is the name that comes to mind."

"And he's not paying. Right?"

"No way a bum like Eddie's gonna give back a million bucks." A short pause. "So . . . Mickey, you can understand my dilemma."

Mickey understood it only too well. "You'd like Panther Studios to reimburse you." He made it a statement, not a question.

"That's correct. An' if you see a way to do that, then you'll save Mr. Kane a lot of grief. Maybe you'll take it out of his salary for the next twenty, thirty years."

"Sounds workable," Mickey agreed amicably.

Carlos was obviously surprised at Mickey's immediate cooperation. "How we gonna handle this? A handshake don't do it for me this time. I'd like a note drawn up sayin' Panther owes my company a million bucks. We can put it down for services."

Mickey nodded. "Good idea. Call in your lawyers. I have the authority to sign on behalf of Panther. One stipulation—it has to be predated. And I have to sign the papers today."

"Done," said Carlos. "My lawyer'll take care of it. No questions asked."

They shook hands—Carlos Bonnatti and Mickey Stolli.

"Be back around two. I'll have everythin' ready," Carlos said. He paused and gave Mickey a long, penetrating look. "You're a very obliging man, Mr. Stolli. A very smart man. Anytime you need a favor . . ."

Mickey nodded modestly. "Thank you."

When Mickey left, Carlos walked around his apartment, considering the action. He pressed his fingers to his temples. Sometimes he wished his father was around. Enzio Bonnatti had always had a way of knowing exactly what was going on. He could immediately assess any situation and explain the whys and wherefors. Santino, his brother, had been a schmuck. All Santino cared about was pussy. He'd been in the right business: porno movies and drugs.

Carlos knew he was smarter than Santino. Shit, anybody was smarter than Santino. But he wouldn't have minded having Enzio around to talk to.

Mickey Stolli had complied too willingly, without so much as a struggle.

Something was going on here and Carlos wasn't sure what. But as long as the papers were drawn up and he got his money, what did he care?

68

Sitting in a private office at Orpheus Studios, Martin Swanson read about himself like a voyeur. His eyes scanned the page of the cheap magazine. He couldn't believe some of the things he was reading.

BILLIONAIRE MARTIN SWANSON!

RAVISHING SUPERSTAR VENUS MARIA!

BEAUTIFUL SOCIETY WIFE DEENA!

And there were all those quotes from supposed best friends and close acquaintances.

Martin had controlled his press for so long that the sheer effrontery of this really shocked him. The ramifications were many. What was Deena going to say? She would be furious when she saw the photograph of him with Venus. How was he going to explain it? It wasn't taken at a function or in a restaurant. It was obviously an intimate photo on somebody's couch.

At least they weren't naked. They hadn't been caught in bed. But you only had to look at the photograph to know they were sleeping with each other.

Thinking about the photographs reminded him of the one of

Deena with Effie's kid. What the hell was Deena doing in Central
Park with Paul Webster?

Not that Martin considered such a callow youth a threat, but it
made Deena look foolish—as if she was desperate or something.

He continued to read the story:

> Sexy superstar, Venus Maria, could teach billionaire tycoon
> Martin Swanson a thing or two about getting to the top.

Oh yeah? What did they know? Who owned this cheap magazine
anyway? He placed a call to his secretary in New York to have her
find out.

"Have you heard from Mrs. Swanson?" he asked.

"I do believe she's in her office," Gertrude replied.

"Has anybody shown this to her?"

Gertrude sounded embarrassed. "I really have no idea, Mr. Swanson."

"If she tries to reach me, tell her I'm in nonstop meetings and that
you can't get to me."

"Certainly, sir."

Now that his affair with Venus was out in the open he was going
to have to be very careful. Was it worth it? Did he wish to continue
seeing her?

She'd been more than aggravating this weekend. Dragging Cooper
along to San Francisco and then complaining about his sexual prowess when they got back. Goddamn it! One moment she was plying
him with hookers, and the next she expected him to put on a record-
breaking performance when he was tired and had a lot on his mind.
At least when you were married, a wife understood these things.

On the other hand, Venus Maria was special. She was universally
desired. Cooper was after her—that was obvious. And *he* had her:
Martin Swanson—Billionaire Lover. Billionaire Stud!

He couldn't help smiling. It was kind of funny, in a way.

It wouldn't be so funny when he had to explain the photograph to
Deena.

A buzzer sounded in the office. "Mr. Swanson," one of the secretaries said, "Mr. White would like to know when you are returning
to the meeting."

"I'll be right there," he said, folding the magazine in half.

Enough worrying about some low-down supermarket tabloid. He'd put his lawyers on to them. He'd kill 'em. He'd break their balls as only Martin Swanson could.

He walked back into the meeting. He was taking over Orpheus Studios. A far more important task.

Side by side on Cooper Turner's desk lay the front page of the *L.A. Times* with the story about Mickey Stolli circled, and alongside it a copy of *Truth and Fact*.

Cooper read about Mickey first. He was amused. It had to have been the funniest scene going. Mickey Stolli arrested with a hooker. Cooper was acquainted with Madame Loretta. Not in a professional sense—but an actress he'd been dating at one time had been playing the role of a prostitute on screen and had wanted to research the part. Ford Werne had arranged an introduction, and Cooper and his lady friend had spent many a pleasant afternoon having tea with the Madame, listening to her outlandish stories.

Cooper wondered how Venus Maria was going to feel when she saw *Truth and Fact*. It would certainly bring her affair with Martin out into the open.

Maybe that was what she wanted. Martin would be forced into making a decision.

Cooper couldn't help raising a cynical eyebrow when he read about Deena with a younger man. Martin wouldn't like that. It would be a blow to his enormous ego.

But all this wasn't his problem. He called the florist and sent Venus Maria two dozen red roses. It was the least he could do.

It soon became obvious that everybody in the rehearsal room had seen the stupid magazine. Venus Maria could tell by the covert little glances coming her way and a certain amount of nervous giggling here and there. Vigorously she launched herself into Ron's latest torture routine.

The Ken Doll wandered in around noon, washed and scrubbed,

tall and bland-faced, wearing a muscle-boy T-shirt and tight blue jeans outlining his outstanding crotch. Obviously the main attraction. She'd been thinking of saying to Ron, "What do you see in him?" But after observing the jeans, she knew exactly what the crowd-puller was.

"Why don't we all have lunch?" Ron suggested, deciding it was about time his best friend and live-in lover got friendly. "You can at least try and be nice to Ken. After all, *I* put up with Martin."

Ha! Ron didn't even know Martin. Only to say hello to. Just to please Ron, she agreed.

"I booked us a table at the Ivy." Ron was obviously delighted.

Venus Maria frowned. "Isn't that a little visible? Especially today?"

"We'll get a table in the back room. In and out before anyone realizes you're there."

At twelve-thirty they set off for the restaurant in the Ken Doll's gleaming Mercedes. Venus Maria hid beneath huge black shades and sat in the back.

"I probably smell like a camel," she remarked. "You too, Ron."

"Count *me* out," said the very pristine Ken.

Anytime, Venus Maria thought.

Lunch turned out to be a drag. Ron turned from his usual acerbic self into a lovesick jerk. Ken was pompous. Ken knew everything. Ken tried to tell her everything. When they got out of the restaurant, she was regretting the whole deal.

By the time they arrived back at the rehearsal studios there was a rapidly escalating group of photographers waiting outside. They began snapping the moment the car drew up.

"Where do they all come from?" Venus Maria sighed, making a wild dash from the car.

"You're front page news today, darling. They're after the real scoop," Ron explained, chugging after her, quite happy to pose.

Ken adored every minute of the attention. "Don't worry, I'll protect you," he said, smiling for the cameras.

Macho Ken Doll.

Stupid Ken Doll.

"What's your comment on the story, Venus?"

"Got anything to say about Martin Swanson?"

"Is it true?"

"Do you love him?"

"Is Martin leaving his wife?"

She ignored all the reporters' questions, and, hidden behind her dark glasses, made it into the rehearsal studio.

69

Lennie brooded his way through the weekend. He spoke to Jess and she told him he was an asshole.

"You always take Lucky's side," he complained. "*I'm* your friend. What the hell is going on?"

"Lighten up, Lennie. You married an unusual woman—stop fighting her."

Stop fighting indeed! What did Jess know? She hadn't had her balls cut off for all the world to see.

Oh, dear. Poor Lennie, he's unhappy. Let's buy him a studio.

Well, screw that crap.

And yet . . . he missed her already. And throwing himself back into the script didn't seem to do it for him this time.

He contacted Brigette, and she met him at Serendipity for lunch.

"You're looking great, kiddo," he said, kissing her on both cheeks. "School agrees with you."

"School does not agree with me," she objected. "I hate it. I can't wait to get out."

"You are out," he said, ruffling her hair.

"Only for the summer," she groaned. "I gotta go back again, huh?"

"If you want to grow up to be smart."

"And then college?"

"Yup!"

"Why, Lennie? It's not as though I need to get a job or anything. I'm going to be inheriting all that money."

"Hey—you want to turn out like your mother?" he scolded sternly. "Getting married and spending money? What kind of life is that? You ought to think about your future."

"I know," she reluctantly agreed.

They sat at a corner table. Brigette ordered a foot-long hot dog and a double-chocolate malted milk.

"No appetite, huh?" he said with a grin.

"It's terrific to see you, Lennie. I'm really excited about Malibu."

"Yeah, well . . ." He stared at the menu. "I got something to tell you."

She gazed at him expectantly.

He hated to disappoint her. "Uh . . . things aren't working out exactly as we planned."

"What's the matter?" she asked, looking concerned.

"Lucky and I . . . well, we've been having some problems, and . . . uh, we haven't exactly worked them out. I'm not sure if we'll spend the summer together."

"Oh, no," Brigette cried, "you and Lucky are so great with each other. Please don't have any problems. *Please.*"

"If life were only that simple." He took her hand. "Listen, I promised you the summer. You'll bring your girlfriend and we'll go to the South of France or Spain or Greece—somewhere. We'll put it together."

"But I was looking forward to being with you and Lucky," Brigette said in a sad little voice. "And Bobby. I *really* miss Bobby. I haven't seen him in ages."

Lennie ignored a blonde at the next table who'd decided to fixate on him. He groped in his pocket for a cigarette. "Yeah, well, life's a bitch, huh?"

"Can I call Lucky?" Brigette asked, staring at the checkered tablecloth, wondering why everything always had to go wrong.

"If she's got time for you," Lennie replied. "She's busy buying a studio."

"A movie studio?"

"Yeah. You'll read about it in the papers. She's bought Panther Studios." He dragged on his cigarette. "My wife the mogul. Not content with running the biggest shipping empire in the world, she now wants to own Hollywood."

"Is that why you're mad?" Brigette ventured.

"Hey—it's a long story. If that's what she wants to do. . . . But I wish she'd told me about it. Where do you think she was for the last six weeks while she was supposed to be in Japan?"

"Where?"

"In Hollywood, playing secretary. She went in undercover."

Brigette's eyes widened. "Really? Sounds exciting to me."

"Yeah, if you don't have any other responsibilities. But Lucky is my wife. I'd like to see her once in a while. I'd like to have her support." He stubbed out his cigarette after two puffs. "Ah, hell. Why am I bothering *you* with this?"

"Because I'm a good listener?"

He laughed. "Yeah, you sure are. Let's change the subject. What's going on with you?"

"Nothing," she said vaguely. "Actually I was going to ask if we could come to L.A. like tomorrow or the day after. Nona's mother is throwing a fit. There's this stupid magazine with a picture of Nona's brother Paul in it with Deena Swanson. She's the wife of that billionaire."

"Oh, yeah."

"Anyway, Paul was photographed with her, and Deena is Effie's best friend—that's Paul's mother. So, as Nona puts it, we've *got* to get out of here. But since you're obviously not going to L.A., I suppose we can't, either."

She looked so deflated that Lennie decided he had to cheer her up. "Tell you what," he said. "We'll eat lunch, we'll talk, and then we'll stop by a travel agent and plan a trip. How's that? You, me, and what's this girl's name?"

"Nona."

"O.K. You got it, kiddo."

"What about Lucky and Bobby?"

Lennie shook his head. "Another time, another life."

70

There were photographers outside the gleaming Swanson building when Deena left. Usually they were only around when she and Martin attended an event. But she smiled anyway and climbed into her chauffeur-driven car.

At Le Cirque she got her usual ebullient greeting from the charming proprietor, Sirio Maccioni, and was led to a table where Adam Bobo Grant sat waiting.

"Darling!"

"Darling!"

They had the Hollywood kiss down pat, New York version.

"You look delightful, as usual," Bobo said, "lime green is your color."

Deena smiled. "Thank you, darling. Martin thinks so too."

"Does he?" said Bobo, waving to people at every table. "And how is the big man?"

"Fine," Deena said. "In fact, very soon we're going to have an exciting story for you."

Bobo raised an eyebrow. "You are? And what might that be, my sweet?"

"Martin would kill me if he knew I was going to tell you, and you have to promise not to print anything until I give you the go-ahead."

"If you can't trust me, who can you trust?" Bobo said in his best sincere voice.

"Martin is taking over Orpheus Studios in Hollywood," Deena announced. "What do you think of that?"

All the better to star Venus Maria in movies, Bobo thought to himself. Was *this* the reason for the romance? "How very interesting," he said, eyes darting around the room, checking everyone out.

"Isn't it just?" Deena smiled; she had lovely teeth. "We'll have to spend more time in L.A., of course. But I think it will be fun. Don't you?"

Bobo nodded. Trust Deena—queen of the understatement. "Great fun, my dear," he agreed.

The wine waiter came by the table and they ordered drinks. Deena decided on a martini. Bobo ordered straight vodka.

"It makes such a refreshing change to lunch with somebody who actually drinks hard liquor," Deena said with a tinkling laugh. "When I lunch with the ladies, nobody touches anything except Perrier or Evian. It's incredibly boring. I rather enjoy a martini before lunch."

Bobo nodded and leaned toward her, speaking confidentially. "Now, Deena," he said lowering his voice, "tell me the situation."

"What situation, Bobo?"

Surely she wasn't trying to hide it from him? "Why, you and Martin, of course."

She looked at him blankly.

"You have seen *Truth and Fact*, haven't you?" He moved closer, daring her to lie.

Deena continued to look blank. "*Truth and Fact?* What's that?"

Bobo was rapidly losing patience. "It's one of those magazines. The kind they sell in supermarkets."

"Oh, you mean like the *Star*, or the *Globe*. I simply adore the *Globe*. 'Headless woman gives birth to triplets'—marvelous stuff. My maid brings it in."

"Then I'm surprised your maid hasn't presented you with *Truth and Fact*."

She gazed at him, perfectly innocent. "Is there something in it I should know about?"

"Yes, Deena, there certainly is." He took her delicate, manicured hand in his pudgy little fist. On his pinky there was an enormous sapphire ring, surrounded with diamonds.

She stared at the glittering ring and sensed she was about to hear something she wouldn't like. "What, Bobo?" she asked, her tone even and well modulated, her slight accent thickening.

"There's a story about your husband and Venus Maria," Bobo said, getting right to it.

Her stomach tightened, but she managed to remain in complete control. "There is?" she asked carefully. "Everybody's always trying to link Martin with some little popsy or other. Surely not another one?"

"There's a photograph of them together," Bobo said. "And the story goes into quite a few details."

"What kind of details?" Deena asked, withdrawing her hand.

"Oh, that they've been seeing each other for several months. And that Martin is supposed to be crazy about her, and that she loves him." He paused, then zeroed in. "I wouldn't bring this up, Deena, but I hardly wish to see you eaten alive by the press. The magazine only came out today, and I'm trying to protect you." He paused again, waiting for her reaction. She remained cool, so he continued, "I'm ready to hear your side of the story. And to report it any way you like."

"There's no story to hear," Deena said through clenched teeth. "I'll have to look at this magazine, Bobo. When I've seen it, perhaps I'll be able to comment."

He reached for the manila envelope he had with him and handed it to her. "It's in here, Deena. Go to the powder room, read it, come back and talk to me."

She took the magazine and, head held high, walked toward the ladies room.

When she read the story her blood ran cold.

When she stared at the picture of Martin with Venus Maria she knew she had to act.

Venus Maria had signed her own death warrant.

Deena Swanson was about to make sure of that.

71

After getting together with all the department heads, Lucky decided she should meet with the various stars who had deals at the studio. She had set up her office in the conference room as a temporary measure, giving Mickey Stolli a couple of days to get out. He'd robbed her of the pleasure of firing him. Too bad.

Morton Sharkey had found an experienced assistant and promptly stolen him from another studio on her behalf. Otis Lindcrest was an efficient black man in his late twenties. He certainly seemed to know his way around, and he worked hard setting appointments and making Lucky feel as comfortable and secure as possible.

There was so much to do that she couldn't quite decide where to start. The most important thing of all was overseeing the projects the studio had in post- and preproduction, and then deciding on the direction of Panther's future.

Out of the executives she'd met with, she wasn't sure whom she could trust. It would take a while to get to know them as individuals and assess their loyalty.

Her immediate plan was to sit down with them one by one over the next few weeks. In the meantime, she'd sent for Lennie's contract and told Morton she wanted it rescinded.

"Send him a letter," she'd instructed, "saying he's out of his deal with Panther. We're releasing him—unless he wants to stay."

"Why are you doing this?" Morton had asked.

"I don't want him thinking he has any obligation to Panther just because I own it. If he decides to come and work here, that'll be great. But if he doesn't, he's free to go elsewhere."

"Lucky, he's an asset," Morton pointed out. "A big one."

"He's also my husband," she replied firmly. "And I can't have him feeling he's tied here."

Flowers began to arrive from various people she didn't know. They were accompanied by warm and welcoming notes. They were from agents, producers, and managers. The stars didn't bother to send them. Being a star meant you never had to send flowers— merely to receive them.

Otis gave her a rundown of all the players. For a young man he certainly knew plenty.

"How long have you been in this business?" she asked curiously.

"Started as a set P.R. Moved on to the mailroom at CAA. Almost got into producing. And I've been personal-assisting for five years."

She noted that he'd like to produce. Somewhere down the line, she thought. Right now Otis was invaluable exactly where he was.

She didn't leave the studio until nine o'clock at night. Boogie handed her a copy of *Truth and Fact* in the car. "I thought you'd want to see this," he said as he drove her home.

She glanced at the magazine, skipped over the stuff about Martin Swanson and Venus Maria. Who cared? She never believed anything she read in these papers anyway. But when she saw the picture of Brigette, she was immediately concerned. After Brigette's bad experience with Tim Wealth, Lucky knew she was far too young and vulnerable to get involved with another renegade. And that's exactly what Paul Webster looked like with his long hair and intense eyes.

"Remind me to phone Brigette first thing in the morning," she said. "And call London and alert Mike Baverstock at British Airways to watch out for Bobby and his nanny. They're flying in on Friday. Oh, and tell Otis to clear Friday afternoon for me, I'll meet them at the airport."

By the time they got back to the beach it was past ten.

"Any messages for me, Miko?" she asked hopefully.

Miko bowed. "No, madame, no messages."

Apparently Lennie didn't feel like calling.

She was too tired to eat. Too tired to do anything except fall into bed and drop off into a deep sleep.

She awoke refreshed and invigorated, showered, dressed, sat down for breakfast. The trades were full of news:

LUCKY SANTANGELO TAKES OVER PANTHER

MARTIN SWANSON MOVES IN ON ORPHEUS

She couldn't wait to get to the studio. There was a lot of hard work ahead, but one thing she knew for sure—running a studio was becoming an addiction.

Johnny Romano was her first appointment. He swaggered into the conference room, entourage hovering close behind.

As soon as he walked in the room he did a doubletake. This woman was beautiful.

"Can we talk by ourselves, Mr. Romano?" she asked.

"Hey, baby, my pleasure." He signaled his entourage to leave.

Lucky got up from behind the conference table and walked over to shake hands. "The name is Lucky Santangelo," she said. " 'Baby' doesn't cut it."

He took her hand and pulled her toward him. "You're a very beautiful lady," he said in a husky voice. "Welcome to my life."

She removed her hand from his. "That's about the corniest line I've ever heard. How many times have you used it?"

He laughed. "It usually goes down pretty good."

"Not with me."

"O.K., O.K., so you're a beautiful woman and I—Johnny Romano—am coming on to you. Such a terrible thing?"

She decided to ignore his remark. "You know, Johnny, your movie grossed big this weekend."

"Sure, baby," he said confidently.

"But I think we'll see a substantial drop next weekend."

He lifted his chin displaying a great movie-star jawline. "What you sayin', baby?"

She didn't hold back. "I'm saying *Motherfaker* is a sexist piece of crap."

Johnny's face darkened. Nobody ever spoke to him like that. "Are you out of your mind, woman?" he glowered.

She shook her head. "No, just giving you some useful advice."

"What's that?" he said arrogantly.

"You *can* take criticism, can't you?"

"You think I can't?" he countered.

"Johnny, you're a sensational-looking guy. Everyone loves you. You're macho, handsome, and sexy. But this movie cancels out a huge audience for you. Kids can't see it, old people won't want to. I don't understand it—for some crazy reason you make yourself into an anti-hero. The result is that everyone ends up hating the character you play. And every other word is 'motherfucker.' You wrote the film, Johnny. Surely you have a larger vocabulary than that?"

He glared at her. "This movie's gonna make a fuckin' fortune for Panther and *you're* criticizing it?"

"I'm saying I know you're capable of so much more. And I'd love you to do another movie for Panther. But I'm willing to tear up your contract and let you walk, because I'm not prepared to make another *Motherfaker*. If you're after a lasting career, you have to build it, not tear it down. What you're saying to your audience is 'Fuck you. I can do what I like and get away with it.' It doesn't work anymore, Johnny."

"You're a crazy woman." He laughed. "I can go anywhere in this town an' get any deal I want."

"Then maybe that's what you should do," she said evenly.

He couldn't believe what he was hearing. Was this broad insane? "O.K., lady, if that's what you want, maybe that's what I'll do."

"Go ahead," she said, challenging him. "But if you're smart you'll listen to me. Don't make an instant decision. Think it over, and we'll talk next week."

When Johnny Romano left the room he was not a happy man.

• • •

Venus Maria was Lucky's second appointment.

The blond superstar breezed into her office with a big grin on her face. "This is really great," she said enthusiastically. "A woman in charge! My wildest dream come true. Howdja do it?"

Lucky grinned back. "I thought it was about time. My plan is to kick a little ass. Are you on for the ride?"

Venus Maria's grin widened. "Oh, have you picked the right star here!"

"I hope so," Lucky said. "I need all the support I can get."

"You *know* so," Venus Maria replied, flopping into a chair and sticking her legs out. She wore cutoff jeans, a Save the World T-shirt, and a long vest covered with pins. Her platinum hair was bunched on top of her head. And on her feet she wore short white socks and Reeboks. "I'm rehearsing," she announced, "for my up-coming video. It's gonna be a trip!"

"I'm delighted you're with Panther," Lucky said warmly. "I know you're committed to do *Bombshell,* and I also know you're not happy with the script."

"How do you know that?"

"Because you told me."

Venus Maria looked puzzled. "*I* told you? Have we met before?"

Lucky reached for a cigarette. "Oh, yeah, we've met. Only you don't remember, do you?"

"In New York?"

"No. Right here at this studio. You bitched to me about the script, and now that I've read it, I couldn't agree more. There's a rewrite in the works. In fact I met with the writer before you came in. He knows what we want."

"He does?"

"Oh, yes."

"Fast worker."

"No point in sitting around. I know the kind of movie you're after. *Bombshell* should be a statement about women and the way they're used. Am I right?"

"Absolutely." Venus Maria looked perplexed. "I still can't figure out where we met."

"Mickey Stolli's secretary."

"Huh?"

"Remember Mickey Stolli's secretary? The one with the pebbled glasses, bad hair style, and terrible clothes? You were really sweet to her."

Venus looked perplexed. "Yes, so?"

"It was me."

Venus Maria jumped out of her chair. "You?" she said in amazement. "Oh, come *on*. You've *got* to be kidding. You!"

Lucky burst out laughing. "Yes, me. I was in disguise."

"No!"

"Yes!"

"Wow!"

"Well, I didn't want to buy the place and not know what was happening, so I worked at the studio for six weeks to find out a thing or two."

"And did you?"

Lucky drew on her cigarette and smiled. "You could say that."

"I bet!"

"I'm telling you because I feel I can trust you. But I don't want the suits knowing. Perhaps I'll tell 'em. Perhaps I won't. Let 'em wonder how I know so much."

"Holy shit!" Venus exclaimed. "This is the greatest. I fucking love it!"

"Anyway," Lucky continued, "the plan is this. We'll get the *Bombshell* script exactly right, and then we're going to make a terrific movie. I've been thinking about directors. How about a female?"

"I love women directors," Venus said. "Only every time I mention it around here they look at me like I'm a zombie!"

"It seems to me a woman director is the only way to go. I have several in mind. Have you heard of Montana Grey?"

"I sure have. She wrote and directed that amazing little movie *Street People*. I think she's great, very talented."

"Good. She's coming in to see me tomorrow. As far as I'm concerned, she'd be perfect. Are you happy with that?"

"Happy? I'm ecstatic!"

"If she likes the idea, I'll set up a meeting for all three of us."

"Anytime."

"And I want to see a screening of *Strut*. I understand there's a rough cut. I'm meeting with Cooper Turner, so I'll discuss that with him."

Venus Maria nodded. "You'll like Cooper, he's a good guy. Don't believe all the stuff you've read about him. Oh—" she added jauntily —"and don't believe all the stuff you've read about me either."

Lucky laughed. "I've had a few headlines of my own. Believe me, I understand."

"So . . . how are the *boys* taking your arrival?"

Lucky took a drag of her cigarette. "I guess they're not used to having a woman walk in and take over."

"No way."

Lucky blew a smoke ring or two. "I always did love a challenge."

72

Emilio Sierra had booked a double room at a fancy hotel in Hawaii overlooking the sea. What he and Rita actually got when they arrived was a room overlooking the vast outdoor parking lot—a far from spectacular sight.

"This is not good enough," Emilio yelled angrily.

"It's fine, honey," Rita soothed. "At least we can see the ocean in the distance."

Dumb broad. Why did he always manage to pick the dumb ones?

"It's not fine at all," Emilio fumed. "I'm kickin' up a stink."

He swaggered down to the reception desk and demanded to see the manager.

Ten minutes later the manager appeared, a tall, thin man with a congenial manner and a constipated smile. "Yes, sir, how may I help you?"

"I requested a room with an ocean view," Emilio said, trying to drag his eyes away from a busty redhead in shorts and a clinging T-shirt as she sashayed on by.

"You're not happy with your room?" questioned the manager, sounding hurt, as if Emilio's complaint was a personal affront.

The redhead swayed out of sight, allowing Emilio to concentrate. "No way, man. It stinks."

"I'm sure it doesn't stink, Mr. —?"

"Sierra," Emilio obliged. "S–I–E–R–R–A," he spelled out. "You've no doubt heard of my sister, Venus Maria."

The manager wasn't sure if he believed him or not. But he looked impressed anyway. "Venus Maria?" he said, with just the right note of reverence in his voice. "The singer?"

"And movie star," Emilio boasted. "I'm from Los Angeles. Well, Hollywood, really. I'm an actor too."

The manager nodded. They'd had bigger celebrities than Venus Maria's brother staying at the hotel. Try the President of the United States.

"Well," the manager said, "right now, Mr. Sierra, we don't seem to have anything else. But I can promise you as soon as something becomes available you will be the first to know."

"Not satisfactory," growled Emilio, deciding he loved having money. It gave him a certain amount of power for the first time in his life.

"It's the best I can do," said the manager, wishing this uncouth-looking person would elect to stay elsewhere.

"Get me somethin' else, or I'm campin' out in the lobby," Emilio threatened, continuing to complain until they moved him into a bungalow on the beach. It cost more, but for once Emilio figured he'd go for the big bucks. Now that he had them, he might as well live it up. Not that Rita appreciated it. She was hot. She was also stupid.

No sooner were they settled in the bungalow than Rita thought she spotted a sand mouse running across the floor.

"Oh, my God!" she screamed hysterically, jumping on top of the bed. "Emilio! Emilio! There's a *mouse!*"

"So what?" he said, completely unconcerned. "It ain't gonna eat you."

"I'm frightened," she squealed, refusing to get off the bed.

Emilio remembered New York back in the good old days when Venus Maria was just a kid and he could boss her around. She'd been frightened of mice too. He and his brothers had caught three one day and stuffed them in her bed under the sheets. When she'd discovered the grisly surprise, she'd screamed for an hour. But he had to admit she'd gotten her revenge. Two nights later she'd cooked a thick and juicy stew with what appeared to be chunks of chicken in it. Only it turned out it wasn't chicken. She'd cooked the goddamn mice and served them up for dinner!

Rita was not to be placated, so Emilio had to march back to the manager and complain again.

Finally, probably to get rid of him and his bitching, they were ushered into the suite of his dreams—two rooms consisting of a luxurious bedroom complete with vibrating bed and a well-appointed living room leading out to a large terrace overlooking a blanket of white sand and a gorgeous blue ocean. This was more like it. Even if it was probably going to cost an arm and two legs.

"Satisfied?" he said to Rita.

She nodded.

Later, he stood on the terrace while she unzipped his jeans and showed him exactly how satisfied she really was.

Sometimes it paid to be extravagant.

The next morning he sent her down to the newsstand instructing her to buy a copy of *Truth and Fact*.

When she brought it back to the room and he read it he was outraged. Where was the story Dennis had recorded? There wasn't even a picture of him—just the one he'd stolen of Venus and Martin. What kind of deal was this?

In a fury he telephoned Dennis Walla in Los Angeles. "Where's *my* story?" he screamed over the phone. "It was supposed to appear this week."

"Next week," Dennis said. "Read the blurb."

"You told me this week, and you've used the picture I gave you," said a disgruntled Emilio. "Listen, man, I've only gotten paid for one week. This is a swindle."

"Hang on a moment, mate," said Dennis, thinking, *Here we go again*. Why were the relatives of the stars so bloody greedy? "You're making plenty of moola outta this. Your story runs when *we* decide to run it. You can't tell *us* what to do."

Emilio slammed down the phone in a rage. Now it would be awkward returning to L.A. Venus Maria had advance warning his story was going to appear. She'd be furious and would certainly be tracking him.

"What's the matter, sweetie?" asked Rita, pirouetting in front of the mirror, admiring her short but otherwise perfect legs.

"Nothing." He wasn't about to confide in her. "Come here."

They made the bed vibrate for ten minutes before going outside to sample the Hawaiian sunshine.

Emilio was disappointed to discover there wasn't much Hawaiian sunshine to sample. It was a cloudy day with strong gusty winds.

He chose two prime positions by the pool and they settled down, Rita in a bikini that attracted the attention of every man within fifty yards.

Emilio was pleased. Maybe she wasn't so stupid after all. He enjoyed being with a woman who scored so much attention.

At lunchtime Rita suggested that perhaps they should go inside. "It may be cloudy," she said wisely, "but there's still a real strong sun coming through. You'd better be careful."

"Me?" he boasted, "I never burn, I tan."

"I don't," she said pulling up her bikini top which was just about to slip and reveal a perky nipple. "Do you mind if I go in?"

He didn't mind. He was too busy enjoying the parade of beautiful women in various small bikinis and great tans.

Come five o'clock Emilio was burned to a crisp.

"Jesus! Why didn't you warn me?" he complained when he finally got back to the suite.

"Honey, I did," Rita pointed out, busily slathering scented cream all over her naked body.

"I don't understand," he whined, feeling sorry for himself. "It was cloudy—how could I burn?"

"It doesn't matter in Hawaii," she explained. "The sun burns right through the clouds. I tried to tell you."

"Were you here before?" he asked suspiciously.

"Once or twice," she said, deciding not to mention her last trip with two stunt men and a bewigged director with a penchant for discipline.

Emilio was in serious pain. Rita rushed down to the pharmacy and came back with soothing lotions. They didn't help. He suffered all through the night, and not silently.

The next morning, when he regarded his lobster complexion in the mirror, he decided they were going back to L.A.

"I'm not spending all this money to lie around in bed," he complained. "We're gettin' outta here."

Rita shrugged. "Whatever you want."

She'd already decided Emilio was only good for a short ride. While he had the bucks, she was there. Who knew how long it would last?

73

"There's a Harry Browning to see you," Otis said. "No appointment. He looks kind of agitated."

Lucky nodded. "It's O.K., show him in."

Harry took a few steps into the room and stopped. He waited until the secretary shut the door behind him and then he stared at Lucky accusingly. "You're Luce, aren't you?"

Finally! Somebody had busted her disguise. "You're the only person who's recognized me," she said. "Pretty sharp of you."

"I thought you were working for Abe Panther."

"In a way, I was. We both thought it was a good idea for me to come in undercover. An interesting exercise. I found out plenty."

"You weren't honest with me," Harry said stiffly, obviously uncomfortable with this confrontation.

She wasn't about to explain things further. "I'd be happy for you to stay at the studio, Harry. We're changing things around here. And I'd also like you to report to me personally."

"Why?" he asked suspiciously.

"Because you want what I want. We're both into making Panther great again. No more exploitation flicks. No more executives playing casting couch with every actress who walks through the door. Are you with me?"

Slowly he nodded.

Shortly after her meeting with Harry, Susie Rush arrived. Susie was used to dealing with male executives. She appeared wearing frills and flounces and a pink ribbon in her hair. Lucky thought she looked like a Kewpie doll.

Susie pursed her lips in a girlish way and said, "Well, this is quite a shock to the system."

"What can I offer you?" Lucky said, playing it nice and friendly. "A drink? Coffee? Tea?"

"An explanation would be nice. After all, when I signed with this studio, Mickey Stolli was in charge. A change is something I hadn't considered."

"The first thing you should know," Lucky said easily, "is that although you have a development deal at the studio, you're free to do anything you want. I'm not holding anybody at Panther against their will."

"Oh," Susie said. She hadn't expected that.

"However, I also know," Lucky continued, "that you're one of this studio's great assets, and as I've told everyone else, my goal is to bring Panther back to the forefront again. And I love your kind of movies. You make films the whole family can see. You're really a wonderful actress."

Susie looked at her suspiciously. She wasn't used to receiving compliments from other women. She also wasn't used to seeing women who looked like Lucky Santangelo in positions of power.

"Here's what I'd like you to do," Lucky said, all business. "Tell me the kind of movie you want to do. I know you're developing a couple of projects at the moment, and if you're happy with those, then we'll certainly consider them."

"Actually," Susie said, "I feel like a change of pace. My career is in a rut. I have the desire to play a different kind of role."

"What kind of role is that?" Lucky asked.

"I want to play the lead in *Bombshell*," Susie said. "As a matter of fact, Mickey promised me I could."

This was a surprise. "*Bombshell* is a Venus Maria project," Lucky pointed out.

"Oh, yes, Mickey had mentioned Venus might be interested. But when I told him I liked the script, he immediately said I could test. I should remind you that normally I wouldn't dream of testing for anything. But I know I can capture this role. She's me."

"I'll tell you what," Lucky suggested. "Venus Maria is definitely set for *Bombshell*. But if you have another script, we'll see what we can work out."

Susie's lips tightened into a thin line. "I want to do *Bombshell*," she said. "I've been offered another film at Orpheus."

Lucky smiled pleasantly. She wasn't about to be blackmailed by stars and their egos. "Susie, if the role is what you want, then I suggest you take it. As I said before, I'm not holding anybody back."

Susie departed, not quite sure where she was at.

So far so good. Lucky's last meeting of the day was with Cooper Turner. He was in one of the editing rooms, and instead of asking him to come to her she decided to run over there.

Lucky was not impressed by movie stars. She'd observed them all her life. When Gino opened his Vegas hotels, they'd come down for special gambling junkets, openings, and all the big parties. And when she was married to Senator Richmond's son, Craven, celebrities had often made the trek to Washington.

Movie stars equaled fragile egos—she was well aware of that. Now, dealing with them on a one-to-one basis was interesting and a definite challenge.

Cooper Turner was better-looking than on the screen, with his boyishly handsome face, rumpled hair, and penetrating ice-blue eyes. He had a devastating smile, which he put into immediate action. "So you're my new boss, huh?"

"Yes," she said, going for a handshake.

He took her hand and gave it an extra squeeze. Behind his horn-rimmed glasses he favored her with a penetrating look. "You're a surprise," he said. "I was expecting a dragon lady."

"Looks don't matter," she said.

"Sure they do," he said casually, removing his glasses. "Beautiful women always get more attention. Not that I'm saying you're not smart, but looks help. And honey—you've got 'em."

She threw it right back at him. "And, honey, so have you."

He laughed. "*Touché*, Miz Santangelo."

"I'm looking forward to viewing a rough cut of *Strut*. When can I?" she asked, getting down to the purpose of her visit.

"How about next week sometime?"

"Sounds good. Was this your directorial debut?"

Without the glasses, his eyes were lethal weapons. "You mean you haven't been following my career?"

She returned his stare, matching his gaze with her black Santangelo eyes. "Let's put it this way—your career has not been the center of my universe."

He laughed again. "No—as a matter of fact, I've directed one dog before, but this one's going to be better. Venus Maria gives a very special performance."

"So I've heard."

"Ah, the rumor is around the studio. That's good."

"It appears your movie is the only decent one we've got going for us. Have you seen *Motherfaker*?"

"My time is valuable. I don't believe in self-punishment."

Now it was her turn to laugh. "I know what you mean. Can we have lunch together next week? There's a lot I feel we need to discuss. The marketing of *Strut* is crucial."

"Why don't I take *you* to dinner?" he suggested.

She put the meeting back on track. "Have you met my husband, Lennie Golden?"

"You're married to Lennie?" he said, surprised.

"You didn't know?"

"Hey—I've followed your career about as closely as you've followed mine."

"My turn to say *Touché*, huh?"

He dazzled her with a movie-star smile. "I guess so. Lunch, then. I'd like that."

The only star she had yet to see was Charlie Dollar, and he was out of the country, due back in a couple of weeks. Charlie had nothing in preproduction. She put out the word: "Find a property suitable for Charlie Dollar. Something sensational."

Her final meeting of the day was with the Sleazy Singles, Arnie Blackwood and Frankie Lombardo.

Arnie, the lean and lanky one with the greasy hair pulled back in a ponytail, and mirrored shades covering watery eyes, was the first to speak. "Congrats, sweetie. This is gonna be a piece of pie."

Frankie, with the freaked-out brown hair and unruly beard, joined in, "Yeah, cutie, we're all gonna work together like we been in bed all our lives."

"Fortunately," said Lucky with a pleasant smile, "we haven't."

They both guffawed.

"She's got a sense of humor," Arnie said.

"What's a good-looking broad like you doing in a job like this anyway?" Frankie asked, collapsing his bulky frame into a chair.

"Probably the same as a handsome man like yourself," Lucky replied sarcastically. "And may I remind you, it's not a job—I own Panther."

Frankie didn't like that.

Arnie walked over to the conference table, put his hands on it, and leaned across it. "Are you here to stay?" he demanded. "Or is this a temporary measure? What's the deal, Lucky? Have you bought the studio to sell out the land and then get out, or what?"

"I'm here to stay," she replied with a cold smile. "How about you?"

"Oh, we're here to stay, all right," Arnie replied, taking off his mirrored shades, polishing them on a corner of his shirt, and putting them back on again.

Frankie brushed his hands through his unruly long hair and pulled on his scruffy beard. Both men appeared to be stoned.

"I'm canceling your two current projects," Lucky said. "I may as well get straight to it—I don't like 'em. They're not the kinds of films Panther is going to continue to make."

"You're doing *what*, baby?" Arnie questioned disbelievingly.

"Aren't I making myself clear?" she replied, cool and in control. "If you need an interpreter I'll be happy to supply one."

"Where have I seen you before?" Frankie got to his feet.

"Let's just say I've been around the studio for some time. I know everything that's going on."

"Everything, huh?" Arnie sneered.

"That's right," she replied, trying to stay calm, although these two assholes could really send her out of control.

"O.K., sweetie, we're gonna give you a break. We won't take you seriously. We got two movies shooting now, an' three in preproduction. Our movies keep Panther in the black. You know what I mean? Our movies score all the profit around here, while your so-called superstars make all the flops."

"Yes," Lucky said calmly. "But I'm here to tell you the system just changed. I don't care for the kind of movies you make. I don't appreciate seeing girls having their clothes ripped off and heads bashed in. Rape and mutilation don't do it for me. Am I making myself clear?"

"Wake up and smell the box office," said Arnie with an insulting leer. "It's what's goin' on out there."

"Ah, but that's the problem," Lucky said. "If that's what's going on—I don't want to film it. I don't like anything you represent. So, Mr. Lombardo, I guess we are just going to have to part company."

Frankie scratched his beard. "Are you telling us to get out?"

"Wow!" Lucky said. "You're beginning to understand me. This is fun."

"You fucking bitch," Arnie said, finally getting the message. "You can't treat us like shit. We're two of the biggest producers in Hollywood. An' what's more, we have a deal with Panther."

"You know something, Mr. Blackwood, Mr. Lombardo? I don't give a rat's ass."

And so ended Lucky's first day on the job. How to make friends and influence people it wasn't. But it was satisfying. And her next project was to put together a team of people who could work together and create the kind of movies she wished to make.

Lucky Santangelo was on a roll.

74

Swanson fever hit like a hurricane—fast, furious, and all-encompassing. It seemed every newspaper and television program in America wanted in on this story. Adam Bobo Grant led the pack. He took everything Deena said and built it into front-page news.

I'LL NEVER DIVORCE HIM!, screamed the headlines. I LOVE MY HUSBAND!

Dennis Walla may have started it, but Adam Bobo Grant was launching it in a big way. An important way. The front page of the *New York Runner* was no *Truth and Fact*. People believed the stories they read in the *New York Runner*.

Bert Slocombe FAXed the story to Dennis Walla in Los Angeles.

Sitting in his Hollywood office, Dennis read it with growing aggravation. He recognized some of his own quotes. Adam Bobo Grant, the faggot hack, was stealing from him! And there was absolutely nothing he could do. It never occurred to Dennis to get angry. What did occur to him was that he might be able to make money out of this.

He picked up the phone and placed a call to Adam Bobo Grant at his newspaper.

An officious assistant informed him Mr. Grant was unavailable.

"Tell him it's important," Dennis insisted.

"I'm sorry," the assistant said, full of his own importance. "If you have an item for Mr. Grant, I can take it."

"Listen," Dennis said with heavy authority, his Australian accent thickening. "I'm not saying this twice. Just go tell him I'm the one who wrote the story in *Truth and Fact* about the Swanson divorce. And comin' up, I have an exclusive story by Venus Maria's brother. We're runnin' it next week. Now I thought he might be interested in some of this information. If he isn't, that's fine by me. Go run it by him, mate."

The assistant left him hanging on the line for a good five minutes before Adam Bobo Grant, gossip columnist supreme, came on the line.

"Mr. Walla," Adam Bobo Grant said.

"Saw your story," Dennis replied. "A nice crib."

Adam Bobo Grant was offended. "I beg your pardon?"

"I said, a nice crib. You stole half the stuff from *Truth and Fact*. *My* stuff—I wrote it."

"Did you phone to complain?" Bobo asked with a deeply put-upon sigh.

"Nah, I'm takin' a shot we can do business."

"Business?" Bobo perked up.

"Yeah, well, you've got items I find interesting, an' you'll find my next story very juicy indeed. It's this exclusive piece running next week, an' I thought—since you're making such a meal out of the Swansons, that you might want to take a peek at my upcomin' story before it runs."

"For a price, of course?" Bobo said crisply.

"Yeah, mate. Whattaya think I am—a charity?"

Bobo thought fast. As successful as his daily column was, it was always nice to make the front pages. "How much?" he asked tartly.

"A bargain price," Dennis replied.

Sure, Adam Bobo Grant thought. But he went for it anyway.

"Photographers are camped outside my house," Venus Maria complained to Martin on the phone.

"Don't think they're not trailing me everywhere, too," he said.

Was it her imagination, or did he sound quite pleased?

They'd talked a couple of times since *Truth and Fact* appeared, but they hadn't seen each other. Now they were attempting to set up a rendezvous.

"We'd better forget about my house. And I'm sure your hotel is a definite no," she said. "But I have an idea. If I can get out without being followed, I can make it to the Bel-Air Hotel. What do you think?"

He thought it was an excellent idea and told her he would book a suite under an assumed name and they could spend the night together.

"Have you spoken to Deena?" she ventured tentatively.

"No. I haven't called her."

"She must have seen it."

"I don't intend to speak to her on the phone. I'll discuss it when I get back. I *am* taking over a studio, you know; I've been kind of busy."

"Oh, yeah. And I'm just lying around doing nothing," she snapped back.

He softened his tone. "I can't wait to see you."

After she put the phone down she planned her escape. In a way it was a kick trying to fool the hovering paparazzi.

She summoned Ron, who dashed over to her house, dying to be in on the game. They dressed one of her secretaries in a platinum wig, dark shades, and one of Venus Maria's outfits.

When they decided she was ready, the girl ran from the house, jumped into a car, and roared off down the hill. Sure enough, the photographers followed.

Meanwhile, Venus Maria slipped out the back into Ron's car. They giggled all the way as he drove her to the Bel-Air Hotel.

Clad in a long coat, a floppy hat, and dark glasses, she went straight to the suite Martin had booked.

He was waiting for her.

The moment she was inside he jumped on her like a randy schoolboy.

She was taken aback. "Martin!" She began to object, but he was having none of it. He kissed her frantically, pawing at her clothes.

She threw off her hat and her platinum hair tumbled around her face.

He buried his hands in her curls. "God, I've missed you," he mumbled, unbuttoning her coat and groping under her sweater.

She'd never known him to be this passionate. Headlines obviously turned him on.

They ended up making love on the floor. It was the wildest she'd ever known Martin.

"Wow! You're hot tonight. What happened to you?" she laughed, when they were finished.

"Are you saying I was cool before?"

She wasn't saying it, but she was certainly thinking it.

"A girlfriend called me from New York today," she said casually. "We're on the front page of the New York papers. And last night there was a story on 'Entertainment Tonight.' Why all this coverage?"

"You're a popular lady."

"It's not just me, Martin. It's you that's captured the imagination of the public. Billionaire this and billionaire that. Hey, you're getting a real stud reputation!"

"Don't be ridiculous," he said. But he didn't sound at all mad.

She bent down and began picking up her crumpled clothes. "I'm going to soak in a hot tub. Shall we order room service? I'm starving!"

"I've already ordered caviar, steak, and ice cream. Does that sound like a feast?"

"This is an adventure! Here we are, just the two of us. And nobody knows where we are. Exciting, huh?"

"It works for me."

She couldn't help smiling. "So I noticed."

She drew herself a hot tub filled with bubbles and luxuriated in it.

Martin strolled into the bathroom carrying two glasses of champagne. He perched on the side of the tub and handed her one.

She lay back. "So . . ." she said dreamily. "What's going to happen? Now that Deena knows, it's a whole different game, huh?"

Martin wasn't about to be drawn into conversation. "We'll have to see what she says."

"How about what *you* say?"

"I've been married to Deena for ten years. It's impossible for me to pick up and go."

"Isn't that what we wanted?"

"It is, but there are ways of doing things. It'll be better if Deena asks me to leave."

"If she has any pride, she will."

He nodded.

"Martin," Venus said, "you *are* going to make a decision, aren't you?"

He nodded again.

" 'Cause if you don't," she added forcefully, "I'm not staying in this relationship. Especially now it's out in the open."

He trailed his hand in the bubbles, touching the tip of her left breast. "You wouldn't be threatening me, would you?"

She smiled seductively. "Would *I* do a thing like that? Come here, billionaire stud. Get in the tub with me."

He couldn't help laughing. "I'm not nineteen."

She sat up, wrapping her wet arms around him. "Pretend," she said. "Let's play pretend."

And in New York, Deena raged around her apartment, angry and humiliated. It seemed she'd been deserted. Which wasn't exactly true, because her phone was ringing off the hook. Everyone had phoned except for Martin, and she couldn't reach him. When she'd called him in California, various secretaries and assistants had told her he was in important meetings and could not be disturbed.

Meetings, she thought to herself. Ha! He was with The Bitch.

Deena had already put her plans into action. She'd activated the private detective she'd hired several months earlier in Los Angeles. His instructions were to give her a complete dossier on Venus Maria, tracking all her movements. The detective had no idea whom he was dealing with. She had set it up by phone, and he reported to a box number.

Deena knew exactly what she had to do, although she hadn't anticipated the amount of publicity Martin's affair with Venus Maria would generate.

She stared at her list of incoming phone calls. Every married woman in New York had called her. They all wanted the inside dish. Adam Bobo Grant had telephoned three times. Did he want more from her? Hadn't he taken enough?

She picked up the *New York Runner* and reread the front-page story. It was different from *Truth and Fact*. Everyone knew *Truth and Fact* was a cheap rag. The story in the *New York Runner* gave it credence.

Her eyes scanned the page.

Deena Swanson, wanly beautiful in a lime green Adolfo suit, refuses to discuss her rival, Venus Maria. Her only comment, "I'm sure Venus Maria is quite talented."

And then farther down:

For a moment Deena is silent as she gazes across the crowded restaurant. A fragile woman. A beautiful woman. A woman about to lose her husband?

At least Bobo had the good grace to put a question mark after that.

She was not about to lose her husband. She was not about to lose anything.

She'd planned what she had to do for the last six months, and now the inevitable was in motion.

75

Nobody could operate like Mickey Stolli. He was a master at the game. He'd excelled even his own expectations.

First of all, he'd outsmarted Abe Panther and Lucky Santangelo by signing a predated note giving Panther the full responsibility of owing Carlos Bonnatti a million dollars—supposedly legally. And then he'd had the document filed neatly away, buried in business affairs.

Second, he'd sat down with Martin Swanson and clinched himself a fine deal with Orpheus at double the salary he made at Panther, plus profit-sharing.

Martin Swanson was a straight talker. "I'm only interested in making money," he'd said. "You can bring with you whomever you want. We're turning Orpheus into a money-making machine."

Business taken care of, Mickey had then returned home to Abigaile. Dear sweet Abigaile.

She was stewing. But what did he care? He had a whole new life ahead of him.

One of the good things about Hollywood was when you failed—you failed up. And being caught in a whorehouse was no big deal. He wasn't committing some heinous crime, he was merely getting laid. Abe Panther's sale of the studio had completely deflated Abigaile. She was almost prepared to forgive him for being arrested.

Not quite. When he'd arrived back at the house after the meeting with Lucky Santangelo, she'd greeted him with a miserable expression—and Ben and Primrose. They were all waiting in the library.

"We have to sit down and discuss everything," Abigaile said very matter-of-factly. "Ben has kindly offered to deal with the lawyers."

"What's to deal with?" Mickey had fixed himself a drink. By this time he was a happy man. And he was about to be a free man.

"Mickey," Ben said, with a long, serious face, "we can't let Abe get away with this."

"It seems to me there's nothing we can do," Mickey replied, downing a hefty shot of scotch.

"Oh, yes, there is," said Ben, the upright family man, who, Mickey knew for a fact, had been boffing a buxom blond starlet who'd worked on one of Panther's movies shooting in London last summer.

"What, Ben?" Mickey said wearily.

"First of all, Abigaile has told me of your problems and you can't walk out on her now," Ben said pompously, pacing up and down. "We're in a crisis situation. We have to present a united front. I've already spoken to my lawyer. He suggests we might be able to have Abe declared incompetent."

"No way," Mickey said. "What's incompetent about Abe? He's walking and talking. This is Hollywood, for crissakes! So he's old. Big deal. Look at George Burns, Bob Hope."

"At least we should discuss it," Ben insisted.

"Discuss *what*? My wife wants me out. So I'm out."

Ben put his hand on Mickey's shoulder. "Think about your Tabitha."

"Listen—I didn't ask to go, get this straight—Abby threw me out. Remember that."

"And now she's asking you to stay."

"Too late."

"We'll have to work this out, Mickey," Abigaile said, her no-nonsense expression firmly in place.

"There's nothing to work out." He shrugged. "I screwed around. I got caught. Now I have to take the consequences. I suggest you see a lawyer."

"Mickey, you don't seem to understand," Primrose joined in, speaking firmly. "Abe has sold the studio. Things are different."

"Stay out of it, Primrose," he warned. "What goes on between me and my wife has nothing to do with you."

"We're all involved." Ben was determined to make his presence felt.

"Not in my private affairs," Mickey said forcefully. "What we do about our marriage concerns me and Abby. It's nobody else's business." He wanted to add, "Get fucked," but didn't deem it appropriate.

Without further discussion he went upstairs to his dressing room and packed a small suitcase. Then he got in his Porsche and drove straight to the Beverly Hills Hotel, where he checked into a bungalow.

Mickey Stolli was back in action.

Forty-eight hours later the news of Mickey's new appointment was all over town. It hadn't actually hit the trades—after all, the deal wasn't even signed. But everybody in the know was aware of it.

Eddie tracked him down at the studio, where Mickey was packing up his personal papers and effects.

"What's happening, Mickey?" he asked feverishly. "Did you hear from Bonnatti?"

"I've taken care of it," Mickey said. "Like I take care of all your fuck-ups."

"Hey." Eddie refused to feel guilty. "It was just one of those things."

"Yeah. One of those things you always seem to get involved in."

"So . . . how did you take care of it?" Eddie asked, trying to sound casual.

"Never mind, and keep your mouth closed. It's no longer your responsibility—there's a deal memo says it's the studio's."

"Really? You fixed it?"

"Forget about it, Eddie. All right?"

"I heard about you and Orpheus." Eddie hesitated before making

470

a pitch. "How about bringing me along for the ride? Am I your good-luck charm or what?"

"Are you shitting me, Eddie?"

"No, Mickey. I need a job."

"You've already got a job."

"Word is Lucky Santangelo is cleaning house." He picked up a script, stared at it blankly, then put it down again. "Take me with you, huh?"

Mickey sighed. When was Eddie going to stop with the favors? "Get clean and I'll see what I can do."

"Clean?" Eddie looked hurt. "I got no problem."

Sure. "I'm telling you, Eddie. You're hooked. Check yourself into some kind of drug rehab and then we'll talk." He took a beat. "By the way, was that your wife I saw at Madame Loretta's?"

Eddie glowered. "Are you crazy?"

"And if it was her, what was she doing there?"

Now he was really furious. "You need glasses, Mickey."

"And you need to straighten out."

"Bullshit."

"Panther's going down when I leave," Mickey boasted. "Everybody's gonna follow me. Johnny Romano, Arnie and Frankie, Susie —they'll all come over to Orpheus."

Eddie scowled. "Yeah. You'll take everybody except me. Right?"

"I told you—clean up your act and you're in."

Clean up his act. Easier said than put into operation. When he was high he felt like he owned the world. And when he was straight he felt like the world wasn't even worth living in.

Why couldn't he carry on the way he was? Why was everyone on his case?

He left Mickey and drove home.

Leslie was showing a realtor around their house. He stared edgily at the two women.

Leslie attempted to introduce him.

"Forget it," he said rudely. "We're not selling."

The realtor looked shocked. "What do you mean, Mr. Kane? I was under the impression we had an arrangement."

"No deal, baby. We've decided not to sell."

"Eddie?" Leslie questioned, her face flushing.

The realtor saw her fat commission fading away. "I feel you should reconsider your decision, Mr. Kane," she said anxiously. "Once you've decided to sell a house, it's never a good idea to stay."

"Scram," Eddie said.

"Mr. Kane—"

"Out!"

The realtor departed.

"What happened, Eddie?" Leslie asked.

"Things got taken care of. I'm off the dime."

"Yes?"

"That's right. C'mon, baby, we're goin' out."

"Where?"

"I'm about to surprise you."

Mickey was emptying his desk drawers into a briefcase when Lucky entered the office. He glanced up and their eyes met. She leaned against the door and stared at him.

"Well, Mr. Stolli," she said, "so you're moving on."

"That's right," he replied shortly. What was this—visiting day?

"I'm glad for you," she said. "Saves me the trouble of firing you, huh?"

He looked at her like she was crazy. "You were going to fire me?"

"Does that seem like such a strange idea?"

"Yeah. As a matter of fact it does."

"How come?"

"A New York broad like you. What do *you* know about the movie business? You need me desperately."

"Is that all you have to say?"

"What do you want me to say? I've spent the last ten years building this studio up, and Abe goes behind my back and sells it to you. I wouldn't work for you, sweetheart, if you were the last broad in town."

She stayed cool. "Really? You weren't exactly a laugh a minute to work for."

He laughed derisively. "Your husband's been telling you stories, huh? Well, let *me* give you the facts. Lennie Golden ain't such a hotshot. Take a look at the dailies."

"I wasn't talking about Lennie."

Brenda, one of Eddie Kane's secretaries, entered the room. She'd corn-rowed her hair. It looked good. "I shredded all those papers you asked me to take care of, Mr. Stolli," she said, glancing at Lucky, checking her out so she could report to the rest of the girls what the new boss looked like.

Mickey shot her a filthy look.

"What papers?" Lucky interjected.

"Personal files," Mickey replied quickly. "Nothing to do with you."

"If it's studio business, I'd prefer you didn't shred anything," Lucky said.

"A little late for that." Mickey smiled triumphantly. Fuck her. Who did she think she was dealing with? "I'm outta here," he said, waving Brenda out of the room.

Lucky walked over and sat in the chair in front of his desk.

Brenda hovered by the door, dying to listen in.

"How's . . . Warner?" Lucky asked casually.

Mickey snapped to attention. "Huh?"

"Warner Franklin. The black cop you were servicing twice a week. Oh, and that kid of yours in Chicago, the one you send a check to every month. Did you ever marry his mother? Or was she only another girlfriend?"

Mickey's skin flushed a dark red. He glared at Lucky and waved a frantic hand at Brenda, indicating she should get the hell out. Brenda exited.

Mickey was furious. "Where did you get all this information?" he asked gruffly.

She lapsed into her best Luce voice. "Working for you, Mr. Stolli. Kissing your ass, Mr. Stolli. You were such a charming boss. A real pleasure to work for."

He glared at her like he couldn't quite believe his eyes. She wasn't . . . couldn't be . . .

"Yes." She nodded, confirming the bad news. "I was Luce. Little

473

Luce, who you kicked around pretty good. It's amazing what a good disguise can do, huh?"

His flush deepened, sweeping upward until even his bald head was red. "You spying bitch! What did you do that for?"

"Abe and I figured it was a fun thing to do. Y'know, see what his favorite scum-in-law was up to. That's what he affectionately calls you and Ben—the scums-in-law."

"I'll tell you something," Mickey said angrily. "You may be a rich broad with a lot of money, but you're going to lose every penny in this business, 'cause this studio's going down. Right to the bottom. I'm taking everybody with me. You'll be left with nothing but shit."

Calmly she walked outside to where Brenda pretended not to be eavesdropping.

"Brenda, dear," she said coolly, "call in the exterminators. I want this office fumigated before I move in."

"Where are we going, Eddie?" Leslie asked for the sixth time.

"It's a surprise. You'll see, babe," he said, leaning across and patting her knee, "just relax."

She wasn't relaxed. She wasn't relaxed at all. Eddie had something on his mind, and she didn't know what to expect.

76

Deena was appalled at the press coverage. She was even more appalled when Martin made no attempt to contact her.

As the days passed her anger grew until she was finally reduced to leaving a cryptic message with Gertrude. "Tell Mr. Swanson if he does not call me back within the next hour, I am making a statement to Adam Bobo Grant he will regret."

It worked. Within an hour Martin was on the phone.

"How nice to hear from you," Deena said coldly.

"My God," he replied. "You have no idea what it's been like here."

"*I* have no idea?" Deena said, her voice like ice.

"I *am* trying to take over a studio," Martin said testily. "I'm in meetings twenty-six hours a day. And it seems every time I get to a phone it's the wrong time to call you."

"Really, Martin?"

"Besides, isn't it best if we talk when I get back?"

"When are you coming back?"

He thought swiftly. "I'll be in New York by the weekend."

"We have a party to go to on Saturday night. Can I depend on you? It would be nice to be seen together in public. Don't you agree?"

He hesitated, reluctant to bring the subject up, but it couldn't be ignored any longer. "You're not mad at me, are you?" he asked.

"That picture in the magazine was a fake. A pasted-together job. My lawyers are looking into it. We're going to sue 'em."

"We are?"

"Don't you think we should?"

"Whatever you want, Martin. As you say, we'll discuss it when you get back."

Did Martin honestly imagine he was fooling her? Did he think she would believe the photograph was a fake?

She was dying to talk to Effie about it. But unfortunately Effie was not taking her calls. Obviously she was still upset about the picture with Paul.

Deena decided to set things straight. She sent her a short note requesting a chance to explain. If Effie was any kind of friend, she would call back.

Paul Webster had telephoned the house three times. Deena had not returned his calls. She had enough on her mind.

Her latest aggravation was Adam Bobo Grant. She was quite upset that he'd betrayed every confidence she'd whispered to him. And now her confidences were spread daily across the front of the *New York Runner*.

Deena Swanson loves her husband and refuses to give him up. "Whatever happens," she said today, "Martin and I refuse to give credence to these ugly rumors."

There were many conversations she and Martin needed to have. And when Martin returned they would have them.

In the meantime, her plans regarding Venus Maria were progressing smoothly.

Soon she would be ready to make her move.

Abigaile was not Abe Panther's granddaughter for nothing. She had a certain amount of craftiness in her, and she soon decided that Mickey Stolli deserved to be taught a lesson. He'd humiliated her and Tabitha. He'd publicly disgraced them, and nobody seemed to care except herself.

Her girlfriends dismissed the news of Mickey's being caught in a whorehouse as nothing more than an irritation. "Just ignore it," they'd advised her. "Most men play around. What difference does it make as long as they don't bring it home?"

Ah, but Mickey *had* brought it home. He could hardly bring it any further home than the front page of the *L.A. Times*.

While Primrose and Ben dealt with lawyers, she sat and brooded. It soon became clear why Mickey did not wish to become embroiled in a fight over Panther Studios. He had a new job. He was taking over as head of Orpheus Studios.

Abigaile frowned. He'd be Martin Swanson's boy, that would be all. Didn't he realize? Mickey had no idea what it was like to work for somebody else. He'd never had to answer to Abe—but he'd certainly have to answer to Martin Swanson.

While she was sitting and brooding, Abigaile began to think about Mickey's secretary at the studio, Luce—the one who'd given her Warner Franklin's number. And then she thought about Warner Franklin, the six-foot black cop. Why had Luce given her the number? And why had Mickey made such a lame excuse?

None of it made sense. And yet, if she thought about it long enough . . .

Abigaile picked up the *L.A. Times* and reread the story on Mickey. It stated he'd been arrested while in the company of an Oriental lady of the night.

Oriental . . . Black . . . Warner Franklin's words began to come back to Abigaile.

"I'm also your husband's mistress," the woman had said over the phone.

Your husband's mistress . . .

Abigaile searched her desk to see if she had jotted down Warner Franklin's phone number. No. However, she did remember where she lived.

Abigaile was anxious to find out more. If Mickey planned to leave her, she wasn't about to let him get away unpunished. He was going to have to pay. Oh, was he going to have to pay!

Abigaile climbed into her Mercedes and headed for Hollywood.

477

77

Lucky's first week at the studio passed quickly. There were meetings, meetings, and more meetings. There were decisions to be made, films to be halted, films to be continued with, distribution discussions, preproduction, post-production, editing, business affairs. Suddenly Lucky found herself immersed in the creative process. She attended script meetings, looked at dailies, viewed rough cuts, went over budgets, and at night, exhausted, she read scripts.

"You don't have to do *everything*," Morton Sharkey told her, amused at the idea that she would want to. "There are employees to take care of the everyday affairs. You're supposed to make only the big decisions."

Lucky was into it. "I *want* to be hands on," she said, full of enthusiasm. "These are *my* decisions."

On Friday she and Boogie drove out to the airport to meet Bobby and Cee Cee, his Jamaican nanny. It was a joyful moment. Her son bounded off the plane straight into her arms.

Bobby was six and a half years old, and gorgeous.

Lucky swept him up and swung him around.

After a moment he got embarrassed. "Hey, Mom, put me down, I'm too big," he objected, struggling like crazy.

She crushed him with a kiss. "You're mine," she sang out, wildly happy. "Mine! Mine! Mine!"

Bobby chatted all the way to the house, while Cee Cee just smiled.

"Where's Lennie, Mommy?" he asked as soon as they arrived.

"He's working, sweetheart."

Bobby was persistent. "Will he be here soon?"

"Sure," she said, although she still hadn't heard from Lennie. Not one word.

It was disappointing. She'd hoped by this time he'd have gotten over his anger and would have called to make things all right.

"Where's Brigette?" was Bobby's next question.

Lucky had tried to reach Brigette on several occasions, but had missed her each time.

"I'll try her again now," she promised. "Maybe we can persuade her to come out here soon. Would you like that?"

Bobby liked it a lot.

Lucky placed another call to the Websters. "You're in luck this time," said Effie Webster. "She's right here. Hang on a second."

Brigette sounded full of high spirits. "Lucky! I'm sorry we keep on missing each other. How are you?"

"Fine," Lucky replied. "More important, how are you? Enjoying New York?"

"Yes, it's terrific. Is Bobby with you?"

"That's exactly why I'm calling. I met him at the airport today, and he's disappointed you're not here. I hope you're coming."

Brigette hesitated. "I wasn't sure you still wanted us."

Did "us" mean she was bringing Lennie? "Of course I still want you. Lennie told me we're all spending the summer together."

"Yes, I know," Brigette said awkwardly. "But Lennie told *me* that you and he were having some sort of um . . . disagreement . . . and so we've made other plans."

"Who's made other plans?"

"Well, Lennie, actually. He's taking me and my girlfriend to the South of France."

Lucky felt a chill. Lennie had made plans to go away without telling her. He was taking off without a word. Was that how much their relationship meant to him? Christ! He really *didn't* care.

"How long are you going for?"

Brigette sounded vague. "Lennie said maybe ten days, or a couple of weeks."

She took a long, deep breath. It wasn't fair to involve Brigette. "Well, that sounds wonderful. Perhaps when you get back you'll come to Malibu."

"I'd love to," Brigette said happily. "Can I bring my girlfriend?"

"Sure." Lucky paused, and then carefully added, "By the way, I saw *Truth and Fact*. Who was that boy you were pictured with?"

"Oh, Paul. He's nobody," she said casually. "Just Nona's brother. You know how these stupid photographers trail me whenever they find out where I am."

"I was just wondering," Lucky said. "I don't want to see you get into any more difficult situations."

"Lucky, I was a kid when all that happened with Tim Wealth. I'm a grownup now."

"Hardly a grownup!"

"I'm seventeen. That's old. You were running wild in the South of France with Mommy when you were almost my age. And then you were married a few months after that."

True. She couldn't deny it. She and Olympia—out of control. Until Gino and Dimitri had come to collect their errant daughters. And then a forced marriage to Craven Richmond. Mr. Personality!

"O.K., sweetheart. It's just that I worry about you."

"You don't have to, Lucky. I can look after myself."

"Good. Call me when you get back."

"Yes, I promise."

Lucky put the phone down and went to find Bobby. He was on the beach and into everything—running, swimming, playing with a neighbor's dog.

He was having the best time. Later, he fell asleep watching television.

She picked him up, carried him to his bed, and tucked him in. Then she brushed the soft, dark hair off his forehead. He looked so like Gino. Olive skin, black eyes, curling lashes—a miniature Gino. God! She loved him.

She kissed him and left the room.

The nights were the loneliest. She couldn't stand the thought that it might be over with Lennie. It was just too painful.

After a while she went to her bedroom and called him—something she'd promised herself she wouldn't do. He was the angry one. It was up to him to make the first move. But so what?

He answered on the third ring. "Yeah?"

She didn't know what to say. It was so unlike her to be at a loss for words. After a long and painful silence she hung up.

If Lennie really loved her he would pursue her. He'd fly out to California and make everything all right.

Sadly she realized he wasn't going to make that move.

She went to bed and slept restlessly. Sleep was not easy. She missed Lennie so very much.

78

Martin Swanson flew back to New York. He had left the city where he lived as a well-known businessman and returned a media superstar. Somehow, Martin Swanson had attracted the attention of a celebrity-hungry public. He was fairly young. He was extraordinarily rich. And sex was involved. What better headline for the eighties?

Deena greeted him as if everything were normal.

"We can't ignore what's going on," he said, getting straight to it. "We're going to have to face it."

"It's you who has to face it," Deena said, trying to keep her fury under control. "Do you want to be with that . . . that . . . woman?"

Was Deena saying he *could* be with Venus Maria *and* keep their marriage intact? That's what he'd like. Maybe it wasn't necessary for things to change.

"I haven't thought about it," he lied, because apart from the successful takeover of Orpheus, he hadn't thought about anything else. "Venus Maria is special," he added unthinkingly.

Deena raised a skeptical eyebrow. "Special?" she sneered. "As special as the ballet dancer, or the author, or the lawyer? How *special* is she, Martin? Is she special enough for you to give up half your money?"

"What are you taking about?"

"If you ever considered divorce, that's exactly what you'd have to do."

"Do you want a divorce? Is that what you're saying?"

"I'm *saying* I do not enjoy being followed by the media and having my personal life written about in the press. It's an embarrassment. I feel foolish and humiliated."

"Yes, well, might I mention that one of the reasons we're all over the newspapers is because you keep giving exclusive interviews to Adam Bobo Grant. Why can't you tell the little fag to back off?"

"Bobo has been a true friend to me. I couldn't even get you on the phone in Los Angeles. That's hardly loyalty, Martin."

"You know what I'm like when I'm closing a deal," he explained.

"Didn't you feel this was important enough to take the time to speak to me?"

"Deena, I'm here now. What more do you want?"

"I want you to stop seeing her."

There! She'd said it. Her words were out in the open. It was the first time she'd challenged Martin about a woman. Now all he had to do was agree, and everything would be all right.

Deena held her breath. This was a crucial moment.

"Give me time to make a decision," Martin said, not looking her in the eye.

Deena sighed. As far as she was concerned, Venus Maria was dead.

Dennis Walla turned out to be right. When Emilio Sierra's revelations about his famous sister hit the stands, *Truth and Fact* was again a sellout. Two weeks in a row. Not bad. He was on a winning streak. It seemed the public couldn't get enough of mega-money, power, and lustful sex. They loved the combination.

Dennis Walla was now in daily contact with Adam Bobo Grant. He fed the New York gossip columnist tidbits, and Bobo used them in his column.

Dennis had two men watching Venus Maria around the clock—a photographer and Bert Slocombe. They reported everything she did.

In fact, they were even getting pretty good at figuring out her various disguises. Sometimes she wore a long black wig. Other times she hid under a huge, floppy Garbo hat and big dark glasses. Sometimes she rushed out wearing her hair in a ponytail, and no makeup, hoping they wouldn't recognize her. Other times she dressed up as the maid.

It was a game. They were winning. Usually she just attempted to ignore them and rushed to her car. When she was particularly irritated she gave them the finger.

They had her house, the studio, and the video-rehearsal hall staked out. She couldn't make a move without their knowing it.

Martin Swanson wasn't such an easy deal. There were two more reporters assigned to him.

A stray paparazzo had managed to snatch a shot of Martin and Venus Maria strolling on the grounds of the Bel-Air Hotel. *Truth and Fact* bought it and planned to run it front page in the next issue with the lurid headlines:

LOVE NEST DISCOVERED!

THE BILLIONAIRE AND THE SHOWGIRL!

A third-week bonanza coming up.

Did Dennis ever have any regrets about invading people's privacy?

No way. He knew he was on to a good thing, and felt no guilt whatsoever.

When he got back from Hawaii, Emilio called him up to whine. "There's a message from my sister on my machine telling me to fuck off. She's furious with me," Emilio said. "And that's before my story has even appeared."

"It's out on the stands now," Dennis said. "Read it. All good juicy. You'll be proud, mate."

The Hawaii trip had cost Emilio more than he expected. He wouldn't mind making a further killing out of this story. After all, it was unlikely Venus would ever speak to him again.

"Uh, I've got more stuff for you," he told an insatiable Dennis.

"Yes? What?" Dennis asked curiously.

"Oh, just some more bits and pieces about Venus I remembered.

Friends she went to school with. Her first boyfriend. That kind of thing."

Dennis was interested. "You have?"

"Yeah. How much can I get for it?"

"Why don't you tell me exactly what you got an' we'll see," Dennis said.

"I just told you. School friends, boyfriends—whatever you're after."

"Give me the day-she-lost-her-virginity story and I'll find out what it's worth."

Emilio decided to get his ass back to New York. With a little intelligent digging, he could come up with anything Dennis wanted.

79

Cooper greeted Lucky at the door to the screening room, dressed casually, and looking as good as ever. There was a showing of *Strut*, and Lucky was anxious to see it. She studied Cooper and idly wondered if she'd ever feel the desire to go to bed with another man again. She'd done as she pleased before Lennie. Now, if their relationship was over, what next? Going to bed with somebody in the eighties was a whole new thing. A dangerous commitment.

"Venus is joining us," Cooper said, taking her arm and leading her inside.

"I was hoping she could come."

"How's everything going? Are you enjoying running a studio?"

"It's time-consuming," she said as she took a seat at the back of the room.

"I hear you bumped the Sleazy Singles," he remarked, sitting down beside her.

"That was Lennie's nickname for them."

"Yeah, it's everybody's nickname for them. Are they hitting you with a lawsuit?"

Casually she shrugged. "Who knows? Who cares? We're in good shape. I told them I was willing to honor their contract—it's just that I won't make any of their dumb movies. If they want to make sexist crap, they can make it elsewhere."

"I understand," he said. "Pretty smart move."

"I don't imagine they've got much of a case, do you? Besides, the rumor is they'll follow Mickey to Orpheus."

He smiled. "Ah . . . Mickey, Arnie, and Frankie. The perfect team!"

Venus Maria rushed in late. "The paparazzi are driving me insane!" she complained. "They're camped outside my house like a band of gypsies. I nearly knocked a couple of 'em down this morning."

Cooper kissed her on the cheek. "Maybe you should have."

"Oh, yeah, great. I can see the headlines now: Venus Maria, the paparazzi killer! Very tasteful!"

Lucky picked up the phone and instructed Harry to roll the film. They settled down to watch.

From the moment Venus Maria appeared on the screen, everybody knew the film was hers. She looked sensational and her acting was captivating. Cooper didn't seem to mind; it made him look good as the director.

"Oh, God! I hate watching myself!" Venus Maria cried, half-covering her eyes. "It's so painful. Do you see how big my teeth look? And my hair—I *hate* my hair!"

Cooper groped for her hand in the dark and squeezed it. "Shut up," he said firmly. "You're a star. Face it."

Cooper wasn't so bad himself. On screen he came across with exactly the right amount of charm and self-deprecating humor. It was a skillful performance.

When the lights went up, Lucky said confidently, "We've got a winner—in spite of the fact that it was made under Mickey Stolli's regime."

"I did have *something* to do with it," Cooper chided gently. "Mickey requested seventeen bare-breasted girls in the opening credits, but I told him, no, let's cool it."

"What does everybody think?" Venus Maria asked anxiously. "Am I bearable?"

It amazed Lucky that Venus Maria had to seek reassurance. Couldn't she see? "You're a natural," she assured her. "You light up the screen. You really do."

Venus's face glowed with pleasure. "Yes?"

"*Yes.* You're going to be a movie megastar. And *I'm* going to make sure this film is handled in exactly the right way."

"Sure," Cooper interjected dryly. "Bud Graham is designing the poster now—a naked amazon surrounded by a dozen nymphets with their tits on fire!"

Everyone laughed. Bud Graham's reputation was legendary.

Lucky suggested the three of them lunch together. They went to the Columbia Bar and Grill, where they pigged out on pasta and spent the entire time discussing everyone at the studio.

By the time they emerged, the paparazzi were gathered in force. Word traveled fast.

"Jesus!" Venus Maria exclaimed, "we can't go anywhere anymore. Hey—come on, Cooper, let's give 'em a picture they won't forget. Lucky, grab his other arm."

They held onto Cooper and smiled for the cameras. The photographers went wild.

Venus Maria giggled. "That's gonna give them something to think about."

"I can't believe the amount of publicity Martin's getting." Cooper shook his head in amazement. "From a conservative unknown businessman in New York he's become a superstud!"

"Not exactly unknown," Venus Maria interrupted.

"Yeah, but not exactly Warren Beatty either." Cooper corrected. "Now he's on the cover of every magazine and newspaper across the country. The Battling Swansons. What's going on with them anyway?"

Venus Maria shrugged. "You think *I* know? One night in the Bel-Air Hotel does not a relationship make!"

"One night?" Cooper questioned.

"He was too busy with the Orpheus deal."

"That figures. Business first."

"Anyway, he's flying back to New York tomorrow. I guess we'll all find out together. I start shooting my new video soon, and that's all I'm into for the next couple of weeks. What Martin decides is up to him."

Lucky found herself liking Venus Maria more and more. The girl had spirit. She did what she wanted to do, and she did it her way. In some ways she reminded Lucky of herself.

Bobby and his nanny settled nicely into Malibu, but Bobby wouldn't stop asking about Lennie and Brigette, and when they were coming. To keep him occupied Lucky sent for one of his school friends from England.

Finally Lennie called.

"Hi," Lucky said, holding her breath, hoping he was going to say, *I'm sorry, I've behaved like a jerk, I'm on my way out there, and we'll get through this together.*

"Lucky, what the hell is all this about my contract?" he asked tightly.

"I thought you'd be pleased," she replied. "Panther is releasing you from all future commitments. You can tear your contract up."

He didn't sound as pleased as she'd hoped. "Oh, really," he said.

"It's what you wanted, isn't it?"

"Sure."

"Now you don't have to worry about anyone suing you."

"Oh, you were thinking of suing me, huh?"

"Not me, Lennie. Mickey. But Mickey's out now, and I'm in." She hesitated for a moment. "If you wanted to, you could be here beside me."

"Hey—Lucky—we've had that conversation."

When Lennie was impossible he was *really* impossible. Her voice hardened. "Why are you calling? To thank me for releasing you from your contract? Is that it?"

"I wanted to say . . . uh . . . Jesus, I don't know. What's going on with us?"

He'd given her an opening, and she went for it. "If you flew out this weekend, maybe we could talk it out. That's what we need to do, Lennie. And I'm prepared to listen to your point of view if you're ready to listen to me."

There was a long silence, then, "No, it's not going to work. I'm taking Brigette to France. We're leaving tomorrow."

Pleading wasn't her style, but Lennie was worth it. "We could all be here together. Isn't that what you wanted?"

"No, Lucky," he said resolutely, as if he'd given it a great deal of thought. "I can't fly in just because it suits you."

"What do you mean by that?"

"You're running Panther. You're in L.A. So now it's convenient, huh? You can fit us all into your busy schedule. But what about next time? How about when you decide to buy a hotel in Hong Kong or India? Am I supposed to sit around and wait? Hey—Lucky, remember this: I'm not the waiting kind."

"Do you want a divorce?" The words almost stuck in her throat.

He came right back at her. "Do you?"

"If we're not together . . ."

"Hey—if it's what you want . . ."

"I didn't say that."

"Yeah, well, we'll talk later." He hung up on her.

She couldn't believe he was taking it this far.

At first she was hurt, then angry. What did he want from her?

A baby.

Barefoot and knocked up.

A proper wife.

Well, damn him! She had things to do first, and if he didn't like it —too bad.

She phoned Mary Lou and asked if she and Steven would like to come out with the baby and stay for a couple of weeks.

"A fine idea," Mary Lou said enthusiastically. "I'll ask baby first, and then I'll run it by Steven."

"How *is* Carioca Jade?"

"Adorable!"

"When does your series start shooting again?"

"You're not going to believe this, but we just got canceled. I go away and have a baby, and look what happens!"

"Are you upset?"

"Sure I am. But Steven's delighted. He wants me at home changing diapers!"

"Of course he does," Lucky said dryly.

"Steven's so traditional," Mary Lou explained. "But I go along with it—makes him feel good."

Lucky thought about Steven for a moment. She missed him. It

seemed like she never had time to spend with the people she really cared about.

"Hey—maybe when you come out here, we'll put you in a movie. How about it?"

Mary Lou laughed. "A movie?"

"You're a big television star. Why not?"

"Suits me," said Mary Lou happily. "I'll tell Steven. He'll kill himself. He thinks I should never work again."

"Men!" Lucky said.

"Yeah!" Mary Lou agreed.

Next, Lucky called Gino and invited him. He was easy to persuade. "I'm feeling tired, kid," he said, sounding weary.

"Have you spoken to Paige?" she asked, knowing that Paige always perked him up.

"Nope. She knows how I feel. If she don't leave Ryder, I ain't seein' her again."

"Oh, come on, Gino. You and Paige have been sneaking into hotel bedrooms for years. What difference does it make if she's got a husband?"

"Hey, maybe in my old age I'm findin' out I got ethics. How about that, kid?"

"I'll believe it when I see it!"

"You'll see it."

"Sure."

He promised he'd fly out soon. She couldn't wait for everyone to arrive. Maybe filling the house with people would take her mind off Lennie.

Meanwhile, business at the studio went on. Out of all the Panther executives, she decided Zev Lorenzo, Ford Werne, and Teddy T. Lauden were the best of the bunch. She knew she was going to have to let Eddie Kane go. And Bud Graham wasn't about to dance to her tune. She hadn't decided about Grant Wendell, Junior.

The Sleazy Singles were definitely out. Naturally they'd threatened to sue.

"On what grounds?" Lucky had asked. "You have a three-year deal that says you make the movies and Panther pays. But the studio has to approve them. Listen, I don't mind paying you the money while you sit here and play with yourselves for three years. How about it, huh?"

They'd told her to shove it and duly departed.

Ben Harrison requested a meeting. He came in and told her he'd be willing to stay and take over Mickey's job.

"*I've* taken over Mickey's job," she pointed out. What did they all think this was? A game?

She decided to keep Ben running the European side of things until she had the time to investigate his skills. Abe had called both Mickey and Ben the "scums-in-law." Maybe he was wrong about Ben.

The important thing was to get the studio headed in the right direction. No more mindless violence against women. No more tits-and-ass specials.

The word soon spread around Hollywood that Panther was the place to take any interesting and exciting new projects and ideas. The scripts began pouring in.

And so business went on while Hollywood watched and waited.

Lucky Santangelo was in charge. It felt good.

80

The second time around, Abigaile knew exactly where to park. She didn't bother driving around the block. She dumped her car in the red zone, walked up to the front of the building, and pressed the buzzer marked Franklin.

"Warner Franklin?" she said imperiously when a woman's voice answered.

"Who's this?"

"Abigaile Stolli. I'd like to come up and talk to you."

There was a long pause while Warner decided what to do. Finally she said, "Third floor, watch the elevator door, sometimes it sticks."

"Thank you," replied Abigaile politely, keeping a hold on herself. This time her heart wasn't beating fast at all. She willed herself to remain in control. Mickey Stolli had lied to her for the last time.

Once on the third floor she marched resolutely toward the apartment.

Warner flung open the door and stared at her.

Abigaile stared back. "Can I come in?" she asked, feeling uncomfortable, but determined to follow through.

"You sure you're not gonna run away this time?" Warner said caustically. "Seems to me you take one look at a black face an' you shit your pants."

"I beg your pardon?" said Abigaile, putting on her best Beverly Hills Bitch face.

"Ah, forget it." Warner was anxious to know what Mickey's wife wanted. "Come in."

Abigaile followed Warner into her small apartment.

"Drink?" offered Warner.

Abigaile noticed a holstered gun thrown casually on a chair, and shuddered. "No, thank you."

"Sit down," said Warner.

Abigaile did so, folding her hands in her lap. Her perfect Beverly Hills manicure glistened. Warner's nails were cut short, and unpolished.

"You told me something before," Abigaile began. "On the phone, do you remember?"

"No, what was that?" asked Warner. She wasn't in a good mood on account of the fact that Johnny Romano, the new love of her life, was not returning her calls. Warner was not used to fuck and run. She didn't appreciate it.

"You said you were my husband's mistress," Abigaile rushed on. "Is that true?"

" 'Was' is the operative word," said Warner.

"Was?" questioned Abigaile. "Does that mean it's over?"

"Hey—you think when I find my man making out with hookers it's going to continue?" Warner asked, surprised. "*You* might put up with it, but *I* certainly won't."

"I see you read about it too," sighed Abigaile.

"No, I didn't read about it," corrected Warner. "*I* was the arresting officer."

Abigaile felt quite faint. "How long have you been seeing Mickey?"

"About eighteen months," Warner replied openly.

Abigaile was horrified. "Eighteen months!"

"You may as well make yourself comfortable," said Warner, thinking to herself that most men deserved everything they got. "And if you like—I'll tell you all about it."

. . .

494

Leslie was used to Eddie's erratic driving. She buckled her seat belt and hoped for the best.

It wasn't his driving that was causing anxiety to sweep over her in great waves. It was when she began to suspect where they were heading.

And sure enough, Eddie finally pulled up outside Madame Loretta's house.

Leslie did not unbuckle her seat belt. She sat perfectly still and waited.

He didn't say a word.

After a few minutes Leslie asked quietly, "Eddie? What are we doing here?"

"Hey," he said, "we're here for tea. Isn't that what you said you used to do here? Tea and a chat."

"Yes, that's right. But I always called first."

"That's O.K., honey. I hear Madame Loretta is *very* accommodating. Always ready to receive people. She'll be pleased to see us."

"Eddie." She looked at him pleadingly. "Why are you doing this to me?"

"Why am I doing what, baby? I don't understand."

"You understand perfectly well."

"Somebody you don't want to see here?" he said, looking around innocently. "Come on, baby. Get out of the car, we're visiting just like you used to."

Slowly she unbuckled her seat belt and climbed out.

He took her hand and marched her up to the front door.

One of the maids answered his ring.

"Is Madame Loretta around?" he asked.

"Who shall I say is calling?"

"Tell her . . . Leslie's here. Tell her . . . Leslie is ready to go back to work."

Leslie turned to him and her eyes filled with tears. "You bastard," she said in a low voice. "When did you find out?"

"Why didn't you tell me?" he demanded angrily.

"Because you wouldn't have understood."

"What makes you think that? You know you should have told me. 'I'm a hooker, Eddie,' that's all you had to say. 'Guys have sex with me for money.' You think that would have made me run, huh? You think I wouldn't have married you?"

"You're a mean son of a bitch."

"What *I* am is honest. What *you* are is a fraud. Now I'm leaving you here, baby, 'cause it's where you belong. Don't bother coming back to the house."

"You can't do this," she said.

"Watch me."

"Don't you love me?" she said sadly. "You always told me you did."

"Hey—I loved the pretty little girl from Iowa. I don't love the hooker who's probably had every guy in town." He turned to leave. "Goodbye, Leslie. Thanks for the free ride."

"Is that the way you want it, Eddie? Because if it is, don't expect me to come back."

He laughed aloud. "Who wants you back? I gotta be out of my head to take you back."

He walked away, swaggering over to his prized Maserati.

Stoned as usual, Eddie didn't really know what he was doing.

81

"There's some guy to see you," Otis said. "Says he knows you. Informs me you're an old friend."

"Does he have an appointment?" Lucky asked.

"Nope. The man drove onto the lot in a limousine with a driver and two other guys in the car. I guess the limo impressed the guards. Nobody stopped him."

"What's his name?"

"Carlos Bonnatti," Otis said. "Sounds like an Italian hood. Looks like one, too. Central Casting couldn't have done better."

"Bonnatti?" Lucky said. "What's Carlos doing here?"

"So you do know him. Shall I show the man in?"

Carlos Bonnatti. A name from her past. The Santangelos and the Bonnattis went way back. Too many years . . .

"Yes. Show him in," she said.

Carlos had the Bonnatti swagger and the same ominously hooded eyes. When he walked into her office, Lucky felt as if she were in some crazy time machine. Suddenly all kinds of bad memories came flooding back. Her mother's murder . . . the time she'd gone to Enzio Bonnatti for money to help finance her Vegas hotel. . . .

Enzio, Carlos's father, her godfather. A man so evil there'd been only one way to deal with him. . . .

She'd known Carlos all her life, and yet she didn't know him at all. Was he like his sadistic brother, Santino? Or did he take after the even more vicious Enzio?

She didn't know. She didn't want to know.

What did it matter anyway? They were both dead. And good riddance.

"Well, well, well." Carlos strolled into her office as if he owned it. "Little Lucky Santangelo, we meet again."

She wasn't about to be polite. "What the hell do *you* want?"

He grimaced. "Nice welcome. Childhood friends an' that's all you have to say?" He paused. "Whaddaya think I want, Lucky?"

"I've no idea, Carlos. Why don't you tell me and get out."

His hooded eyes darted around the office. The Mickey Stolli chrome-and-leather look was still very much in evidence.

"Nice place," he said. "Word is you're the new owner around here. Seems like you did pretty good for Gino's dumb little kid."

"Give it up, Carlos, and get the fuck out."

"Still the perfect lady, huh?"

"You wouldn't know a lady from a ten-cent hooker."

He stared at her. "Right."

She contemplated buzzing Otis to throw the asshole out—but why start trouble for no reason?

"Panther owes me a million bucks," Carlos said, sitting down. "It'll be a pleasure taking your money."

Lucky stood up. "Out," she said sharply. "I'm not in the mood for blackmail."

"I'm not sure you understand," he replied, making no attempt to move.

"Oh, yes, I understand perfectly well. I know all about what was going on here before I took over. You had a deal with Eddie Kane, and Eddie stole from you. Right?"

Carlos regarded her from under drooping eyelids. For a moment an image of Enzio flashed before her. Enzio's face, just before she shot him . . .

It was self-defense. The case never even came to trial.

But still . . . his face . . .

"Get out of my office," she repeated.

"Lucky, you got it all wrong. My company performed certain services for Panther, *legitimate* services. An' in return they signed a note. Your studio owes me a million bucks. I'm here to collect."

"Panther owes you nothing."

They locked stares.

He reached into his pocket and withdrew a copy of an official deal memo which he placed on her desk. "Read it," he said, standing up. "I'll be back to collect."

Without another word he walked out of the office.

Otis put his head around the door. "Everything all right?"

"Yes, Otis. Thank you."

"Who was that guy?"

"It doesn't matter."

She picked up the document and began to read it. It appeared to come from a legitimate firm of lawyers in Century City.

Her eyes scanned the page. It was a legal paper stating Panther Studios owed Bonnatti Inc. a million dollars for services rendered. And it was signed by Mickey Stolli.

What services? What kind of scam was this?

She looked at the date. It was dated a month earlier.

Impossible. It couldn't be true. As Luce, she'd sat in the outer office listening in on every conversation. She knew Eddie Kane owed the money and that Mickey had refused to accept responsibility for Panther. If this deal memo existed, how come Mickey had backed off? He must have known about it.

Something was going on. The document had to be a phony.

She called up business affairs and reached Teddy T. Lauden.

"Teddy," she said, "can somebody check through the files on outstanding debts? Let me know if we've got anything on Bonnatti Incorporated. If so, send it over."

Sure enough Teddy sent over the original of Bonnatti's deal memo. He attached a note stating this was a Mickey Stolli deal that he, Teddy, wasn't aware of.

So Mickey had paid old Abe Panther back and stuck it to her at the same time.

Son of a bitch!

She had no intention of giving Carlos Bonnatti one red cent. She knew what was right and what was wrong, and there was no way she was going to give in to this.

As far as Lucky was concerned it was a matter of principle.

82

The media bombarded them. Everywhere they went, Deena and Martin Swanson were swamped with questions from intrusive journalists.

"I can't live my life like this," Deena said icily. "I'm going away to a health spa."

"The Golden Door?" Martin asked.

"No. There's a new place in Palm Springs I hear is excellent. I need to get away, Martin. You've been honest with me and I appreciate it. Now I must be alone."

He nodded. Deena was taking this better than anticipated. He hadn't actually come right out and said he wanted a divorce; he'd merely asked for time to make a decision. But if he were truly honest he'd admit he was quite enjoying all the publicity. It was a real ego boost to be regarded as a Don Juan. And, quite frankly, it wasn't so bad for business either. Orders for his new car, the Swanson, were pouring in. And that was before they'd even presented it to the public.

A divorce. He'd never thought about it seriously before. But if Deena was prepared to let him go . . .

Not that he'd pay her half his money. She must be crazy to even contemplate that. But the lawyers would work out a fair settlement.

"So you're not coming to Detroit for the launching of the Swanson?"

"Definitely not," she replied coolly. "I'm sure you'll manage on your own."

"How long do you plan to be away?"

"Ten days or so." She gave him a long, cool look before adding, "And you'll be in Detroit?"

"Yes. And then I'll fly to Los Angeles to make arrangements at Orpheus. When I get rid of Zeppo, I'm putting Mickey Stolli in to run it. I'll oversee appointing the other executives while I'm there."

"Martin," she said quietly, "promise me one thing."

"What's that?"

"Don't make a decision until I return. Or any statements. If we're going to separate, then we have to announce it together in a dignified fashion. Agreed?"

He nodded. "I wouldn't embarrass you."

"It will certainly embarrass me if you see Venus Maria while you're on the Coast. So kindly don't. When we make our decision you'll be free to do whatever you want." She paused. "It's not much to ask, is it?"

He nodded again. "As you wish."

She fixed him with her dead blue eyes. "I'm asking for your promise."

"Isn't—?"

"Your *promise*, Martin."

"Very well," he said reluctantly.

"Thank you."

Upstairs in her bedroom she instructed her personal maid about which clothes to pack for her trip.

"Will you be away long, Mrs. Swanson?" inquired the maid.

"Just long enough."

When the maid was gone, she went to her safe and selected a few pieces of jewelry to take with her. Hidden in the back was the gun she'd purchased under an assumed name six months earlier. Just in case. It was always good to be prepared, although she hadn't really expected the day would come when she'd be forced to use it.

Locking herself in her bathroom she expertly loaded the weapon, clicked on the safety catch, and hid it in the bottom of her carry-on bag.

When she reentered the bedroom, Martin was preparing for bed. He wore blue silk pajamas and a satisfied smirk.

She stared at her errant husband. What had forced him into the arms of other women? Had she been such a terrible wife? She was attractive, perfectly groomed, beautifully dressed. She loved him, looked after him, she was available for him sexually if he wanted her. What was it?

"Did you see this?" He handed her a magazine in which he was profiled. "The photo's not so good. They caught my bad side."

Who did he think he was, a movie star?

Hollywood was going to Martin Swanson's head. His publicity was taking over.

In the morning, Martin left for the office before Deena departed. She'd told him she wished to use the Swanson jet, and it was waiting at the airport. She boarded, nodded to the captain and crew, and sat quietly in a window seat. When this was all over, she decided, she would redecorate. First the plane, then their New York town house, followed by their summer retreat, and then their house in Connecti-cut.

The plane flew her directly to Palm Springs. It was a smooth flight. She read a few magazines and slept a little.

When they arrived, there was a car and chauffeur to meet her. It took her straight to the Final Resort Health Spa.

What an aptly named place, she thought to herself.

The Final Resort . . .

Emilio strutted around his old neighborhood like a king. He'd bought himself a camel-hair coat and a white fedora with a black headband. He wore the fedora gangster style, and the coat flung casually over his shoulders.

To really blow everyone's mind, he'd brought Rita with him. Rita, the Hollywood starlet. Red hair, fine ass, and a lot of attitude.

"Wear clothes that show it all off, honey," he'd encouraged her. "I want 'em to see what I got."

"I *know* what you got," she giggled, always the flatterer.

Emilio had booked them into a hotel. He didn't fancy staying at his father's house, knowing his brothers would all try to come on to Rita. It ran in the family. But what could he do? The Sierra men were a horny bunch.

When he and Rita appeared for Sunday lunch, relatives and friends crowded the house.

"Where's Venus?" they all asked when he arrived. "Isn't she coming?" Disappointment was in the air. Wasn't it enough they had the great Emilio, fresh from Hollywood, with his beautiful starlet girlfriend?

"Venus sent me instead," he said magnanimously, shrugging off his coat. "She's kind of busy right now, but I got a few days off before I start work on my first movie."

"A movie?" shrieked one of his second cousins. "You?"

"Yeah," boasted Emilio. "A Stallone movie. I'm playin' Sly's best friend."

Rita shot him a look. She'd heard of lying, but Emilio was an expert.

As expected, his brothers were all over her. When he checked out the women they'd married he could understand why. Thank God he'd made the decision to follow Venus to Hollywood. Thank God he'd gotten out of Brooklyn.

"I've been readin' about you," his father said, patting his swollen beer belly.

"You have?" Emilio tried to appear casual, but he did love being the center of attention.

"Yeah, that *Truth an'* somethin' shit. Your picture's in it."

"It was taken special," Emilio said modestly, as if his photo turned up in magazines all the time.

"They pay you?" his father asked, scratching his balls—a Sierra family habit.

Trust his father to ask about money.

"Sure they paid me, Pa," he boasted. "They paid me pretty good."

"So, when ya gonna put some in my direction?"

Emilio hadn't been planning on doing so, but since he wanted to look like a big man, he took out a couple of crumpled hundred-dollar bills and handed them over. "Here's cash, Pa. There's more where that came from."

His father looked at it, was about to make a derogatory remark, changed his mind, and stuffed it in his pocket. He knew he was in luck to get anything out of Emilio. The boy had always been a cheapskate.

One by one, Emilio took the old gang aside and questioned them. "*People* magazine has asked me to write a piece for them," he lied. "On Venus. What do you remember about her? Like when she was a kid. What was she doing? Who was she friendly with?"

"She was a good girl," said Uncle Louie.

"She was a little slut," said his wife.

"She studied hard," said one of his cousins.

"She played hooky from school all the time," said another.

"I knew her well," said a friend from school who Emilio remembered was Venus's dreaded enemy.

"We were best friends," said a girl who hadn't even been in the same grade.

Emilio pumped his brothers for information. "Who was that greasy guy she was seeing in school? Did she make out with him? Was he her first boyfriend?"

"Yeah, I remember him," said one of his brothers. "Scrawny little fucker. I caught them necking in the kitchen one night. Hadda throw him out."

"What was his name?"

"Vinnie somethin' or other," said one brother.

"Nah," corrected his older brother, "it was Tony Maglioni. He's drivin' a cab now, hangs out at the pizza parlor every Saturday night."

Rita was bored. She didn't appreciate getting pinched by Emilio's father and his three brothers. She wasn't enjoying the experience. At first it had been fun. She could act like a star and tell them all about Hollywood. But now it was a drag and she wanted to leave.

"Come on, Emilio, let's go," she whined.

"Come on, Emilio, let's go," imitated one of his brothers with a sly nudge to Emilio's ribs. "Hot stuff," he whispered. "I wouldn't mind a piece of that."

"You gotta wife an' kid," reminded Emilio.

"I can wish, can't I?" drooled his brother, making sucking noises with his lips.

Emilio took Rita back to the hotel.

If he could get hold of this Tony guy, maybe he'd have a story.

Martin took his plane out of New York the next day and flew straight to Detroit ready to launch the Swanson. All the publicity linking him with Venus Maria had only helped the enormous press coverage he was receiving. If it sold more cars, why object?

It occurred to him if he'd persuaded Venus Maria to attend, the publicity would really explode. That would be something, except that Deena would be furious.

He contemplated what it would be like to be married to Venus Maria. Exciting, that was for sure. Different. Stimulating.

He'd be sorry to lose Deena. In a way she was an asset. But he was forty-five years old and it was time for a more exciting life.

Martin reveled in being headline news.

Settled into the health spa, Deena felt perfectly calm. She had a simple solution, and soon she would put it into action.

She was getting closer every day.

83

Saxon was fixing Venus Maria's hair at her home in preparation for a major shoot with the great Antonio.

"I feel like a prisoner," she complained. "I can't take a step out of here without being stalked. It's ridiculous."

"I know," Saxon agreed sympathetically.

How could he possibly know what it was like to be emblazoned all over the supermarket rags?

God! If she ever got hold of Emilio again, she'd personally strangle the traitorous son of a bitch. How dare he! *How dare he!*

She'd tried to find him, but it appeared he'd run off to hide, for all she could get was his goddamn answering machine.

The second installment in *Truth and Fact* was a real put-down. A lot of crap about how she wore curlers in her hair, walked around without any makeup, admired herself in the mirror for hours, sometimes wore men's underwear, and liked to swim naked. She felt as if someone had broken into her home.

Saxon strutted around her. Moussing and blow-drying, tossing his own mane of thick hair, which was more impressive than most of his clients'.

"Are you gay?" she asked curiously.

"No, darling, just happy," he replied, without taking a beat.

"Seriously," she demanded.

He massaged the creamy mousse into her scalp. "That's a very personal question."

Ha! Did he want to talk personal? How would *he* like to be all over the papers?

The truth was he'd probably love it!

"Well, are you?" she persisted.

"I don't think it's any of your business," he replied, frothing her hair with his hands.

"Come on, Saxon, tell me," she teased. "Maybe we could get it on."

"You're such a bitch."

"And so are you."

"If you must know," he said, enjoying her attention, "I swing both ways."

"I *love* that expression," she squealed. "It's so old-fashioned. "Swing both ways. You know, it kind of brings back memories of the playground. Playing on the swings and the roundabouts—that choice—right? What exactly does it mean? And isn't it awfully dangerous right now?"

"You ask questions nobody else would dare."

"That's why I'm me. Anyway, what *is* your preference?"

He began to laugh. "None of your business."

"Aw, come *on*," she wheedled, "if you had a choice between, well, say, me and Ron, who would you choose?"

"Both of you," he said, wielding his brush.

That shut her up. Grinning, she watched him in the mirror as he attended to her hair.

Saxon had a lot of admiration for Venus Maria. Not only was she a superstar with a full work schedule, but she also found time to support causes and charities she believed in. She worked hard for AIDS and also Mothers Against Drunk Driving and the Rape Crisis Center. She preferred to keep her efforts quiet so they would not be construed as publicity opportunities.

"Since we're on the personal-question kick," he ventured, "what's happening with you and Martin Swanson?"

"Now you sound like Ron," she groaned. "That's all he wants to know."

"You can confide in me. Who am *I* going to tell?"

"Oh, just about every woman in Beverly Hills. Your salon is gossip heaven. Isn't that what goes on there, Saxon? Everyone talks about everyone else? It's a hotbed of scurrilous rumor!"

"I can't control it."

"That's because you love it."

He brushed against her. She glanced at his jeans in the mirror. They were almost as tightly packed as the Ken Doll's, and that was saying something.

"I bet you hear some great scandal in the salon," she pressed.

"Let's put it this way, we hear it first." He smiled proudly.

"Was everybody talking about Mickey Stolli when he got himself arrested with the hooker?"

"You could say it was a hot topic of conversation."

She laughed. "But I'm more of a topic, huh?"

"Not so much you as Martin Swanson. They all love Martin Swanson."

"They love his money," she corrected.

"True. They love his money *and* they love his power. To be a Hollywood Wife you have to marry a man with both those things, and apparently Martin has more than anybody." He gave a wicked laugh. "*Does* he have more than anybody, darling?"

She laughed back. "I never screw and tell!"

Yves, her makeup artist, arrived next, followed by two stylists and Ron, dragging the Ken Doll behind him.

The Ken Doll had on his usual skintight jeans and a white fifties T-shirt, all the better to show off his muscles. He flexed for the stylists.

"He's been shooting a beer commercial, doesn't he look divine?" Ron said, establishing ownership up front.

"Divine," Venus Maria said sarcastically. "You know Saxon, don't you?"

"Do *I* know Saxon."

"We were just discussing his sex life," Venus Maria said wickedly.

"Really?" said Ron, all interested. "And how are all those little thirteen-year-old schoolboys, Saxon, dear?"

Saxon shook back his mane of hair and laughed. "You've got it all wrong. That's *your* territory, Ron."

"Oh, God. There's nothing worse than bantering fags." Venus Maria giggled.

At noon the great photographer Antonio arrived, accompanied by several hardworking assistants.

"Baby!" Venus greeted.

"*Bellissima!*" gushed Antonio.

They hugged and kissed.

Antonio was extremely famous, extremely temperamental, and extremely tight-fisted. Fortunately he rarely had to put his hand into his pocket because the magazines who assigned him to photograph the various stars always paid. *Style Wars*, for whom this shoot was taking place, didn't pay as much as other publications, but that was because *Style Wars* was way ahead of the pack. A combination of *Vanity Fair* and *Interview*, it was the magazine of the moment—a must for the avant-garde.

Antonio prowled around her house followed by his minions, deciding where he would shoot the cover picture. Usually Venus did not allow photo sessions at her home, but for Antonio and *Style Wars* she'd made an exception.

"What do you think, darling?" Antonio asked. "The bedroom? Miss Venus Maria in the center of her bed, naked, with only the black silk sheet to cover her beauty."

Venus Maria almost got off on the idea of nothing except a thin silk sheet between her and her voracious public. "Yes," she said. "I like it."

"Why not, darling? You are the big star. Glamour is everything."

"What do *you* think, Ron?" She turned to her closest adviser.

"Sounds good to me," he replied, busily thinking about the surprise birthday party he'd planned for her. She was going to be twenty-six in three days' time, and he'd been planning the party for six weeks. It was going to be a fantastic affair if all went according to plan.

"Imagine," Antonio said, gesturing wildly as he spoke. "Your body, *bellissima*, one leg exposed. Your blond hair piled on top of your head. And black silk up to your chin. Maybe we go wild and one breast escapes."

"No nudity," Venus said firmly. "I've never done it in photographs, and I never will."

"For Antonio, you change your mind."

For Antonio she'd do a lot of things, but she'd decided right at the beginning of her career she would never take her clothes off for media consumption.

Not that she couldn't if she wanted to. She had beautiful breasts. Not too big. Not too small. Just perfect.

Perfect Venus Maria breasts. She smiled to herself.

Antonio described to Saxon how he wanted her hair to look.

Saxon understood perfectly. A tumble of wild curls, the hair piled on top of the head, a few tantalizing strands escaping each side.

"You'll look great, Venus," he enthused.

"Naturally she look great," Antonio announced. "Antonio—he say so."

While her hair was up in heated rollers, the makeup artist went to work.

Antonio checked out the clothes the stylists had brought with them, just in case he decided she should wear anything at all. He discarded everything, obviously in love with the black silk sheet idea.

In the middle of it all, Martin called. Her feelings were ambiguous. Since the rush of publicity he'd been particularly cagy about seeing her. They'd spent one night together in the Bel-Air Hotel, and apart from that he'd told her he was too busy with the Orpheus takeover, and that he felt he was being followed and had to check with his lawyers because he didn't want to give Deena cause to take him for everything he had. And then he'd returned to New York.

Understandable, but still it pissed her off. Either Martin committed himself or he didn't. She wasn't going to be the Hollywood girlfriend any longer.

"I'm in Detroit," he said, assuming she was anxiously awaiting news of his whereabouts.

"Really." she replied coolly.

"You sound mad."

"I am mad, Martin. I refuse to sit around waiting for you any longer. When you were out here we saw each other once—it's not enough. Now you've been back in New York for almost a week and I've heard nothing from you. What's happening with you and Deena?"

"It's no good talking on the phone," he said, sounding very businesslike. "I need to be with you."

"In that case you'll have to make a choice."

"I've made a choice."

"You have?"

"Yes."

"Are you going to let me in on it?"

He took a deep breath and announced, "I'm leaving Deena."

She'd been waiting months to hear him say those words, and yet when she heard them she felt a chill. Did she really want to be with Martin all the time? Was this the relationship of her dreams?

"Well?" he demanded impatiently. "Don't you have anything to say?"

"I'm shocked," she managed.

"Why are you shocked?"

"Because I never thought you'd do it."

"I'm doing it for you. I'll launch the Swanson, and then I'm flying out to see you."

"Are you coming here for me or for Orpheus?"

He conveniently forgot about his promise to Deena. She'd never find out anyway. "You, Venus. We'll be together and discuss our future."

"Sounds serious."

"I *am* serious. Very serious."

"Hmm . . . we'll see."

"Who was that?" asked Ron when she returned to her dressing room.

"You're so goddamn nosy. You know perfectly well who it was. Martin, of course."

"Ah. And is Superstud flying to your side?"

"Good guess."

Ron's mind started racing. If he could arrange to have Martin at the surprise party, it would really make her evening.

While she'd been on the phone, Antonio had obviously fallen in love with the Ken Doll.

"We shall put him in the background," Antonio decided, pouting in the Ken Doll's direction. "You, Venus darling, on the bed. Ken, he lean against the headboard. It will look marvelous, so . . . how you say? macho. Ken, unbutton the top of your jeans." He clicked his fingers for one of the stylists. "And we tear the T-shirt. Very Marlon Brando, very sixties."

"I think you mean fifties," corrected Ron, eager to score points. "Of course I wasn't born then, but you would know, wouldn't you?"

Antonio ignored Ron.

"Mmm . . ." murmured Saxon. "I sense trouble in paradise."

Venus Maria was primed and painted. Her platinum hair was curled and pinned atop her head, her body was smoothly covered with makeup. Clad in a brief pair of bikini panties and nothing else but her hands to cover her modesty, she arranged herself under the black silk sheets the stylist had draped on her bed.

She knew what Antonio was after. The classic pose. One leg provocatively snaking out, while she sat up, holding the sheet to her chin, her shoulders exposed, a seductive smile. The Venus Maria look. She'd perfected it. Over the years she'd studied carefully.

"Bellissima, darling," cooed Antonio peering through his lens. "And now, Ken, you move a little close."

Slouching against the wall in the background, Ken and Antonio experienced serious eye contact.

Hovering on the sidelines, Ron could see what was going on. Venus Maria observed his mouth go into a thin, tight line, a sign of deep trouble.

Somebody put Stevie Wonder on the stereo, and the house was flooded with music.

Venus Maria knew how to make love to a camera better than anyone. She licked her lips, somehow making them fuller and more seductive. Her eyes radiated sensuality. Her expression was pure sex.

She gazed at the camera reveling in every minute.

84

Gino arrived in L.A. before Steven and Mary Lou. Lucky took the day off and met him at the airport, taking Bobby with her.

When Gino walked through the terminal she almost didn't recognize him. Where was the Gino strut? Where was that famous Santangelo grin? Where was Gino the Ram?

Oh, God, was it possible that Gino was getting old? Her father, her wonderful, vital father, who'd always been so much younger and stronger than everyone else.

She hugged him. "Hey, what's going on?"

He hugged her back. "I told you, kid. It's finally gettin' to me."

"What?" she asked anxiously.

"Old age, I guess. I'm wearin' out, kid. I'm wearin' out."

She was dismayed to hear Gino talk that way. "*You*, Gino. Never!"

"Hey, Grandpa!" yelled Bobby, clamoring for attention.

"Hey, Bobby!" Gino greeted, hugging his grandson.

Boogie drove them to the beach house while Bobby chatted excitedly about his school in London and what he'd been doing.

"My friend is here, Grandpa," Bobby announced proudly. "I told him he couldn't come to the airport 'cause I had to see my grandpa first."

"That's right," encouraged Gino. "And don't you forget it. I'm gonna teach you a thing or two this trip."

Bobby couldn't have been more thrilled. "Yes, Grandpa. What?"

"I'm gonna teach you how to be a Santangelo."

"He's not a Santangelo. He's a Stanislopoulos," Lucky pointed out.

"Bullshit," argued Gino. "Bobby don't look like a Stanislopoulos, he looks exactly like a Santangelo."

She laughed. "You're right. Bullshit!"

"Thank you."

They grinned at each other.

"So . . . what have you been up to?" she asked.

"Aw, nothing," Gino said. "I sit around the apartment, take a walk. Sometimes I put a poker game together."

She hated to see her father inactive. Since he'd sold out the bulk of his companies he didn't seem to be interested in business anymore.

"You know what we should do?" she suggested.

"Yeah. What?"

"Build another hotel. We did it with the Mirage and the Magiriano, but they don't belong to us anymore. Why don't we build a new hotel and call it the Panther? We'll make it bigger than the Mirage. Better than the Magiriano. What do you say?"

"I wouldn't build another hotel if you paid me," he said, shaking his head.

"Why not? You loved it. You were one of the first in Vegas."

"That was a long, long time ago. It's a different world today."

"It's not so different. We'd do it together. I'd love to build a new hotel."

"Yeah, you're gonna fit it in between doin' studio deals, huh?"

"I've got a lot of energy."

"Don't even talk about it. I'm too old."

Gino admitting he was old: something was wrong somewhere, she thought.

She waited until they were back at the house and Bobby had raced off to play with his friend before mentioning Carlos Bonnatti.

"He came to see you?" Gino asked, concerned. "Did he threaten you in any way?"

"Are you *kidding?* I wouldn't allow that asshole to threaten me. I know this is a phony debt, and I'm not paying it."

"You know what, kid? Pay it, get him off your back. We don't need more trouble with the Bonnattis. There's been enough over the years."

She was surprised. "I can't believe this is you talking, Gino. Pay a debt we don't owe? Let the Bonnattis get the better of us? *No way.*"

"Life's too short to worry about these things. You got the money —pay him."

She narrowed her black eyes and stared her father down. "I said no way."

Something had to be done about Gino. He was in a slump. She had to come up with a brilliant way to snap him out of it.

After playing with Bobby for a while, Gino decided to take a nap. Lucky went straight to the phone and called Paige. A maid answered.

"Is Mrs. Wheeler there?" Lucky asked.

"One moment please."

When Paige picked up the phone, Lucky was delighted. "Hi, this is Lucky Santangelo. How are you?"

"Lucky," exclaimed Paige. "How nice to hear from you. Congratulations. I'm thrilled about the Panther deal, although Ryder's not so thrilled. He loved doing business with the wonderful Mickey Stolli. But I hear you're planning good things."

"I hope so," Lucky said. "I want to make films that give women a chance to show their strength."

"You will," Paige said warmly. "You always manage to do whatever you set your heart on. When your father and I were together, Gino never stopped boasting about you."

Lucky was pleasantly surprised. "Really?"

"Always," Paige assured her.

"Can we meet?" Lucky asked. "I'm not into doing lunch, but maybe if it's convenient for you we could have a drink or something."

"Fine," said Paige. "I'd love to see you. When?"

"As soon as possible."

85

The South of France was glorious. Hot sunshine, beautiful women, wonderful restaurants, and a carefree atmosphere.

Lennie was miserable. All he could think about was Lucky. He sat around the pool at Eden Rock watching Brigette and Nona. The two girls were having a great time. They'd met plenty of friends, and spent most of the day either in the pool or waterskiing. He saw them only for lunch when they joined him and his friends, Jess and Matt Traynor, who'd flown out to keep him company.

Jess, his best friend, counseled him a lot. "You're being very childish about this whole thing, Lennie," she scolded. "Lucky's not your average woman. You knew that when you married her. You love her. You want to be with her. And now you're playing hurt little boy because she bought a studio without asking your permission. Big deal!"

"She should have told me," he said stubbornly.

"Why?" Jess wrinkled her snub nose. "It was a surprise. For you."

Nobody understood. "Not for me, for her. She gets off on being in charge."

"No," Jess argued. "She did it to make you happy because you were always bitching about your contract, the movie, and the people you had to work with. She thought it would be fun. And let's face it —she can certainly afford it."

He tried to explain. "It's like she's buying me, Jess. You understand what I'm saying?"

"What kind of crap is that? You're her husband, for crissakes—give the girl a break!"

"I'm trying."

"How?"

"By staying away."

Jess gave him a look. They knew each other too well to get away with lying.

"Lucky Santangelo is the best thing that ever happened to you," she said firmly. "Wake up and realize it before it's too late."

He grimaced. "Hey—you and Matt make it work pretty good. Howdja do it?"

"When you get married you commit yourself," Jess answered seriously. "I failed once—so did you. When you do it a second time you know exactly what you're getting into. I want to be with Matt because I love him. Don't you love Lucky?"

Yeah. He loved Lucky. He loved her more than anything in the world.

But could he live with her? That was another question.

"There's one thing about you, Lennie," Jess said, sighing with exasperation.

"What?"

"You're pretty damn good at screwing up your life."

"Thanks!"

"Think about what I'm saying. Did Lucky do such a terrible thing? It wasn't like she ran off and slept with the Lakers, for God's sake!"

"She lied to me."

Jess was getting impatient. "She lied to you for *you*, asshole. Why don't you at least go see her, and maybe the two of you can work it out. I hate to see it end like this. You're both too stubborn—that's the problem."

Later, alone in his hotel room, Lennie thought about what Jess had said. Yeah. He was stubborn. And so was Lucky. But it didn't mean they couldn't talk.

Jess was right. He loved Lucky. And he wasn't about to give up on their relationship. It was about time he did something about it.

"You're fired," Lucky said.

Eddie twitched. "Why?"

"Because I don't approve of the way you do business."

Eddie couldn't believe he was getting canned by a woman. "Oh, you've been here five minutes and you don't approve of the way *I* do business, huh?" he said nastily.

"Eddie, I know what's been going on around here."

"Hey, hey, hey, no big deal. I've been offered a job at Orpheus."

"Then I suggest you take it."

"I'm packing up today."

"Oh, and do me a favor."

"What's that?"

"When your drug dealer arrives, the lovely Miss Le Paul, give her a message from me, will you? Tell her if she ever sets foot on this lot again she's gonna find her ass in jail."

Eddie glared and twitched and left her office.

Later she met with Paige. Paige was such a vibrant woman, full of life and fun. Lucky could certainly understand why Gino missed her.

Paige ordered a Campari and soda before settling back. "You look wonderful, Lucky," she said. "Hollywood agrees with you."

"Thanks. You never change, Paige."

Paige fluffed out her copper-colored hair. "I try to keep it all together. How's little Bobby?"

"Absolutely great."

"And Lennie?"

"The same." She wasn't about to spread the word on their separation. "By the way, guess who's out here?"

"Who?" said Paige, knowing full well.

"Gino. He's staying at the beach with me and Bobby."

Paige sipped her Campari. "He is?"

"He's getting older, Paige."

"Ah, Gino, he'll never be old," Paige said, smiling warmly.

"Without you he's *definitely* getting older."

Paige fiddled with a heavy gold bracelet. "It wasn't me that stopped seeing him," she said. "It was the other way around."

"I guess he had to have you to himself. You know Gino."

Paige continued to smile. "He always *was* greedy."

Lucky got right to it. "So, are you leaving Ryder, or what?"

"Is that what you're here to find out?"

"It's a pretty good reason, isn't it?"

Paige attracted the waiter's attention and ordered a second drink. "Did Gino send you?"

"He doesn't know I'm here. He'd kill me if he thought I was interfering."

"Ah, yes, he would indeed."

"So?"

"You Santangelos are so pushy. . . ."

"Think about it, Paige. Will you do me that favor?"

"I'll think about it, Lucky."

"That's all I needed to hear."

86

Deena hired the car a couple of days before she needed it. It was a sedan. A Ford. Dark brown. Ordinary.

The girl behind the rental desk would never remember her. Deena wore a long black wig, dark glasses, jeans, and a denim jacket. Her own mother would not recognize her.

She produced a phony driver's license with the appropriate picture attached.

"How long will you need it?" the girl asked, chewing gum and daydreaming about her truck-driver boyfriend.

"A week or so," Deena said, trying to disguise her accent. She paid cash.

"O.K." The girl behind the desk couldn't have cared less. "Sign here."

Deena wondered if it was necessary to bother with the disguise any longer. Probably not. But she had every detail of her plan worked out, and there would be no trails leading back to her.

Once the car was hired, she drove to an underground parking lot, collected a ticket, and left it there. Also parked in the lot was the silver Cadillac she was using, supplied by the Final Resort.

Getting into the Cadillac, she drove to Saks, entered the ladies room, removed her wig, dark glasses, and denim jacket, and emerged as Deena Swanson.

After making a few minor purchases, she headed back to the health spa in the Cadillac.

The Ford could take her anywhere she wished to go. And nobody could ever connect it to her.

Her next step was to use it.

87

When Ron so desired he could be incredibly organized. And his plans for Venus Maria's surprise twenty-sixth birthday party were proceeding full tilt. The trick was keeping it a surprise. But he'd personally invited every guest and sworn them to secrecy. And then, to be absolutely sure, he'd sent them a discreet little follow-up card, beautifully printed on Tiffany stationery, with "Be there. Keep your mouth shut!" engraved on it.

He'd invited three hundred guests—everyone from Cooper Turner and the other Panther stars to Mickey Stolli and his merry band of executives. Of course, he'd invited them before he knew of the upheaval about to take place at Panther.

Now he'd also invited Lucky Santangelo, who said she'd be delighted to attend.

The cake had been ordered—a huge three-tiered affair with Venus Maria's image on the top tier, and fake records hanging from the sides with the names of her hits.

The icing on the cake was to be the presence of Martin Swanson. If he produced Martin for her, it would make her evening.

Ron was throwing the party in the tented back garden of his home. He'd arranged to have exotic flowers, soul food, three different live groups, and a discotheque—all of Venus Maria's favorite things. Included in the guest list would be her dancers, personal staff, friends, and people she didn't know that well but might like to know better.

Unfortunately he'd made the mistake of inviting Emilio. He'd issued the invitation long before her brother's scummy revelations.

Surely the dumb brother wouldn't have the nerve to turn up?

No. Ron didn't even consider it a possibility.

To make sure everybody would have a good time, he'd also invited twenty beautiful girls and twenty good-looking boys to keep the husbands and wives of Hollywood happy.

The boys had been rounded up by Ken. He'd invited young actors, friends, and the best-looking male models in town.

"Try to make sure half of them are straight," Ron had instructed.

"You want I should personally test them?" Ken had replied.

Bitch! Ron had shaken his head in exasperation. "Never mind."

The girls he'd taken care of himself. He'd contacted Madame Loretta, who without a doubt had the most beautiful supply of girls in town. "For once they won't have to put out," he'd told the dear Madame. "Just dance, have a good time, and look utterly gorgeous."

There was nothing like beautiful people to make a party go over with a bang. And Venus Maria would adore the underlying humor of having the hookers mixing with the wives.

Ron had elected Cooper Turner as his co-conspirator, as far as getting Venus Maria to the party was concerned.

"At least if she thinks she's going out with you she'll look fabulous," Ron had explained. "I wouldn't care to put up with her wrath if she walked in here not looking her best. As it is, I've bought her a divine new Gaultier outfit as a birthday present. She can change when she arrives."

The party was on Monday. Only two days to go. It was difficult keeping the secret. But he'd kept it this long—he could surely manage another two days.

Warner Franklin marched up to the front door of Johnny Romano's Hancock Park mansion and rang the bell.

One of his entourage answered. He didn't recognize Warner as the six-foot black woman Johnny had been frolicking around with recently. All he saw was a very tall uniformed cop.

"Mr. Romano," she said, all business.

"He's not available," replied the gofer.

Warner could be very stern when the occasion called for it. "Do I have to come back with a warrant?" she said.

The gofer shifted uncomfortably. "What's it about?"

"That's for Mr. Romano to know. If you value your job you'd better bring him down here."

The gofer hurried off, muttering under his breath. Five minutes later he returned with Johnny. Handsome Johnny. Sloe-eyed Johnny. Sexy, macho, and son of a bitch Johnny.

To Warner's annoyance, he didn't recognize her.

"Yeah?" he said. He was clad in a terry-cloth robe, with several gold chains nestling for position around his neck. His long hair curled over his collar. Two bodyguards hovered in the background.

She remembered what he was like in bed and she wanted him.

Removing her large black sunglasses she stared at him. "I've been trying to reach you," she said. "You're impossible to get hold of."

Recognition dawned. "Holy shit!" he exclaimed. "It's you! Get an eyeful of the uniform!"

Warner knew there was something about a uniform that turned some men on. That's why she'd kept hers. Obviously Johnny was one of them.

"Why haven't you returned my calls?" she demanded.

"Honey, who knew you called?" He waved his arms vaguely in the air. "Hey, Chuck—did Warner call me?"

"Dunno, Johnny, I'll take a peek at your messages."

Johnny couldn't help grinning. He admired her balls, coming to his front door as if it was her right. "I'd ask you in, but I'm like—uh . . . entertaining," he said.

She wanted to let him know she wasn't just another pass-in-the-night groupie. "When *can* I see you?" she pressed. "I'm through trying to reach you on the phone."

He thought quickly. There wasn't much going on in his life. Upstairs he had blond twins rolling around on his bed. They would do for tonight, but after that . . .

"Tell you what, babe. I'm goin' to a big party Monday night. I'll take you with me. How's that?"

"Yes," said Warner.

"You got it," said Johnny, remembering her incredible tits.

Warner was satisfied.

He stretched out his hand and fingered the front of her uniform. "Whaddya say—maybe next time we stay in you'll bring the uniform, huh?"

She nodded. "Maybe."

Johnny was satisfied.

"Gimme your address. I'll have a limo pick you up. Eight o'clock Monday night. Put on something sexy."

"For you?"

"Who else, baby? Who else? Doncha know? Johnny Romano—he's the king."

88

In his Century City penthouse Carlos Bonnatti began to brood. Lucky Santangelo . . . treating him like shit . . . making him wait for money that was rightfully his. Fuck her, and fuck her father, Gino. The Santangelos had always thought they were better than everybody else. If it wasn't for that goddamn family . . .

He remembered growing up and Enzio complaining about Gino. *That lousy son of a bitch. Thinks he's smarter than everybody else. Doesn't want to get into drugs and hooking. Thinks just 'cause he takes money for loan sharking and skims the casinos clean, he's a good guy. Fuck him. I'm gonna show him a thing or two.*

When Enzio was murdered by the Santangelo bitch, Carlos had backed off. He didn't care to get involved in the family grudges. He wanted to run his businesses his own way. And when Santino vowed revenge, Carlos said to himself, Fuck Santino, he's a moron, and he had distanced himself from his brother. Eventually Santino had gotten himself killed too. But Santino was always a dumb schmuck, more interested in pussy than anything else.

Carlos had his priorities straight. Money came first. Money came before everything. And now the Santangelo bitch was going head to head with him.

It was time he laid down the rules.

Twenty-four hours, bitch. And if you don't pay . . .

89

Although the Beverly Hills Hotel was one of the most luxurious hotels in the world, it was not quite the same as living in one's own mansion. Mickey Stolli soon discovered that.

He'd installed himself in a bungalow. But what was the use of having a kitchen when there was nobody to cook your meals?

Room Service and he soon became very close indeed.

On Saturday, Tabitha insisted on visiting him.

"I wanna go out by the pool, Daddy. There's a lot of cute boys by the pool."

"There's no cute boys at the Beverly Hills Hotel," Mickey said flatly. "Just old producers."

"Like you, Daddy?"

"I'm not a producer."

Tabitha wore baggy shorts and a floppy shirt. Once they got out by the pool she removed both items of clothing, revealing a much too small bikini for her size. He hadn't realized his daughter was developing so fast. If it wasn't for the glint of steel around her teeth you would never know she was only thirteen.

"Put your shirt on," he scolded.

"I wanna sunbathe, Daddy."

"I *said* cover yourself."

Tabitha made a face and reached for her shirt. "When are you coming home?"

"Who says I'm coming home?"

"Mommy says you are."

"She did, did she?"

"Yes. Mommy says you'll never stick it out on your own."

"Does she want me back?"

"I dunno."

He waved to a few acquaintances as they walked to the restaurant by the pool and sat at an outdoor table.

Tabitha decided to order everything on the menu. Mickey made her settle on a club sandwich and chocolate malt, while he ordered Eggs Benedict.

"Can I have my Sweet Sixteen at Orpheus?" Tabitha asked, eyes lustfully following a Mexican busboy.

"Who knows?" Mickey said irritably. "Jesus, what are you asking me now for? Your sixteenth birthday isn't for another three years."

"I'm planning ahead," his daughter announced. "Mommy says we always should. She taught me to do that."

Tabitha stared at the busboy.

He stared back.

This was Beverly Hills; there was no chance of their ever getting together.

"Did you know that when Grandfather dies he's leaving me a whole lot of money?" Tabitha asked.

Mickey perked up. "Really?"

"All the money he got for the studio he's divided between me, Aunt Primrose's kids, and Inga. When Grandfather dies, we get everything. Everything, Daddy. I'm gonna be like really rich."

"Good. You can keep me in your old age."

"You can keep yourself. You're rich."

Not as rich as he'd like to be. "What about your mother?" he asked curiously.

"I dunno. She gets interest or something until I'm twenty-one, and then I get everything. I'm gonna buy a Porsche, a Corvette, and a red Thunderbird. Whaddya think, Dad?"

Just like her mother—spending it before she had it.

Tabitha grabbed a roll and stuffed it into her mouth. "What's Orpheus like? Is it as nice as Panther? What movie stars work there? Tom Cruise? How about Matt Dillon? Can I meet Rob Lowe?"

"I haven't even signed the contract yet," he said irritably. "Gotta wait till Zeppo gets out. He's making noises."

"What noises?"

Was it his imagination, or did the busboy wink at her? "Threatening to sue, contract disputes. As soon as it's all sorted out, I'll be there."

Tabitha fidgeted in her seat. "Can I come visit? What movies will you make?"

"Leave me alone," Mickey said gloomily. "I'm not in the mood."

"You've gotta be nice to me," Tabitha said, chewing on a hangnail. "I'm a deprived child now that my parents are separated." She slurped her milkshake. "Can we go to a movie? Can we go to Westwood? Can we go to Tower Records?"

"Can *you* shut up?"

Was this what it would be like every Saturday?

Mickey had a feeling he was going to dread weekends.

Warner phoned Abigaile. "I did as you suggested," she said excitedly.

"I told you it would work," replied Abigaile.

Warner giggled. "He was *really* surprised to see me."

"I'm sure he was."

"He's invited me to a party on Monday."

"How nice."

"You know, Abby," Warner said warmly, "I really misjudged you. The things Mickey told me. He made me think you were the bitch of Beverly Hills! God knows, when I was a traffic cop I met enough of them. If only I'd known the truth about you, I would *never* have had an affair with your husband."

"I understand, dear," said Abigaile soothingly. "After all, Mickey can be very persuasive. Perhaps we'll lunch one day. The Bistro Gardens, wouldn't that be nice?"

"The Bistro Gardens? I've never been there," said Warner. "What a treat!"

"Good," said Abigaile. "Call me anytime."

She put down the phone and nodded to herself. Better to be friends with the enemy. It was an advantage. And Abigaile always enjoyed having an advantage.

"We're going to a party," Madame Loretta informed a select group of her special girls.

"For entertaining purposes?" asked Texas, a delicate blond twenty-two-year-old.

"No, you don't have to entertain," replied Madame Loretta. "This is strictly a pleasure trip." She turned to Leslie. "The perfect opportunity for you, my dear."

"What kind of opportunity?" Leslie asked listlessly. Since Eddie had left her, she'd had no desire to do anything.

"The perfect opportunity to find you a husband," said Madame Loretta. "The place will be overflowing with rich, successful men, and Leslie, dear, much as I'd like you to resume working for me, I'd sooner see you settled. You're what I call the marrying kind."

Leslie nodded and wondered how Eddie was managing without her. He'd been so mean to her—and yet she couldn't help thinking about him.

"Monday night," Madame Loretta told the assembled girls. "Make sure we all look our very best. We're going to the hottest party in town!"

90

Being surrounded by her family—Gino and Bobby, Steven and Mary Lou and Carioca Jade—made Lucky feel good, although it wasn't the same as Lennie's being there. Having everyone around only made her miss him more.

She wondered where he was, what he was doing, if he was happy.

Things at the studio seemed to be falling into place. *Bombshell* had already been rewritten and the new script was excellent. Venus Maria had read it and loved it. Montana Grey visited the studio and met with both of them. She was an interesting woman. Tall, smart, and most of all, extremely talented. Lucky had hired her to direct the film.

She'd read two other scripts she liked and put them into development. And she'd also come across a black comedy which would take Susie Rush away from the sweet-little-thing roles she was so tired of playing.

Susie was interested but she'd already made a commitment on another project at Orpheus.

"Is the deal signed?" Lucky had asked, and finding out it wasn't, had offered Susie more money and extra points in the picture.

There was nothing like the mention of extra money to change an actress's mind. Besides, this was the opportunity Susie had been waiting for. She said yes.

In the short time she'd been at Panther, Lucky felt she'd accomplished plenty.

One of the things she'd attended to was reviewing the footage of *Macho Man*. If Lennie was prepared to work on it again, it was certainly salvageable.

Maybe she should call him.

No.

Maybe *he* should call her.

Just as she'd predicted, *Motherfaker* was failing dismally at the box office. Although there had been a rush of business the first weekend, word of mouth soon killed it stone dead.

Johnny Romano was not a happy superstar.

The weekend came as a welcome break. After lunch on Saturday, Steven suggested he and Lucky take a walk along the beach.

"I wanna come too," announced Bobby.

"No," said Lucky.

"Yes," pleaded Bobby.

"No. I want to be with your mommy alone," Steven explained. "I never get to see her. This is our one opportunity."

Lucky grabbed his arm. "That's not true, big brother."

"Oh yes it is!"

"I'm here now."

"That's why we're taking a walk."

They set off along the beach.

"I'm so glad you and Mary Lou could make it. Not to mention Carioca Jade—she's totally gorgeous!" Lucky squeezed his arm. "You're right, Steven, we don't get to see enough of each other."

"She's admitting it!"

"O.K., father of the year, what else have you been up to?"

"More to the point, what have *you* been up to?" He studied her for a moment. "I heard about your undercover scam. You're really something, Lucky."

"Yeah," she said ruefully. "And look where it got me. I gained a studio and lost a husband."

Steven stopped walking. "What does *that* mean?"

"Haven't you heard? Lennie went berserk when he found out

what I'd done. He's not thrilled about my owning Panther. In fact . . ." She hesitated. "We're talking divorce."

Steven shook his head. "No way."

"I'm afraid so."

"Your problem is you always expect to get your own way. No roadblocks."

"Oh, like you've known me all my life, right?"

"Hey—it hasn't been that long, but I feel real close to you. Having you as a half sister is an experience."

"Yeah. You too. Remember when we first met? The elevator?"

He couldn't' stop grinning. "Ah, the famous elevator. When we were trapped during the big New York blackout. Two strangers with nothing in common—little did we know. . . ."

"I was pissed off about Gino coming back into the country from his tax exile. And you were *really* uptight!"

"Yeah, and you were a crazy one. There we were, stuck in the dark, didn't even know each other, and all you could talk about was sex—and I'm thinking to myself, Who is this insane woman I'm trapped with?"

She laughed ruefully. "That was when I was wild and young."

"Hey, Lucky—nothing's changed. You're still the same pain in the ass!"

She gazed at him earnestly. "Is it such a terrible thing I've done to Lennie?"

"Well . . . it's not exactly sharing a relationship, is it? Mary Lou taught me that to make a marriage work you have to do things together. Confide in each other. Don't hold back."

"So you're saying I shouldn't have surprised Lennie with Panther? I should have told him and let him be part of it."

"That's it, kid."

"Steven! You're beginning to sound just like Gino!"

"Not such a bad thing."

"Can you imagine growing up with Gino as a father? Do you realize how dull and boring most people's lives are? And I had Gino —the most exciting father in the world."

"Sorry I missed out."

"You've got him now. He loves you, Steven." She reached up and kissed him. "And so do I."

"Mutual, kid."

"*Stop* calling me kid!"

They resumed their walk.

"Do you think Lennie will come back?" she asked wistfully.

"For sure."

"How do you know?"

"Because you're you. And no guy's gonna walk away from you."

She grinned. "Thank you, Steven. Just what I wanted to hear."

"I'm a lawyer. I give good advice."

"Am I about to get some?"

"Not that you'll listen."

"What?"

"When Lennie comes back, tell him you'll sell the goddamn studio if that's what he wants."

"Hey, hey, hey—hold on—I'm not about to become the little woman at home."

"Lucky—give marriage a chance. There's nothing *wrong* with sharing, remember that."

"I'll try."

Back at the house, Carioca Jade gurgled in her cot, Mary Lou sunbathed, and Gino slept, while Bobby dragged buckets of sand up from the beach and dumped them on the deck.

Miko gave Lucky a pained look.

"I told Mr. Bobby not to bring the sand up, but he informed me you gave him permission."

"No big deal, Miko," she replied casually. "It's a weekend. Let him have fun."

"If you say so, madame."

Miko certainly wasn't enjoying this influx of house guests. But Lucky was loving every minute.

"We're flying back to America," Lennie said.

"What?" Brigette jumped with surprise. "We've only been here a short while. Why are we leaving?"

"Don't you want to see Lucky and Bobby?"

"Wow, I'd love to, but I thought you and Lucky weren't talking."

"You know something?" Lennie said. "Life's too short. It's about time we tried to work it out."

Brigette nodded happily.

"So you and Nona get packed, and I'll take care of the arrangements. Not a word. I want to surprise Lucky. O.K.?"

The call came at noon on Sunday. Lucky picked up the phone as she sat at the pool. Carlos Bonnatti's low, grating voice was unmistakable.

"Pay up, bitch," he said. "I'm tired of waiting. I'm giving you twenty-four hours. If I don't get my money by then—you're in deep trouble. The Santangelos have fucked with the Bonnattis long enough, an' now it's time for retribution. So pay, bitch, or you know what's gonna happen."

She didn't say a word. She replaced the receiver and glanced over at Gino. He seemed so relaxed lying in a beach chair, his head back, catching the sun, Bobby playing nearby.

Screw Carlos Bonnatti and his threats.

Lucky Santangelo wasn't intimidated by him or anyone else.

She could handle it. She'd think of a way.

91

Tony Maglioni was a handsome, slick-haired, big-nosed hood who sat in the neighborhood corner pizza parlor and held court. Emilio made his entrance dragging Rita behind him.

"What are we doing in this piss palace?" Rita asked in disgust.

"Securing my future," Emilio replied, wondering where she'd learned such a colorful turn of phrase. "So try be nice to everybody, 'cause we're gonna score big."

Rita scowled. She was fed up with being nice to everybody. She'd thought that when she'd finally arrived in Hollywood she'd left all the old neighborhoods behind. Especially Brooklyn.

Vaguely Emilio remembered Tony, even though the guy was younger than him.

"Yo, Tony!" he greeted. "Emilio Sierra."

Tony was no slouch in the remembering-names department. He leaped up from the table. "Emilio, my man. How ya doin'?"

"Found myself in town. Didn't wanna miss seein' ya," said Emilio.

Getting a firsthand look at Tony, it was all coming back to him. Venus Maria had liked this guy a lot. She'd had a real schoolgirl crush, trailed him for months, and eventually nailed him in the kitchen one evening when everyone was out.

"I hear you're drivin' a cab now," said Emilio. "Takin' over Manhattan, huh?"

Tony laughed. "Yeah, I drive a cab. I part own it, y'know? An' I got a few other things goin' on the side. I do O.K. An' you, Emilio —what's happenin' with you?"

Emilio shrugged modestly. "I live out in Hollywood, an' like I'm doin' a movie. Playin' Sly Stallone's best friend."

Tony was duly impressed. So was his girlfriend, a frizzy-haired, miniskirted bimbo with cross-eyes and nice tits.

Rita gave a disgusted sigh. What was with Emilio and this Sly shit he kept coming out with?

"Mind if we join you?" said Emilio.

"Sit down, sit down," replied Tony, anxious to impress. "This is *the* pizza place. I gotta piece a the action." He thrust a greasy slice of pizza at Emilio. "Eat. Enjoy."

Emilio sat down, pulling a reluctant Rita into the chair next to him.

"Yeah, well, I always knew you was gonna be a big shot," Emilio replied, gingerly biting into a stale piece of pepperoni. "No way Tony Maglioni wasn't goin' places."

Tony nodded. This Emilio was a smart guy. "So—" he smirked— "how's your sister?"

Emilio smirked back. It was all-guys-together time.

"She's doin' pretty damn good."

"Yeah, little Virginia . . ." mused Tony.

"You two used to go together, right?"

"Well—" Tony gestured expansively—"I took her out a few times. She was a wild kid."

"Bet you didn't think she was gonna become a big friggin' movie star, huh?"

Tony threw back his head and laughed. "Who would have guessed?"

"Ya know, if ya ever come out to Hollywood," Emilio said, laying the bait—"Venus an' me—we got a big house there. You could come visit us, she'd love to see ya. Talks about you a lot."

Tony looked eager. "Yeah?"

His girlfriend leaned forward. "He ain't goin' nowhere without me," she announced.

"Ya wanna shut up?" said Tony, turning on her viciously. "You wanna keep your mouth tightly closed? We're havin' man talk here."

Rita wasn't about to take that. "Emilio," she said. "Let's get out of here."

Emilio didn't say a word. He kicked her under the table, warning her to be quiet.

"You know—" he continued speaking to Tony—"Venus never married. I gotta feelin' she's still hankerin' after you. In fact, I know."

"Me?" Tony grinned, exhibiting two crooked front teeth, the only flaw in his handsome face.

"Well, you gotta admit—you two were pretty tight for a while."

Tony gave a dirty laugh. "Nobody tighter!"

His girlfriend frowned. "Tony!" she complained. "Tell the man we're gettin' married. Go on, tell him!"

Tony turned on her again. This was his opportunity, and he was taking it. "You know what, baby? I just broke the engagement."

92

What did you do with the million dollars, Eddie Kane?

He asked himself that question every morning when he awoke. It was a difficult one to answer. All he knew was that he was broke. No money in the bank. No money in his pocket.

Surely he couldn't have snorted the whole bankroll?

No. He'd had expenses. There was the house, a closetful of designer clothes, marrying Leslie, his prized Maserati. A man had to spend to make it big.

What did you do with the million dollars, Eddie Kane?

The question haunted him. Since he'd dumped Leslie he'd been on a downward spiral. Most nights he spent over at Arnie and Frankie's house, where there was always a party going on. The drugs were plentiful and so were the girls.

And yet . . . none of them compared to Leslie.

He thought about her a lot. Her wide eyes, luscious body, open, friendly smile.

Shit, man. She was a goddamn hooker. He'd been right to dump her.

Maybe.

But now he wanted her back, only he couldn't figure out a way to go about it and still save face.

Maybe cocaine would help him find an answer.

Snort enough and he could come up with the answer to almost anything.

Deena established a routine at the health spa. She was svelte and limber. Her body was pampered with the most expensive lotions and creams. In fact, she was in peak condition and really didn't need to be at the health spa at all. But that wasn't the point.

Every morning she would swim a few lengths in the outdoor pool, have a leisurely massage, and then partake of a light lunch in the dining room. After that, she made sure she disappeared into her private suite until the next morning.

A routine. Establish a routine. That was the most important thing of all. She avoided contact with the other women staying there, barely spoke to the staff, and kept herself to herself.

Naturally, everyone knew who she was.

Monday morning the new edition of *Truth and Fact* hit the stands. On the front page was a giant color photograph of Venus Maria and Martin, strolling in the grounds of the Bel-Air Hotel, gazing up at each other and holding hands.

SECRET RENDEZVOUS FOR LOVERS! blazoned the headlines.

Deena stared at the photograph for a while and knew for sure she'd waited long enough.

"Hey, yo, Dennis! It's your friend, Emilio, back in town."

Hang out the flags, Dennis thought sourly. Was there no getting rid of the guy?

"What you got for me?" he asked.

"What *haven't* I got for you?" Emilio replied arrogantly. "I got the real goods this time. I got her first make-out with a guy an' all the details."

"Who's the boyfriend?"

"Fuck you!"

"We can't print the story if we don't know his name."

"I'll give you the story an' *then* I'll give you the name. After I've gotten my money, of course." Emilio was getting smart in his old age.

"What's the matter? Don't you trust us by now?" Dennis complained.

"I don't trust nobody," Emilio said contemptuously.

"How do I know this is genuine?"

"Am I selling magazines for you, or what?" Emilio demanded in disgust. "Do I have to go through a third degree every time I give you somethin' ?"

"Your *sister* is selling us magazines," Dennis pointed out. "Without her you got nothin', mate."

"Shit!" Emilio said, "Maybe I should go to the *Enquirer*. Could be they'll treat me better."

Dennis sighed wearily. "O.K., let's meet," he said. "I'll listen to the details and we'll arrange a price."

Triumphantly Emilio hung up.

Rita was primping in the bathroom mirror. She appeared to have moved into his apartment—her stuff was everywhere. He hadn't noticed how it happened, but it *had* happened.

Emilio didn't really mind. He'd never had a girl live with him before. Especially one as pretty as Rita.

"Your sister's mad as hell," she said, walking into the bedroom.

"How do *you* know?"

" 'Cause I played your answering machine. I heard her. She's steaming."

"She'll get over it. In fact—you know something? I got a little treat for you tonight, baby."

"What's that?" she asked, hoping it wasn't his body.

"I'm gonna take you to meet Venus. Her fag friend, Ron, is throwing a surprise birthday party for her."

"Oh, yeah?" Rita sneered sarcastically. "She'll *surely* want to see you."

"I was invited," Emilio said cockily.

"When?" Rita asked, full of suspicion.

"A while ago. You gotta remember I'm her brother. Of course she'll expect me there."

"So? All the more reason for her to be mad."

He hated it when a woman had something to say. His father had been right. Women were put on earth for three reasons: cooking, cleaning, and fucking. End of story. "Whadda I care? I wanna go to the party, don't you?"

Rita's eyes gleamed. "Is it a big party?"

"Big enough."

Rita nodded. Try and keep her away! "Whatever you say, Emilio."

On Monday Deena followed her usual routine. After lunch she vanished to her room. Once there, she made her preparations. She took out her long black wig and the denim outfit, and finally she removed her gun from its hiding place.

Very soon she would slip out unnoticed, get into the Cadillac, drive to the parking lot where she'd left the Ford, transfer into that, and drive straight to Los Angeles.

Tonight she was going to kill Venus Maria.

93

Ron surveyed the scene at his house. There were people running around everywhere. It was total chaos.

He turned to Ken. "I hope she's going to appreciate it," he wailed. "They're wrecking my bougainvillea!"

"She will," Ken assured him. "It'll be wonderful."

"It can't be just wonderful," Ron fretted. "It has to be *the* party of the year."

"It will be."

"Do you really think so?" Ron was a nervous wreck. It had taken so much planning and time. The good news was he'd located Martin Swanson in Detroit, and Martin had promised to fly in a day early to surprise Venus at her party.

"Will there be any photographers present?" Martin had asked, remembering his promise to Deena.

"Absolutely not!" Ron had said. "This is a private affair. We might have one of our own photographers, but I'll make sure he has instructions not to photograph you and Venus together."

"Excellent," Martin said. He'd just been shown the new edition of *Truth and Fact.* When Deena saw it, there was going to be even more trouble. But still . . . he wasn't going to have to answer to Deena for much longer.

Ron was having a terrible time trying to decide on his seating arrangements. He wasn't place-carding the tables—that would be too difficult. But he was giving people table numbers so they'd know exactly which table they were at.

He placed himself, Ken, Lucky Santangelo, Cooper Turner, and of course Martin, at Venus Maria's table. Maybe he'd add another major star or two.

Nervously he went outside to inspect the tent once again. Everything looked marvelous. The tent was black with a sea of fairy lights strung around it. At night they'd look like a thousand tiny stars. The rest of the decor was black and silver, a dramatic theme Venus Maria would love. And the flower arrangements were exotic blooms imported from Hawaii.

Huge screens were erected on the sides of the tent. Hidden projectors would flash giant blowup photographs of Venus Maria all night long.

"You must relax." Ken put a soothing hand on his arm.

Ron shook it off. He had not been pleased with Ken since the eye incident with Antonio. "No more flirting," he'd warned him.

"As if I would," Ken had replied, quite affronted that Ron even imagined he was doing so.

"I've never given a party like this before," sighed Ron. "What a responsibility!"

"It will be successful," Ken said. "I can promise you that."

"I don't care about successful," Ron said irritably. "I already told you—it has to be the most talked-about party of the year."

"Same thing," said Ken.

Ron shot him a look. What did he know?

Abigaile had no intention of hiding herself from public life just because Mickey had done something most other men in town probably did all the time but were smart enough not to get caught doing. She had every intention of attending the surprise party for Venus Maria. Her problem was, who could she get to escort her? Abigaile had no male friends; all the men she knew belonged to Mickey.

Sitting in Ivana's, having her hair attended to by Saxon, she came up with a brilliant idea.

"Saxon, dear," she said, slightly condescendingly, "how would you like to attend a glamorous Hollywood party?"

Saxon couldn't believe Abigaile Stolli was about to invite him out. It certainly wasn't the first time a client had come on to him, but he'd never expected it from her.

"Well?" Abigaile said impatiently, waiting for his reply.

He stalled for time while he thought it over. "Well what, Mrs. S.?"

"Do you want to come to a Hollywood party with me or not?"

Like he hadn't been to ten thousand of them. "Uh, I . . ." He didn't know what to say. Maybe he should say yes. She looked desperate. "Sure, what party did you have in mind?"

"A birthday party for Venus Maria."

"I'm already invited to that, Mrs. S."

"You are?" She was surprised. Hairdressers weren't supposed to get invitations to important events.

"Yeah, I do her hair. She's a good friend."

"She is? I didn't know that. You've never mentioned her."

He grinned. "I'm discreet."

"Well, then, if you're already going, perhaps you can escort me."

Saxon saw no way out. This was really going to blow everyone's mind! He couldn't wait to see Venus Maria's face when she realized he was with Abigaile Stolli! It might be worth it for a laugh.

"It'll be a pleasure, Mrs. S.," he said. "Shall I pick you up?"

Abigaile suffered from car anxiety. "What car do you drive?"

"A Jaguar."

She thought a moment before deciding a Jaguar was acceptable. "Hmm . . . very well."

"About what time?"

"What time does it start?"

"Ron wants everybody there by seven-thirty. He's planning the full surprise bit. So I'll pick you up around seven-fifteen. You'd better jot down your address for me."

Abigaile did so and left the salon feeling quite lightheaded. If Mickey could have an affair with a six-foot-tall black policewoman, she could certainly appear at Venus Maria's party with an exceptionally good-looking hairdresser.

Why not? All was fair in love and marriage.

After mulling it over, Mickey decided he'd go to the party for Venus Maria. He had nothing else to do. Sitting in a hotel room night after night, as luxurious as it was, had not turned out to be a laugh a minute. At home he had his own personal Olympic-size swimming pool, his sauna, his steam bath, his gym, and his magnificent private study leading into his screening room.

Ah, the comforts of home. How he missed them!

If he was going to divorce Abigaile, he'd better think about buying himself a house. And fast. Hotel living was not for him.

Martin Swanson was screwing him around. He couldn't reach him. Every time he called, he got one of Martin's many assistants who gave him the Zeppo White story. Apparently they had to handle Zeppo carefully. Zeppo had an extremely lucrative contract with Orpheus, and he had no intention of leaving. At least not voluntarily.

"How long is this going to take?" Mickey had asked.

"Soon," was the reply he received.

"Soon" was getting to be a word he hated.

He didn't even have the energy to return to Madame Loretta's. Every time he thought about getting laid he remembered a hand clamping him on the shoulder and a voice saying, "You're under arrest."

Talk about putting a man off sex!

And as for Warner, he missed the sex, the compliments, and the uncomplicated pleasure of being with her.

But it was over. Of that he was sure.

94

Rita wore a red dress that emphasized every curve of her quite spectacular body. She pirouetted for Emilio, showing off. "You like, honey?"

He whistled. "Hot!"

Pleased with his reaction, she twirled a couple more times. "What are you going to wear?" she asked.

Emilio had a new pair of brown leather pants and a matching leather jacket. He planned to wear the outfit with a dusty-pink frilled shirt.

When he put on the leather pants, they clung unflatteringly to his thighs, making him look plumper than he already was. Rita didn't care to point this out because Emilio was a vain one, and she wasn't about to piss him off.

"Do *I* look hot too?" he asked, strutting peacock-like in front of her.

"*Veree* hot," she replied—not such a lie, because he'd already started to sweat. "Are you sure your sister's going to be pleased to see you?" Rita worried. "She screamed 'Fuck you' on the answering machine. It doesn't exactly sound like you're the person she wants to be with. Especially with the new issue of *Truth and Fact* out today."

"Will you quit? She loves me," Emilio boasted. "The Sierras stick together."

"O.K." Rita wasn't about to argue. This was going to be an amazing party and she didn't want to miss it. She'd get there somehow. With or without Emilio.

Warner went out and splurged on a gold-spangled dress. If her idol, Magic Johnson, ever saw her in it, he would die for her. She added a matching jacket.

Parading in front of the mirror, she decided Johnny Romano was definitely going to like what he saw. But just in case he didn't . . . she folded her old uniform and stuffed it in an overnight bag, along with her handcuffs and gun.

When the limo arrived to pick her up, she had the driver place her bag in the trunk.

"When we get to Mr. Romano's at the end of the evening," she said with a pleasant smile, "make sure I don't forget it."

"Certainly, ma'am," replied the driver, looking her over and deciding she had the best tits he'd ever seen.

"Thank you." Warner climbed in the car, exhibiting plenty of leg. "Are we picking Mr. Romano up?"

"We're on our way," said the driver, happy with his view.

"I'm a movie star," recited Johnny Romano, admiring himself in the mirror. "Hey, man, I'm a movie star."

There was nobody else in the room, but Johnny liked to hear the sound of his own voice. It turned him on, gave him a charge. "Hey, man, I'm a movie star." He repeated the words a third time and grinned at his reflection. Cool. He was looking cool.

A model he'd dated a couple of times had turned him on to Armani, and the Italian look really suited him. Sharp tailoring. Black suit, black shirt, white tie. And with his black hair, olive skin, and dark eyes, he certainly looked like a movie star.

The entourage waited downstairs. The entourage did everything for him.

Being a movie star meant never having to lift a finger.

He could remember when it wasn't that way. Oh, could he remember! Johnny's first job in Hollywood had been parking cars. Big, sleek, expensive automobiles.

Most people whose cars he parked had treated him as if he didn't exist. Some of the nicer ones gave a decent tip, but most of the time he was fortunate to make the two-dollar parking fee.

Sometimes, at parties, he saw the very same people whose Rollses and Porsches he used to park. What a kick it would be to tell them, "Hey, man—I pissed in your trunk. I ripped off your radio. I stole your cassettes."

They wouldn't appreciate the joke. But he liked it a lot.

That was before stardom. Before he was Johnny Romano. Before he was a movie star.

One last look in the mirror. The man was hot. The man was gonna kill 'em! In spite of abysmal reviews of his movie and an ominous drop at the box office.

What did he care? People loved him. They'd be back.

He flung open the door to his bedroom. "Hey, Johnny Romano is ready," he yelled out. "Let's go!"

The entourage snapped to attention.

The Sleazy Singles had sort of adopted Eddie Kane. He was their kind of guy.

"You going to that party?" Arnie asked him. "It's like a surprise thing for Venus Maria. We may as well pick up broads. Best place in town to do it."

"Sure," agreed Frankie. "You'll come with us."

Vaguely Eddie remembered he'd been invited several weeks ago. God! Several weeks ago seemed like a lifetime. "Yeah, why not?" he decided. "I'll take a ride to my house and change. I feel like a shower."

"Why don't you shower here?" said Frankie, ever the generous host.

"Yeah, why don't you fuckin' move in?" guffawed Arnie.

They all laughed.

"Hey, guys, I'll see you there. Gimme the address."

Frankie scribbled it on a piece of paper and handed it over.

Eddie drove back to his house. On the way he called Kathleen Le Paul. "I need to make a buy," he said. "Can you come by my house?"

She was short with him. "What do you think I am, your runner? I happen to be busy tonight."

"And I happen to be one of your best customers," he reminded her.

"Yeah, one of my best nonpaying customers. You still owe, and until I get paid—no more deliveries."

He slammed the phone down in a fury. Bitch!

The Maserati ripped up the highway. God, he loved his car. He'd sell his house, he'd sell his clothes, but he'd never sell his goddamn car.

"We're going to a party," Lucky informed Gino.

"Aw, come on, I'm partied out," he said, groaning.

"Don't sound like such an old grouch. We're going to a real Hollywood bash, and we'll have a great time."

"A great time, huh?" He looked at her like she was nuts. "You know how many of those things I went to when I was with Marabelle Blue? And how about when I was married to Susan? She dragged me to three a night! Christ. A great time—you gotta be kiddin'."

"Will you quit with the bitching? I want you to meet Venus Maria. She's a fabulous woman."

"Hey, kid, when you reach my age you've seen everythin', you've done everythin', an' you know something? You don't wanna see nothin' else."

"Stop talking like that. You're getting on my nerves. We're going, O.K.?"

Gino shook his head. "You're a tough broad."

"Yeah, yeah, yeah, I know, and I got a smart mouth. So you've always told me. I'm just like my daddy!"

They both laughed.

"Lucky, you really turned out to be somethin'."

"And so did you, Gino. So did you. Now go change—I want to see you in a suit."

Mary Lou and Steven had taken little Carioca Jade, Cee Cee, Bobby, and his school friend to Santa Barbara to visit one of Mary Lou's aunts. They were staying overnight.

Lucky had given Miko a few days off before he had a nervous breakdown. The place was a mess, but she didn't mind as long as everyone was having a good time.

Prowling through her closet, she decided on a white tuxedo with nothing underneath. When she was dressed, she looked strikingly beautiful with her unruly mass of jet curls, black gypsy eyes, wide, sensual mouth, and weekend suntan.

"Hey, kid," Gino said when he saw her. "What am I gonna tell you? You make me proud."

"Thanks, Gino . . . Daddy."

Their eyes met, father and daughter. They were truly united.

"Let's go party," Lucky said, smiling.

95

"Kill her," Carlos Bonnatti said.

"Who?" asked Link.

Carlos Bonnatti paced around his Century City penthouse. "Lucky Santangelo, that's who."

"It's as good as done."

"I hope so."

"Don't worry, the lady is already dead."

"She's no fuckin' lady, she's a Santangelo. It's to be done within the next twenty-four hours. And it better look like an accident."

"You got it, boss."

Carlos nodded. The time had finally come to take revenge.

96

Cooper arrived on time to pick up Venus Maria.

"What's so important that we have to go out to dinner?" she asked. "I'd really like to stay home. It's my birthday tomorrow and Martin's coming in. I need an early night."

Cooper shrugged. "I'll bring you home by midnight—just in time to wish you a happy birthday. How's that?"

"Very funny, Cooper."

"My aim is to amuse."

"So, what's the big secret? Why were you so insistent we get together tonight?"

"When I explain it, you'll understand."

"Is it something about Martin?"

"In a way. Remember when you asked me to talk to him?"

"That was a while ago. Everything's changed since then."

"So I noticed. But I still think we should discuss some of the things he said."

She sighed. "O.K., Cooper, if that's what turns you on."

He didn't crack a smile. "Yes, it is."

She reached for her purse. "We're awfully serious tonight."

"I'm practicing for when you announce your wedding."

"Would it bother you?"

They exchanged a long silent look before Cooper changed the subject and said, "Is that what you're wearing?"

She was clad in ripped-at-the-knee jeans, a tight white T-shirt, and an oversized man's jacket. So much for Ron's theory that if she was seeing him she'd wear some incredible outfit.

"Oh, I'm so sorry," she said sarcastically. "Doesn't this cut it for Hamburger Hamlet?"

"I booked a table at Spago."

"Not again! I can't be photographed with you every time we go out. Once or twice is a laugh, but this is ridiculous. Martin's going to get pissed off."

"Martin couldn't care less about you and me. We're just friends, remember?"

"I'm not changing," she said stubbornly.

"Have it your own way. Don't say I didn't warn you."

She looked perplexed. "Warn me about what?"

"Not to worry."

"You're acting strange tonight, Cooper."

"Yeah?" He stared at her. She was the most desirable and stimulating woman he'd come across in a long time and she belonged to somebody else. "Why do you think that?"

"You're just like, uh . . . jumpy."

He glanced at his watch. "Come on. The sooner we go, the sooner I'll get you home."

"Charming! Maybe we *should* stay out until midnight."

"Why the change?"

"I told you—it's my birthday at midnight."

"You should have told me before, I would have bought you a present."

"That's all right, you can send me flowers tomorrow. Orchids. I'm crazy for orchids." She took his arm. "Let's hit the road. I'm starving!"

Lennie booked the girls into the Beverly Hilton. He didn't deem it appropriate to turn up for a reunion with Lucky dragging Brigette and Nona along.

They loved the idea of staying in a hotel. Room service and cable television. They were perfectly happy.

"You're sure you're going to be O.K.?" he asked them for the fifth time.

"Will you get out of here, Lennie?" Brigette said, giving him a little shove toward the door. "We're not kids, you know."

"I know that," he said. "But you've got to promise me—no boys in the room."

Nona giggled. "What makes you think we'd bring boys up here?" she asked innocently.

"I was your age once. The memory doesn't go—just the body. Know what I'm saying?"

Both girls nodded and laughingly escorted him to the door. "Yeah, yeah, Lennie, now get the hell out. Good*bye!*"

He felt really good, as if a weight had been lifted. It was all going to work out. He knew it.

Downstairs he had the doorman get him a cab, then set off for the beach. He tried to think of a great opening line. How about "I'm home"? That should do it.

Martin Swanson was met at the airport by Ken, who was proud to be assigned such an important task.

"Venus Maria has no idea you're going to be at the party," Ken offered. "In fact, she has no idea about the party."

"No photographers. You're sure about that?"

"Absolutely sure," replied Ken, guiding Martin to a waiting limousine.

"I can't be photographed." Martin repeated his fears. "I've had it with the press. Publicity is exactly what I don't need. It's becoming ridiculous."

"Oh, yes," agreed Ken, wishing the press would hound *him*. "We understand perfectly."

"Good," said Martin. He was not in a talkative mood.

"The surprise will be worth it," Ken said, putting on his Ray-Bans, even though it was after dark.

"I'm sure," replied Martin, less than modest.

. . .

Although none of them were aware of it, they passed one another on the highway, Lucky and Gino heading for Beverly Hills, Lennie in a cab on his way to Malibu.

When Lennie arrived at the house, he was disappointed to find it empty. After letting himself in with his key he looked around. The place was a mess. Had Lucky been entertaining?

He yelled for Miko a few times, then realized that even he wasn't home.

Shit! He should have told her he was coming. What made him think she was sitting around every night hoping he'd appear?

Goddamn it. Well . . . she'd be home eventually, and he'd be waiting.

And on another highway a short distance outside Los Angeles, Deena sat behind the wheel of her rented Ford and headed toward her destination.

97

The throbbing rhythms of a half-naked bongo player welcomed the guests into Ron's somewhat eclectic home. He had a passion for high ceilings, black granite, mirrors and other huge expanses of glass. His home was dramatic, to say the least.

The guests had been instructed to arrive before eight, giving Ron plenty of time to see that they were served drinks and a wonderful array of hors d'oeuvre.

An army of servants worked full force while a parade of Hollywood luminaries kept arriving at the door. Ron didn't know everybody, but Venus Maria's name was enough to get them all out.

Among the first to arrive were several married couples: the Tony Danzas, the Roger Moores, and Michael Caine with his dazzlingly beautiful wife, Shakira. They were followed by a smiling Susie Rush in the company of her husband. Singing star Al King entered next, with his exotic-looking wife, Dallas. And then came a few studio executives, including Zeppo and Ida White, Mickey Stolli, and a disheveled-looking Eddie Kane, whom Ron couldn't remember inviting.

The vibrations were good. There was a definite buzz in the air.

Ron personally greeted legendary film director Billy Wilder with his elegant wife, Audrey, unquestionably the chicest woman in town, and waved at the Jourdans, Poitiers, and Davises. The evening was shaping up.

Johnny Romano's silver limo snaked its way along the driveway. Warner sat beside him, knees firmly together, skirt riding high somewhere near the tops of her thighs.

"Hey, baby, how about a little feel?" Johnny encouraged, trying to wriggle his hand between her tightly closed knees.

"Not now," she objected. "Later."

"*Now*, baby," Johnny said, fingers fighting their way toward his goal. "Johnny says so. C'mon, baby, open up for Daddy."

She slapped his hand away.

"Oh, boy, you got a sharp slap."

"I've been practicing."

He grinned. "Yeah?"

His bodyguards traveled in the car behind. At private functions they attempted to make themselves unobtrusive. Not easy, but insisted upon by most of the hosts.

"You ever fucked in the back of a limo?" Johnny asked, leering all over her.

She didn't want to tell him that this was the first time she'd been in a limousine, although she'd given out a few tickets in her time. "No," she said.

"Hey, baby—Johnny says your education is not complete. Johnny's gonna help you out!"

"Not now," she repeated vehemently.

"When?" he demanded. "Tomorrow? You want I should send the car for you in the morning?"

She was planning to spend the night. "I'll be with *you* in the morning, won't I?"

"Oh, yeah, sure, baby, if that's what you'd like."

"That's exactly what I'd like, Johnny." Warner Franklin was not about to get fucked in the back of his car and sent home.

"O.K., I'll tell you what, baby. We'll drop by the party, stay an hour, an' when we leave I'll fuck you in the back of the limo. Hey— I'm gonna fuck you all the way home. How about *that?*"

Warner couldn't help getting excited at the thought. As long as it was *his* home.

There was something about Johnny Romano that turned her to jelly.

Adam Bobo Grant wouldn't have missed this party for the world. He'd got word of it in New York, telephoned Ron personally and requested an invitation.

Ron had been only too delighted to oblige. Bobo had hopped a plane and flown right out. He was certainly not regretting it. There were stars everywhere. Enough to fill his column for a month.

He cruised the room with a happy little smile and a retentive memory.

"Amazing house," he complimented Ron. "Simply . . . different."

Ron was pleased. "Do you really like it?"

"I just said so, didn't I?" Bobo said tartly, spotting Lionel Richie and his pretty wife, along with Luther Vandross and the Bacharachs.

"Then maybe you'd consider being my house guest, perhaps sometime in the future?"

Bobo didn't commit himself either way. He waved at Tita and Sammy Cahn, who were just coming through the front door, and took off in pursuit of Clint Eastwood.

Eddie wandered around looking for people he knew—for anyone who would talk to him, in fact. Word spread fast, and it was general knowledge he was out at Panther.

He bumped into an actor friend.

"Hey, man, how you doin'?" said his friend.

"Good." He nodded, managing to control his twitch.

His friend glanced around before asking, "Got any blow?"

What was he? A fucking dealer? Why was this schmuck asking *him*? As a matter of fact, he didn't have any, and if he did, he certainly wouldn't share it with this asshole.

He tried to spot Arnie or Frankie, but they were nowhere to be seen.

LADY BOSS

Mickey was at the bar speaking to Zeppo White. Eddie was surprised they were still talking. He'd heard that Zeppo had no intention of quitting Orpheus without a battle. Right now Mickey was out of a job—unless Martin was paying him for doing nothing.

But this was Hollywood, and in Hollywood you put on a good face and hoped for the best. Mickey was a survivor—just like Eddie.

A long line of cars approached the driveway.

"Are you sure we're invited?" Rita asked yet again, anxiously checking her reflection in her compact mirror. "What if we're thrown out? I mean, I couldn't stand it, Emilio. I've never been thrown out of anywhere in my life." Which wasn't strictly true, because Rita had been fired from three jobs and thrown out of a topless bar for refusing to sleep with the owner. This of course was in her past, long forgotten. After all, she'd had three speaking roles in movies. She was an actress now.

"What's the matter, don't you trust me or something?" Emilio snapped. "I'm telling you, me and Venus are real tight."

"Did she give you her permission to write all these things about her?"

Emilio wished Rita would quit with the nagging. "I don't have to ask. She understands. When I get the money I'll probably share it with her."

"Oh, like she needs it. Right," said Rita sarcastically.

"So I won't give her any. It don't matter. We're family. Will you shut up?"

Rita sighed. "If you say so. But what about the new story? All that sex stuff Tony told you? Like how she is in bed, and the first time she did it—all of that?"

Christ! What did he have to do—gag her? "Who cares? She won't."

"I don't see how they're going to print it anyway," Rita added, clicking her compact shut.

Emilio wished he could click her mouth shut. She talked too much.

Their car reached the front of the house and valet parkers leaped to attention, opening both doors.

Rita slid from her seat, stood still for a moment, and pulled her dress down over her hips. Two of the valet parkers nearly collided. And then, head held high, she took Emilio's arm and entered the house.

"Who the fuck is that?" Ron muttered, watching Rita sashay into his front hall. She looked like a Hollywood Boulevard hooker. At least Madame Loretta's hookers presented themselves like ladies.

Ron inwardly groaned when he noticed Emilio on her arm. This kind of move took balls. And Emilio didn't have any.

As Ron began to head toward them he was cut off by Antonio. "Ah," said the diminutive photographer, "where is your friend? I talk to him about the photo."

Ron was enraged. Was this midget Italian creep still after Ken? "He's not here," he said disdainfully.

"Not here? I don't understand," replied Antonio, confused.

"Do you have a message?" Ron said. "I'll see he gets it."

Antonio was not to be fobbed off. "Ah, no, I promised to talk with him personally."

Lecherous little brute. Ron stalked off, forgetting that his purpose had been to throw Emilio and his trampy girlfriend out.

By the time he remembered, they'd vanished into the crowd.

Rita was hot to cruise. They'd actually gotten into the party, and she wasn't about to hang around with Emilio in his cheap leather outfit. He resembled a Hollywood Boulevard pimp.

"Get me a drink, honey. I'm going to the powder room," she purred. "I'll meet you at the bar."

Before he could object, she wriggled off.

Heads turned as she passed. She knew she looked outstanding. Why else were they staring? Tonight was the night to make a very big impression. A career impression. Rita was all set to knock 'em on their Hollywood asses!

98

When Saxon arrived to collect Abigaile Stolli he was faced with a truculent thirteen-year-old girl.

"Who are *you*?" Tabitha demanded, staring him down.

What a precocious child. "Saxon," he replied.

"You don't look like any of my mother's friends," Tabitha said rudely.

Thank God for that, Saxon thought to himself. "Is your mother around?" he asked. "I'm supposed to be taking her to a party."

Tabitha laughed. "*You're* taking Mommy to a party? Huh! Wait till Daddy hears about this."

"Aren't your parents separated?" Saxon remarked.

"None of your business," Tabitha sneered.

Fortunately Abigaile chose that moment to appear, quickly waving Tabitha away.

But Tabitha was having none of it. She glared at her mother. "You look stupid," she said. "Why've you got all that makeup on? It doesn't suit you. It's gross. Ugh!"

"Good night, dear," Abigaile said through clenched teeth.

In the car she apologized for her daughter's behavior. "Tabitha's upset. It's been a most embarrassing time for all of us. I'm sure you heard about my husband's . . . indiscretion."

Heard! The entire salon had talked of nothing else for days! He shrugged. "These things happen."

Abigaile was wearing a chic Valentino suit, lots of real jewelry, and an abundance of *Joy*.

"You smell good, Mrs. S.," Saxon said, sniffing the air.

"Thank you." She stared straight ahead. It wouldn't do to encourage him too much. After all, he was merely her escort for the evening, nothing more.

When they arrived, she noticed a few heads turn. Saxon was tall, good-looking, and hardly the man anybody would have expected to replace Mickey.

Ha! Abigaile reveled in the attention.

Spotting Zeppo and Ida White, she took Saxon by the hand and dragged him over.

Ida's lecherous eyes checked him out. Then she drew Abigaile to one side and whispered in her ear, "You came with your *hairdresser?* It's not on, darling, don't do it again. I know you must be desperate to get back at Mickey—but this kind of behavior is not acceptable."

Abigaile bristled. How dare Ida White give her advice, the permanently stoned old cow.

"He's not my hairdresser, he's my lover," she spat.

Ida's eyebrows shot up. She was shocked. "I'm sorry, I . . . I didn't realize," she stuttered.

Abigaile smiled. "Why do you think Mickey had to go to a whorehouse? *I* haven't slept with him in months. Saxon and I are *very* close." She leaned toward Saxon and gave him an intimate squeeze.

Saxon was as surprised as Ida.

"Come along, darling." Clinging to his arm, she led him away, leaving an openmouthed Ida behind.

It was almost time for Venus Maria to arrive. Ron checked out the guests. Everybody appeared to be having fun, and most people seemed to have got there on time. The only person missing was Martin, but Ken would be bringing him from the airport in time to surprise Venus Maria.

Ron knew Cooper had the plan down pat. He was to collect Venus Maria, make out they were going to dinner, and, in the car, say, "I have a surprise for you," blindfold her, and bring her straight to the house.

Venus Maria would go for it. She loved intrigue.

When she arrived, Ron had instructed, everyone was to be quiet. He planned to take her into the middle of the room, whip off the blindfold, and have everybody scream "Surprise!"

He made a little announcement to that effect. There was a smattering of applause and some laughter. But they would go along with it. This was Hollywood, after all. And Venus Maria was a superstar.

Warner held tightly onto Johnny Romano's arm as he made his usual flamboyant entrance. Heads turned. What a couple!

Warner wished her family in Watts could see her now, strolling into a big Hollywood party on the arm of a movie star. And not just any old movie star. Johnny Romano! The King!

She wondered how many people in the room she'd given parking tickets to when she was a traffic cop. This was something. This was *really* something. Warner Franklin and Johnny Romano!

Johnny had a big smile on his face. Tonight was an important night for him. It was the first time he'd been out in public since the *Motherfaker* receipts had dropped so disastrously at the box office.

Gotta put on a face.

Gotta show them that he didn't give a flying fuck.

And with Warner by his side, he felt pretty damn good. She wasn't just another Hollywood bimbo. She was a woman. All woman. Six feet of woman.

The first person they ran into after Ron greeted them was Mickey Stolli.

Mickey was shocked.

Warner was delighted.

After saying hello, Mickey was about to make an excuse and escape, when who came up behind them but Abigaile, dragging some long-haired hunk behind her!

She ignored Mickey altogether. "Warner, dear!" she exclaimed, as if they were the oldest of friends. "How *are* you? And Johnny, you're looking handsome, as usual."

Mickey could hardly believe this little scene. When had this group gotten all pally?

He threw Abigaile a low aside. "What are *you* doing here? And who's the creep?"

"Creep?" She looked puzzled. "I've no idea *what* you are talking about."

"The jerk with the heavy metal hairstyle?"

"Oh, do you mean Saxon? Haven't I ever mentioned him to you before? Saxon owns that wonderful salon on Sunset. Ivana's. Are you *sure* I haven't mentioned him, Mickey?" At which point she grabbed Saxon's hand and squeezed it. "Darling, meet my soon to be ex-husband, Mickey Stolli."

Saxon towered over Mickey, as did Warner. "Hey, man, nice to meet you," he said. "Heard a lot of things about you."

"Come on, Saxon," Abigaile said gaily. "We have to circulate." She favored Mickey with a triumphant smile and swept off.

He didn't believe what was going on. Abigaile? Enjoying a party? Smiling? Dragging some guy around?

Abigaile was supposed to be sitting in her Hollywood mansion, sulking.

Mickey Stolli decided this wasn't his night.

Rita caught Mickey on the rebound. "I know you," she said, excitedly pouncing. "I saw your picture in the paper. You're . . . you're Mickey Sully. Yes?"

"Stolli." He stared at the cheap-looking girl in the red dress. Too tight. Too much makeup. Too much hair. "Who are you?"

"I'm Rita."

"Rita who?"

"Rita, the girl who's gonna be the next Venus Maria," she said, taking a random shot. "I dance, I sing. In fact"—she moved in a little closer—"anything you want, *I* do." In case he didn't get the message she added, "And I mean *anything*."

Before Mickey could reply, Emilio marched over and yanked her away. "I was waitin' for you at the bar," he said accusingly. "Where were you?"

Rita looked at Mickey apologetically. "My friend—he's a little uptight," she tried to explain.

"Who the fuck's uptight?" Emilio exploded.

"Please excuse us, Mr. Scully." She hesitated. "Uh . . . are you casting? 'Cause if you are, I'd appreciate it if you'd think about me. Rita. I sing, I dance, I—"

Emilio dragged her off.

In the car heading toward Ron's house, Cooper suddenly pulled over to the side of the road.

"Oh, no!" Venus Maria mocked. "Remember what happened last time we pulled over?"

He began to laugh. "This is different."

She put on her businesslike voice. "O.K., what is it this time?"

"I want you to do something for me."

Now she was back to teasing him. "A blow job is out of the question, Cooper."

"Will you shut up."

"Why?"

"Just shut up and put on this blindfold. I've got a surprise for you."

"Ooooh," she squealed with delight. "I get off on surprises."

"I know. So be a good girl and do as you're told."

"I love it when you're firm with me, Cooper."

He took a silk scarf from the glove compartment and tied it around her eyes.

"This is sexy," she said. "I'll have to remember this one. Where will I end up, Cooper? Naked in your bed?"

"You're such a flirt, you really are. And another thing—you're all mouth."

She was amused. "Hmmm, don't you wish."

"Can I concentrate on my driving?"

"Can you?" she teased. "Just thinking about me naked in your bed—"

"Enough," he said sternly.

"Tell me where we're going."

"And spoil the surprise? Forget it."

Deena drove down Sunset. The doors of her car were locked. She'd studied a street map of L.A. and Beverly Hills and knew exactly where she was going.

When she reached Doheny Drive she turned right and drove up into the hills.

Very soon she would be outside Venus Maria's house.

99

Lucky thought about telling Gino of Carlos Bonnatti's threat, then decided against it. Why worry him? She could handle Carlos. She could handle anything that came her way.

In her evening purse she carried a small gun for protection. It was a habit she'd acquired, and it certainly made her feel more secure. Especially now.

"Goddamn it," Gino groaned. "I hate these parties. Why'd I let you talk me into it?"

"Maybe you'll meet a beautiful movie star and she'll whisk you away from New York and you'll come out here to live," Lucky teased.

"Big deal," he snorted. "You've seen one movie star, you've seen 'em all."

"Whatever happened to Marabelle Blue?"

"She married a bullfighter, and then she married a singer, and after that I don't know."

"Is she still around?"

"Who cares?"

"If you like, I'll find out."

Gino burst out laughing. "What for? I'm lookin' forward to a quiet life. I'm an old man."

"Will you stop saying that? It's really pissing me off. One moment you're telling me you're forty-five forever, and the next you're an old man. What happened in between?"

"Nothin' happened, kid. I faced up to reality."

They made it into the party five minutes before Venus Maria arrived and settled by the bar.

Lucky was a born voyeur. She loved watching the action as the stars jostled for position.

"Isn't this fun?" she whispered to Gino as Al King walked by.

"About as much fun as root canal in a heat wave."

"Surprise!" The yell went up.

Venus Maria snatched off her blindfold and gasped. "I don't believe this! Who arranged it?"

"Who do you think?" said a proud Ron by her side.

"Oh, my God! What a wonderful surprise. *Everybody's* here!"

"Naturally, my princess. And you should *see* the presents. Oh, are we going to have fun opening them!"

"Thank you, Ron." She turned and kissed him. "You're the best friend a girl could possibly have."

"I've got another birthday present for you. It's a fab outfit. You might want to change," Ron suggested.

Ruefully she glanced down at her ripped jeans and oversize jacket. "Shit! Cooper—why didn't you tell me?"

"Come along, sweet. I'll take you up to my bedroom."

"Oooh, Ron," she joked. "You *really* know how to turn a girl on."

They walked upstairs to Ron's bedroom, receiving a chorus of "Happy Birthday!" on the way. Standing in the middle of the room waiting for her was Martin.

She stopped short.

"Surprise, surprise!" said Ron, delighted. "Just the way we planned it."

"Happy birthday," said Martin.

She smiled. "Are you my gift?"

"One of them," interrupted Ron. "Now I'll leave you two alone. But only for a minute. Hurry up and join the party. Here's another present." He indicated a large gift-wrapped box on the bed.

"Thank you, Ron."

"My pleasure."

He left them alone together.

Venus Maria sauntered slowly over to Martin, entwined her hands around his neck, pressed her body against his, and gave him a long, deep soul kiss. "Mmmmm," she said. "Welcome back."

They kissed for a few moments, then Venus asked him in a breathy voice—reminiscent of the early Marilyn Monroe—"Have you missed me?"

"Oh, yes," he said.

"Prove it," she said.

He thrust himself toward her. "Here's your proof."

She laughed softly. "Oooh, Martin, you've *really* been saving up."

And then she slid to her knees, unzipped his pants, and before he knew what was happening, had him in her mouth.

That was what he liked about Venus Maria. It was her birthday, and he got the present.

Downstairs Ron caught Antonio and Ken in deep conversation. He hurried over and possessively grabbed Ken's arm.

"Antonio says my photos came out great," Ken said enthusiastically. "It's going to be a big career boost to be in photographs with Venus Maria. Don't you agree?"

Ron sighed. Why did he always have to find the ambitious ones? Wouldn't it be nice if Ken was happy to stay home and just look handsome.

"Very nice," he said resolutely.

Ken leaned anxiously toward Antonio. "When can I see them?" he asked. "I can't wait."

"Tomorrow. You come to my studio," Antonio said, shooting Ron a triumphant look. "My house is my studio. We have a light lunch and I show you the pictures."

"Great," said Ken.

Ha! Ron thought, glaring at Antonio. Why don't you unzip your pants and show it to him now?

. . .

Madame Loretta's girls mingled easily. They were certainly among the most beautiful women in the room. Madame Loretta had an eye. She picked them fresh off the train or plane. They came to Hollywood to be stars. A little hooking on the way did nothing to harm their careers.

Madame Loretta's stable was famous. Several of her girls had already married movie stars and producers, and another was engaged to an Arab billionaire. It gave her a great sense of satisfaction.

Leslie was certainly one of the most special girls she'd ever had, and she wanted to see her well looked after.

Tonight Leslie was paired with Tom, one of Ken's male model friends. They'd been told to circulate and charm everyone in sight.

"Are you getting paid for this?" Tom asked.

"Why would I be getting paid?" Leslie replied defensively.

"There's a rumor going around that some of the girls here are— look, I'm not saying *you* are, but some of the girls work for Madame Loretta."

"There's also a rumor that some of the guys are gay," Leslie retorted. "Are *you* gay?"

Tom blushed. "I'm an actor."

"Are you trying to say there's no gay actors?"

"I'm bisexual," he explained.

"I guess that covers a multitude of sins," she murmured.

When Venus reappeared with Martin by her side, a buzz traveled around the room. She'd transformed herself from a waif in blue jeans into the Venus Maria everyone knew and loved—the sexy, strutting, outrageous video queen. Challenging, vampy, unafraid. Now she had on her birthday present from Ron, a Jean-Paul Gaultier tunic dress, over which she wore a jeweled vest, and on her wrists, several red-and-black-enameled bangles.

"Everyone's staring at us," she whispered to Martin. "I guess they're surprised to see you."

"No photographs," he warned.

"Don't be so paranoid. Ron wouldn't allow photographers at a party like this."

572

A waiter handed them champagne. Martin squeezed her hand. "I'm here to stay."

She sipped the champagne and wrinkled her nose. "Really?"

"It's what you want, isn't it?"

She smiled. "Oh, yes, Martin. It's what I want. It really is."

But even as she said it, she knew she wasn't sure.

100

"**A**re we having fun?" Cooper asked dryly.

Lucky smiled at him. "I always make the best of everything. It's an interesting party."

"If you like parties," Cooper said restlessly.

"And you don't?"

"I'd sooner be home in bed reading a good book."

"From what I hear, the last thing you do in your bedroom is read a good book."

He gave her a perplexed look. "Why is it that everyone thinks I'm this insatiable stud?"

"Because you are!"

"You know that for a fact, do you?"

"I've read plenty about you."

"And you believe everything you read, of course?"

She grinned. "Naturally. Don't you?"

He moved on. "How come I never see you with your husband? Where is Lennie anyway?"

"He's in Europe right now."

"What do you two have? One of those marriages where he goes his way and you go yours?"

"It's really none of your business."

"I see. It's perfectly O.K. for you to discuss *my* love life—but when it comes to yours, hands off, right?"

She sighed. "Right now we're having a . . . problem or two."

That's all Cooper needed to hear. He'd been attracted to Lucky from the first time he'd seen her. "I'm very good at solving problems. It's my specialty."

"I'm sure it is. But I can solve my own, thank you."

They locked eyes. If it wasn't for Lennie, she would find Cooper Turner irresistibly attractive, in spite of his lethal reputation.

So what? In her time she'd had a reputation too.

"You're a very intriguing woman," Cooper said, refusing to break the stare.

Lucky did it for him. "Tell me," she said, "do you have a generic line? Or do you come up with something new for every occasion?"

Gino was over at the bar getting a refill.

"Hello, Gino."

He turned around and discovered himself facing Paige. "Hey— what're you doin' here?"

"The same as you. Having a lousy time."

"Are you with Ryder?"

"No."

He noticed she was not wearing her wedding ring, and he began to wonder. "Who *are* you with?"

She put a perfectly manicured hand over his. "There's something I've been meaning to ask you, Gino."

He could smell her musky scent. "Yeah?"

"Did you keep that ring?"

"What ring?"

She rolled her eyes. " 'What ring?' he says. The big diamond ring, remember? The one you handed me when you asked me to leave Ryder."

He took a slug of scotch. She was making him hot. "No, I took it back. Why do you wanna know?"

"Pity," she said quietly.

"What's goin' on here, Paige?"

She licked her full lips. "What do *you* think?"

"I got a feeling you're—"

She finished the sentence for him. "Ready to go home with you, Gino."

"Permanently?"

"Yes."

He burst out laughing. "About time!"

"Martin, perhaps I can get a quote from you."

Martin recoiled in horror. What the hell was Adam Bobo Grant doing here? Ron had said there was to be no press, absolutely none.

"Good evening, Bobo," he said amiably, smart enough not to let his displeasure show.

"I'm so very sorry to hear about you and Deena," Bobo gushed, placing a sympathetic hand on his arm. "But what must be must be."

Martin glanced around the room, desperately searching for Ron. When he found him, he was going to strangle him. If Bobo wrote anything about tonight, Deena would try to take everything he had.

Hovering near the fireplace, Mickey and Abigaile came face to face.

"You're disgusting," Mickey hissed.

"*I'm* disgusting," Abigaile replied. "What about you and that . . . that whore?"

"It's better than being with a hairdresser. He's younger than you. How can you put yourself in this ridiculous position?"

"Don't tell *me* what to do, Mickey Stolli. You walked out, and when you walked, you closed the door behind you. My life is my own now."

"I want to walk back in again," Mickey blurted, surprising himself.

"You do?"

"Yes, I do. How about it, Abby?"

Dinner was served. There was a long buffet table loaded with everything from fresh lobster to Southern fried chicken, barbecued spareribs, pan-fried potatoes, creamed corn, hot, crusty garlic bread, and huge salads.

"All my favorite foods!" Venus Maria said excitedly. "Ron, you really pulled out all the stops. I'm so happy. This is a *sensational* evening. How did you ever keep it a secret?"

"It wasn't easy," he replied. "But you're worth it."

She sat between Ron and Martin, reveling in all the attention. Nobody had ever thrown her a birthday party before, and she was touched.

Lucky came over and sat down with a plate piled high with food. "Soul food—my favorite," she said.

Venus Maria grinned. "Mine too. By the way, have you met Martin Swanson?"

Lucky extended her hand. He returned her firm grip with a limp handshake. Hmmm. When she was at school, the girls used to joke about guys with limp handshakes. Limp handshake, limp dick, they'd all said. If it was true, what was Venus Maria doing with him?

Lucky kept her thoughts in check. "I've heard lots about you," she said.

"I knew your late husband," Martin replied. "Dimitri was an interesting man."

"Did you ever do business with him?" she asked.

"We talked, but never got around to it."

"Just as well. Dimitri was a killer."

Martin raised an eyebrow. "I'm not exactly a pussycat."

"I didn't say you were, but Dimitri was a *real* killer in business."

"I understand we're going head to head," Martin remarked.

"What do you mean?"

"You've bought Panther. I'm taking over Orpheus. In fact, Mickey Stolli is going to run it for me."

"If you ever get rid of Zeppo."

577

"Oh, I'll get rid of him." He waited a beat. "You must be sorry to lose Mickey."

"Yes," she said sadly. "We'll really miss him at Panther."

"And I expect you'll be even sorrier to lose Venus."

"Who said she's losing me?" Venus interrupted.

"We haven't discussed it yet," Martin said smoothly, "but I have wonderful plans for you at Orpheus."

"I'm very happy at Panther," Venus replied, waving to Angel and Buddy Hudson. "Lucky has had *Bombshell* rewritten for me. And *Strut* is terrific. Wait until you see it. I'm not moving anywhere."

Martin smiled politely. "Now is not the time to discuss it," he said. "I'll tell you what we have planned for you at another time."

Venus began to back up. "Martin, I don't care *what* you've got planned. I'm with Panther, period. O.K.?"

He didn't pursue the subject. Once he got Venus Maria alone, he would educate her on the facts of life. If they were to be married, she would be an Orpheus star. No argument.

A waiter tapped Lucky on the shoulder. "Miz Santangelo?"

"Yes?"

"I have a message from your father."

She accepted a scrawled note from Gino.

You're on your own kid. Paige and I have gone off to the Beverly Wilshire. Don't hold your breath. Maybe I'll be back tomorrow! P.S. You were right. I'm not as old as I thought!

Lucky grinned. Gino was back in action. Just where he belonged.

The cake was tremendous—so big it had to be wheeled in on its own special trolley.

As Venus blew out the candles, a naked boy burst through the top.

"Oh, my God!" she exclaimed. "Just what I always wanted!"

Hundreds of balloons fell from the ceiling as twenty Brazilian dancers formed a conga line through the room.

Venus turned to Ron. "This is really amazing," she said, hugging him.

"A party to remember," he replied. "From one old friend to another."

They looked at each other, remembering the early days.

"Thanks, Ron," she said warmly. "I love you so much."

And nobody noticed the man called Link slip in among the guests.

101

For all our sakes we should hope that day never comes. Deena thought about her words to Steven Berkeley and Jerry Myerson. How many months ago had she said them? And deep down, had she ever imagined that the day would come?

Probably not. But it was here, and Deena didn't shirk the task that lay ahead of her.

She sat in the Ford outside Venus Maria's house, parked a few yards away. She knew the house was empty except for the housekeeper, who slept in the back. And she also knew what kind of alarm system there was, where the beams were located, and exactly what it took to trigger it off. The information she'd paid for had been very thorough.

Venus Maria. The girl's image danced in front of her eyes. A tramp. A little tramp. A bitch. *The* Bitch.

What did Martin see in her? He didn't love her—she merely represented sex. And Deena knew she had to save him from Venus Maria's venal clutches. When The Bitch arrived home, she was going to take care of the problem forever. And nobody would ever suspect her. Deena was far too smart for that. Besides, as far as everyone was concerned, she was asleep in her room at the health spa in Palm Springs. How could they possibly track her to Los Angeles?

Deena allowed her mind to drift back in time.

Fourteen . . . she'd been fourteen when she'd caught her father in bed with another woman. . . .

Deena Akveld was a coltish-looking girl. She had a serious, pale face, long, red hair, and lived for the weekends she spent with her father. The two of them always went off together. Her father liked to hunt and fish, and since Deena was an only child, and he'd never had a son, Rione Akveld took her everywhere with him. She could run like a boy. She could fish like a boy. She could shoot like a boy. Her father was proud of her.

Deena had even remained flat-chested. Quite a feat, when all the girls around her were sprouting breasts. She was proud of the fact that she was as strong and surefooted as any boy.

Rione Akveld ran a small inn outside Amsterdam. It was a kickoff point for people who desired to go hunting and fishing. He gave his guests room and board, and supplied them with camping facilities.

When she wasn't in school, Deena helped around the inn. She made beds, did washing up and light cleaning. It was not hard work. And as long as she had the weekends with her father to look forward to, she was perfectly content.

On this particular weekend she'd been fourteen for just a month.

Her mother, who worked during the week as a translator at the American Embassy, arrived home tired. "You can't go with your father today," she said. "You're to stay here and help me."

Deena was crushed. It was a Sunday, their best day together. "But Daddy expects me to join him," she cried.

"Not today," her mother repeated. "You will help me. There is plenty to do here."

Deena was furious, but as the day progressed her mother began to feel a little better, and seeing that her daughter was so upset, she finally gave permission for Deena to join her father in their one-room hunting lodge an hour away.

Deena thanked her mother, kissed her, hopped on her bicycle and set off. She had several new jokes to tell her father. She'd heard them at school the previous week and remembered them for him. It was so nice when they were out in his boat, the sun shining and the breeze blowing—just the two of them alone together.

Deena was happy. Whistling to herself, she rode her bicycle as fast as she could.

When she arrived at the lodge she was delighted to see her father's small black car parked outside. Good. He wasn't down at the lake without her.

She entered happily, ready to surprise him.

He was surprised, all right. He was naked in the center of the bed, crouched over, his bare behind rutting up and down like a wild pig, and he was making horrible groaning noises.

For a moment Deena didn't understand. What was the matter with him? Was he sick?

And then she saw the woman spread out under him. A naked woman with huge breasts and a massive amount of pubic hair, her mouth wide open, making little sighing noises. "Oh, I love it. Give me more—more—more!"

Deena was perfectly calm. She picked up her father's hunting rifle, which was propped next to the door.

Her father seemed to sense her presence, and moved off the woman just in time.

Deena fired the gun.

A bullet smashed into the woman's chest, killing her instantly. Deena scored a direct hit, just as her father had taught her.

"Oh, Jesus!" her father screamed, rushing toward her and knocking the rifle out of her grip. "What have you done? What in God's name have you done?"

Deena stared at him blankly. It had all happened so fast she wasn't sure what she'd done.

"You killed her! You killed her!" her father yelled.

"Can we go fishing?" she asked very quietly, very calmly.

A while later, when he got over his shock, her father sat her down and talked to her in a low, quiet voice. "You will tell nobody what happened here today, do you understand me? You will tell nobody, because if you do, they will put you in prison and throw away the key and you will never be free again." He took her by the shoulders and shook her vigorously. "Deena, are you listening to me? Do you understand what I'm saying?"

Blankly she nodded. "Yes, Father. Can we go fishing?"

He shook his head in despair.

The woman in his bed was a hitchhiker he'd picked up earlier that day. Nobody had seen him with her. There was nothing to connect the two. He made Deena help him wrap her in the sheets until she was nothing more than a bundle of blood-soaked linens, then they wrapped the sheets in plastic and placed the body in the trunk of his car.

When it was dark, they took her down to the river. Her father weighted the body with bricks, and finally they threw it in the cold, dark water.

"This never happened," her father said fiercely. "Do you understand me, Deena? This never happened."

"Very well, Father," she replied. "Can we go fishing tomorrow?"

"Yes," he said.

Neither of them had ever mentioned the incident again.

Deena could afford to be patient. She knew Venus Maria had to come home eventually.

And when she did, it would all be over.

Nobody crossed Deena Akveld.

102

Lennie prowled around the house a few times. He had no idea where Lucky was, or where anybody else was, for that matter. Even Miko had failed to appear. Some reunion, he thought ruefully.

He raided the fridge, discovering cold roast beef and potato salad, which he wolfed down.

Now that he was back he couldn't wait to talk to Lucky. But it seemed he was going to have to. He should have called and warned her he was on his way. Shit! Dumb move.

By eleven o'clock he was tired. He decided he'd do what she had done to him in New York, so he entered their bedroom, stripped off his clothes, and got into bed. Before doing so, he removed the light bulb so she wouldn't be able to spot him when she came home. This way he'd surprise her. She'd get into bed, and there he'd be!

He figured he'd lie down and close his eyes for a few moments, but before long he fell into a deep sleep.

Eventually it had to happen—Venus Maria spotted Emilio before Ron was able to have him and his loud girlfriend removed. She stared at the offending couple across the room and really began to steam. "Ron. What the hell is *he* doing here? Get him out. And fast. He's a sniveling sneak. I never want to set eyes on his fat face again!"

Ron summoned two security guards and pointed out Emilio and Rita.

"Get rid of them discreetly," he instructed the guards—which would have been O.K. if Emilio had harbored any intention of going discreetly.

But no—this was not to be. "Get your hands off me!" Emilio yelled, when, after trying to persuade him to leave quietly, the two guards shifted into action.

People turned to observe.

"Excuse me a moment." Suddenly Venus Maria jumped up from her table and marched over to them. She glared at her brother.

Rita offered a futile little wave. "Hi, my name's Rita. Emilio said it was O.K. for us to come here tonight. I'm a big fan. I'm—"

Venus silenced her with a steely glare. "Emilio," she said in a cold voice, "get the fuck out of my party. And do it now."

"Hey—little sis—what've I done?" Emilio whined plaintively. "Nothin' so terrible, huh?" He added a hurt expression. "I'm your brother. We're family. It's like we should be close. In fact I think we—"

She hauled back and slapped him across the face. "That's for selling me out," she said fiercely. "Goodbye, Emilio. Don't bother coming back."

Emilio snapped. Public humiliation was not for him. "Who the fuck you think you're talkin' to?" he yelled, red in the face. "You ain't no big star to me. I know all about you—an' I'm gonna spit it out to the highest fuckin' bidder. So watch out, little sis—I'll get your high-an'-mighty ass. An' I'll get it good."

Venus Maria turned her back on him. "Take him away," she ordered the guards.

They attempted to grab Emilio, but he shook them off. "I can *walk* outta here," he said harshly. "But that don't mean I won't be back."

"Well," commented Ron, watching Emilio depart, a pathetic Rita trailing behind. "I guess that takes care of *him*." He gestured to the watching guests. "Let the party continue." Then he turned to Venus Maria. "Are you all right?" he asked sympathetically.

She nodded. "Hey—one less brother to worry about. He's history."

Lucky, Cooper, Venus, and Martin all began to leave the party at the same time. Ron escorted them to the door.

"You really pulled this off," Venus Maria said affectionately, throwing her arms around his neck. "And my presents—what an amazing haul. I can't wait to rip 'em open!"

"Come by in the morning and we'll do it together," Ron suggested, dying to take a look at her gifts.

"Don't you *dare* touch anything. I know you!"

"As if I would."

"Honestly! It was the best night of my life, Ron. I had the greatest time."

Lucky agreed. "Fantastic party."

"Apart from Emilio," Ron said with a grimace.

"Forget it." Venus Maria shook her head. "He's nothing."

"I notice it didn't take your father long to get connected," Cooper said dryly, looking at Lucky.

She smiled. "Ah . . . the great Gino. In the good old days his nickname was Gino the Ram. He's probably been connected more times than you, Cooper."

Everyone laughed.

"I do believe he was coming on to me earlier," Venus Maria said. "He's got those sexy dark eyes. Wow! He sure must've been something when he was young."

"Oh, yes," Lucky agreed, nodding.

"So, how are we doing this?" Cooper asked. "Maybe I'll take Martin. Lucky, you go with Venus. And Ron, you can end up with whomever you want."

They all laughed again.

"Seriously, though—" Cooper put his arm around Lucky's shoulders—"you're not driving back to the beach by yourself. I'll take you."

"I'm perfectly all right. I've got a car and driver somewhere."

"I said, I'll take you," Cooper repeated.

She felt particularly vulnerable. And there was something about Cooper. . . . "Well—as long as you don't expect me to ask you in for coffee."

"What is it with all you women lately? I take Venus home, she tells me nothing's going to happen. Now I escort you, and before we're even in the car you're giving me the same speech. Have I lost my touch or what?"

"I'm a married woman."

"Yeah, I can really see your husband around all the time."

"That's not the way it is."

"So I'll drive you home. Nothing's going to happen."

Once upon a time plenty would have happened. Cooper was an incredibly attractive man. But Lennie was still on her mind.

"Where's Ken?" Ron looked around peevishly.

One of the parking valets offered the information that Ken had left with Antonio.

Ron did not take the news well. "Are you sure?"

"Yeah—I know who Ken is. They were in Antonio's Cadillac."

Venus Maria sensed Ron's pain. "Just remember—he was never good enough for you," she whispered, squeezing his arm.

Ron tried to hide the hurt he was feeling. "You're right," he said. "I spent far too much money on him. The next fortunate contender will have to be richer and older. *I* want to be taken care of, for once."

"Quite right," Venus Maria concurred. "Go for it, Ron. You deserve the best."

Martin was waiting for her by the limousine.

She glanced over at him and then back to Ron. "Would you like me to stay?" she asked. "I will if you want."

"No. I'm a big boy. I can handle it," he replied, putting on a cheery face. "You run along. Mr. New York is waiting."

"Let him wait," she said recklessly. "I don't care."

"Happy birthday," Ron said, kissing her on the mouth. "We've both come a long way."

"We certainly have," she agreed, before joining Martin.

Meanwhile, Lucky got into Cooper's Mercedes.

Ron turned and walked slowly back into his house. As far as he was concerned the party was over.

When Johnny Romano was horny there was no stopping him. In his limo on the way home he was all over Warner.

She attempted to push him off, but he was having none of it. "Spread 'em, baby," he said, and then laughed at his own joke. "Isn't that what you say to all the criminals? Spread 'em."

"Johnny, don't." She attempted to keep her dignity, but her skirt was so short he had it up around her waist with no trouble.

With one hand he expertly removed her panties.

"What about the driver?" she objected.

"He ain't watching," Johnny said, thinking to himself, He's seen it all before.

And then with one quick lunge, he was on top of her, thrusting away as the limo proceeded down Sunset Boulevard.

On the one hand, Warner enjoyed it. On the other, she kept thinking, *Oh, God, I hope we're not pulled over and stopped.* The embarrassment of being arrested for doing it in a car would be too much to bear.

"If that little rat writes anything, I'll sue his ass," Martin muttered as the limousine sped down the hill.

"Who?" Venus Maria asked, snuggling up to him.

"That asshole Bobo Adam Grant, or whatever his name is."

"Bobo's harmless."

"He's about as harmless as Johnny Romano's cock!"

"Martin!" She broke up laughing. "I never knew you could be so funny."

"Neither did I," he said grimly. "Look, I may as well tell you, I made Deena a firm promise that I wouldn't see you this trip. If Bobo prints anything, she's going to be mad as hell."

"So what? You're leaving her, aren't you?"

"Yes, but I'd like it to be amicable. And I don't intend to end up giving her half my money."

Is that all he ever thought about—money? "Legally you wouldn't have to do that, would you?"

"No, but once a woman gets mad she gives her lawyer incentive to kill. I made her a promise, and I suppose I should have kept it."

"A little late to be thinking of that now, Martin."

"You're right."

"I'll tell you what," she suggested. "I'll call Bobo in the morning and give him an exclusive on something else. I'm sure he'll listen to me if I ask him to lay off us. Does that please you?"

"Yes. But it still pisses me off. I warned Ron, no press."

"Nobody regards Bobo as press. He's like part of the scene."

"He's not part of my scene. What's he doing out here anyway? He's usually in New York."

"Show Bobo a party and he's there."

The limousine drew smoothly into her driveway.

"You should have a better place than this," Martin remarked. "There are no electric gates. Anyone could follow you in."

"I have an alarm system."

"That's not enough protection for someone like you. And it's certainly not enough for me. Tomorrow you'll start looking for a new house. My birthday present to you."

Didn't he realize she was a working woman? "I don't have time. *You* find one."

"Why don't we look together? I'll have a real estate person line up some suitable properties. We can do it next weekend."

She wasn't sure she wanted to move. She liked her house.

"You're staying tonight, aren't you?" she asked.

"Of course."

They dismissed the limo and entered the house.

"So, Mr. Swanson." She turned to face him. "It's my birthday. What have you got for me?"

Martin smiled. "What *haven't* I got for you. Come here."

She walked slowly over to him, putting her arms around his neck and pulling him very close.

He managed to peel down the top of her dress, touching her breasts.

"Oooh, I love the way you do that." She shivered with anticipation. "Touch me like it's my birthday. And don't let it happen too soon. Let's take our time. Tonight I want to do it slowly. Very, very . . . slowly."

He began to kiss her in earnest.

She gasped softly and fell back onto the couch. "Unzip me."

He did as she asked. Underneath she wore nothing but minuscule black bikini panties.

Martin shrugged his way out of his jacket, loosened his tie, and bent to kiss her again.

Neither of them heard Deena enter the room.

Venus Maria threw her arms back over her head and sighed voluptuously. "*Oooh*, Martin, I really get off on the way your mouth feels. I adore it when you touch me. . . ."

Neither of them heard the click as Deena took the safety catch off the gun.

Venus Maria reached for his pants and pulled down the zipper. "Satisfaction . . . guaranteed . . ." she teased, releasing him.

"Oh, God, I love you," he groaned, as she began to please him with her tongue.

Martin's words struck Deena like a lethal blow.

He loved her?

Martin loved The Bitch?

Impossible.

Unthinkable.

The ultimate betrayal.

"I've been waiting to hear you say that," Venus Maria murmured softly. "Do you mean it, Martin? Do you *really* mean it?"

"Oh, yes, baby, oh, yes."

The sound of a gunshot drowned out any further conversation.

103

"You're not driving fast enough," Lucky said.

"Are we in a hurry?" Cooper asked, glancing over at her, a quizzical expression on his handsome face.

"It's one o'clock in the morning. I have to be back at the studio in six hours."

"So do I. Wouldn't it be convenient if I stayed the night?"

She began to laugh. "Didn't I tell you? No staying the night. No coming in for coffee. No nothing. I'm a married lady."

He reached out and placed his hand lightly on her knee. "You're a very beautiful married lady."

"Let me ask you something," she said, deftly removing his hand.

"Go ahead."

"Do you always feel obliged to make a pass at every woman you find yourself alone with?"

He smiled. "Why not? When you've got my kind of reputation, women expect it. If I don't make a move, women begin to wonder what's wrong with them. And the last thing I want is you thinking you're unattractive."

She burst out laughing again. "Cooper, I can assure you I'm a *very* secure person. You don't have to worry about me."

"Oh, but I do."

"Such a gentleman!"

"Thank you."

"Anyway," she said, "I'm very intuitive."

"Yes?"

"And I know you like Venus."

"She's my friend," he said defensively.

"She's your friend and you like her a lot, right?"

"Venus is with Martin."

"Oh, yeah, he's a real prize."

"They're very happy."

"Come *on*, Cooper. You and I know it's not a match made in heaven. How long before he starts screwing around again? That's his way of operating, isn't it? Make a conquest and on to the next. A lot of high-powered businessmen are like that. It's the chase that turns them on."

"Maybe," he said carefully.

"Listen, trust me, I know what I'm talking about. I used to be like that myself."

"Like what?"

"Oh, you know—the thrill of the conquest was everything, and then on to the next. My father was always telling me I conducted myself just like a guy. If a man came along I wanted, I'd have him. It was the don't-call-me-I'll-call-you syndrome. I didn't want to get involved. Of course, that was in the good old seventies, when it was safe to sleep around. Now not only do you have to get a Dun and Bradstreet on them, you also have to know their medical history for the last seven years. Not to mention keeping your favorite condom manufacturer in business!"

"You're a straight talker, aren't you?"

"Sure, it's the only way."

"It's refreshing."

"Thanks."

"In fact—"

"Yes, Cooper?"

"Can I call you one of the boys?"

She laughed. "Sure. Call me anything you like. Lennie and I will be your new best friends."

"I'd like that."

If he ever comes back, she thought with a deep sigh.

The Mercedes roared down the Pacific Coast Highway.

"Make a left here," she instructed. "The house is in the Colony."

Cooper made the turn and asked if Gino was returning home.

"I sincerely doubt it," she said. "When he and Paige get at it there's no telling when they'll stop."

"You mean . . . at his age?"

"*You* should be so fortunate."

"Hmmm."

"Thinking it over, you probably will be."

He pulled the car to a stop in front of her house.

"O.K.," she said firmly, "you *can* come in for a cup of coffee, but that's all you're getting."

He smiled. "I appreciate your generous offer, but I'm not taking you up on it."

She smiled back. "Good night, Cooper."

He leaned over and kissed her on the cheek. "Good night, Lucky."

She got out of the car, walked over to the front door, waved and let herself in.

Cooper waved back, revved the engine, and took off.

Neither of them noticed the black sedan slide past and stop a few yards down the street.

She hadn't been inside the house two minutes when the doorbell rang. Thinking it was Cooper, she flung open the door.

She had no chance to defend herself. Link grabbed her before she could scream, roughly covering her mouth with his arm.

Frantically she tried to bite him.

He hauled back and smashed her in the face with his other fist.

Lucky slumped into unconsciousness without a sound.

104

Rita ranted and raved all the way home. "I've never been so embarrassed. How could you do this to me? There were important connections at that party, Emilio, and *you* got us thrown out. How could you?"

"Don't worry, you'll read all about the dumb party in *Truth and Fact*," Emilio said sourly. "I'm going to expose every one of these uptight assholes. Show 'em up for the phony bums they all are. Nobody throws Emilio Sierra out."

"What are you going to do when you run out of stories?" Rita jeered. "That's all you've got going, Emilio. You make enemies of these people, an' you're never going to work in this town."

"What do *you* know?' he snapped.

"Plenty."

Their argument escalated, and by the time they got back to his apartment, Rita was ready to move on. She got all her stuff together and called a cab.

"You'll never find another guy like me," Emilio screamed after her.

"And I never want to," she screamed back.

. . .

And in the Beverly Wilshire Hotel, Paige kissed Gino on the lips and snuggled into his comforting embrace.

"Goodnight, Gino," she sighed contentedly.

"Hey—what's so good about it?"

She shook her copper-colored curls. "We're together, aren't we?"

His hand reached down her leg, and traveled up it with his fingers. "For keeps?"

"I want my ring!"

"Sweetheart—you got it! Tomorrow we go shoppin'."

They embraced again and settled down under the covers.

"What took you so long?" he asked curiously, stroking her thigh.

"I was frightened."

"Of me?"

"Of making another commitment."

"Well, this is it."

She smiled happily. "I know, Gino. I know."

"Get used to it, kid."

"I already am."

"It's good to be home," Mickey said.

"You're not home yet," Abigaile replied tartly. "You can keep your bungalow at the Beverly Hills Hotel until we're both quite sure. You're here on probation, Mickey."

"What is it with the probation bit? We've been married long enough to know we belong together."

"If we do decide to reconcile, it has to be different from before," Abigaile said. "No more mistresses. No more whores. I've been thinking, maybe we should see a marriage counselor."

Mickey roared incredulously. "A marriage counselor! You and me? We'd be laughed out of town."

Venus Maria had departed, but there were still plenty of guests left. Ron wished they'd all get the hell out. He was destroyed about Ken's taking off with Antonio. They'd been together almost a year. Loyalty, ha! It didn't exist anymore. Ken was a taker. Venus Maria had been right about him all along. The Ken Doll. What an apt description.

Adam Bobo Grant approached him. "Sensational party, Ron. You certainly do things with style."

"Thank you, Adam."

"Tell me, where's your . . . friend?"

"He's not my friend anymore."

"Really?"

"Really."

"You have beautiful hair," Saxon said, reaching out to touch.

"Thank you," Leslie replied, backing away.

"In fact, you're a very beautiful girl. Are you an actress?"

She stared at him, wide-eyed and luscious. "No. Are you an actor?"

He tossed his mane of hair. "Do I look like one?"

"You're certainly handsome enough," she said shyly.

"Who did you come with?"

"Friends. Who are you with?"

"A married lady about to get a divorce who changed her mind and reconciled with her husband tonight."

"Do you always take out married ladies?"

"They're kind of . . . attracted to me." He stared at her fresh beauty. "Why, are you married?"

She lowered her eyes. "I'm not sure."

Frankie and Arnie had picked up four girls. "We're goin' back to the house to party," Arnie said, grabbing Eddie. "Get your ass in gear."

Eddie had been pacing around all night long. He'd spotted Leslie early on and kept an eye on her. Now she was talking to some long-haired asshole, and it pissed him off. He hadn't spoken to her because he didn't know what to say.

"Sure, sure, I'll be with you in a minute." He waved Arnie away.

"We're outta here now," Frankie said. "See ya later."

Eddie went to the john one more time. He laid out the last of his coke on the mirrored top, neatly arranged it into three thin lines, and snorted it through a hundred-dollar bill.

As the cocaine exploded in his brain, he had a revelation.

Eddie Kane was going straight.

Leslie was going to help him.

Fuck everybody else. He'd made his decision.

And so the party slowly wound down. One by one the staff finished off their duties and went home for the night. The musicians packed up and left. The valet parkers produced the last of the cars.

Eventually there was peace and quiet.

The party was over.

105

In Venus Maria's house a shaking hand groped for the phone and desperately dialed 911.

"Help," a frantic voice gasped. "Please . . . please help us. Someone's been shot. Get here as fast as you can."

Something woke Lennie. He didn't know what it was. Still half asleep, he reached out to see if Lucky was in bed beside him. She wasn't. Where the hell was she?

Rolling out of bed, he wandered into the bathroom, glancing at his watch on the way. It was past one o'clock.

There was something wrong. He had a feeling. The kind of gut feeling you get when you wake up after a real bad nightmare.

He checked around the house. There was still nobody home. It occurred to him that the waves breaking on the shoreline sounded awfully loud.

He went into the living room and found the doors leading out to the deck were open.

Strange, he couldn't remember the doors being open before.

He walked across the room, and was just about to close them when he saw a man, illuminated by the moonlight, dragging a body into the sea.

LADY BOSS

Instinctively Lennie yelled out, "Hey! What are you doing?"

The man turned around, dropped the body, and began to sprint off along the beach.

Lennie raced down the steps onto the sand and ran toward the raging surf, heading in the direction the man had been standing.

By the time he got there, whoever it was had vanished into the darkness.

Lennie waded into the surf. He couldn't see anything, and yet he was sure the guy had been hauling a body into the ocean. Another wave crashed in and then subsided.

Suddenly Lennie spotted a body lying there, slowly being dragged out to sea.

It was Lucky. Oh, Jesus Christ, it was Lucky!

Stumbling and filled with panic, he managed to grab her under the arms, and little by little—because she felt like a dead weight— he slowly pulled her up onto the sand.

Was she breathing? He couldn't tell.

Frantically he tried to remember everything he'd ever learned about CPR. Drowning . . . drowning . . . what the hell were you supposed to do when somebody was drowning?

Get the water out, turn her upside down. Do *something*. Oh, God! This was his worst nightmare come true.

And the worst thing of all was that he had no idea if he was going to be able to save her.

599

106

The funeral was a somber affair. The mourners wore black. And a huge crowd overflowed the church.

Martin was there, ignoring the crazed paparazzi as he walked inside, head bowed.

Several illegal helicopters hovered overhead, jostling for air space as photographers leaned dangerously out.

Ahh . . . the price of fame . . .

"I still feel like I went ten rounds with Mike Tyson," Lucky joked, speaking carefully. Her jaw was bruised where the unknown assailant had smashed into it with his fist, and her arm was broken. Apart from those two injuries she was fine, although Lennie had insisted that she stay in bed for a few days.

"If anything had happened to you—" Lennie began to say.

She silenced him with a finger to his lips. "I'm here, you're here. That's enough. Don't let's think about what could have been if you hadn't come back to me."

He looked at her quizzically and shook his head. "I guess you and I—we were meant to be, Mrs. Golden."

Ruefully she smiled up at him and responded with a simple "Yes, Mr. Golden, I guess we were."

. . .

"She was a fine woman," said the reverend. "Fine and respected. And she will be missed."

Martin stared straight ahead as the reverend continued with the eulogy.

Yes, she would be missed, and so would Venus Maria. She'd run off to Mexico City and married Cooper Turner two days after Deena had turned the gun on herself and blown her brains out in front of them.

Fate.

Who could control it?

Not even Martin Swanson.

He'd been publicly disgraced and humiliated, all within days. It reflected badly on his image.

But he would rise again.

Nothing could hold Martin Swanson back. A tarnished image could regain its luster. He was working toward that goal.

They watched the funeral on television.

"Tough break," Lennie said quietly.

"For whom?" Lucky asked.

"All of them."

She nodded in agreement. "Yes, I guess so."

"Listen," Lennie said, "I talked to the police again. They've still got no lead on who your assailant was. Are you sure you don't know anything?"

"I have no idea," Lucky said, casually picking up a magazine and glancing through it.

Lennie wasn't certain he believed her, but what could he do?

Bobby raced into the room. "Grandpa's gettin' married," he yelled. "Grandpa's gettin' married." He leaped on the bed and began bouncing up and down.

"When?" asked Lucky, throwing down the magazine.

"Soon as he can," shouted Bobby. "And I'm his best man. He told me, he said so."

Brigette followed Bobby into the bedroom. "It's true," she said, full of giggles. "Gino says he and Paige are getting married the minute her divorce comes through, and they're going to live in Palm Springs."

"Gino will hate Palm Springs." Lucky frowned and shook her head.

"If he's with Paige, Alaska will do it for him," joked Lennie.

Brigette jumped on the bed too. "Can Nona and I borrow your car, Lennie? We're meeting Paul at the airport."

"The Ferrari? No way. Take the Jeep."

Brigette pulled a face. "I *do* drive a stick shift, you know," she said haughtily.

"Good for you. Take the Jeep."

"Can I come with you?" yelled Bobby.

"Keep the noise down, your mother's supposed to be resting," Lennie said.

"Can I?" screeched Bobby, jumping up and down.

"Come on, brat," replied Brigette. "Catch me if you can."

They raced noisily out of the room.

"Hmmm," Lucky said. "And you want more kids? Aren't these two enough?"

He smiled. "I thought I did, but now that I know what it's like to almost lose you, we can do whatever you want. It's your call."

"And I made it."

"Huh?"

"I've got another surprise for you."

He mock-groaned, "What this time?"

She couldn't wipe the grin off her face. "You'll like it."

"What? Tell me for crissakes."

"Lennie . . . we're pregnant."

"We're *what?*"

"Yup. We're pregnant, and we own a studio, and we're going to make your screenplay, and we're still married, and hey, do you realize we've been married almost a year?"

He shook his head in amazement and grinned. "A year, huh? And they said it wouldn't last."

"Spring open the champagne, husband."

"You got it, wife."

Their eyes met and they both smiled. Two stubborn, crazy, smart people.

A new adventure was just beginning.

EPILOGUE

Mickey and Abigaile Stolli reconciled.

Mickey eventually became the head of Orpheus Studios, although by that time it was owned by a Japanese conglomerate.

Abigaile continued to give tasteful dinner parties. Mickey continued to fool around.

Tabitha celebrated her fourteenth birthday by running away with an eighteen-year-old Hispanic waiter.

Abigaile and Mickey were unamused. They sent her off to L'Evier, a strict girls' boarding school in Switzerland, and hoped for the best.

Johnny Romano took Lucky's advice and made a simple, heart-warming comedy in which he played the hero. He did not say "motherfucker" once.

The film—a Panther production—went through the roof.

Johnny celebrated by asking Warner Franklin to marry him in the middle of a promotional tour of Europe. He'd taken her along for company.

On the night before their wedding in Italy, she met a six-foot-ten American basketball player and fell madly in love.

Johnny Romano was left waiting at the church.

. . .

Emilio Sierra sold as many stories about his sister as he could, until there was nothing left to say.

When his money ran out, he returned to New York and got a job as a bartender in a hot discotheque, where he met an aging Euro-trash contessa, who took a shine to his somewhat sleazy charm.

Emilio accompanied her to Marbella and learned how to tango.

They made an odd couple.

Eddie Kane tried for a reunion with his lovely wife.

Leslie wanted to get back together with him—after all, he needed her, and he'd faithfully promised to clean up his act. But something held her back and she told him they had to wait.

On his way to the beach house, high on yet another final blast of cocaine, his prized Maserati ricochetted out of control and hit a solid concrete wall head-on.

Eddie Kane did not survive.

On his eighty-ninth birthday, Abe Panther married his longtime companion, Inga Irving.

His granddaughters Abigaile and Primrose were heartbroken.

After a short, abortive affair with Adam Bobo Grant, and still upset over the loss of the Ken Doll to the thieving arms of Antonio, Ron was granted his wish, and met an older, richer, and by far wiser man. His new friend was the owner of an important record company and reveled in megabucks.

For once in his life, Ron found himself on the receiving end, and he happily accepted a Rolls-Royce, a solid-gold Rolex, and a small Picasso in fast succession.

Venus Maria was thrilled for him.

. . .

Leslie Kane went to work at Ivana's as a receptionist. This enabled Saxon to keep a watchful eye on her.

Unfortunately Eddie had left her nothing but debts.

One day Abigaile Stolli spotted her and thought she was the most exquisite creature she'd ever seen. "Are you an actress, dear?" she asked.

Leslie said no, but Abigaile insisted Mickey test her for his latest epic.

On screen, Leslie's beauty was incandescent.

Within a year she was a star.

Brigette Stanislopoulos met the grandson of one of her grandfather Dimitri's business rivals. He was tall and blond and destined to be even richer than she.

When she announced her engagement, Paul Webster stepped into the picture and declared his love for her.

Brigette was becoming wiser every year. "Too late," she said. "Try someone not so close to your own age."

When Steven first heard the news of Deena Swanson's bizarre suicide he felt almost responsible.

"You couldn't have done a thing," Mary Lou consoled. "The woman was obviously bent on self-destruction."

"But maybe I should have tried to talk to Martin or something," Steven fretted.

"No," Mary Lou said firmly.

To his partner Jerry Myerson's dismay Steven found out the firm still had Deena's million-dollar retainer, and after a long-drawn-out discussion he made Jerry donate the entire amount to charity.

After that he felt a lot better.

Gino Santangelo took care of business by making one phone call. It was enough.

Carlos Bonnatti suffered an unfortunate fall from the nineteenth floor of his Century City penthouse.

Nobody could figure out how it happened.

While Link, the former right-hand man of Bonnatti, was shot in an apparent mugging.

The perpetrators were never found.

Meanwhile Gino and Paige finally made it legal. She became his fourth wife.

Gino was seventy-nine years old.

And very happy.

Martin Swanson slowly put his life together again after the scandal. He missed Deena—she'd been his true partner and a help in every way.

He did not miss Venus Maria—too much of a responsibility.

When his business empire began to crumble because of shady investments in junk bonds, he moved to Spain to avoid being arrested and became involved with a voluptuous opera singer.

Gradually he began to plan his triumphant return to New York.

Venus Maria and Cooper Turner remained the darlings of the tabloids.

What an explosive mix!

Everything they did was chronicled in great detail.

Their marriage was happy. But the paparazzi kept up a constant vigil.

Waiting . . . watching . . . ready to pounce.

Lucky and Lennie became the proud parents of a dark-haired, dark-eyed baby girl.

They named her Maria.

Together they ran Panther Studios, united in their quest to make challenging, entertaining, intelligent movies of all kinds. From comedies to gritty dramas, they excelled, and they gave women new opportunities at every level.

And just as Lucky had promised, Panther Studios became great again.

A year after Maria's birth they had another child—this time a boy. They called him Gino.